SAM STARED DOWN AT HER IN FRUSTRATION

"Lady, you are really starting to annoy the heck out of me!"

Catherine felt downright warm and cozy. When a man started repeating himself, you knew you had him on the run. She shrugged as best she could, given the grip he had on her upper arms. "So?"

"So give me just one good reason why I shouldn't handcuff you and gag you for the rest of the trip. And if you're smart, Red, you'll give it to me quick, because I'm just about out of patience."

By God, she was tired of his arrogant threats. She'd won this round, and he couldn't stand it, pure and simple, so he was throwing his weight around. Catherine's chin jutted up. "I suppose because it would make us too conspicuous, and you'd have to answer too many questions."

Abruptly Sam stepped back, then scooped up the bags, grabbed her arm, and started walking back to the bus. "Right," he muttered. "Like you aren't already conspicuous enough on your own."

Ha! She'd made the big, bad bounty hunter back down.

Baby, I'm Yours

SUSAN ANDERSEN

AVON BOOKS  NEW YORK

AVON BOOKS, INC.
1350 Avenue of the Americas
New York, New York 10019

Copyright © 1998 by Susan Andersen
Inside cover author photo by Teresa Salgado Photography
Published by arrangement with the author
Visit our website at http://www.AvonBooks.com
Library of Congress Catalog Card Number: 97-94412
ISBN: 0-380-79511-6

First Avon Books Printing: May 1998

AVON TRADEMARK REG. U.S. PAT. OFF. AND IN OTHER COUNTRIES, MARCA REGISTRADA, HECHO EN U.S.A.

Printed in the U.S.A.

WCD 10 9 8 7 6 5 4

This one's for the guys in my life
Dedicated with love
to Steve,
who still rocks my gypsy soul
and
Christopher,
who fills my heart with pride

And in memory of Linda Ann Bell
I think this one might've finally knocked
Present Danger off the top of your list

Prologue

∼∼∼∼∼ SAM MCKADE RAN down the airport
concourse toward the boarding area, arriving just in
time to see Flight 437 roll away from the gate. He
skidded to a halt.

"Son of a *bitch*!" Slamming a fist through the air
in frustration, he spun around, then brought his
hands up to ram all ten fingers through his hair, glaring off into the distance. He was blind to the people
giving him a wide berth as they carefully skirted
around him.

He wanted to hit something. *Man*, did he want to
hit something! A golden opportunity had just
dropped in his lap . . . and then been snatched away
before he could grasp it.

Trying to calm down, he told himself to look on
the bright side. Hell, it was strictly by chance that
he'd spotted Kaylee MacPherson in the first place.
He'd been coming back from a meeting with the
North Carolina bankers who were financing the fishing lodge he wanted to buy, and the last person he'd
expected to see at the airport was a bondsman's cli-
ent. Yet there she'd been, and while he'd stopped

dead to watch in amazement, she'd undulated down the concourse with that killer walk of hers, her suitcase bouncing off her shapely calf.

Unable to credit his eyes, he'd failed to react immediately. But it was impossible to mistake her— earlier in the week he'd been in the office picking up a check while the bond bailsman who employed him made arrangements to be at Kaylee's arraignment to post bail. Sure as heaven made catfish, there weren't two women in Miami with hair that color or a body like that. And Sam knew damn well that by leaving the area, she was breaking the terms of her bail.

Man oh man, he'd thought, there was a God after all. The bounty on her bond would put him over the top for the last of the financing he needed for the lodge. Then it would be good-bye, dregs of society and humid, gritty streets, and hello, serenity on cool, misty mornings. Talk about easy pickin's.

Which just went to show what happened when you underestimated the job at hand. It gave unwelcome teeth to that "famous last words" thing—no way in hell he should have assumed nabbing MacPherson was going to be a piece of cake.

She was such a dim bulb, though, that she hadn't even attempted to tone down or change her appearance, let alone travel under an assumed name. Hell, looking at her, a man could all but hear the sultry bump-and-grind drumbeat set up by those well-rounded, spandex-encased hips. Not to mention the enormous wealth of red hair that blazed so brightly. There might as well have been a row of flashing neon arrows overhead to point out the way. He could keep her in sight merely by following the path of turned male heads.

A fat lot of good it had done him.

He hadn't anticipated the new hire who had hung him up at the checkpoint, and for that he had only himself to blame. Now he had no choice but to buy a ticket to Seattle and try to pick up a trail that would undoubtedly be stone-cold dead by the time he got there. God, he wanted a cigarette. *What a damnfool time to quit smoking.*

He called the office to let them know where he was headed, to make arrangements to have the fugitive's bond undertaking messengered to him, and to get all the information on MacPherson he could garner. Then he went to the ticket counter, where he finally got lucky in a good-news bad-news sorta way. The good news was, he could catch a flight that would land him in Seattle less than an hour after Mac-Pherson. The bad news was, it blew his budget all to hell and gone. But that couldn't be helped.

Somehow he'd have to find a way to economize on the return trip to Miami. The thought caused Sam to utter a soft, unamused snort of laughter. That ought to provide one mother of a challenge—considering the high-maintenance woman he'd have in tow.

1

CATHERINE MACPHERSON'S FIRST impulse, when the doorbell rang, was to ignore it. She wasn't feeling particularly sociable.

Self-pity, on the other hand, was such an unattractive trait, and one that filled her with guilt—in spite of the permission she'd given herself to take one full day to wallow in her misfortune. The doorbell pealed again, relentlessly, insistently, and in the end, years of self-discipline won out. She went to answer the summons.

The last person she expected to see on her front steps was her identical twin. "Kaylee," she said blankly, and simply stood there for an instant, staring dumbfounded at her sister.

"*Surprise!*" Kaylee exclaimed in the breathy contralto she'd perfected when they were fifteen years old. With the shoulder strap of her purse sliding down her arm, her suitcase ricocheting off the doorjamb, breasts jiggling, she tripped into the foyer. Dropping luggage and handbag, she flung herself at Catherine, enveloping her in a lush and fragrant embrace.

4

Catherine's arms automatically closed around her sister to return the hug, but she couldn't suppress the little voice in her brain that whispered, *Uh-oh. I smell big trouble in River City.* Patting Kaylee's shoulder, she disentangled herself from the embrace and stepped back.

Kaylee's gaze took in the foyer and she peered into the living room, then looked back at Catherine, one eyebrow sardonically quirked. "Ever the Suzy Spotless, I see," she commented with lazy amusement. "A place for everything, and everything in its place."

It was like having a bruise poked with a careless finger, and Catherine replied stiffly, "Actually, it's much neater than usual. I was supposed to leave for Europe last night, but when I arrived at the airport, I discovered my travel agency had gone bankrupt and taken my money with them."

"Ouch," Kaylee sympathized.

"I saved forever for that trip, Kaylee." Catherine's chin wobbled for an instant but she summoned her resolve, biting down hard on her molars until she had herself under control once more.

"Yeah, that's tough luck," Kaylee said. Then she shrugged and added blithely, "But you'll get it straightened out, Sis. You always do." Picking up a fragile sculpture from the little table in the foyer, she studied it dispassionately for a moment, then looked over at her sister. "The thing is, Catherine"—she carefully replaced the sculpture—"I'm in really big trouble, myself."

Oh, hey now, there's a huge surprise. It just popped into Catherine's mind, and yes, she knew such sarcasm spoke ill of her own character, but she just couldn't seem to work up a decent regret. It wasn't an accident that she lived as far away from her sister as it was possible to get in the contiguous United States.

For as long as Catherine could remember, it had fallen to her to take care of family problems. She could never quite recall how the responsibility had come to be hers, but most likely it boiled down to one basic fact. Before anything could be accomplished, someone first had to be willing to do it— and no one else in her family ever volunteered. Her father had usually been off chasing one of his get-rich-quick schemes, letting the devil—and everyone else—take the hindmost. Mama had been deaf and perennially immersed in her fundamentalist church group, only emerging from it long enough to admonish Catherine and Kaylee about the dangers of displaying their sinful bodies. Warnings of that nature had been issued with numbing regularity, but day-to-day problems had somehow been ignored. It had been left to Catherine to see that the utility bills got paid, that meals got on the table. It had been up to her, too, to bail Kaylee out of the various scrapes her twin got herself into.

Catherine had wished for a lot of things during her adolescent and teenage years, but most often she'd wished that Mama wouldn't preach so about their sinful bodies. It only made her self-conscious about her own and sent Kaylee overboard to display as much of hers as was legally allowed. Her sister's motto had seemed to be *If They Say No, Do It. And If It Feels Good, Then Do It 'Til You Drop.*

It made Catherine weary just thinking about it. Cleaning up after Kaylee's excesses had once occupied most of her energies, for her sister could rarely be depended upon to think before she acted. Catherine needn't even close her eyes for an entire montage of incidents to flash with dizzying, strobe-light speed across her mental screens.

Catherine's patience wasn't what it once was, but that didn't negate the fact that, like Pavlov's dogs, she'd been conditioned to react to a given set of stimuli. In her case it was to begin searching for solutions the instant a dilemma was presented to her. Experiencing that old uneasy mix of love, anger, and frustration, Catherine suppressed a sigh and bent to pick up her sister's suitcase. "Come on into the kitchen," she invited wearily, "and tell me all about it."

"You overheard *what*?" she demanded incredulously a few moments later. Twisting around, she stared over her shoulder at her sister.

"A murder being arranged."

"Oh, my God, Kaylee, that's what I thought you said." Catherine turned back to the stove to set down the teakettle. Shock rendered her fingers clumsy, and the kettle clattered loudly against the element as she fumbled it onto the burner. The cups she picked up to carry to the table rattled slightly in their saucers, and the sunlight pouring through the miniblinds seemed suddenly garish and inappropriate. "When? Where? *Whose*?"

Kaylee stared blankly at the dainty floral cup her sister set in front of her, then looked back up at her twin's pale face. "Tea?" she demanded incredulously. "I tell you I heard a murder being planned, and you give me *tea*? Jayzus, Cat. Don'tcha have something a tad stronger? Scotch or bourbon maybe—anything?"

Jayzus, Cat. It was their father's voice Catherine heard, his face she envisioned, with its ready smile and florid complexion. *Jayzus, Caty-girl, you gotta learn to lighten up a little. I'm sure you can scrape together somethin' real fine for dinner. The way you act, you'd think I spent all the grocery money.*

She refrained from pointing out it was a bit early for booze; instead, she silently rose and went to the cupboard where she kept the pint of whiskey left over from Christmas. Handing it to her sister, she watched as Kaylee twisted off the cap and added a healthy dollop to her teacup. Then Catherine resumed her seat opposite her twin.

Kaylee took a large sip, swallowed, and coughed delicately. She looked across the table at Catherine. As if seeing her for the first time, her mouth tilted up wryly on one side and she shook her head. "Good God, Cat, you dress just like a nun. Mama would be so proud."

Catherine looked down at herself. It was true her white blouse was on the boxy side, but that was because having her breasts faithfully delineated drew too much unwelcome attention. Her bicycle shorts, however, were second-skin Lycra. She looked over at her sister, who wore spandex from cleavage to mid-thigh, and three-inch, spike-heeled pumps to Catherine's Keds, and conceded that compared to Kaylee she probably did look fairly parochial. "You really want to talk about my wardrobe?"

"No, I s'pose not. Where were we, then?" Kaylee immediately waved the question away with a flip of her slender, flame-tipped fingers. "Never mind, I'll start at the beginning. Three days ago, I was stuck at the club without wheels because of this bitch who . . . well, that's another story and small spuds in the long run, compared to the trouble I'm in now."

The club, Catherine knew, was the Tropicana Lounge, where Kaylee was a showgirl. As far as Catherine could tell, that meant Kaylee stepped synchronously about a stage with other showgirls, wearing costumes that were large on headgear and small on material. Mama always used to refer to Kaylee as a dancer, because she'd seemed to feel it held less-wicked connotations. In her view "showgirl" might as well have been "stripper." But that was Mama.

"The Trop is really nice," Kaylee continued. "But the dancers' dressing room shares a wall with the men's loo, and I tell ya, Cat, it's a thin one. There are just some bodily functions I woulda been as happy never hearing." She shrugged. "Anyhow, I was coolin' my jets waiting for Maria to finish flirting with this guy out in the lounge and give me a ride home when I heard Hector Sanchez, who owns the place, talking on the other side of the wall. He was jawing with Chains about Alice Mayberry, who everyone knows is carrying on a hot and heavy romance with him. And while I'm standing there sort of enjoying eavesdropping and hopin' to hear some really juicy gossip, Hector puts out a *contract* on her."

"A contract," her twin echoed in a faint voice.

"A hit, Catherine, an execution. Ordered by my boss ... and carried out by Jimmy 'Chains' Slovak. He's the Trop's head of security. And, um"—she cleared her throat, eyeing her sister cautiously—"my boyfriend Bobby LaBon's boss."

Catherine choked on the sip of tea she was taking and hastily set her teacup down. "Your *boyfriend*? Your boyfriend works for a hit man?"

"Bobby's a bouncer, Cat. And I sure didn't know Chains was a hit man. Hell, he's *not*. At least he wasn't before now, as far as I know."

Catherine wasn't listening. She was staring in amazed horror at her sister. "And you came *here*? Kaylee, are you crazy? You must realize this is the first place those people are bound to look for you."

"No, they won't." Kaylee's eyes narrowed. "And what exactly do you mean by 'those people,' Catherine? You sound just like Mama."

"I do not. I just tend to get a little tense when you lead contract killers to my door."

"Jayzus, girl, get a grip. Sanchez and Jimmy Chains don't have a clue about you."

"Yeah? Well, what about your boyfriend, Kaylee? You said he works for this Chains person, this— you'll forgive me for belaboring the point—hit man, and *he* must know about me."

"Nope. He doesn't."

Catherine felt some of the tension leave her spine.

"Oh." She nodded her comprehension. "A new boyfriend, huh?"

Kaylee blinked her big green eyes. "Oh, no, Cat, he's a *long*time lover. We've been seeing each other four whole months."

Four whole months. Imagine that. In carefully noncombative tones, Catherine said, "And in all that time, you never once felt compelled to mention you have a twin?"

Kaylee shrugged. "Not really. Conversation's not a real big priority when we get together, if you know what I mean."

Did she ever—it was the knowledge of Kaylee's sometimes indiscriminate sexuality that had reined in her own, the few times it threatened to run away with her. What if she let herself go and turned into her sister? The thought scared her to death and had kept her, if not exactly pure, at least cautious.

Kaylee rummaged through her purse and pulled out a compact. Glancing up from a critical survey of her reflection, she must have seen something in Catherine's expression, for she hastened to assure her, "I mean, it's not like we've *never* had a conversation. We talked about lots of stuff. Like I know he has a couple brothers and he does know I have a sister. We just never got around to swapping the small details of our family trees. Or our address books." She gave the bulging purse in her lap a complacent pat. "And I made sure to bring mine with me when I left." Her foresight clearly made her proud.

Catherine refrained from grinding her teeth, but just barely. Thrusting her fingers through her hair to hold it off her forehead, she planted her elbow on the kitchen table and stared at her sister. "Perhaps you'd better back up," she suggested in a neutral voice. "I'm a little confused."

"Okay. Bobby caught my act at the Tropicana my first night and it was, like, instant chemistry between us, you know? Oh, I wish you could see him, Sis," she digressed enthusiastically. "He's like this *god*, six-foot-two if he's an inch, with the blackest hair, shoulders out to here, and eyes to *die* for, they're so—"

"Kaylee! I don't care about your squeeze's attributes. Tell me about the thing with Alice Mayberry."

"Okay, sure, where was I?" She recollected her scattered train of thought. "Oh, yeah. So, when I first heard Hector offering Chains money to knock off Alice, I figured it for black humor, you know? I mean, Hector and Alice had been so lovey-dovey I thought it was just something along the lines of 'Girlfriends, can't live with them, can't shoot 'em—' "

"Exactly what did Sanchez say?"

"He said Alice was causing him grief, and he'd give Chains ten thousand dollars to make the problem disappear. And he told him where to bury the body when the deed was done."

"And you thought that was a *joke*?"

"Well . . . yeah. I mean, who'd believe it could be real? That sort of stuff just doesn't happen."

"So what'd you do?"

"I caught a ride home."

Catherine moaned and got up to rinse out her tea-cup—not from any sudden desire for tidiness, but to keep her from reaching across the table and shaking her sister silly. How could Kaylee hear something like that and just walk away? It was hard to believe she and her sister had once shared the same egg. Catherine doubted two more disparate personalities could be found if she searched the world over.

"Catherine, do you honestly believe I would have gone calmly home if I thought they were *serious*?"

Drawing a calming breath, Catherine put the rinsed cup in the drainer and turned to face her sister, who was watching her with accusing eyes. "No, of course not," she said, and felt ashamed because the truth was that for a moment she had believed exactly that. Responsibility was never Kaylee's long suit. "And perhaps you're right, anyhow. Perhaps the murder was never executed." She winced at her poor word choice and knew she was indulging in wishful thinking. Kaylee hadn't come all this way for nothing.

"That's what I hoped, too," Kaylee said. "But I must have called her a dozen times and never got an answer. And Alice quit coming to work, Cat. I know it's because she's dead."

Catherine sagged back against the counter. She tried to think. "What possible reason could Sanchez have to kill her? There has to be some sort of motive, or else it doesn't make sense."

"I've thought about it and thought about it, and I've got a sick feeling that maybe Alice threatened to go to Mrs. Sanchez to expose the affair."

"Why would she do that? At the very least it would lose her her job, wouldn't it?"

"Yeah, but Alice had ambitions beyond strutting around a stage."

"Dancing," Catherine corrected automatically, and Kaylee flashed a sudden warm grin at her sister.

"Boy, did Mama ever brainwash you." Kaylee barely had time to see her sister's crooked grin of rueful agreement before she sobered again. "Maybe Alice thought it was a way to force Mr. S to dump Mrs. S and marry her."

Catherine gripped the counter at her back as she stared down at her sister. "Okay, but it still doesn't seem like much of a reason to kill her."

"Mrs. Sanchez controls the purse strings in that family, Cat."

"Oh. Shit."

"Amen to that, sister."

"Okay, we have possible motive. But if you were in the dressing room, Kaylee, with a wall between you and the men, why would they have reason to suspect you'd overheard anything?"

"I ran into Jimmy Chains out in the hallway afterward." The look on Catherine's face made Kaylee say defensively, "I thought they were gone! I heard both of 'em leave, but Chains musta forgot to pee or something. That would be just like him—the guy's entire brain could be high-grade cocaine, and it wouldn't retail for enough cash to buy a tube of lipstick in a discount drugstore. Anyhow, when I left the dressing room to go find Maria and get the hell outta there, he was coming back down the hall."

"If he's not particularly intelligent, perhaps he won't make the connection."

"He probably wouldn't, on his own," Kaylee agreed. "But he loves to talk, and I'm scared to death he'll mention it in passing to Hector. And if that happens, Catherine, I'm as dead as Alice." She looked up at her sister. "That's no exaggeration. I heard Hector tell Jimmy Chains where to bury the body. Without a body, there's no crime. With one—and testimony tying Hector to it—he probably goes to jail for years. I left all those messages to call me on Alice's machine. If Hector's heard them, and he even *suspects* I overheard his plans, I am literally dead."

Catherine pushed away from the counter. "You have to go to the police, Kaylee."

"Well, um, about that, Caty-girl . . ." Her twin couldn't quite meet her gaze.

"Oh, no." Catherine straightened. "What? What have you left out?"

"I was, like, kind of arrested earlier in the week."

"You were *what*?"

"Arrested. It wasn't my fault, Cat."

"Oh, of course not, it never is with you, is it?" Catherine gritted her teeth. How many times had she heard those words in her lifetime? It was the primary reason she'd snapped up the position at the Briarwood School when it was offered to her four years ago. Seattle seemed so wonderfully far removed from Miami. "Just once before we're old women," she said bitterly, "it would be really sweet if you'd accept responsibility for your actions." God. Twenty-five minutes in her sister's company, and it was as if she'd never gotten away. It shouldn't be like this.

It hadn't always been.

"Oh, get the stick outta your butt, Catherine," Kaylee snapped back. "God, when the hell did you turn into such an old fuddy-duddy?"

"When the hell have I ever had the chance to be anything else?" Dropping into her seat, Catherine glared across the table at her sister. "I was always too freaking busy cleaning up after your messes."

"Yeah, okay, so maybe I haven't always been all that—whataya call it—*accountable* in the past. But that was then, and this time it wasn't my fault, I'm tellin' you. The arrest was totally bogus. See, Bobby had to go out of town, and he left me his new car to drive. Only it turns out it wasn't his to lend, and I ended up being charged with grand theft auto on the say-so of some bimbo with a legal registration and a bad attitude."

"Then how—?"

"Oh, I made bail. But that's the problem, Cat. I'm restricted to Florida by the terms of the bond, and the minute I figured out that the contract to kill Alice wasn't a sick joke after all, well, naturally I emptied out my bank account and came straight here." She reached across the table and squeezed her sister's fingers. "Come on, Cat, please. This is serious, and I really need your help."

A car door closed out in the street, and Catherine glanced out the window. There was a sedan parked halfway between her house and the neighbor's, and a man was bent over it, locking the driver's door. Probably someone looking at the house for sale next door. Catherine looked back at her sister. "I'll do what I can to straighten out the situation, of course," she agreed wearily. "But you still have to turn yourself in."

Kaylee released Catherine's fingers. "Dammit, Catherine, I just explained why that's impossible."

"No, you explained how matters became complicated. The fact remains, however, that you overheard a murder being ordered. A *murder*, Kaylee, that to the best of your knowledge has since been carried out. And according to your own words, you're the only one who knows where the body's buried. This is not exactly a penny-ante mess you've gotten yourself into this time."

"Read my lips, Catherine. When I left Florida I jumped bail. I can't go back."

"You have to."

Clearly not liking what she was hearing, Kaylee started to push away from the table, but Catherine reached over and grabbed her by the wrist, hanging on until she had her sister's full attention. "If you don't turn yourself in, you're not only going to be running from this Chains person or your Bobby LaBon, or whomever, but from the law as well. Trust me, you don't want everybody hunting you. You need someone on your side."

"Yeah, I know. That's what I've got you for."

"For God's sake, Kaylee, I'm a teacher for the deaf! What do I know about hit men or your legal standing in a matter this complicated? You need people trained for this sort of situation if you hope to remain safe." Glancing out the window again, Catherine noticed the man had straightened and was studying the house next door. He was arresting, with his dark hair, dark brows, and a well-knit body clad in slacks and a white dress shirt, the sleeves of which were rolled up his forearms. She got a swift impression of energy and strength.

"Come up with something else," Kaylee demanded, recapturing Catherine's attention. "I can't go back."

"There is nothing else."

"There's gotta be. Nobody's gonna believe me if I go back. Sanchez is a respected businessman. He's well-known in the community." Kaylee rubbed at the furrows between her eyebrows. "Dammit, I was so thrilled that, for once in my life, I'd found a gig at a really upscale lounge. I thought it was my big chance. Think of something else, Cat. I know you can—that's why I came here."

"For heaven sake, Kaylee, what did you think I was going to do, make you disappear into thin air? Wave my magic wand and make the whole thing go away?"

"I don't need your sarcasm, Cat, I need your help! Going back's a no-win situation."

"I'm sorry, but it's the only solution you have. You said it yourself, this is serious, and you can't just sweep it under the rug." Seeing the belligerent angle of her twin's chin, knowing Kaylee didn't want to hear what she had to say, Catherine nevertheless reiterated through gritted teeth, "You-have-got-to-turn-yourself-in!"

Kaylee stubbornly refused to meet Catherine's eyes, her gaze sliding past her to the window. Abruptly, she pushed away from the table and rose jerkily to her feet. "I gotta use the loo." She grabbed her purse and her suitcase and trotted with knock-kneed awkwardness down the hallway.

Catherine buried her face in her hands. Maybe they should call a lawyer before they called the police. And did one call the local police or the Miami police or—*Wait a minute.*

Why did Kaylee need her suitcase to go to the bathroom?

Catherine was down the hall in a flash. Bursting through the door just in time to see her sister drop from the windowsill to the brick patio outside, she dived for the open window. "Kaylee!"

It came out less than the peremptory order to halt she'd intended when her diaphragm made forceful contact with the sill. Simultaneously, a loud crash sounded at the front of the house, and a male voice roared, "FREEZE!"

Identical shocked green gazes clashed and held as both sisters did exactly that. Then Kaylee's paralysis broke and she snatched up her address book from the patio where the contents of her purse had exploded. She tucked in the wad of cash that had tumbled out of the address book and rose to her feet, tucking it under her arm. She rubbed a circle on her chest with her closed fist, American Sign for *I'm sorry.* She hesitated for a moment, then simply reiterated, *I'm sorry, Cat.* Then she turned and ran, leaving purse and suitcase behind.

No! It was a silent scream in Catherine's head as she renewed her efforts to get through the window. She had nearly succeeded and was fervently hoping she could break her fall with something other than her head when the bathroom door crashed against the interior wall.

"Hold it right there, sister!" Hard hands clamped down on her hips and hauled her back into the room.

Catherine opened her mouth to scream, only to find her vocal cords had frozen. So, taking a tip from the one and only self-defense class she'd ever taken, she did the next best thing. She lashed back with her foot and experienced a savage burst of satisfaction when she felt it connect with the hard bone of her interloper's shin.

2

"SON OF A *bitch*!" Sam McKade had had it. Would this fuckin' day never end? It felt like the woman had bruised his shin right down to the bone.

Sam leaned over the lush redhead in his grasp and thrust his head through the window he'd just hauled her out of. Squinting against the sun, he saw the suitcase and purse on the brick patio and accepted it as indisputable proof that MacPherson had, indeed, been in the process of escaping. He straightened back into the room, lifting his chest off her back, then slammed the window shut and locked it. "I gotta hand it to you, lady, you are some piece of work." He moved her over a step, shoved her up against the wall, and, inserting his foot between hers, kicked them wide of each other.

She made a soft choking sound when his hands swept her shoulders and ran down her sides. When his fingers brushed the sides of her breasts, however, she went silent and stood very, very still, as if she imagined he'd stop patting her down if she were simply quiet enough.

Sam didn't feel particularly sympathetic—she'd

run him ragged today and cost him a bundle he couldn't afford. He brought his hands around front and ran them up between her breasts to her collarbones, then whisked them impersonally down the full, thrusting slopes of her breasts. Skimming his fingers around the elastic waistband of her bicycle shorts an instant later, he frisked her from waistband to crotch seam, front and back.

"Oh, don't," she moaned. "Please."

"Relax, Red. All I'm interested in here is concealed weapons." He squatted to run his hands down her hips to where her shorts gave way to bare skin, and then brought them around to run a reverse pattern up the inside of her legs, which were long, firm, and smoother than premium whiskey. The impression had no sooner registered than his hands snapped wide of her body and he rose to his feet. "Okay, you're clean. Turn around."

She slowly pivoted to face him. The way she clutched at the button placket of her blouse like a horrified maiden auntie was a nice touch, Sam thought cynically. He could almost believe she didn't have a clue why he was here.

"Listen," she said breathlessly, staring up at him with huge green eyes, "you've made a terrible mistake."

He laughed without humor. "How many times have I heard that one before? Come on, Sister, let's go grab your stuff. Then you can tell it to the judge in Miami."

The judge? Catherine sagged with relief. Oh, thank goodness. If he was transporting her to face the Florida judiciary system, he must be a policeman and not LaBon.

Not that she would ever in a million years mistake the big ape for a *god*, or anything. It was just that, remembering Kaylee's description and given the man's height and those shoulders, plus the midnight darkness of his hair, she had just sort of automatically assumed . . .

He hauled her willy-nilly down the hallway to the foyer, where he closed and locked the front door, and then back up the hallway and through the kitchen to the back door. She trotted along docilely in his wake for the moment. This wasn't as bad as she'd feared then; everything would be all right. It wasn't ideal, of course; *that* would have been her sister sticking around to turn herself in voluntarily. But at least Catherine was left to deal with the right side of the law. That was certainly a relief.

"Listen, you've made a mistake," she repeated when he came to a halt out on the patio. He gripped her wrist with one hard-fingered hand and squatted to scoop the contents of Kaylee's purse back into the handbag with his other. "You have the wrong woman. My name is Catherine MacPherson. I'm Kaylee's twin."

He stilled for a moment. Then he slowly straightened until he was once again towering over her. She had time to notice that his eyes were golden brown and more piercing than an osprey's on the hunt. Then he reached out his free hand, gave her a patronizing little tap on the cheek with his rough-skinned fingers, and agreed dryly, "Sure you are."

"Listen to me! I'm more than willing to cooperate with you, but my name is Catherine MacPherson. I'm a teacher at the Briarwood School for the Deaf, and this"—her gesture encompassed the sun-washed yard, the back of the house—"is my home."

"Do I look like I was born yesterday?" he interrupted impatiently. "My first stop was at the Briarwood School for the Deaf. And guess what, Red? Your sister left yesterday for Europe on a trip she's been planning for years."

"I was *robbed* of that trip," Catherine said bitterly. "And my name is not Red, it's Catherine Mac-Pherson. That's *Ms.* MacPherson to you."

Flipping open the wallet he'd picked up off the bricks, Sam thrust a section containing picture ID close to her face. "Says here your name is Kaylee MacPherson." He snapped the wallet shut but continued to wag it in front of her nose. "And Kaylee MacPherson is a showgirl at the Tropicana in Miami."

Catherine slapped the wallet aside. "Dancer," she corrected automatically, and then could have bitten her tongue in two. Mama had been in denial up until the day she died, and her repeated, stubborn insistence had made naming Kaylee's occupation thus second nature to Catherine. Blurting it out at this juncture, however, merely made it sound as if she were defending herself. "And it doesn't say that on her driver's license, anyhow," she added, and then grimaced. *Weak, Catherine, very weak. You're making everything worse.*

She gave her wrist an experimental tug, but he

didn't set it free. Instead, he took a step closer, which made Catherine very nervous. "Look," she said desperately, "let's go into the house, and I'll show you *my* driver's license. I'll show you an entire stack of— *What do you think you're doing?*"

He'd abruptly collapsed cross-legged onto the bricks and pulled her down after him to lie face-down across his lap. Holding her in place with one strong, splay-fingered hand, his free hand went to the waistband of her bicycle shorts. In a single economical movement, he had them peeled down. "According to my file, *Miz* MacPherson, you've got a quarter-sized tattoo of little red kissy lips right"— one of his fingers slid beneath the lacy high cut leg of her panties—"about"—he jerked aside the fragile fabric, exposing one rounded cheek—"here." His callused thumb rubbed across the spot.

Catherine froze. He was a madman. Then she exploded into a frenzy of motion, reaching back and raking his hand with her nails, knocking it aside and scrambling to her feet. Fumbling to straighten her panties, her shorts, she turned—she feared with all four cheeks blazing—to face him. "My God," she choked. "What sort of person are you? To think I have an entire curriculum teaching my children that policemen are our friends! I can't believe you would do something so ... my God, so utterly ... *sleazy*—"

"Oh, give it a rest, will you, Red? You know who I am, I know who you are, so let's not turn it into an opera, huh? Here, take your purse. We've wasted enough time as it is." He shoved it into her hands and leaned down to grab the suitcase. Then he grasped her hand and hustled her around the side of the house. "I've got a schedule to keep."

Batting a trailing vine out of his way, Sam rounded the corner of the house and emerged into the front yard, dragging his prisoner an arm's length behind him. What the hell did she take him for, he wondered moodily, a complete moron? The woman had obviously seen far too many soap operas.

Sam's mother used to watch the soaps. Lenore McKade had sat around their dingy, fourth-floor walkup for hours on end, glued to the programs on their small-screen TV. With a mother who much preferred daytime fantasies to coping with reality, Sam was more familiar than he wanted to be with the old evil twin/angelic twin story line. He hadn't bought the concept when he was a kid—he sure as hell didn't buy it now.

Did MacPherson think he'd just fallen off the rhubarb truck? Hell, it wasn't *him* who was the dim bulb around here if she seriously believed she could render herself unnoticeable simply by scrubbing off her makeup and brushing out her hair until it was smooth and shiny instead of big and fluffy. He'd give her credit for making an effort to tone down the flamboyancy—even if it was only done as a self-serving attempt to blend into her sister's middle-class neighborhood. But get real. While her nondescript blouse did its best, the conservative garment hadn't yet been designed that could effectively disguise a hootchie-kootchie body like that one.

"You've got to listen to me," she yammered at him, dragging against his hold on her wrist. "Kaylee's in big trouble. She overheard a contract being put out on a woman who has since disappeared, and if the body's been buried where she heard them say it was going to be, she's in a position to bring to justice both the man who committed the murder and the man who ordered it done. That means she's in serious danger."

Oh, for Christ's sake. Sam hauled her over to the car parked at the curb and jerked open its passenger door. "Watch your head," he advised, placing his hand on the crown of her head to protect it while he assisted her into the sedan. Her hair felt hot and slippery beneath his fingers, and he pressed against her skull to get her moving. He wanted her inside the car so he could take his hands off her. He didn't like the impulses that ran through him every time he touched her.

Catherine didn't budge. Refusing to cooperate, she instead pivoted to glare up at him. "Dammit, mister, will you *listen* to me?"

"Oh, I heard you, Red. You can tell that to the judge, too."

"I want to see some identification," she demanded. "And I want to see it now." Inwardly, she quailed as she watched the sullen cast of McKade's full mouth and the way his black eyebrows pulled together over those narrowed amber brown eyes. He glowered at her as if he would just as soon snap her in two as look at her. Catherine swallowed hard. "I want to see your ID," she repeated determinedly and tried to ignore the way heat emanated off his big body in waves.

He swore under his breath, but his hand slid away from her head to slap down on the roof of the car, effectively penning her between him, the automobile, and its opened door as he reached in his hip pocket with his free hand. He didn't bother to step back, and Catherine lowered her eyes, focusing on his Adam's apple while she waited. Was it really necessary that he stand so close? She could smell the laundry soap in his oxford cloth shirt and the faint, underlying suggestion of clean male sweat.

"Here," he growled, thrusting his opened wallet in her face.

She read the identification. Then she blinked and read it again with growing disbelief. "Bail enforcer?" To her mortification, her voice cracked. She took a deep breath, expelled it, and craned her head back to stare up into McKade's fierce golden eyes. "Why, you're not a policeman at all," she accused. Her voice grew louder with each word. "You're nothing but a lousy *bounty hunter*!"

He swore again. Then he muttered, "I don't have time for this, lady." In one smooth movement, he pulled her away from the open car door and tucked her firmly under his arm. Slamming the passenger door, he hustled her around to the driver's side, where he pulled the door open and stuffed her inside the car. He crowded in behind her and, closing his door, activated all the locks from the panel on the armrest. "Buckle up," he ordered and fit the key in the ignition.

Catherine panicked at the sound of the engine roaring to life. "Let me out of here, McKade!"

The look he turned on her had Catherine shrinking back into her corner. "I said buckle up, Red. Or do you want me to do it for you?"

No way in hell was she providing him with an excuse to put those wide-palmed, long-fingered hands on her again. Catherine buckled up. "You can't get away with this, you know."

McKade snorted. Accelerating away from the curb, he fished a folded sheet of paper out of his shirt pocket. He shook it out and held it up for her to read. It was a certified copy of Kaylee's bond undertaking. "Traditional common law says this is sufficient evidence to make an arrest," he disagreed.

"*If* I were Kaylee MacPherson, perhaps," Catherine said through her teeth, as he drove away from her neighborhood. "But my name is Catherine."

"Dammit, Red, I've heard all I'm going to hear about that. Give it a rest, or I'll gag you." He wouldn't, of course. But if he knew women, the threat alone should be enough. Nothing females hated more than having their power of speech imperiled.

Catherine stilled. *All right. That's it.* Fury surged through her, suffusing every cell in her body. *He'll gag me? Gag me? That is the absolute, final frontier. And he's just stepped over the line.*

All her life, she had played by the rules. And this was her reward: a cretin who didn't hesitate to lay his big hands on her or use his strength to intimidate her. Worse, he was just like her father, out to make himself a buck any way he could . . . and the hell with anyone who got in his way. Well, she was finished trying to convince Mr. Sam-know-it-all-McKade she wasn't the woman he thought she was. What she instead was going to do, from this moment on, was any and everything in her power to impede their progress to Florida. The specifics of accomplishing that might be a bit vague at the moment, but come hell or high water, she'd find a way. First, however . . .

She turned to face him head-on. "You are a pig," she said, enunciating very clearly. He took his gaze off the traffic a moment to scowl at her, pinning her in place with his whiskey-colored eyes. The muscles in his neck and shoulders grew taut, which made him appear even larger than he had before, but Catherine didn't back down. She leveled on him all the contempt at her disposal.

"You've made a huge mistake, McKade, and somehow, some way, I will make you pay for it."

Sam made a rude noise. "Oh, yeah, I'm gonna lose a lot of sleep worrying I've got the wrong woman." He changed lanes then glanced back at her. "As for making me pay, Red, give it your best shot. The day I'm wrong about someone like you—"

Catherine bristled. "Excuse me? Someone like me?"

"Someone who prances around in a big hat and a couple of sequins for a living."

"Oh, as opposed to an upstanding citizen like yourself, I presume. Well, sugar, I hate to break it to you, but you're not the cream in my bottle of milk, either. You're just a bottom-of-the-barrel bounty hunter who likes to pretend he's a real cop."

That flicked him on the raw. "At least I've got a nodding acquaintance with the truth," he said stiffly.

"Oh, that's rich. You wouldn't recognize the truth if it bit you on the butt."

Sam felt his jaw growing rigid. "Like I was saying, Red. The day I'm wrong about someone like you is the day I'll eat my shorts."

"Well, prepare to chow down then, bud," Catherine snapped. "Because sometime soon I'm going to serve them to you on a big ol' silver platter."

3

◠◡◠◡ ONLY HOURS OLD and already this case had disaster written all over it. *Mom, it's a cryin' shame you're no longer with us,* Sam thought grimly, doing his best to ignore his sulky, curvaceous passenger and focusing instead on the heavy downtown traffic. *You would've just loved the hell outta this.*

Not only did this situation involve elements straight out of Lenore McKade's favorite viewing material, it played nicely into her pet defeatist "nobody-escapes-the-niche-they're-born-in" theory.

It wasn't that she'd wished him or anyone else ill. She'd simply never believed that people could improve their lot in life. She'd worked hard, and all it had gotten her were long hours and low pay, an ultimate pink slip with no retirement benefits, and a stint on welfare. In other words, right back where she'd started. So, she'd taken in ironing, watched TV, and warned Sam to resign himself to the fact that he, too, would end up where he'd begun. According to her you could take the boy out of the projects, but sooner or later life would kick him in the head and he'd be back at the bottom again.

32

Sam had disagreed. He'd joined the army, become a military policeman, and for more than a dozen years had proven his mother's predictions wrong. Within the environment of structure and order, he'd thrived. Then his partner Gary Proscelli had taken a bullet meant for Sam and was left a paraplegic as a result.

And Sam had wondered if maybe his mother wasn't right after all. Look what he was doing now.

But damned if he'd just give up, tuck his tail between his legs, and slink off into the sunset. He'd quit the service when he'd learned the brass planned to transfer him to Oakland Army Base. Just who the hell had they expected to get Gary settled if he was sent to the other side of the continent? There had been reams of paperwork that accompanied an army discharge and reams more for establishing disability benefits. Not to mention his friend's need of someone to help ease the transition into a new way of life.

God, the guilt of watching Gary struggle to put his life back together had just about eaten Sam alive, and he'd known he had to do something. Once he'd had them situated in a small, ground-floor Miami apartment, he had looked around for a way to realize a dream they'd been kicking around for years.

They had always talked about putting in their twenty-five years, then taking their service retirement and buying themselves a fishing lodge. Frankly, it had been an ambition that seemed far off in some distant, dimly envisioned future. But when the plan was shot down by the same bullet that par-

alyzed Gary, Sam had needed a way to make money
fast.

There weren't a lot of prospects for a grunt with a
high-school education and too few college credits.
Crime was out, and law enforcement didn't pay
enough, not if he hoped to realize their goal anytime
in this century. That was too bad in a way, because
he thought he'd like being a cop—he'd sure liked
being an MP. But this wasn't about him. It was about
taking care of business so Gary's future was secure.
Bounty hunting seemed the fastest way to make
money. The fact that Sam had no desire to become a
bail enforcer and had come to hate the job the longer
he was in it was immaterial.

He was dead tired of the daily contact with Miami's lowest life-forms. But after a year and a half it
was paying off for him, for just a few weeks ago the
fishing lodge of his and Gary's dreams had come on
the market. It was the site of some of their best times,
the vacation getaway in North Carolina they'd returned to several years running. It was a little slice
of heaven right here on earth, and they'd never expected to see a For Sale sign on it.

Sam was going to get it for them. The down payment was steeper than he'd expected, but he had
thirty days to come up with the amount needed before their option ran out and it went to an alternate
buyer.

He glanced over at his prisoner, who was moodily
watching traffic out the side window. At least this
one didn't have a history of violence, unlike most of
the jokers he brought in. He was kind of surprised,

in fact, at how high her bail had been set. It was her tough luck to have drawn a judge with a hard-on against the entertainment element, he guessed. But that wasn't his problem. In fact, from his point of view, the higher her bail the better, since his cut upon delivery was a straight 10 percent.

First, however, he had to get Red back to Miami without any more screwups like this morning's. Sam reached for the street map and shook it out.

Catherine heard him grumbling to himself and glanced over. Whenever they came to a red light, which seemed to be about every two minutes, he bent his head over the map on the console between their seats and muttered extremely rude words beneath his breath. She caught herself staring at the huge hand he'd spread out over the tangle of paper. It was long-fingered and powerful-looking, and she had to hurriedly direct her attention back out the window when she experienced a savage spurt of satisfaction upon seeing the red welts bisecting the back of it. Dear God. She never thought she'd see the day when she'd feel *good* about inflicting that sort of damage on someone.

The streets they traveled were cast in preternatural gloom by the buildings that loomed on either side, and for the first time she took note of the scenery that had been passing by outside her window. She'd been too upset to pay attention when they'd exited off the freeway, but realized they were in downtown Seattle.

Whatever for? SeaTac Airport was a good ten miles to the south.

Several blocks later, her captor made a rumbling sound of satisfaction deep in his throat and turned the car into a Thrifty Rental Car lot. Within seconds he'd parked their vehicle and had himself, Catherine, Kaylee's luggage, and his own duffel bag all lined up at the counter inside the miniscule agency shack. While he talked to the counterman about turning in the car, Catherine discreetly attempted to extricate her wrist from the hard fingers that encircled it. Sam immediately stopped what he was doing and turned those piercing golden brown eyes on her, using a subtle shift of one large shoulder to block the counterman's view.

"We can do this one of two ways," he informed her in a low voice. "We can handle it nice and friendly-like, or I can slap the cuffs on you and very publicly drag you kicking and screaming if necessary. Frankly, Red, I don't give a rat's ass about your dignity, so the choice is up to you."

Catherine's arm went slack in his hold. Seething quietly, she trailed obediently behind him when he left the rental agency a minute later and strode up the street. Noting the way he favored his left leg, she congratulated herself on at least preventing his job from being a complete walk in the park. Giving him a limp and a scratched hand, however, hadn't noticeably improved her own situation. He was still dragging her off to . . . where was he taking her, anyway?

A block later they paused in front of a tan marble-tiled building on the corner of Eighth and Stewart. When he opened the door to admit them, Catherine came to a dead halt and stared up at the blue-and-white sign overhead. *"Greyhound?"* she said incredulously. "We're taking a *bus* to Miami?"

To Catherine's amazement, a dull red flush crept up Sam's throat and over his strong jaw to the smooth, flat planes of his cheeks. He glowered off at some distant point beyond her left ear, refusing to meet her eyes. His obvious discomfort gave her back something she hadn't possessed since the moment he'd exploded into her life: a modicum of control. She quirked a brow at him. "What's the deal here, McKade? Aren't you big, bad bounty hunter types given a travel allowance?"

His fingers tightened around her wrist for an instant, but he merely growled, "That's cute, Red, I'm amused," before he dragged her over to the ticket counter. Fifteen minutes later, he was tucking their tickets into the chest pocket of his white shirt and leading her to a row of molded plastic seats that were bolted to the floor outside the game room. He dumped their luggage. "Take a load off."

"My. How could I possibly refuse an invitation so charmingly put?" Picking out the cleanest chair, she sat.

He kicked their luggage nearer to her seat, then plunked himself down next to her. Leaning forward, he planted his elbows on his widespread thighs, his shirt stretching tight across his shoulders and his large hands dangling between his knees as he stared down at the gritty red tiles between his feet. His left thigh infringed on Catherine's space.

She sat stiffly upright, with her ankles aligned and

her knees pressed primly together and angled point-edly away from the muscular leg encroaching on her territory. She knew she probably looked prissy in the extreme, but she didn't care. It was all she could do at the moment to keep her flip-flopping emotions in check. Listening to the electronic trills and beeps coming from the video arcade at her back, she stared off into space.

Sam watched her out of the corner of his eye and scowled. She had a way about her that made him feel like a mannerless ox. The way she sat there like royalty among the hoi polloi, it was hard to remember she made her living strutting her stuff in the minimum of clothing. What an actress. He was tempted to press in a little closer with his left thigh just to see what she would do about it.

But that probably wasn't such a hot idea. Damn. What was it about her that kept enticing him to set aside his professionalism?

He bent down and snagged his duffel bag, lifting it to his lap. Opening the zipper, he began pulling out the contents to run a brief inventory, and his mood took an upward swing. He wasn't nearly as bad off as he'd feared he'd be.

"What on earth are you doing?"

He looked over to see that she had turned to face him. She was staring at the pile of jeans, T-shirts and underwear in his lap, and at the shaving kit balanced on top of it all.

"Checking to see what I've got here."

"Why, did your wife pack it for you or something?"

Sam's snort of laughter was brief and unamused. "Lady, do I look like the product of wedded bliss to you?"

Her big green eyes were level as they met his. "I don't think you really want to know what you look like to me, McKade. You do, however, appear marginally intelligent enough to remember what you threw in a bag last night or this morning."

For some reason, the insult made him smile. He had to hand it to her, she wasn't a mealy-mouthed little whiner. "The bag's been in the trunk of my car for . . . I can't remember how long," he said. Its permanent place there had prevented him from being caught short on more than one surveillance. "I'd left the car at the overnight lot, so I had just enough time before my flight left this morning to retrieve the bag. A lucky thing for me, too, or I would've had to outfit myself at gift-shop prices when you got away from me at MIA."

"MIA? Oh, please, what's that, bounty-hunter speak for missing in action?"

Right. Like you don't know. "Okay, I'll play the game," he said with a show of patience. "Miami International Airport. Where we both came from this morning." Hell. So much for his good mood. He could have gone the whole damn day without a reminder of how much she'd already cost him in airline and bus tickets.

A little towheaded boy climbed up onto the chair next to Catherine. "Hi!" he said. Hanging on to the back of the molded plastic seat with one chubby hand, he inclined toward her, the grape drink in his free hand tilting precariously near the rim of his cup.

"Tommy! Leave the lady alone." An exhausted-looking blonde in worn discount-store clothing took the seat on the other side of her son.

To Sam's surprise, Catherine smiled at both mother and child. "It's okay," she assured the woman, then, focusing on the boy, added softly, "Hello, Tommy."

"Know what?" the tyke demanded. "I'm gonna be fo' years ode next week." He grinned and then further informed her, "Me an' Mommy's goin' to Pote'land." He made an expansive gesture with the hand holding the juice. "We's gonna live with my granny. How 'bout you? Where you goin'?" Grape juice sloshed from the cup with the final question, arcing through the air to splatter the front of Catherine's blouse, her bare knees, and the floor. Sucking in a startled breath, she leaped to her feet, plucking the soaked cotton away from her chest.

"Oh, Tommy, look what you done!" the mother wailed. "I'm sorry miss, I'm so sorry." She got up to dab ineffectually at Catherine's stained blouse with a paper napkin. Her escalating distress communicated itself to the boy, and his whimper of surprise turned into a full-fledged wail.

"It's okay. Really. It's an old blouse." Catherine took the damp napkin from the woman's hand and blotted juice from her legs.

Sam was surprised by her restraint. He would have pegged her as a woman who'd fly off the handle over something like this. He climbed to his feet.

"Come on," he said, picking up their bags. "You can clean up in the rest room."

Leaving the woman babbling apologies and the boy sobbing, Sam took Catherine by the elbow and escorted her up the ramp to the women's rest room. He shoved open the door and stuck his head inside, checking to make sure there were no exits she could shimmy out of. A woman drying her hands at the sink gasped in outrage, but he ignored her and handed Catherine the suitcase. "Go get yourself cleaned up."

Catherine used tap water and a handful of paper towels to clean sticky trails of grape juice from her skin. She peeled off her blouse, and after a regretful examination, tossed it in the trash can. It was simply stained beyond repair. Squatting down, she snapped opened Kaylee's suitcase and flipped back the top.

For a woman who had spent her entire adult life disguising her too-lush curves, the choices presented within were agonizing. She tried on one top after the other, and each seemed to her more revealing than the one before. She finally settled on an emerald green baby-T, but seeing her reflection in the mirror, she tugged self-consciously at the skimpy fabric in an attempt to make the shirt's hem reach the waistband of her shorts. And oh, dear Lord, if only it would conform less to the shape of her breasts! She gave the contents of the suitcase a final, futile search. Didn't Kaylee own one article of clothing that didn't glitter, shine, or fit like it was sprayed on?

Heavy pounding on the rest-room door made her

jump. "Open up, Red," McKade's voice said. "You've been in there long enough."

She charged over to the door and yanked it open. "Back off! I'm not your trick poodle; I'll be out when I'm finished."

His eyes zeroed in like heat-seeking missiles on her breasts. Then his gaze was all over her, and she watched his Adam's apple take a slow slide up and down the strong column of his throat. "Um, yeah. Sure. Okay," he agreed vaguely. He dragged his gaze up to her face, and his dark brows snapped together above the strong blade of his nose as he recollected himself. "You got two minutes, MacPherson."

She slammed the door in his face. "Do this, Red, don't do that," she mimicked bitterly. "I really need some lowlife bounty hunter dragging me all over hell and gone, telling me what to do." She repacked Kaylee's suitcase, then rose to her feet and looked around.

What on earth had she been thinking, to waste time worrying about the fit of her sister's clothes when she had a minute alone to figure a way out of this mess? Damn! She could kick herself. Was there a window in here? She looked around. No, no window. All right, then, think. What else? Lipstick! She'd write an SOS on the mirror. Maybe someone would read it and call the FBI or something.

She pawed through the purse for Kaylee's industrial-sized makeup bag. Digging a tube of Woodrose Creme out of the bottom, she thumbed off the cap and swiveled up the base. Bracing one hand on the sink, she leaned into the mirror.

The door whipped open behind her.

"What *is* your problem?" she demanded of Sam's reflection. Holding his gaze, she rounded her lips and stroked on creamy color. "Is the men's room out of order or something?" She watched him watch her blot her lips with a tissue and saw his gaze drop down to the thrust of her bottom. Then it bounced back up to her image in the mirror. She formed a little moue with her mouth and stood back to study herself critically in the mirror. Briskly, she dropped the lipstick into her purse, turned, and gestured toward the stall. "It's all yours."

He was across the room in a flash, slapping his big hands down on the countertop on either side of her hips, crowding her up against the sink. "You don't want to push me, Red."

Her chin angled up. "Or what, you'll drag me across the country and throw me in jail?"

A muscle jumped in his jaw. Then he stepped back, his eyes cool once again as the fires were abruptly banked. "Come on. The bus will be here soon."

Panic blasted through Catherine's system. With the moment of departure at hand, everything suddenly felt much too real, and her brief rebellion ended not with a bang but a whimper. No! She couldn't allow this to happen! She'd built a life for herself here, a *safe* life untouched by the messy extremes her sister always seemed to find. And now, because of Kaylee, she was about to be . . .

"No!" She broke for the door, a futile move, a stupid move—she knew that even before Sam snagged her with one arm around her waist, plucking her off her feet. She wasn't capable of calm reasoning at the moment, however. She reacted instinctively and struck out wildly, aiming fists and feet at any part of his body she could reach, until both his arms wrapped around her and he shuffled them a few steps to the right. The next thing she knew, she was pinned too tightly between the stall wall and his unyielding musculature to inflict further damage.

"Calm down," he ordered, his voice rumbling up from his chest to speak directly into her ear in a tone that was surprisingly lacking in aggression. "Get ahold of yourself, Red." He made an adjustment that freed the use of one of his hands without allowing her to budge an inch. Cradling the top of her head in it, he held her immobile, her forehead pressed to his chest, and the warmth of his wide palm and long fingers spread through her hair to the skull beneath. Then he smoothed his hand down the length of her hair. "Stop and think about this a minute," he instructed her in that same brisk tone. "This isn't getting you anywhere." Heat from his body began to penetrate her locked muscles.

Sam felt her small movement of surprise. He wondered what she'd think if he told her he'd expected this, or something like it anyway. There always came a point when prisoners realized they were well and truly headed back to jail to face the trial they'd thought to escape. Reaction to that realization was universal—they all tried to bolt. The men he simply subdued with brute strength and the use of his gun, if necessary. With most of the women he tried to be a little gentler, provided they didn't get aggressive with him first. Red was the only prisoner, however— male or female—he'd ever left uncuffed.

Not that she was special or anything—it wasn't for her benefit. They had a long way to go, and his profit margin couldn't afford the price of airline tickets to get them there fast. He didn't for a minute believe her wild tale of overheard murder plots, buried bodies, and hit men. But he was a cautious man, and on the outside chance there was a kernal of honesty in the woman, he wanted to get them across the country as inconspicuously as possible. It only took one look at Red to know chances of her escaping notice were pretty slim, and the shrink-wrap clothing she'd just changed into didn't improve their odds. Add handcuffs to the mix, and he might as well just park it right here and wait for one of the phantom bad guys to show up and take her off his hands.

His expression hardened. That wasn't going to happen, not while he was on the job. And not while he had a fee to collect and a lodge to buy for Gary.

He unwrapped himself from around her and stepped back. She swayed a little, and he braced his hands on her shoulders to steady her against the stall wall. "Come on," he said roughly. "It's time to get a move on."

She blinked. "What?"

Sam's mouth tightened when he took in those big, haunted eyes. Man. She really had missed her calling. She could have made a killing in Hollywood—

and wouldn't have even had to expose 95 percent of her body to do it.

He didn't know why the thought of that kept sticking in his craw.

The door behind them opened. Sam's head whipped around as he abruptly realized he'd left himself in a position where he couldn't quickly reach his gun. A woman came through the door but stopped in her tracks when she saw him. Her eyes narrowed as she looked from him to Catherine.

"You two go somewhere else to neck," she snapped. "There are those of us who like to know when we come into a women's room that there'll only be women in it."

"Come on, Red." He picked up their suitcases and slid an arm around her shoulders, escorting her past the disapproving woman. He guided her down the ramp to the departure door. "The bus is gonna be here in a few minutes." He glanced at his watch. It read 5:40. That reminded him it was closing on dinnertime, and they were going to be on a bus for hours before the next scheduled stop. "You want something to eat?"

She shook her head.

"We probably have time to get you a Whopper." He nodded toward the Burger King that had an entrance into the bus station.

She gave a tiny shudder and looked away.

"Okay, no burger. I think I'll pick up a few things to take with us, though. You might change your mind once we're on the road." He pulled her over to a group of vending machines and made several selections, which he tossed in his bag. Then he guided her outside, where other passengers were either standing around smoking or simply milling about as they waited for the bus. Sam patted his chest pocket for his own cigarettes before remembering he'd given the damn things up.

The bus rumbled into the lot a moment later. Coming to a halt, the door wheezed open. Sam ushered his prisoner on board and soon had their bags stored on the shelf overhead and Catherine settled in a window seat. He sat down next to her.

She didn't speak. She didn't so much as acknowledge his presence. Head averted, she gazed out the window as the bus pulled out of the station. He might as well not exist.

That was just fine with him. The less they talked, the better. It wasn't as if he were dying to get to know her. The lights of the city gilded her profile as the bus headed for the freeway, and Sam scowled. She was just merchandise to him—that funny clench he'd gotten in his gut when he'd watched her putting on her lipstick notwithstanding. Hell, that was probably just hunger anyway—she might not have wanted a hamburger, but he sure could have used one. *Merchandise*, he repeated silently. *She's merchandise.*

A package he needed to deliver before his goal could be accomplished.

4

KAYLEE STOOD IN front of the closet in her sister's bedroom. Didn't Catherine own one article of clothing that had a smidgen of pizzazz? She rattled through the hangers. Sage green, antique gold, *brown* for God's sake. And not a style among 'em that made a girl want to strap on her highest heels and strut her stuff. How could Cat wear this shit? With a long-suffering sigh, Kaylee exchanged her glittery purple tube top for a boring little bronze blouse. Okay, the color flattered her complexion. But it sure as hell didn't showcase her pretty boobs or tiny waist to their best advantage.

Still. If the neighbors caught a glimpse of her, it was necessary they believe they were seeing Catherine. Kaylee needed a place to catch her breath while she figured out what to do next.

She'd recognized the bounty hunter from the day she'd made arrangements for her bail. He hadn't said a word to her in the bondsman's office that afternoon, but she always noticed a sexy man, and God knew those big broody types had sex appeal to spare.

Today she had hidden in a neighbor's carport until

he'd taken Catherine away. Then she'd crept back to her sister's house and looked in all of Catherine's traditional hiding places until she'd located the spare house key. As she'd let herself in the back door, she'd briefly felt guilty about the situation she'd placed her sister in. But Catherine would handle it; she could handle anything. Kaylee was the one who always needed a little help.

Standing in Catherine's bedroom, however, she was beginning to doubt the wisdom of her actions. She told herself her sister would be fine. It would be one day, two at the most, out of Catherine's life. Hell, she'd get a free trip to Miami, where she'd set 'em all straight in no uncertain terms about her true identity.

It was the idea of Cat anywhere near Miami, however, that made Kaylee nervous. Oh, God, what had she been thinking? Sanchez had leverage, connections—he knew people from all walks of life, with varying degrees of influence. He'd undoubtedly concocted some story and had the word out he was looking for her, and if someone at the courthouse, say, spotted her twin and told him, he wasn't going to stop to ask Catherine's name.

He'd figure he knew it already and would take steps to see Catherine didn't draw another breath. Oh, man. She'd really screwed up this time.

The last thing Kaylee expected, as she paced nervously through the house a few hours later, was to look out the window and see Bobby LaBon parking at the curb.

He found me! How in God's name did he find me? Her

first impulse was to run. But she checked herself. *Think.* She had to do what Cat would do. She had to *be* Catherine.

Kaylee stilled. That was it. She had to be Catherine.

She raced into the bathroom and scrubbed her makeup off with a washcloth. She whipped a brush through her hair and anchored it on top of her head in a sloppy ponytail. Then, buttoning Catherine's blouse up to her throat, she dashed back to the front door. Taking deep breaths, she opened the door before Bobby had a chance to knock on it or kick it in or whatever it was he planned, and reached for the paper she'd heard hit the porch earlier. Straightening, she gave a start. "Oh! Hello. May I help you?"

His gaze slid over her. "I came to take you back, baby."

"*Excuse* me?" Kaylee congratulated herself on the tone of voice. It was Cat's tone, the one that used to make her and Pop say, *Jaysus, Caty-girl, lighten up.*

Bobby frowned. "Kaylee?"

"No, I'm Catherine, Kaylee's sister. Who are you? Hey!" she protested when he shoved past her into the foyer. Oh, God, what would Catherine do in this situation? Kaylee headed straight for the phone and picked up the receiver. She managed to punch out 9-1 before he depressed the cutoff switch with two fingers.

"Show me some proof you're who you say you are," he demanded.

She didn't even have to think twice, she *knew* what Catherine's reaction to that would be. Her chin shot up in the exact manner her sister's would. "In a pig's eye I will," she said frostily. "This is my home—I don't have to prove my identity to you." She thrust out an imperious arm, pointing at the door. "Get out of my house."

He pulled out a gun. He didn't point the thing at her, but the threat was implicit. "Show me some proof."

On the other hand, her sister had never been inflexible to the point of stupidity. Chin in the air, Kaylee led the way into the living room, where she handed him two framed photographs from the bookshelves. One was a glamour shot of herself, in which she looked damn good, if she did say so herself. "Kaylee," she said. The other was a framed photo of her sister at the ocean. The face was hauntingly similar to that in the glamour shot, but the differences were also apparent. "Me." She held it up to her face, then picked up Catherine's purse and extracted the driver's license from the wallet within. She handed it to him and waved a hand down her body, indicating her clothes, which Bobby had good reason to know she wouldn't be caught dead in under ordinary circumstances. "Also me."

He gave her a slow once-over, his gaze lingering on the smooth length of her legs. "Nice."

Oh, you no-good, lousy, two-timing sonofabitch. It was all Kaylee could do to stand still and return his look with a bland one of her own. *If I weren't so terrified you're going to hurt me, I'd cut your black heart out for that.*

"Where's Kaylee?" he demanded.

"I wouldn't know. Who *are* you?"

"Bobby LaBon." He paused. "Her boyfriend."

"Okay, I've heard of you." Kaylee drew back. "But why are you here?" There could only be one reason, couldn't there, given the gun. *Oh, Bobby.* "Did you two have a fight or something?"

"Listen, don't play dumb with me. I've been tracking her all day, and I know she's been here. Now for the last time, where is she?" He narrowed his eyes at her. "Don't make me pull my gun again."

"I don't know where she is," Kaylee said, and knew when his eyes suddenly narrowed on her that she had somehow made a mistake. Brain spinning, she thought back. *Oh, shit.* It was the voice. She'd reverted to the throaty voice she had worked so hard over the years to make second nature.

He towered over her. "Okay, Kaylee, what's the deal? I'd know that voice anywhere."

The part of her that wasn't numb with terror was gratified to know he could tell her apart from her twin sister. She wasn't, however, about to admit to anything. "Catherine," she corrected him frostily. "My name is Catherine."

"Like hell. You had me goin' for a minute there, but I know who you are now." His tone softened. "Listen, baby, I'm not here representing Sanchez or Chains or anyone else. I didn't come to hurt you. I came on my own as soon as I got your note, because I was worried about you."

Inside, she sagged with relief, but outwardly she maintained her composure. "Yes, of course you were. That's why you pulled a gun on me."

"What, this?" Bobby looked at the pistol, and then

tucked it away. "That was just to get your attention when I thought you were your sister. Hell, I didn't even buy it until after I got back to Miami and read your note. I got it to protect you, baby, not hurt you."

"I'm certain that would be very reassuring, Mr. LaBon, if I were my sister. However, I am not. For the last time, my name is Catherine."

"Yeah?" The next thing she knew, he'd wrapped his hands around her upper arms and tugged her up against his chest. "Well, let's just try a little experiment," he suggested. Lowering his head, he kissed her.

And kissed her. And continued to kiss her.

To within an inch of her life.

Kaylee gave it her best shot, but she was a sucker for a forceful man, and she had never been able to resist Bobby's kisses in particular. By the time he raised his head, she was limp all over. If not for the support of his hands holding her upright, she was sure she'd slip right down his body and across the floor like one of those Slinky toys.

Bobby's own eyes were heavy-lidded as he stared down at her. "Hey, baby," he greeted her huskily, and licked his bottom lip. "I missed ya."

That snapped her back to reality with a vengeance. Shoving back, she linked her fingers together and swung for his head as if it were a ball she intended to send into the stands.

Bobby dodged, and her clubbed fists glanced off the side of his head. Had his reflexes been the slightest bit slower, the blow would have knocked him off his feet. "Jesus, Kaylee." He rubbed at his temple. "You coulda killed me."

"I was arrested! You told me it was your car, and I was arrested!"

"Yeah, I'm sorry about that. I don't know what happened."

"I know what happened—you stole the damn car and I took the rap!"

"Hey, I didn't *steal* it. It was just there, baby, singin' a siren song, and I knew Babette was out of town, so I sorta . . . borrowed it for a while, that's all. I meant to bring it back, but when that trip came up I got to thinking how cute you'd look driving it around, and I guess it kinda slipped my mind that it wasn't actually mine. It was an honest mistake, Kaylee."

"Honest mistake, my butt. And exactly who the hell is this Babette bimbo to you, anyway? When she came down to the station after I was arrested, I got the distinct impression she knew you."

"Yeah, well—" Bobby eyed her warily. "She does in a way. She's kind of an old, uh, girlfriend."

"An old girlfriend?" Kaylee was furious. "An old *girlfriend*? I don't *believe* you, Bobby! Good God, I don't believe *me*—I don't believe I've been sleeping with a guy who'd date a woman named Babette."

"It was a long time ago, baby."

"I don't care if it was the last century—your taste sucks. What's her problem, anyhow?"

"Dog in the manger, babe. The fact that we broke up didn't bother her at all. But when she saw what a fine woman I replaced her with, she couldn't handle it. She probably took one look at you and knew she couldn't come close to matching you for looks and style, and it made her green with envy.''

''Oh, stuff it, Bobby. I'm in big trouble because of you. I need help here, not flattery.''

''We'll get it straightened out, babe.''

''And just how will we do that? Didn't you read the note I left you? I overheard Sanchez and Chains discussing murder! I can't go back to Florida, and you aren't exactly Mr. Upstanding Citizen yourself.'' A sudden thought occurred to her, and she studied him with speculative interest through narrowed eyes. ''So, you're here strictly because you want my forgiveness, huh? That's the only reason—you want to kiss and make up?''

''More than anything.'' Bobby moved in, crouching a little to bring their faces to an equitable level, surrounding Kaylee with his heat and scent, running his hands up and down her arms.

She felt her knees start to go weak and braced herself against his effect. ''Well, I'll consider it,'' she agreed smoothly. ''Just as soon as you help me rescue Catherine.''

Bobby straightened up, his hands dropping to his sides. ''Rescue Catherine from what?''

She briefly explained. ''I shouldn't have let him take her, Bobby, but I wasn't thinking beyond not letting him get me. Now we've got to get her back.''

''Are you crazy?''

Her eyebrow elevated. ''So much for kiss and make up, I guess.''

Bobby rammed his fingers through his hair. ''I

don't see what one thing has to do with the other!"

"You don't have to see—those are my terms. Cat said that just once she'd like to see me take responsibility for one of my messes. Well, Bobby, I'm in this one because of you, so make up your mind. Either you're going to help me or you're not. What's it gonna be?".

"Yeah, sure, whatever. What's the bounty hunter's name?"

"How should I know?"

"Whatta ya mean you don't know? How do you expect me to—never mind. Let me think a minute." They were both silent for several moments. Bobby began absentmindedly to crack his knuckles, making Kaylee shudder.

"Bobby, do you mind!"

"Quiet! I'm trying to think."

She rolled her eyes but kept silent.

A moment went by before he looked over at her. "Okay, what's the bailsman's name?" She told him, and he asked, "Where's the phone?"

"There's one in the kitchen. Why? What are you going to do?"

"Call Scott Bell in Miami. Guy's a wizard with the computer. With the bailsman's name he can find out who your bounty hunter is. Once he knows that, he can tap into the airline records and find out what flight the guy and your sister are on."

"Oh. Good thinking." Kaylee picked up Catherine's purse and riffled through the wallet. She was pleased to see it contained one of her favorite items in the whole world, a gold card. "You start on that, and I'll be back in a while."

Bobby, on his way to the kitchen, stopped dead in his tracks. He turned and stared at her. "Where the hell you going?"

"Shopping. Look at me, Bobby." She spread her arms wide and stared down at the little bronze blouse in distaste. "I have got to pick up some decent clothes."

5

CATHERINE AWOKE TO find that sometime during the night, she'd gravitated in Sam's direction. She was partly curled against him, her cheek resting on the hard curve of his biceps. His arm then stretched down across the divider between their seats and culminated in his big hand cupping her thigh. Long, callused fingers spread heat where they curled lightly around her inner knee. And his thumb, she realized as she came more fully awake, was lazily rubbing back and forth on her bare skin.

Her eyes snapped open and she found herself staring up into his face. It was rough with dark stubble and there was a blatantly sexual droop to his full bottom lip. Opening her mouth to demand just who the hell did he think he was, she realized his eyes were barely slitted open, and they were focused with drowsy concentration on the sight of his own weathered thumb moving in slow, measured strokes against her pale skin. Clearly he wasn't fully conscious.

She knew the moment he was. His thumb stilled, and the arm beneath her cheek tensed. She could sense him lowering his chin to look down at her, and she hastily closed her eyes, feigning sleep. It was sheer impulse, and a childish one at that, but once she'd made the decision she was stuck with it. And if pretending to be asleep might save her an awkward moment or two, that worked for her.

He slid his hand free and eased her off his arm. A moment later he rose from his seat and pulled his duffel bag from the baggage rack overhead. Then he was gone, presumably to the rest room at the back of the bus.

Catherine opened her eyes and sat up. Stiff and groggy, she stretched in place in an attempt to work out the worst of the kinks. Sitting as tall as possible, she braced her fingers in the small of her back, thrust back her shoulders, and arched her back to stretch out her spine, angling her chin up and to the left. When she swiveled her head to the right, she found herself looking directly at the man across the aisle. He, in return, was staring with glazed eyes at her breasts.

Her first inclination was to hunch in her shoulders to disguise their fullness as best she could. But a kernel of something—irritation? defiance?—stopped her. She immediately amended her provocative posture, but there was no use hoping for concealment in her sister's skintight top. So she did the next best thing. She continued to regard the man levelly until his gaze unglued from her chest. When he noticed her watching him with unsmiling eyes and a raised eyebrow, he flushed deep red and quickly looked away.

It afforded her a small surge of empowerment.

She turned back to stare out the window, although the scenery that streamed past went largely unnoticed. Last night's panic-induced numbness was gone, and she had decisions to make. One option was simply to allow herself to be hauled cross-country like a good little soldier. She could remain inviolate within the walls of her hard-won good manners, play by McKade's rules, and straighten everything out once they reached Miami. It's what she most likely would have done yesterday.

She didn't like that option today.

McKade had turned her world upside down, all for the sake of a lousy buck, and she saw no reason to facilitate his job for him. He was obviously in a great burning hurry to get her to Miami and collect his fee, although for the life of her she couldn't quite figure where Greyhound fit into the scenario. But their mode of transportation was an accomplished fact, and she needed to stay focused on the point. And the point was, if McKade was in such a huge rush, then her object should clearly be to do whatever it took to slow the journey down. She knew only one way to accomplish that.

The idea of behaving as she knew Kaylee would in the same situation made Catherine cringe. She'd spent her entire adult life developing a respectable niche for herself that was worlds removed from the exhibitionist milieu that was her twin's.

Still, sometimes being the nice, well-behaved woman didn't pay off. Just look where it had gotten her so far. McKade was so damn smug, so almighty cocksure he knew just who it was he had on his hands. That being the case, she really shouldn't disappoint the man, should she? He insisted she was Kaylee; then, Kaylee he would get.

In spades.

Sam made his way carefully back up the aisle. *You are not to touch the merchandise,* he warned himself for the umpteenth time since he'd left Red sleeping and escaped to the rest room. *You got that, McKade? You've got a job to do, and you are not going to screw it up.* He snorted softly. Appropriate word, that, given the red-hot urge the feel of her skin had raised in him and the temptation to follow that urge to its natural conclusion.

But he hadn't followed it, and it wouldn't get to the point where his urges turned into a problem— he'd see to that. Hell, he'd just been half-asleep, that was all, and she'd been there. It was a knee-jerk reaction to having awakened with his hand on a woman's long, firm, incredibly soft-skinned leg; the result would have been the same with any woman. He'd been a long time without sex and was sure as hell gonna remedy the situation once this job was complete. Meanwhile, he'd just be grateful that Red had slept through it. Keep her quiet and keep a low profile, that was the ticket.

He saw his prisoner step into the aisle and reach for the overhead luggage rack, displaying her spectacular body from her fingertips right down to the tiptoes she balanced on as she stretched for her bag. Three men tripped over themselves to be first in line to lend her a hand.

She didn't even look at them, which surprised Sam. It didn't cajole him from the flash of temper that surged through him, however, and in a few giant strides he arrived at the cluster of passengers blocking the aisle. He elbowed two of the men out of his way and reached over the head of the third for Catherine's bag. "I've got it," he growled in the face of the man's persistence, and his tone was such that Red's little helper finally got smart and backed off.

The angle for lifting was an awkward one, and Sam felt a twinge in his back as he lowered the suitcase. "What the hell have you got in here?" he demanded, setting it on her seat. He'd bet the lodge it wasn't books.

"More interesting stuff than the pitiful heap of belongings in your bag, you can bet." She unsnapped the locks and flipped open the top.

Sam's heart sank. He only caught a glimpse, but the contents all seemed to either glitter, shine, or be about the size of his wallet. It was the latter that really worried him, since it meant serious expansion would be necessary to cover those killer curves of hers, and you could bet the fit would therefore be the next best thing to spray paint. She bent over to paw through the case, and he growled in frustration to notice the man across the aisle and the guy behind him, too, craning their necks to get a better look at the sweet, full, inverted-heart shape of her butt. He moved to block their view.

"Ah," she murmured in satisfaction, and Sam watched her wrestle free a case from within the case. She unzipped it and he realized that this was most likely the source of the added weight. It sure as hell wasn't her clothing—she probably didn't have a single piece in there that weighed in at more than three ounces. That left either the several pairs of skyscraper heels or the bag of cosmetics and toiletries. While he watched, she assembled a washcloth, one of those mysterious bottles of girly lotion that women swear by, a toothbrush, and toothpaste. She juggled her booty for a few moments, then gave up and tossed everything back into the cosmetic case. Lifting it, she straightened and turned her head to look up at him.

"Rest room's in the back, right?"

He grunted.

Watching her stroll down the aisle, he scowled to see the number of men who stared at her with avid eyes as she approached, and then twisted around to observe her from the back as she passed by. Friggin' wonderful. He could kiss the low profile good-bye.

At least she'd only used a fraction of the ten pounds of cosmetics in her case, he noted with relief when she returned. She'd applied lipstick and mascara, but that appeared to be all. And she hadn't reverted to the big hair she'd worn yesterday at the airport, thank God. But Sam knew he was grasping at straws. She'd brushed her hair and put it up in a conservative little knot on the crown of her head. It should have been demure, dammit. Already, however, it had tilted to one side, and bright strands had slid free down the curve of her nape and along her long white throat, and it made her look instead as if she'd just rolled out of some guy's bed.

His last stubborn hope of remaining inconspicuous died a quiet death.

At least she was being pretty docile. He'd take his blessings where he could find them and be grateful for that. Sam stood aside to allow her to slip into her seat.

She turned to look at him. "How long does it take to get to Florida?"

"Three and a half days."

He thought he saw a flash of panic in the depths of her eyes but if so, she got a firm handle on it, for she merely nodded. "I'm hungry," was all she said.

"We'll be stopping for breakfast in about ten minutes. Can you hold out until then, or do you need something to tide you over?"

"I'll wait." Catherine was happy to wait, for it meant a few minutes' reprieve from what she planned to do. Her stomach lurched, but hunger wasn't really the problem. Nerves were, and the slow, deep breaths she took in an attempt to quell them were only partially successful.

The bus rolled into Boise ten minutes later and into a café parking lot five minutes after that. "Breakfast stop, folks," the driver announced, and opened the door. "You've got forty-five minutes, and I advise you not to dawdle. I keep a strict schedule."

Up the aisle, a small white-haired woman struggled to shove an awkwardly shaped parcel onto the overhead storage shelf. People jostled her as they streamed around her, mumbling with impatience. Sam, to Catherine's astonishment, stopped at the woman's side.

"Here, ma'am, let me get that for you," he offered, and lifted it from her hands to slide it easily onto the rack. Giving it a thump of accomplishment, he brushed aside her thanks, flashed a crooked self-deprecating smile, and waved her ahead of them.

Catherine studied him from beneath her lashes as they walked into the cafe and settled into seats at a small table by the counter. He looked large and mean, with that black stubble, sullen mouth, and those fierce golden eyes, and Lord knew her experience with him had done nothing to dispel the impression. Who, then, would have thought he could possess such a charming smile? For about thirty seconds it had made him look sort of shy and sweet. She shook her head and accepted a menu from the waitress. She must be more nervous than she thought, to imagine a fool thing like that.

Catherine perused the menu, looking for the most expensive item. Her reward was Sam's pained expression when she gave her order. *Get used to it, McKade* she silently advised him. *I'm going to hit you right where it hurts the most—in your precious timetable and your almighty wallet.*

The thought of what she was about to do made her breath come faster and shallower, and she forced herself to draw it in deeper and hold it longer until her heart rate slowed a little. Timing was everything, and as much as she'd like to get this over with, she wasn't going to mess it up by rushing it. No way would she risk allowing Sam enough time to get the problem straightened out before the bus had to leave. She looked around the crowded café.

It was filled to capacity with bus passengers. Harried waitresses rushed around, taking orders and filling coffee cups. The one handling their table stopped by just long enough to top off Sam's cup and set down two sets of flatware wrapped in paper napkins. Catherine unrolled hers and placed the napkin in her lap.

Fifteen minutes later the waitress was back, sliding their orders onto the table in front of them. "Be careful, folks, the plates are hot. Enjoy your breakfast."

Catherine ate little. Pushing her food around her plate, she kept her gaze locked on the bus driver seated two tables away.

"Dammit, are you gonna eat that, or are you just going to play with it?" Sam demanded irritably, and she started, her gaze swinging back to look at him.

"I'm not as hungry as I thought," she managed to respond with credible coolness.

"Then give it here. Maybe you grew up in the lap of luxury, Red, but where I came from we didn't waste food."

Catherine stared at him incredulously. "No right-thinking person would call the neighborhood where I was raised the lap of luxury." Hearing herself, she emitted a delicate snort. "But then I forget, we're talking about you."

"Yeah, my standards are kind of low, all right." He deliberately chose to misunderstand the insult as he reached for her plate. "Hell, if you knew where your next meal was coming from seven days a week, I'd say you had it pretty cushy." Transferring all but a small portion of her breakfast onto his plate, he passed it back to her. "Here. Eat that."

"I told you, I'm not—"

"I said eat. You didn't have dinner last night, and I'll be damned if I'll let you get sick on me."

"Oh, no, we certainly mustn't inconvenience the fearless bounty hunter," she snapped, and stabbed up a forkful of hash browns. Anger steadied her nervous stomach and she cleaned her plate. Then she looked across the table. "Give me back some of that steak."

He cut the remaining piece in half and passed it to her.

Too soon, their meal was finished, their coffee cups had been refilled, and Catherine's personal clock had ticked down to the zero hour. It was time to act. She shoved to her feet. "I have to use the rest room."

"Hold it." Sam reached across the table to grab her purse. "Hand over your lipstick."

"Excuse me?"

"Don't play dumb, Red. Give me your lipstick."

Catherine heaved a sigh but did as he requested, digging out a tube and passing it to him.

"All of them, Red."

She located three more and handed them over. "Satisfied?"

"I'll be satisfied when I collect my fee in Miami." Then he accompanied her to the rest room, where he opened the door and stuck his head inside, making sure there wasn't an alternate exit.

There wasn't. It was a closet-sized, windowless room with a toilet, a sink, and a cupboard full of supplies. Catherine slammed the door in his face, locked it behind her, and went to stand over the sink, her hands braced against the cool porcelain. She let her head hang as she drew in deep, controlled breaths. Then, exhaling, she raised it to meet her own gaze head-on in the flyspecked mirror.

Okay, she could do this—how hard could it be, after all? She just had to cause one itsy-bitsy scene, make a fuss that the bus driver wouldn't want to waste time trying to straighten out. She could and would do it, if it meant throwing a crimp into Sam's cherished schedule.

Don't think about how foolish it will make you feel. She took another deep breath, straightened her shoulders, and turned to the door. She was reaching to unlock it just as someone pounded on it from out in the hallway. Jumping a foot, she snatched her hand back.

"Open up, Red. It's time to go."

Staring at the lock, Catherine took a step backwards. *Oh, my goodness, that's it.* She didn't have to make her scene out in the cafe at all. Why hadn't it occurred to her before? She could do it from right here.

"Red! Open up!"

"No." It came out weak, soft, and she cleared her throat and tried again. "*No.*"

There was an instant of silence. Then, low and menacing, "What did you say?"

"I said no. I am not coming out."

His fist smacked the panel hard. "Get your butt out here, or I'll break down the damn door!"

"Hey now," an irate female voice demanded. "What's going on back here?"

"This doesn't concern you, lady," Sam growled.

"I own this place, mister—it darn well does concern me. Especially when I hear a patron threatening to destroy my property."

"Listen, you don't understand—"

"Ma'am?" Catherine called through the closed panel. "Please, won't you make him go away? He got me pregnant," she improvised. "And he said he'd take care of me. I thought that meant we'd get married, you know? But he's taking me to a clinic, where he expects me to . . ." She let her voice trail away. "He says little Sammy isn't even his, even though he knows I haven't been with anyone else—"

"That's a damn lie!" Sam couldn't believe this. A crowd was gathering, the woman who owned the place was glaring at him as if he were the lowest life-form to walk the face of the earth, and the bus driver was consulting his watch. "I never laid a hand on her."

Somewhere in the growing crowd a man snorted with disbelief, and Sam swung around to glower at him. "What?" he demanded in the face of the stranger's patent skepticism.

"We've all seen her, buddy," the man said. "And we've seen you hovering over her. You expect us to believe you've been keeping your hands to yourself?"

"I don't give a flying . . . flick . . . what you believe, Jack. It's the truth. And if I've 'hovered' it's because I'm a bail enforcer and she's my prisoner."

Another man emitted a sound of cynical amusement. Sam recognized him as the clown from across the aisle, the one so enamored of Red's ass. "Nice work if you can get it," the guy commented dryly. "You and your prisoner sure wrap together pretty tight to sleep . . . but I imagine that's just part of the job, huh? Wouldn't want her gettin' away or anything." He looked past Sam to the closed rest-room door and smiled lasciviously. "Can't say as I blame ya. I wouldn't mind playing 'bounty hunter' with that one myself."

"Three minutes, folks," the bus driver called out.

Sam swung around and pounded on the door again. "All right, Red, this has gone far enough. You come out now, or I'm kicking down the door."

"You do, and you'd better be prepared to pay for it," the owner said.

"Jesus." He wanted badly to hit something but reined in his temper. "You got a screwdriver, then? I could take the hinges off."

"No."

He didn't have a prayer of doing it in three minutes, anyway. Sam thumped his forehead down on the door panel and strung together several creatively linked vulgarities.

"Time to board, folks."

"Sammy?" Catherine's voice drifted through the portal. "Don't be mad at me. Please. If you don't wanna marry me, then you gotta let me go home to my momma. It's your *baby*, Sam. I can't just get rid of him."

Sam felt the mood of the crowd shift from amusement to something darker and knew Red had won this round. He turned to the driver. "Let me get our bags off the bus."

"I can't be opening up the storage compartment," the driver informed him unhelpfully. "We got rules about that."

"This won't violate your rules. They're inside on the overhead rack."

"Okay, then. Last call, folks. Bus is leaving."

Sam grasped the driver's arm as the passengers boarded the bus. "What about our tickets?"

"Talk to Darcy." The driver indicated the café owner. "She has the local concession. She'll reissue your tickets for the next bus."

"Which will be here when?"

"Do I look like a walking, talking schedule to you? Talk to Darcy." Impatient to leave, the driver shook off Sam's arm and climbed aboard. "C'mon," he snapped when Sam didn't automatically follow. "You got thirty seconds to get your bags. I've got a schedule to keep."

Sam was off in twenty and the door immediately wheezed closed behind him. A moment later, the bus rumbled out of the parking lot in a cloud of diesel smoke and disappeared around the corner.

Red was the first sight to greet his eyes when he shouldered open the café door again. She was seated at the counter, sipping a cup of something steaming while Darcy fussed over her. Three waitresses sat with their feet up in a corner booth, lingering over cups of coffee and cigarettes. He wondered what the chances were of bumming a smoke. Probably pretty slim. Dropping the bags with a thump, he stalked up to the café owner, careful not to look at his treacherous prisoner for fear he'd lose it entirely and ring her luscious white neck. "The driver said you'd reissue our tickets."

"Hmmph." Darcy gave him a disapproving glance. But she left off patting Catherine's back and moved around to the end of the counter, where a computer was set up. She asked a few questions and tapped in the keystrokes that accessed the functions to reproduce his tickets. Her businesslike demeanor lasted the length of the transaction. Then she went back to regarding him as if he'd just crawled out from under a rock.

"You've had your fun with that young woman," she snapped contemptuously as she handed him the tickets. "It's time now to be a man and accept your responsibilities."

Between the street toughs in his old neighborhood and his DIs in the army, Sam had been hassled by the best, and usually he could take about anything dished out to him with a stoic lack of response. Never let the assholes know they're gettin' to you was his motto. But something rebelled at the unfairness of hearing that disparaging tone from a total stranger. "Let me see if I've got this straight," he growled, leaning toward the café owner. "You don't know me from Adam, but you think I oughta marry Red and raise her kid."

"According to her, it's your baby, too, mister."

He laughed without humor. "Right. My baby. The one I got on her having my *fun*." That was rich. He'd been hanging on to his professionalism with both hands—and for what? So he could have the name without even a taste of the game?

Well, the hell with it. Red made a big mistake when she picked that particular method of fighting, because two could work this angle. He swallowed his temper and summoned half a smile. "Well, Miss Darcy, what can I say? When you're right, you're right." Stuffing the tickets in his shirt pocket, he turned on his heel and headed straight for the red-head at the counter.

Catherine had been keeping a wary eye on him and swiveled to face him fully when she saw him stride straight for her. She felt pumped by her victory but shaky, and she braced herself, unsure what to expect. He had to be ten kinds of furious, and he hadn't even heard yet about the schedule for the next bus. She didn't know whether to thrill at her success or fear for her life when he did hear the news. She couldn't read anything except determination on his face, but that didn't necessarily mean blood wouldn't flow.

The last thing she expected was for him to swing a leg over her thighs to straddle her where she sat, curl both big hands in her hair to hold her steady, and clamp that sullen mouth over hers.

Inexplicable white-hot sensation shot through her like a laser. Shock rocketed hard on its heels. Vaguely aware of the waitresses' gasps, Catherine reached up and grasped his wrists to pull his hands away, but it was like trying to dislodge stone, and he was already lifting his head anyway. His mouth was slow to leave hers, however. It clung to the last instant, an insistent suctioning heat that tugged at her lips. Desperate to deny the response she had no business feeling, she pulled harder at his wrists, but his palms remained cupped around her nape, his thumbs firm on her cheeks, his fingers splayed against the back of her head. The instant his lips cleared her mouth, she shoved at his chest and demanded, "What do you think you're doing, Mc—"

"I'm a pig," he murmured, and tipped his head to press his mouth to the vulnerable hollow behind her ear. His hands held her head high as he dragged his mouth slowly down the middle of her throat. "You were right on the money yesterday when you said so." He opened his lips and drew a portion of her neck against his teeth. Releasing it, he rubbed his thumb over what Catherine very much feared was the resulting red spot, and gazed up at her with those intense golden eyes. "I'm sorry, honey. I'll take care of you and the baby. I promise. You tell me what you want, and I'll do it."

Catherine stilled. Oh, the cad. The unprincipled, brazen cad. He'd taken her own story and used it against her. She squeezed her thighs tightly together. And for a minute there, to her eternal shame—

He stepped back suddenly and pulled her off her stool, whirling her around and enfolding her in his arms, her back against his chest and one of his huge hands spread across her stomach and abdomen to pull her into the hard heat of his thighs. A hard ridge poked insistently at the small of her back.

Oh, man, wasn't it awfully warm in here all of a

sudden? Looking at Darcy, Catherine decided that it wasn't only her, for the older woman, too, seemed to be dealing with a sudden rise in temperature. She was staring at them with her mouth agape while dabbing at her throat and nape with a handkerchief.

"When's the next bus, Miss Darcy?" The rumble of Sam's voice vibrated between Catherine's shoulder blades.

Darcy had to clear her throat twice. "Um, nine o'clock. Tomorrow morning."

Catherine felt every muscle in Sam's body tense. "Tomorrow?" His voice was dangerously quiet. "There's not a bus out of here until tomorrow?"

"Not heading east."

His hold grew uncomfortably tight around Catherine, and she made a small sound of distressed protest. His arms immediately loosened their grip, but the musculature surrounding her remained unyielding as stone. "Is there a motel nearby? Something on the cheap side?"

The waitresses all tripped over themselves to give him the information. Minutes later, he had both bags in one hand and a hard grip on Catherine's wrist with the other. "Well, hey, I'm real sorry we can't invite y'all to the wedding, but if you're ever in Florida, look us up. Sam and Kaylee McK—"

"Catherine," she interrupted. She gave the women a solemn look. "My name is Catherine. He seems to have a difficult time distinguishing me from my sister."

An unholy smile lit his face. "Only in the dark, darlin'," he said, and pulled her out the door. It was

quite clear he relished having had the last word—
not to mention the looks of horrified fascination his
comment had left on the waitresses' faces.

The smile faded, however, as he strode across the
lot with Catherine digging in her heels an arm's
length behind him. She had a bad feeling that his
anger was just a scratch below the surface—and if
he was attempting to walk it off, the program didn't
appear to be meeting with noticeable success. That
fact was driven home when he stopped suddenly
and swung around to face her. Their bags hit the
ground, raising a puff of dust.

"Little Sammy?" He grabbed her by the shoulders,
looming over her. "Where the blazin' hell did that
come from?" His eyes narrowed with sudden suspicion and he demanded hoarsely, "Oh, shit, Red.
Tell me you aren't really pregnant."

Catherine's chin tilted up. "Of course I'm not pregnant. Do try not to be any more ridiculous than you
can help, McKade."

"Hey, I don't happen to find it ridiculous, lady—
I find it scary. Things are bad enough as is. I sure as
hell don't need a boyfriend hot on our trail looking
to make an honest woman out of you." Then he
made a rude sound. "Though that would be a challenge I'd pay to see."

"Oh, right. Like the Tightwad of North America
would ever leave off pinching his pennies long
enough to actually part with one."

Sam pulled her up onto her toes. "Damn, you're a
pisser!"

"I try." Feigning boredom, Catherine nonchalantly picked a piece of lint from his shirt.

"Tell me where that baby business come from."

She gave him a dirty look. "Originally I planned to tell the driver you were a white slaver transporting me across state lines for salacious purposes. The pregnancy thing just sort of came to me when you were pounding on the door with your usual savoir faire, and I decided to go with that instead. There was a chance you could've talked your way out of my first idea with those stupid papers of yours, but my second story was a lot harder to argue, wasn't it?" He glowered, and she shrugged. "It seemed the expedient thing to do at the time." Suddenly remembering the way he'd called her bluff, she rolled her shoulders uneasily, eager to dislodge his hands. "Let go of me."

If anything, his grip tightened. She felt his chest brush her breasts with every angry breath he sucked in. "Jesus," he said between his teeth, "you are the biggest liar I've ever met."

Catherine shrugged. "You have a point?"

"My point is you're a brat. A low-class, expensive little brat."

Catherine yawned in his face. "Gee," she murmured. "However will I sleep nights, knowing you hold such a low opinion of me?"

6

STARING DOWN AT her, Sam snarled with obvious frustration, "Lady, you are really starting to piss me off!"

Catherine felt downright warm and cozy. When a man started repeating himself, you knew you had him on the run. She shrugged again as best she could, given the grip he had on her upper arms. "So?"

"So, give me just one good reason why the hell I shouldn't handcuff *and* gag you for the rest of this trip. And if you're smart, Red, you'll give it to me quick, because I'm just about out of patience."

That knocked the amusement out of her in a hurry. What patience? And by God she was tired of his arrogant threats. Catherine's chin jutted up, and for about five seconds as she stood nose-to-nose with him in the dusty parking lot, with the morning heat starting to shimmer up off the blacktop in visible waves, she fought an imprudent temptation to openly defy him. She'd won this round, and he couldn't stand it, pure and simple, so he was throwing his weight around. Staring up into those narrowed eyes, her knee-jerk reaction was to say, "Go ahead then, you big bully. Bring on your handcuffs and gag if you're so all-fired determined."

Fortunately, the impulse passed. She hadn't yet lost all semblance of reason, so instead she considered the question. And finally said with thoughtful slowness, "I suppose because it would make us too conspicuous, and you'd have to answer way too many questions."

His hands tightened, lifting her up onto her toes. Then, abruptly, he released her and stepped back, all expression erased from his face. He grabbed her arm, scooped up the bags, and started walking again. "Right," she heard him mutter. "Like you aren't already conspicuous all on your own."

Hah! She'd made the big, bad bounty hunter back down.

The thought brought her up short and garnered her a jerk on the arm, which got her trotting along in his wake again. Good grief, what was getting into her all of a sudden? Had she actually *enjoyed* matching wits with the big coyote? Lordy, Lordy, Lordy. And who said she'd made him back down from anything anyhow? For all she knew, he was simply retrenching to consider his options. This was not smart behavior on her part. Perhaps she ought to just be quiet for a while and allow him time to cool down.

Sam steamed as he hauled her down the road to the nearest cheap motel, checked them in, and let them into their room. He tossed their bags on the swaybacked mattress closest to the door, and watched as Red immediately transferred her case to the other bed, flipped it open, and began sorting through it.

He was determined to maintain his distance, to recoup his professionalism. After watching her for several long moments, however, curiosity got the best of him. "What the hell are you doing?"

She barely spared him a glance. "I'm going to take a shower and change into clean clothes."

The image of soapsuds slithering down naked curves was immediately, ruthlessly suppressed. Turning his back on her, he stalked over to the window and tweaked back the curtain, squinting against the glare reflecting off the cars parked in the dingy courtyard. A warning buzzed in his brain when he heard her walk from the room, and he dropped the curtain, turning back to look at her. "Hold it right there, Red." When she continued to walk away, he snapped, "I said wait a damn minute."

Her back was to him as she halted, but Sam saw her shoulders move beneath the force of the impatient sigh she heaved. "Now what?" she demanded. He'd never realized two short words could be imbued with such long-suffering martyrdom.

Not bothering to reply, he moved past her and opened the bathroom door, leaning in to check the size and placement of the window. Then he stepped back and held the door open for her. "Okay. It's all yours."

"Gee," she said snidely. "There's a window in here. Aren't you afraid I'll jump out it?"

He gave her a thorough once-over. "Not with those hips, honey."

The look Catherine gave him was full of sheer feminine outrage. "What's wrong with my hips?"

Not a damn thing. But he wasn't about to tell her that. He merely quirked an eyebrow at her.

"You think they're *fat*?"

"Go take your shower, Kaylee."

"My name is Catherine, you son of a bitch!"

Why the hell had he started this? He plowed his fingers through his hair. "Red, go take your damn shower."

"Fine, I'm going." Her belongings clutched to her breast, she whirled around. "I wouldn't hold my breath waiting for any hot water to be left for you though, McKade." She slammed the door behind her with a muttered, "Fat, my Aunt Beatrice."

Sam exchanged his slacks for a pair of jeans, flopped onto his back on the bed, and stacked his hands beneath his head. He listened to the shower kick on in the other room and scowled up at the ceiling.

Kissing her in the café had been a big, big mistake. Hell, barely half an hour earlier he'd been giving himself a lecture on keeping his hands off the merchandise, and good, solid advice it had been, too. But had he then had the presence of mind to listen to it? Hell no, Brother—he'd seen an opportunity to beat her at her own game and thought himself pretty damn clever to take it. Now he knew it for what it was: one of the dumbest moves he'd made in recent history.

And God knew, he'd been making his share.

He knew her taste now—rich, smooth, like the finest blended whiskey, the kind that slid down a man's throat real slow and easy and exploded heat everywhere it touched. It was knowledge he would sure as hell be happier without, but he'd just have to work around it. He had a job to do here.

He'd failed Gary once. Damned if he was going to let him down again. And despite his friend's insistence that another opportunity would come along if the deal on the North Carolina lodge fell through, Sam knew whose fault such an eventuality would be. No unruly surge of hormones was going to divert him from his goal.

It'd sure as hell help if she owned some baggy clothes, though. He resented the hint of desperation that colored the thought as he watched her emerge from the bathroom ten minutes later. But the truth of the matter was, if her clothes displayed her figure just a little less faithfully, then maybe he wouldn't keep getting so distracted.

She had on a pair of cutoff jeans that exposed an acre of firm, creamy white skin. Her hair was wet and slicked back from her face, and the ends dripped onto her forest green skinny-knit tank top. Was she wearing a bra under that thing? Hell, he didn't see where there was room for a bra.

"Well, you were wrong as usual," she informed him coolly, glancing up briefly from her foray through the makeup bag. "It was my shoulders that wouldn't fit through the window. My hips slid through slicker than butter." She gave one of the full curves under discussion a satisfied little pat.

He turned the startled laugh that erupted into a

cough. Damn. He should have known she'd give the window a try—the woman had proven to be a doer from the moment he'd first clapped eyes on her. He'd only made the remark in the first place because his nose was out of joint. It had been one of those throwaway cheap shots, feeble payback for having been bested. And he should have realized she would treat it as a personal challenge. Damn lucky thing for him that his space-relativity skills were better honed than hers were, or she'd be miles down the road by now.

He watched her through slitted eyes as she sat down on the worn chenille spread that covered the other bed and began pulling bottle after bottle of nail polish from the makeup case. She commenced to line them up on the cheap blond-laminated nightstand next to the bed, switching and shuffling them around like little tin soldiers until she had them in some aesthetic order understood only by her. Next, she propped her right ankle up on her left knee and commenced stuffing cotton balls between her toes. After considering her polish collection carefully, she looked up at him. "What do you think, McKade, should I use Satin Mauve"—she picked up a bottle and shook it in his direction—"or Renegade Red?"

Okay, he'd play the game. "Renegade Red." That seemed fitting.

"Satin Mauve it is," she agreed.

Should have known, fool. He grunted and pulled his gun from its holster.

Catherine's hands flew up in surrender. "Whoa. I think the Mauve goes better with my skin tones, but

if you feel that strongly about it, Samuel, all you
gotta do is say so.''

"That's real witty, Red. I can't tell you how
amused I am.'' Reaching for his duffel bag, he riffled
through it. He located his gun-cleaning kit and stu-
diously kept his attention away from her as he broke
down his revolver and laid the parts out on a piece
of newspaper. He was nevertheless highly aware of
every creak the old springs made each time she
shifted her weight on the other bed. When she whispered a mild curse, he gave up the fight and glanced
over at her.

And wished immediately that he hadn't.

She was sitting with her heel pulled in close to her
butt, her long white thigh supporting the weight of
her upper body as she leaned forward to carefully
wipe a smear of color from a cuticle. Sam's mouth
went dry at the provocative picture she made.

The frayed hem of her cutoffs brushed her firm
thighs, and her breast was pressed back against the
wall of her chest by the leg she hugged to it. Creamy
flesh swelled above the neckline of her top, and as
he watched, a droplet of water dripped from the end
of her hair and rolled over her collarbone, along the
swell of exposed breast, and into her cleavage. A fine
dusting of goose bumps rose in its wake and the nipple not hidden behind her updrawn leg tightened,
poking at the clingy material that covered it. Without
missing a stroke of the polish she was meticulously
applying, she shivered.

Sam's sudden leap up off his bed caused Catherine's hand to jerk in surprise, and polish slopped in
a jagged slash across her toe.

"Hey!" Scowling, she raised her head to give him hell, only to feel her mouth drop open. She closed it with a snap but swallowed drily when she saw him staring down at her as he ripped his shirt off in three impatient movements. What on earth did he think he doing? What was he—*Oh . . . my . . . Gawwwd.*

Heart thudding dully, she found herself staring at his bared torso as if mesmerized, unable to look away. He was . . . something. Big. Muscular without being muscle-bound. His skin was a lot darker than her own, sort of a toasted brown, and the same black hair that feathered his forearms covered his chest in a fan from collarbone to the bottom of his pectorals. It then dwindled to a line that bisected his tightly muscled diaphragm and abdomen before disappearing into the waistband of his low-slung jeans.

She felt her eyes grow larger with every purposeful step he took in her direction. There was something in his amber eyes that was fierce and unsettling. When his arms suddenly lashed out toward her, she flinched back. But his white shirt merely snapped out and billowed like a sail over her head for a second before drifting to settle over her shoulders. He pulled it closed around her with a decisive tug. "You looked cold," he muttered, as his big hands slid from the fabric. He turned away to pull a T-shirt out of his bag, and Catherine watched the muscles in his back ripple as he pulled it on over his head.

"I, um, was, a little. You must be a mind reader." Her voice was embarrassingly hoarse, and, self-consciously, she cleared her throat. "Thank you." Carefully returning the cap with its attached brush to the bottle of nail polish, she set it aside and slid her arms into the sleeves of the shirt. Slowly, she rolled back the cuffs.

The oxford cloth retained the warmth of his body heat and carried his scent. Feeling decently covered for the first time since she'd had to relinquish her own blouse in the Greyhound depot, Catherine tugged her wet hair from beneath the shirt's collar and gave the sleeve covering her right arm a surreptitious sniff as she watched Sam settle back onto the other bed. The shirt smelled of both laundry soap and man. Its owner, she noticed, didn't so much as glance in her direction as he picked up a blued-steel pistol part and resumed cleaning his weapon. She reached for a cotton swab and the bottle of polish remover to clean up the mess on her toe.

Lord have mercy. She didn't get this guy at all. He threatened her with a gag and handcuffs in one breath, then gave her the shirt off his back with the next because he thought she might be cold.

She could call it a split-personality disorder, except what did that say about her own?

She hadn't been behaving at all like herself since he'd barged into her life. Insurrection tended to be Kaylee's specialty—it was something Catherine generally avoided, as it only got her in trouble. Yet here she was acting with the same reckless abandon that had marked the night she and her sister had wound up with matching tattoos on their butts. And if that wasn't a perfect illustration of bad judgment, she didn't know what was.

Even without the permanent reminder, that was a night Catherine would never forget, if for no other reason than the rare, perfect solidarity she'd briefly shared with her sister. Rebelling against Mama's ubiquitous lectures and buzzing on too much cheap wine that Kaylee had liberated right out from under Papa's nose, it was Catherine who had come up with the idea of the much regretted kiss-my-ass tattoo. As an unspoken rejection of Mama's constant warnings, the little red pursed lips had seemed so funny and fitting at the time.

Which just went to show what happened when she allowed her impulses free rein. She hadn't been laughing when she'd awakened the next morning with a pounding head and a very sore, very permanent mark on her rear.

She reminded herself grimly that if she didn't watch her step now, she was going to land herself in something equally unpalatable.

And yet . . .

Part of her liked that tattoo. And she was tired of being so proper all the time, especially if this was her reward. Besides, while she'd always found Kaylee's lackadaisical refusal to accept responsibility irritating, she'd also harbored a secret admiration for her lack of inhibitions. She herself so often felt self-conscious. It must be very liberating just to thrust it all out there and say to hell with those who disapproved. The closest she'd ever come was when she'd improvised on the spur of the moment to get her sister out of trouble. But that was role-playing, pretending—not the same as being comfortable having your real self on display.

It wasn't the same thing.

Well, perhaps she'd never know that exact feeling of liberation, but damned if she wasn't going to get *something* out of this debacle. She had sworn to hinder Sam's progress to Miami in any way she could, and she still intended to do that. But this was supposed to have been her vacation, and she'd decided in the shower that she was going to derive whatever enjoyment she could squeeze out of the situation. Thus, the rosy new paint job on her toenails.

This sort of primping was more Kaylee's bailiwick, but what the hell, she had a lot of time on her hands, not to mention all the ingredients for an entire makeover at her disposal. It was fun and such a small thing, so why not indulge herself? Catherine looked down at her newly pedicured toes, tilting her feet first left, then right, for the complete overview. They looked pretty good, if she did say so herself.

As for wrangling with Sam—well, he needed to be kept on his toes. Catherine glanced over at him, watching the twist and bunch of muscles in his brown hands as he reassembled the gun. He was way too arrogant. It wasn't as if she *enjoyed* sparring with him, for heaven's sake—she simply didn't believe it was wise to allow him to grow too complacent. She did what she had to do to prevent him from running roughshod over her.

Really.

Looking at his hands again, big and tanned,

scarred by her fingernails, and so masculine with all those hard tendons and standing veins, she felt an inexplicable clenching in her stomach, a tightening that worked its way down deep between her legs. She hastily looked away.

She just had to pick her moment, that was all, she assured herself. Until she found it, there was certainly no disgrace in indulging herself with Kaylee's makeup kit. It would fill the minutes and hours while she watched and waited for the exact right moment: when he'd finally relax his vigilance and she could get the hell out of Dodge.

"Kaylee din't show for rehearsal again today, boss."

Hector Sanchez placed a manicured fingertip on the liquor invoice to mark his place and looked up, directing his attention to the man who had spoken. Jimmy Chains stood in the doorway, resplendent in a custom-made summerweight suit, a shirt unbuttoned to mid-chest, and a multitude of the various weight gold chains from which his nickname had derived. Hector reached out his free hand for the cigar that smoldered in the ashtray and brought it to his mouth, taking a satisfying drag. "If she misses this evening's performance, that'll make three nights in a row. We might as well put the word out that we need two new showgirls instead of just one, because Kaylee's obviously skipped town. Angel told me about her arrest."

"Yeah," Chains agreed. "I heard about that, too. And I ain't seen her since I ran into her in the hallway outside the girls' dressin' room Wednesday night."

Hector slowly lowered his cigar. "Since you did what?"

"Din't I tell ya, boss? I thought I told ya."

"No," Hector said through clenched teeth. "You didn't tell me."

"Oh. I coulda swore I did. In any case, I remember on account of our meetin' Wednesday night. Hell, it couldn'ta been five minutes later that me 'n her practic'ly had a collision. I still ain't sure how we avoided it, the way she came racin' outta that dressing room like a bat outta hell. She was sure off to somewhere in a big damn hurry."

The motel didn't run to telephones in the rooms, which was why Sam found himself in the phone booth outside the office, dialing home and trying to forget the look on Catherine's face when he'd snapped the handcuffs on her to secure her to the bed frame.

The receiver at the other end was picked up. "Yowser," came the greeting in Gary's distinctive raspy voice.

"Hey, it's me."

"Sambo! Where the hell are ya, man?"

"Idaho. I've got this showgirl handcuffed to the motel-room bed whose—"

"Well, all right, Sam! I guess I can finally quit worryin' about you, after all. Didn't know you went in for that bondage stuff, but if it works for you, it works for me. Is she a blonde? I bet she's a blonde."

"No, she's a redhead, but listen—"

"No shit? That's even better than a blonde. I love redheads. She the kind with freckles all over her body?"

"No, she's got skin so white, you can see her veins through it in places." *Sonofabitch!* Sam scowled at the neon sign that blinked the motel's name off and on. This conversation wasn't going at all the way he'd intended. It was supposed to have taken his mind *off* Red's body, not detail the highlights for Gary's entertainment. He wondered if the motel office had a cigarette machine—he could sure use a smoke to settle his nerves.

"She's cargo, Gare," he insisted flatly. "Merchandise I've got to transport back to Miami. Her bond is gonna be our ticket to the lodge."

There was a moment of silence. Then, "Damn, boy, we gotta get you a life."

"Hey, I've got a life!"

"No, you've got a job," Gary disagreed. "You work like a dog, you fuss over me, and that's about it. When's the last time you had a date? *I've* got a healthier social life than you do. And it's for damn sure my sex life is livelier."

"Yeah, well, just as soon as I get us the lodge maybe I'll find me a nice woman who bakes cookies and likes kids. Stranger things have happened."

Once again silence filled the line. Then, "Wait a minute, let me see if I've got this straight." Gary's raspy voice was incredulous. "You've got a redheaded showgirl, who by definition probably has tits like torpedoes and legs up to here, chained to your bed. But you think, if you're really lucky, that maybe somewhere down the road you'll get to meet *Betty Crocker*? Well, yeah, sure, I can see where that'd be preferable." Gary made a noise like a steam engine about to blow. "Are you out of your fuckin' *mind*? Go for the showgirl!" A moment later he said quietly, "Or is she one of the violent ones? She do something really ugly?"

"Nah. She just thugged a car."

"Then I don't see the problem. Man, the first thing *this* kid'd do is let her know I can still get it up with the best of 'em, and she can ignore the wheelchair unless it's to climb aboard. On second thought, go for Betty. Bring the redhead home for me."

Sam made an involuntary sound of dissent, which, to his eternal disgust, Gary immediately latched on to.

"Ah. Like that, is it? I'd like to meet this woman. I say go for it, Sambo. For once in your life go for it. I'm not suggesting you have to marry the woman. Frankly though, bud, your criteria for what constitutes a good date is kinda skewed, if you ask me. Homemade cookies are overrated, man—trust me on this. You can find a decent bakery just about anywhere you go."

7

BOBBY GENTLY RESEATED the telephone receiver and went in search of Kaylee. He found her in Catherine's bedroom, giving herself a bikini wax. Wincing as he watched the wax strip get ripped away from the vulnerable area, he said, "You aren't gonna believe what I just found out, baby."

"What's that?" She rent a second strip from the other thigh.

"How can you *do* that?" he demanded. His eyes watered just watching her, and he found himself pressing his thighs together and hunching over a bit. "Damn, Kaylee, doesn't that hurt?"

"Not really. It's kind of like plucking your eyebrows—it hurts the first few times you do it, but then it toughens right up." She tossed the used wax strips into the bedside wastebasket and reached for some lotion to soothe the newly exfoliated area. Then she looked up at him. "What aren't I going to believe?"

"Huh?" He forced his gaze from the spread of her smooth white thighs and the sweet, silk-covered delta at their apex. When his eyes finally rose all the way up to meet hers it was to find her watching him

93

with a Don't-even-think-about-it-Buster expression. Man, she could hold a grudge. "Oh. Scott called—my computer guy? You're never going to believe how McKade and your sister are traveling back to Miami."

"He found them?" Kaylee jumped up off the bed. "Where are they?"

"In Idaho."

"Idaho?" Kaylee's eyebrows drew together over her slender white nose. "What on earth are they doing in Idaho?"

"They're traveling by—you're gonna love this—Greyhound bus."

Kaylee smacked his chest with the flat of her hand, shoving him back a step. "Dammit, Bobby, quit joking around! I'm worried about her."

"I'm not kidding, baby. They're on a Greyhound bus. Actually, this is their second bus—something happened to make them either miss or get kicked off the first one."

"Catherine!" Forgetting for the moment that she was through with men in general and Bobby in particular, Kaylee reached out and squeezed his forearm. She laughed, that rich, deep-in-the-throat, tickled-to-death gurgle that never failed to elevate Bobby's blood pressure. "She's slowing him down. Cat's really smart, and she thinks fast on her feet. She woulda made a great con artist if only she weren't so damn determined to have a Brady Bunch life." Kaylee shook her head, mourning her sister's lost opportunities. "When we were kids she always came up with the most unique stuff to get us—well, me, mostly—outta trouble." She grinned in remembrance. "I bet she's pissed as all get out, and when Cat gets mad—look out." Recalling herself, Kaylee let her hand slide away from Bobby's arm, took a giant step backward, and gave him a look. "So what do we do next?"

"Catch the three o'clock puddle jumper at Boeing Field, rent a car in Pocatello, and track them down."

Hector Sanchez hung up the phone and sat staring at it in thoughtful silence for a moment. Then he fished a cigar out of the humidor, clipped off its end, and lighted it. Muted laughter filtered through the office wall as this week's headliner expertly worked the audience.

A bail enforcer named McKade had Kaylee in custody and was bringing her back to Miami to stand trial on the auto-theft charge. Sanchez could make sense of that part, although he was frankly far from happy to hear it. But Greyhound? Why the fuck would the bounty hunter transport her by bus?

It was a question to which there might never be an answer, and Hector supposed it didn't actually matter anyway, since in the long run it would undoubtedly work to his benefit. If McKade had done the normal thing and flown her back, most likely they would have arrived by now, which meant Kaylee would already be in the county jail. And the minute she was in the lockup, his own chances of getting to her were considerably diminished. This was not an acceptable possibility. Kaylee MacPherson was a question mark that needed to be erased. He had an excellent life going for him here, and he'd be damned if he'd allow some bimbo showgirl to screw it up for him. God only knew what song the worthless bitch would sing to the DA if she thought it would save her own sorry butt.

Well, it wasn't a scenario worth considering, let alone expending perfectly good energy worrying about, because it was simply not going to happen. She was being transported cross-country by bus, and that opened a whole world of opportunities to remove once and for all the threat she represented.

He sure wished there was someone other than Chains to send, though. Jimmy Chains Slovak was dumb as a brick. As Tropicana's head of security that was of no particular import—it had, in fact, a certain advantage. He was loyal and easily manipulated. Tell him what needed to be done and Chains did it without question. As an independent thinker, however, the man was a dead loss. Hector shuddered to think of all that could go wrong with Chains in command.

Any way he looked at it, though, Sanchez knew he didn't have a helluva lot of choice. It wasn't as if he had mob connections or could just go to the friggin' Yellow Pages and look under *Hit Men* when he wanted a job taken care of. And Jimmy had performed competently with the Alice Mayberry affair. Hector would simply have to trust he'd do equally well with the Kaylee MacPherson problem.

But this time Chains would be far away, beyond Hector's ability to control, and solely dependent upon his own brainpower.

It was enough to scare the crap out of any right-thinking individual.

"You're wearing *those*?" Sam watched in fascinated horror as Catherine stood on first one foot and then the other while she worked a pair of three-and-a-half-inch-stiletto-heeled shoes onto her feet. Jesus, it was bad enough when she'd walked out of the bathroom in that jade green spandex microdress; all it *needed* to make them totally conspicuous was the addition of a pair of glittering gold fuck-me shoes. When she didn't so much as glance in his direction, he stepped closer and wished immediately that he hadn't. She smelled great. "How come you're not wearing your Keds?"

Catherine looked right through him as she brushed past to the suitcase on the bed. Rummaging through it, she pulled out the huge bag of toiletries.

Sam watched her every move. "Ah, I get it. The silent treatment, huh?"

She brushed by him once again to return to the bathroom. Since she didn't bother to close the door, he followed in her wake and propped a shoulder against the jamb as he watched her lean into the sink. The skintight dress rode up the back of her thighs until it was just a hairbreadth this side of legal, and he didn't have to stretch his imagination at all to visualize the little red tattoo on her ass. He resolutely blinked the apparition away while she shook a bottle of foundation and tipped some out onto a small sponge.

Sam watched in increasing dread as the war paint

mounted up. When she flipped her hair upside down and started doing something to it that resulted, once she was right-side up again, in a sizable French-looking, I've-just-been-screwed hairdo with pieces tumbling free all over the place, he could no longer hold his tongue.

"This is because I cuffed you to the bed, isn't it?" He shoved upright from the doorjamb. "Well, I'm sorry I had to do that, but it was necessary. Hell, I turned you loose the minute I got back."

She blew by him again, and he slugged the door-frame in frustration, then shook out his fingers and swore. Sucking on a split knuckle, he glowered at her. Dammit, what was the matter with him anyway? He had nothing to apologize for. He was doing his job, and if Miz MacPherson didn't like the way he did it, that was too damn bad. She was his prisoner, not his houseguest.

"Pack your suitcase," he snapped, stepping back into the main body of the room and fumbling the fastenings closed on his own bag. He carried it to the motel-room door and impatiently waited as she slowly complied.

An hour and a half later they arrived at Darcy's café. It was loud with conversation and clattering dishes, and Catherine blinked at the sudden on-slaught of noise as she attempted to shrug out from under Sam's proprietary arm. It was amazing how fast one grew accustomed to quiet surroundings.

She still hadn't spoken one word more than nec-essary, and the café where he'd taken her for break-fast was a world removed in decibel level from

Darcy's. They'd eaten without speaking, their attention either directed at their plates or out the plate-glass window. And the silence that she'd instigated apparently seemed perfectly workable to Sam.

But from the moment they'd approached Darcy's café, where they were to catch the bus, he had been acting like the soon-to-be-husband he'd yesterday convinced the café personnel that he was. He hugged her to his side and held her there with the casual splay of one big hand over her hip. Discreetly, she dug an elbow into his side in an attempt to gain herself a little space.

His arm tightened warningly. She left off trying to squirm free, but casually swung one of her spiked heels over his instep and bore down hard.

He bent his head and lovingly nuzzled her ear, lipping the lobe into his mouth and giving it a gentle tug with his teeth. "You don't get that friggin' thing outta my foot, Red," he growled, "I'm gonna have to get mean."

Catherine tried to crush his jaw by sharply hunching her shoulder to her ear. To her satisfaction his mouth moved away, but not without a final blast of warm breath and a quick flick of his tongue at her lobe.

"And this is supposed to be something new?" she demanded. She reluctantly removed the spiked heel from his instep, cursing her heightened awareness of him. By rights he should leave her stone cold. But except for the crop of goose bumps that rose all along her right side in response to the feel of his breath insinuating itself down the sensitive whorls of her ear, she was anything but. Nervously, she tried again to step away, but his grip merely tightened until she found herself plastered from shoulder to calf against unyielding, heat-producing muscle and bone.

He tilted down his chin to look at her, cupping hers in his free hand and watching with apparent fascination the contrast his dark-skinned thumb made as it rubbed back and forth against her pale flesh. "Honey, I've been a pussycat up until now. You don't even want to make me mad."

Catherine managed to keep her expression impassive. What she *wanted* was to hurt him. Badly. She longed to rake her nails down his arrogant face, to bite and punch and kick and scream until he begged for mercy. She had all this impotent rage bottled up inside of her, and it was making her feel slightly crazed.

"You realize this is war, don't you, McKade?" For a couple of hours yesterday she had nearly forgotten that. The truth had been driven home like a stake through a vampire's heart when he'd calmly produced his handcuffs and left her manacled to the bed frame while he'd gone out to make a phone call.

Sam pressed his thumb against her lower lip. "Wouldn't have it any other way, MacPherson. Oh. Excuse me—*Miz* MacPherson, I mean." His voice was a rough murmur, and Catherine could have ground her teeth right down to the gum line. She just knew that to an outsider he looked as if he were spouting sweet nothings in her ear.

She had never in her life experienced such a feeling of helplessness as when she was locked to that bed last night. She wasn't accustomed to being without defenses—one way or another she had always managed to take care of her own problems, and everyone else's as well, and she knew herself to be a capable, competent woman. But with a single click of a chrome handcuff, she'd become completely vulnerable.

She wouldn't forgive him for that.

She had donned Kaylee's look-at-me apparel with definite defiance this morning. The shoes were killing her after that trek up and down the highway, and the makeup and big hair were embarrassing, to say the least, but she would live with it because she knew it made her increasingly conspicuous—if not stand out like a hooker at a Baptist wedding—which in turn drove Sam right up the wall. And *that* had become a reward all its own.

So, instead of responding to Sam's insolence, she jerked her head away from his caressing fingers, crossed her arms beneath her breasts, and turned as far away from him as his hold allowed. Pointedly ignoring him, she watched the crowd.

That's when she saw the woman using American Sign.

Actually there were two of them, but a suitcase rested by one woman's feet, which made Catherine believe she might be catching the same bus that they were. Reading their conversation, she soon saw that this was so. With a lift of her hopes, Catherine tried to decide how to use the woman's knowledge of sign language to her own advantage.

She couldn't tell from the hand conversation which

of the women was deaf. Hopefully, the one traveling with them could speak; communication between the deaf and the hearing was difficult without the spoken word.

"Five minutes, folks," the bus driver suddenly called out.

Once again Catherine tried to pull free of Sam's grasp. "I have to use the bathroom."

Sam snorted. "Forget it. You can hold it until we're on the bus. No way in hell I'm going through a repeat of yesterday."

"Oh, get a grip, McKade. You spiked that ploy when you publicly announced your willingness to marry me and give baby Sammy a name, so it would be pretty damn lame for a repeat performance with the same people, now wouldn't it? Just how stupid do you think I am, anyway?"

He didn't answer beyond a cynically raised black eyebrow, and Catherine's lips tightened. But damned if she was going to let him reduce her to childish sulks. She'd simply have to come up with a way to turn things around.

It truly was unfortunate that the only thing she could come up with on such short notice was to flaunt her body, but a woman had to work with the tools she was given. The minute Sam released her and bent down to grab their bags, she smoothed her dress over her hips, thrust her shoulders back, her chest out, and looked around until her gaze alighted on a young soldier who was staring at her thighs and hips with glazed eyes. She gave him an encouraging smile that she knew darn well he'd never see, since she simultaneously executed a little hip wiggle guaranteed to keep the young man's gaze from ever climbing that high. The important thing was that Sam straightened in time to see it, and she had the satisfaction of hearing him say something truly obscene beneath his breath.

Turning to see who she was smiling at, he latched on to her arm and pulled her close. His mouth assumed its familiar sullen slant and his black brows snapped together as he glowered at the soldier until the young man took notice. Flushing a painful dull red, he turned away.

Catherine felt immensely better. Nothing like destroying a man's complacency to cheer a girl up. And for one brief moment, at least, she hadn't felt the least bit self-conscious. Rather, she'd experienced an unaccustomed flash of feminine power.

"Time to board, folks."

Catherine and Sam passed by the women she'd watched conversing in sign. Catherine saw them hug; then observed as the nonpassenger gripped the other woman's shoulders and held her at arm's length. "I'm going to miss you, Mary," she heard her say with the slightly atonal, foreign-accented-sounding intonations of the deaf.

The departing Mary reached out and brushed her fingertips along her friend's cheek. "I'll miss you, too. We are not going to let so much time pass before our next visit. I promise."

The smallest of smiles curled Catherine's lips. Perfect.

There was a slight commotion at the door of the

bus. An elderly woman was frantically assuring the driver she'd had her ticket when she'd gotten off for breakfast. A bottleneck built as the other passengers slowed down to catch the driver's eye, flashed their own tickets, and then edged with varying degrees of patience around the woman.

Sam stopped at the woman's side. She was teary-eyed and frantic as she scrambled through her purse, and he took her elbow in a gentle grasp to move her out of the doorway. "Take a deep breath, ma'am," he instructed when she looked up at him in panic. After she'd done so, he said, "Now. Your ticket is bound to be here somewhere. Where do you usually put it?"

"In my pocketbook, but it's not there!" Her breathing started to accelerate again.

"Easy now, it's okay. Would it be all right if my friend took a look through your bag? Sometimes it helps to have fresh eyes on a search."

The purse quivered when the woman held it out, and Catherine gently removed it from her fingers. She unzipped the side compartment and checked the contents.

"Check your pockets, ma'am," Sam advised, while Catherine methodically searched the handbag, and the woman calmed somewhat with something constructive to do. She chattered nervously as she went through the pockets of her cotton jacket. "I always keep it in my pocketbook so I'll know right where to find it, but this time when I went to find it, it was gone . . . oh. Oh, my goodness!" She laughed in embarrassed relief as she withdrew the ticket from a pocket. "Here it is! Oh, my goodness gracious, I remember now—I was going to put it in my handbag but then that nice young soldier offered me a hand down the bus stairs and I stuck it away so I could take his arm. Oh, *thank* you, young man! Thank you so much." She accepted her purse back from Catherine. "And you too, miss."

Catherine climbed aboard the bus in the woman's wake. "Don't go thinking," she muttered to Sam out of the side of her mouth, "that just because you did one nice thing, I'm gonna start believing you're a decent guy." *But damn you, I prefer my villains one-dimensional.* She certainly preferred them without this confusingly sweet soft spot for little old ladies in distress.

"Wouldn't dream of it," he agreed. "Anyway, I'm thinking I just might kick the next little ol' granny I see."

"Much more in keeping with the guy I'm used to dealing with." She took a deep breath, expelled it, then straightened her shoulders. "I suppose even Hitler had his moments."

"There you go. I knew you'd find a way to square it with your personal view of me if you just thought about it hard enough."

The bus lurched into gear as they arrived at their seats and Catherine's balance in her skyscraper heels was thrown off kilter. Arms windmilling, she toppled backwards.

Grabbing at the overhead rack with one hand, Sam snaked out his free arm and wrapped it around her waist, hauling her in with a yank. Catherine slammed up against him. Their position was a precarious one, with her bent backwards from the waist, tightly clutching at Sam, who loomed over her. Eyes locked, hearts suddenly kicked into overdrive, for one hot suspended moment neither one moved.

Then they straightened, shoved apart. Catherine spotted the woman who knew sign near the rear of the bus and didn't slide into her seat when Sam stiffly stood aside and gestured for her to enter. She self-consciously straightened her dress. "I've got to use the rest room," she said, and mortified by the breathlessness of her voice, cleared her throat and added with acerbity, "Since you so rudely denied it to me in the café."

"Fine and dandy, Sister. Just hand over your purse."

She tossed it at him. "We've really got to get you one of your own, McKade," she said, and continued down the aisle, aware of those golden brown eyes boring a hole in her back.

Her pace was glacial because of the treacherous height of her sister's heels, but that ultimately worked in her favor. Heads popped up row by row to watch her mincing, hip-swiveling progress down the aisle, and all that activity eventually caught the attention of the one woman whose attention Catherine desired.

The moment the woman looked up, Catherine discreetly placed her right fist on her left palm and lifted both hands together. She then pointed her right index finger at herself. *Help me.*

The woman's eyes widened but she pressed the

backs of her fingers together, fingertips pointed at her own chest, and rolled them over until they were facing Catherine, palms up, little fingers pressed together. *How?*

My name is Catherine MacPherson. Call police next stop. The man I'm with is holding me against my will. Please. Help me.

The woman nodded her fist. *Yes.*

With heartfelt gratitude, Catherine touched the fingertips of her right hand to her chin, then snapped the hand down. *Thank you.*

Catherine let herself into the tiny rest room and leaned back against the door while her heart rate settled. Catching sight of herself in the mirror, she leaned in closer and grimaced. God, that makeup. It was much too much and would more likely hinder her cause rather than help it, if the afternoon went at all as she expected. She pumped water into the miniscule basin and, using dispenser soap and paper towels, managed to wash most of the cosmetics off. Next she climbed out of Kaylee's heels with a sigh of relief. Carrying them with her, she let herself out of the rest room.

Back at their seats, she tossed the shoes in Sam's lap. "I want my Keds."

Sam's eyes rolled toward the ceiling. "Thank you, God," he said fervently, and promptly rose to his feet to pull her suitcase off the overhead rack. When he sat down again, he handed her the shoes, and said, "Hey, you washed off all the war paint." His eyes narrowed. "And I have to ask myself why. Just what the hell are you up to now, Red?"

Ignoring him, Catherine plucked pins from her hair and bent forward to brush all the teasing from it. She gathered it into another French twist, but this one was smooth and conservative.

Sam poked a long finger in her side. "What are you cooking up in that busy little brain, lady?"

Blinking up at him with feigned innocence, she speared the pins into her hair to anchor it in place.

"Red?" he persisted.

Catherine turned her head and stared out the window.

"Back to the silent treatment again, are we?" Sam shrugged and settled back. "Okay. I can live with that. In fact it's kinda peaceful. It's the only time I can be halfway certain you aren't lying through your pearly white teeth."

8

◌◌◌◠◠◠◠ THE BUS STOPPED in Pocatello for lunch. Continuing on its journey forty-five minutes later, it had barely hit the expressway on-ramp before sirens were heard wailing up the freeway. Passengers on the left side of the bus craned their necks to watch the Highway Patrol car that flashed by, blue lights swirling, siren shrieking. Then the siren abruptly moaned into silence and a voice that emanated from a speaker atop the vehicle ordered the bus to the shoulder of the road.

The pneumatic door whooshed open a moment later and a highway patrolman boarded the bus. He spoke to the driver, who in turn plucked a handheld mike from its hook on the dash. His magnified voice seemed to boom in the sudden hush. "Will Mary Sanders please come forward?"

Catherine's contact made her way to the front of the bus and conferred with the state patrolman. They both turned to look at the passengers at one point and then turned back while the woman said something in a low, urgent voice. He replied at length. Then they started down the aisle, Mary in front, the patrolman resting a casual hand on the butt of his pistol as he brought up the rear.

Without sparing them so much as a glance, Mary passed the section where Catherine and Sam sat. The patrolman, however, stopped in front of their seats.

"Will you come with me, please, sir, ma'am?"

Sam's gut clenched. Oh, son of a bitch. What had Red done now? And how the hell had she pulled it off? Resisting the impulse to shoot her a glance, he asked, "What's this about, officer?" His tone was carefully neutral and sitting forward, he reached for his hip pocket to produce his ID.

His wallet had not yet cleared the pocket when he found himself staring down the barrel of a pistol.

"Keep your hands where I can see them, sir!" The highway patrolman stepped back, putting himself beyond Sam's reach. He was young and visibly tense. "Now, slowly, slide out of your seat."

Sam complied.

"Turn around and put your hands on top of the overhead rack." The officer patted Sam down, sliding Sam's weapon into his own waistband when he came across it. Some of the tension left his posture.

Sam's position left him facing Catherine. He paid no heed to the other passengers gawking at the drama being played out, for his attention was focused exclusively on her. If there truly was a God in heaven, Red would drop dead on the spot.

She was alive and well, however, as she returned his intense regard with a slow blink of her big green eyes. Continuing to drill her with his furious gaze, he watched for a response as his hands were pulled behind his back one at a time and secured with handcuffs. He kept expecting to catch a glimpse of triumph, at the very least. But her face remained blank right up until the moment he sensed the cop's attention shift past him to her.

"You okay, ma'am?"

Sam watched her expression turn helpless as a toddler's on a busy street corner as she gazed up at the young patrolman. "Yes," she said faintly. "I'm just so glad you're here."

He was going to kill her.

Taking a deep breath, Sam expelled it in one harsh blow and turned to the Smokey. Clearly this was not a good time to allow rage to govern his actions. "Listen," he said reasonably, "you're making a mistake. Let me show you some identification; I'm a—"

"You can give me the whole sad story down at the station, bud." The patrolman took Sam's elbow and moved him out of Catherine's way. "Ma'am," he said politely. "After you."

"Could we get our bags, at least?" Sam demanded, and glared at Catherine as she made a production out of hesitantly edging past him. She immediately turned to the patrolman, her behavior while she pointed out the luggage that of a survivor who'd almost given up hope to her avenging hero.

Sam grunted when the strap to his duffel bag was suddenly dropped over his manacled hands. Catherine's suitcase, he noted sourly as the cop herded him along, was solicitously carried by the Smokey.

In the patrol car he once again attempted an explanation and was once again advised to save it. He shut his mouth and stared out the window.

By the time they reached the Highway Patrol barracks he had a brittle hold on his temper. When the Smokey ushered them into a large room crammed with desks and bade them sit, he took a seat as directed, but then demanded to speak to a senior officer. He half expected the young man to refuse, but after a brief hesitation the patrolman turned on his heel and walked away.

Sam immediately turned to Catherine, who awarded him with a little three-cornered smile that pumped his blood pressure right into the red zone. "I don't know how the hell you pulled that off, Sister, but sooner or later they're going to let us out of here. And when they do—"

"No talking!" barked an officer at a nearby desk, and Sam subsided back into his chair. His cuffed hands bumped against the molded plastic seat back. As he shifted in search of a more comfortable position, he breathed deeply through his nose, trying to get a grip on his emotions. Jesus. He'd always considered himself a fairly easygoing guy. Right now, however, he could happily do her bodily harm. In his own defense, he'd never met anyone quite like this woman. She could drive a Quaker to violence and seemed to have some instinctive knowledge of how to push his buttons in particular.

When the young patrolman returned to where they waited, he was accompanied by a man with a steel grey military brush cut and ramrod posture. Obviously the senior officer, he had a no-nonsense bearing and steady eyes. "My name is Major Baskin," he said briskly. "Let's get to the bottom of this situation, shall we?"

"Oh, Major," Catherine immediately exclaimed before Sam could so much as open his mouth. "I can't tell you how relieved I am to be here. This *man*"— her tone suggested *animal* would perhaps be a more suitable word—"kidnapped me from my home in Seattle—"

"No, sir," Sam interrupted. "I legally removed—"

"And has repeatedly molested me—"

Sam swung around to stare at her. "What?"

"He *stripped* me of my shorts and my underpants and *touched* my exposed bottom, and he publicly *forced* his attentions on me while telling people we're to be married—"

"Now wait a damn minute! She's twist—"

"And, oh, dear God, Major." Catherine rode right over his protest. "Worst of all, last night he handcuffed me to a motel-room bed. And I was utterly, completely helpless to prevent him . . . Oh, dear God, to prevent him from—" She choked, as if too overcome with horror to continue.

Sam erupted out of his chair in a red rage. "You're saying I *raped* you?" Jesus, those lips of hers looked so innocent, but every time she opened them, lies, lies, and more fucking lies came out. Blind to all reason, he lunged forward. He'd shut her up if it was the last thing he—

Hard hands slammed him back in his seat. The cuffs on his wrists, ramming against hard plastic, ground into his wristbones, and the resulting jolt of pain served to snap some sense back into his head.

Chest heaving, he shook himself free of his consuming fury and blinked the major's face into focus as the man bent over him.

"Attacking a defenseless woman is not the best way to state your case, son," the state patrolman informed him calmly. The three officers who'd jumped up to lend assistance holstered their guns once again—all except the junior Smokey who'd brought them in. He continued to point his at Sam's head.

"*Defenseless*?" A sharp bark of laughter exploded out of Sam's throat. "Oh, shit, that's beautiful. You could throw her into a tank full of *sharks*, and I bet they'd clear a path for her out of professional courtesy! She's about as de*fense*less as a mama barracuda." Breathing heavily, his attention was suddenly pulled past the major to the young patrolman still pointing a gun at him, and Sam's anger solidified on this new target. "Get that thing the hell out of my face," he snarled. "Jesus, kid, if you'd just allowed me to say a few words back there on the bus, we could have avoided all this."

"Just for the record, ma'am," the major said briskly to Catherine without removing his steady gaze from Sam. "Are you accusing this man of sexually assaulting you?" He turned his head to look at her.

"No, of course not," Catherine replied, as if amazed they could have ever reached such a conclusion. "I merely said he handcuffed me to the bed, and I was helpless to prevent him from doing so." She appealed sadly to the major. "But you must see how chancy his temper is, Major. The least little word just sets him right off."

"Yes," the major agreed drily. "And I'm sure it owes nothing at all to the inflection you gave your handcuffed-to-the-bed story."

"It's not a story, sir; it's the truth! And God, it was about the most degrading moment in my life." Her eyes held the senior officer's gaze. "The only ones that have been worse can also be attributed to this man."

Major Baskin didn't know quite what to make of her. Years of dealing with people had given him excellent instincts, and those instincts led him to recognize manipulation when he saw it. She'd skillfully played on her alleged abductor's emotions. The man had reached the *exact* conclusion she'd intended him to reach. At the same time, there was a ring of truth to her tone when she talked about the degradation she'd received at McKade's hands. It was an interesting conundrum.

Sam sucked in all his anger and frustration, grabbed a deep breath, and blew it out. Ignoring everyone else, he focused his attention exclusively on the major.

"Please," he said with hard-forced calm. "I'm just trying to do a job here. In my right hip pocket is my wallet. In it you will find my identification and my permit to carry concealed. In the money section is a bond undertaking for this 'poor, degraded' woman."

"You're saying you're a bail enforcer?" Hands reached around him to slide his wallet free from his pocket.

"Yes, sir, I am."

Major Baskin eyed him steadily for a moment, then looked down at the wallet in his hand. Flipping it open, he riffled through the contents until he came upon proof of Sam's claim. Removing three items, he turned and passed them to the young patrolman. "Did the prisoner attempt to tell you this when you apprehended him?" he demanded.

The patrolman looked up from the papers he held, his expression faintly sick. Sam's respect for him escalated, however, when the young man met his superior's gaze head-on and answered without excuse, "Yes, sir. I wouldn't allow him to speak."

The major's hand sliced the air in Sam's direction. "Get those cuffs off him," he commanded. "Now." Then he drilled his subordinate with displeased eyes. "I'd be interested in knowing why, Johnson."

Sam believed in assigning blame where blame rightfully belonged. "Probably because Ms. Mac-Pherson is one hell of an actress as well as a pathological liar," he said flatly before the young patrolman could even attempt to defend himself. "I doubt an honest word has passed her lips since the day she was born. I know for a fact that one hasn't since I arrested her in Seattle."

"That is completely false," Catherine disagreed. "Not to mention slanderous."

"Oh, I'll give you this, Red, you're damn good." Sam didn't quite trust himself to look at her as he made the concession. He carefully rotated his shoulders forward when his wrists were freed and he could finally move his arms. Rubbing his wrists, he looked up at the major. "She's so convincing, in fact, that this is the second bus she's managed to get us kicked off of." Then he did swivel in his chair to look at Catherine. Anger still percolated deep in his gut, but he at least was able to face her without fearing he'd snatch her up by her slender white throat and shake her like a terrier with a rat. "Just out of curiosity, how the hell did you manage to get the cops called in?"

She eyed him levelly but didn't respond. It was Major Baskin who replied to his question.

"We received a call from a Mrs. Mary Sanders. She said a woman using sign language communicated to her that she was being held against her will on Greyhound Bus Number 1175."

"Which is all perfectly true," Catherine contributed calmly.

Sam's stomach began to churn. *Sign?* She actually knew sign language? "When was this?" he demanded, staring at her, willing her to just once tell him the truth. "When you used the rest room on the bus?"

Once again she ignored him and spoke directly to the senior officer. "My name is Catherine Mac-Pherson," she said, and launched directly into her Teacher-of-the-Deaf, Twin-Sister-to-Kaylee-MacPherson story.

Sam rolled his eyes, and said, "Oh, boy, here we go again."

But in truth, for the first time since he'd taken her into custody he wasn't one hundred percent certain he had the right woman. Never in this lifetime would he have expected a chorus girl to know sign language.

"Where did you learn how to sign, Ms. MacPherson?" the major inquired. "In college?"

For the first time since the patrolman boarded the bus, Catherine's confidence faltered, and she hesitated, shooting a speculative glance at Sam.

He sat up straight, inexplicable excitement making his heart pound in his chest. What? What did she think he might know that would preclude her lying for once? And why would she think he knew it?

Her hesitation lasted another heartbeat before she admitted, "No, sir. I already knew how to sign before I began college. I learned it from my mother, who was deaf."

Yes! The sick, sinking feeling in his gut disappeared. Hell, he never should have doubted himself—he was an excellent judge of character. "Miss MacPherson does have a twin sister who teaches the deaf, Major. But when I went to the school that employs her, I was informed Catherine MacPherson is in Europe."

Catherine opened her mouth to tell them how her travel agent had robbed her of that trip but shut it again, the words left unspoken. As if they'd believe anything that came out of her mouth at this point, especially with Sam relating in that no-nonsense way of his how he'd then discovered her fleeing through the bathroom window, Kaylee's suitcase and a purse that identified her as her sister already strewn before her on the patio.

She'd made a huge mistake getting caught up in

their game of wits. She should have immediately established her identity instead of giving Sam the chance to make her look like a natural-born liar.

It took another two hours and fifty minutes, but the Highway Patrol ultimately managed to intercede to have their bus tickets replaced. Twenty minutes after that, the young patrolman who'd brought them in, pointedly all business with Catherine this time, dropped them at a modestly priced motel.

It occurred to Catherine as Sam hustled her to the motel office that failing to tell the police of her canceled European trip was a serious misjudgment on her part. Here she'd been in a place rife with the resources to varify things like that, and she'd allowed a momentary discouragement to prevent her from availing herself of them. She was going to have to do better than this at thinking on her feet.

Sam shoved Catherine into the room ahead of him and tossed their bags on the nearest bed. He was furious and wired and knew if he had an ounce of intelligence he'd just lock her to the bed frame and go take a walk until he cooled down. Instead, without even attempting to curb the nasty curl of his lips, he gave her a feral grin. Neither did he resist the temptation to needle her a bit. "Thought the information about your deaf mother was in my file, didn't you, Red? Ah, man, ain't justice a sweet thing?" He stepped closer and gave her a patronizing little chuck under her chin. "Guess what, darlin'—that was the one bit of information not covered in there." He lowered his head until their faces were only centimeters apart. Arranging his face in solemn lines, he said with false commiseration, "Don't you just hate it when your lies turn around and bite you on your pretty little butt?"

It was at that moment their former bus pulled into its scheduled dinner stop.

Across the lot, Kaylee leaned forward in the front seat of the rental car. "C'mon, c'mon, c'mon," she urged under her breath, as each passenger who exited the bus turned out to be someone other than Catherine. Staring through the windshield, she silently willed her sister to appear, and it took several moments before it finally sank in that no one else was going to get off the bus.

"She's not on it?" Incredulous, she turned to Bobby, her voice beginning to rise, her eyes to accuse, as she demanded frantically, "Where is she, Bobby? Oh, God Jaysus, where the hell is she? She's not on the bus!"

"I don't know, baby." Bobby was as mystified as she. "Scott said she and the bounty hunter were supposed to be on this one." He reached over to smooth his fingers down Kaylee's flushed cheek, but as usual whenever he tried to touch her these days, she slapped his hand away. He flung himself back behind the wheel. "What the hell am I doing here?" he demanded testily.

She shot him a look. "Kissing and making up was how you sold it to me, chum."

"Yeah? Well, there sure hell ain't been a whole lotta kissin' going on, so maybe what I'm really doing here is making a mistake." He didn't need this shit. He didn't need it at all. No sir. There were always more women where this one came from. Hell, yes, plenty more—women *loved* him.

Kaylee apparently didn't, however—at least not anymore. Her look drilled right through him. "Nobody forced you to come along," she informed him coolly. "If this is too much trouble, just say the word and I'll drive you back to the airport in Pocatello."

"Keep pushin' me, Kaylee, and I will." It was what he ought to do. If he was smart, he'd bail right out while the bailing was good and leave this cranky redhead and her stupid, sister-hunting wild-goose chase behind.

Hell, it was only pride that had brought him running after her in the first place. Well, okay, there'd been concern, too, for the mess she was in, but mostly it was pride. He'd seen her getting away, and it had threatened his perfect record, and that had chafed.

He possessed charm in abundance, and it had enabled him to walk away from every relationship he'd ever had and still remain friends with the woman involved. After the screwup with the borrowed car, Kaylee had been the ultimate challenge, that was all, and this was just his pride demanding he figure out a way to make her forgive him. That was the only explanation that made sense as to why he'd felt so compelled to follow her across the country.

Well, maybe he ought to just forgo getting her avowal of eternal friendship and hit the highway back to his real life.

Kaylee smacked him on the arm. "Why are you

just sitting there?" she demanded. "What do we do now?"

"There's a phone booth over there. I'll go call Scott again."

Five minutes later, he climbed back in the car, loath to share the latest news, which was actually no news at all.

Kaylee, of course, exhibited her usual patience. "Well?" she demanded. "What's the story?"

"Scott's not home."

"*Bobby*!"

He turned on her, slamming his palm down on the steering wheel. "Just what the hell do you expect me to do, Kaylee? He's not *home*—I can't control that."

She continued to glare at him for a moment, then suddenly her anger collapsed. She reached out a hand to trail conciliatory fingertips down his forearm. "I know you can't. I'm sorry. I'm just worried about Cat, and I'm frustrated because once again I've screwed everything up, and I don't know what to do to clean up this mess I've made."

Bobby didn't quite know how to deal with the funny little double clutch his stomach performed. "We'll figure it out," he heard himself promising and ground down hard on his back teeth. *Shut up, LaBon.* Reaching out, he ran his fingertips down her cheek again, and felt inexplicably gratified when this time she allowed it. "You hungry, baby?"

She shook her head despondently.

"You haven't had much rest," he observed next and wondered a bit frantically just when the hell it was he'd turned into such a Nurse Nancy. "Why don't we go grab a motel room while we decide what to do next."

"Whatever." Kaylee shrugged indifferently.

"Listen," Bobby heard himself say, "you've told me yourself that Catherine is nothing if not careful."

Kaylee turned to face him, pulling one knee up onto the seat. "It's the one thing you can always count on with her," she agreed earnestly. "Oh, she's resourceful, for sure," she rushed to say, as if he'd argued with her assessment. "But the one fact that is above all, A-1 guaranteed in my sister's life is that she is always, but always, very, very careful." She gave him a tentative smile, and Bobby had to check himself from sliding out from under the wheel to reach for her.

"So, she'll be okay."

"Yes, she'll be okay," she agreed. She gave a thoughtful little shimmy that caused a ripple effect from her rounded white shoulders, down her arms, to her rounded, spandex-covered breasts. "Let's go get that room," she suggested with renewed confidence. "I could use a shower, and I definitely need to redo my makeup. You're right, Cat'll be fine. After all, prudence is the girl's middle name."

9

LOOKING INTO SAM'S mocking eyes, only centimeters from her own, Catherine knew the prudent thing to do was allow him time to regain his customary command of his temper. It didn't take a genius to figure out that underneath that cock-of-the-walk arrogance, he was still furious.

The day had been too long, though, this motel room was too depressingly dingy, and she felt restless, *reckless* . . . not to mention the way his crowing was beginning to get on her last good nerve.

Smacking both hands against the solid wall of his chest, Catherine gave a shove to get him out of her face. Relieved when he backed up a step, taking his heat and his scent with him, she drew her first comfortable breath and edged around him to reach for her suitcase. Throwing it on the worn bedspread, she opened it and pulled out the shirt he'd lent her yesterday, which she'd appropriated as her own. She rammed her arms into the sleeves and then looked over at him. "I'm getting sick and tired of having you call me a liar," she informed him with more heat than she'd intended. With each button she fastened,

124

her confidence level rose. It felt good to again be wearing something that didn't cling to every last molecule of her body. "You know, McKade, it seems to me that after being treated like a congenital liar yourself all afternoon, you'd be a little less free about bandying that word around."

A muscle ticked in his jaw. "The difference here, Sister, is that you *are* a liar. I, on the other hand, was railroaded by your ability with a quick story."

"Oh, for crying out loud!" Catherine's hands fisted on her hips. "I defy you to point out one word I said today that wasn't the absolute truth."

One minute there was a respectable amount of space separating them, and the next Sam was towering over her, crowding her away from the bed and close to the wall. Once again she found herself standing with her nose practically pressed into his collarbone.

"That your name is Catherine MacPherson, for starters," he growled above her head.

She pulled herself erect and jutted out her chin, aiming for a more equitable height ratio between them. "It *is* Catherine MacPherson," she informed him coolly. His nostrils flared and his amber eyes were hot with wrath as he stared down at her, and she was filled with a sudden heedless urge to goad him into losing his temper entirely. She'd liked it when he'd lost it at the state barracks earlier. No, she'd *reveled* in it. She'd had so little control over her own life since this man had barged into it, that it was exceedingly gratifying to see him thrust into a Tilt-A-Whirl world for a change. His frustration when his authority was removed from his hands had been a pretty sight to see . . . even if only temporarily. "Did I lie when I told them you pulled my pants down and touched me where you had no business touching me?" she demanded. "I don't think so."

"You know damn well that was strictly to verify that you have a tattoo on your lily-white ass!"

"So you say. But we both know you could have verified it without touching me. And may I remind you that you're the one who keeps mentioning the color of my butt? Why is that, I wonder? I think you just get some perverted sort of thrill out of feeling up helpless women."

"Bull!" Sam's hot breath hit her mouth, her nose, her cheeks, as he thrust his face aggressively near. "That's total bullshit. And I think we've pretty much established that you haven't been helpless since the day you were born, Red, so why don't you just drop that act. Ain't nobody who's been in your company for more than an hour gonna believe it anyhow." Black lashes suddenly narrowed over his eyes. "You know what I think, lady? I think you like seeing how many men you can get all hot and bothered."

Indignation roared through her veins. "Oh! You are so full of it! Just because you can't keep your hands to yourself or get your mind out of the gutter doesn't mean the rest of us share your lowlife pre-occupation with sex!"

"Oh, I think you do. Maybe you're one of those women who doesn't deliver in the end, but you sure do like to tease. Just look at what you do for a living."

"Teach deaf kids?"

"Wear G-strings and feathers. I think you really like stickin' those 38 Double Dee extravaganzas in everybody's face—"

"Thirty-four D!"

"—and shaking your butt in those tight little numbers you're so fond of wearing, and seeing just how many guys you can make slobber all over themselves."

"You know what, McKade? You're beginning to sound just like my mother. She used to harp on displaying our sinful bodies, too."

Sam was highly insulted to be compared to a nagging mother, but he gritted his teeth and confined his response to a reasonably mild, "Yeah? Well maybe you should have listened to Mom."

"Oh, I did," Catherine assured him. "It was one of the main reasons I chose the field I'm in today."

"Getting back to that, you might want to watch your habit of gettin' the guys all riled up. They just plumb hate it when you get 'em all in a lather and then refuse to put out. In fact, they've got a name for women like you—"

"Oh, no, no, no, no, no, no." Catherine thrust her nose up under Sam's. "Huh-uh, buster—no *way* you get away with that one. You're not gonna twist this around on me because you're some uptight cop wanna-be who can't handle the sight of a healthy female body!"

"And yours is certainly healthy, darlin'." His gaze was insolent as he leaned back to slowly run it up

and down her body. "Well fed, some might call it."
Well rounded, well filled out. *Nice.*

"Oh! You are such a coyote! I am not overweight,
so don't even think you can make me feel like a
heifer."

"I wasn't—"

"The hell you weren't! And the really nasty part
is that I doubt you even go for the skinny, anorexic
type. I bet you *fantasize* about G-strings and feathers
all the time you're sneering at the dancers who wear
them. Just because you're some repressed, Calvinistic
prude—"

One black eyebrow shot up. "Logical as ever, I see.
Make up your mind, Red—am I a repressed prude
or a degenerate sex maniac?"

How dare he be amused by her? Focused on that
sardonic eyebrow, Catherine missed the signs of temper gathering in his eyes, the muscles bunching
along his jaw. Her face hot, her heart pounding, she
said wildly, "Both! You're a repressed, sex-crazed
hypocrite who wouldn't have the first idea what to do
with a willing woman—provided you could ever
find one in the first place."

Grabbing her upper arms in his big hands, he
hauled her up onto her toes. Belligerence was written
all over his face as he once again thrust it close to
hers. "Women happen to like me just fine," he said
through gritted teeth.

She shrugged, and the motion brought her breasts
into fleeting contact with his chest. Her glance
dropped swiftly to his sullen mouth before lifting
once again to meet his furious gaze. Her heart was

drumming so fast and so loud it was a wonder people weren't pounding on the connecting walls of their room to demand they hold it down in there.

"So you say," she managed to reply with spurious calm around the pulse pounding in her throat. This was surely the time to pull back and defuse the situation, but somehow all the words she knew she should suppress just boiled up out of her. "But we haven't seen any evidence of that, have we, McKade? I bet the truth is that you hang out in seedy little strip joints, all hunkered down like a troll at the bar, drooling over the dancers while righteously belittling the morals of women who take their clothes off for a liv—"

Sam slammed his mouth over hers to shut her up—at least that's what he told himself in his brief moment of lucidity. One second he stood there gripping her arms, his head pounding, pounding, pounding—with rage, with the excitement that was never far beneath the surface in his dealings with her, with a carnal curiosity so powerful he thought it might cripple him—and the next thing he knew he had her pressed up against the wall and his mouth was on hers, and he was kissing her—holy Christ, kissing her like a starving man presented with a sudden feast.

And she was kissing him back.

He felt her mouth open to him, and he groaned. Then he was inside her, and her taste was hot and sweet, and *God*, he wanted more. He insinuated his tongue deeper and his body closer, loving the lush weight of her breasts flattening beneath his chest, and the grip of her smooth, white arms as they wrapped around his neck and clung.

His hands thrust into her hair, dislodging pins. Slippery strands tangled around his fingers, and the scent of shampoo, fresh and seductive, was released into the air. Inhaling a sharp breath through his nostrils, he clamped her head between his hands. Then he raised his head fractionally, stared down at her slumberous eyes and reddened lips for a moment, and, changing the angle of his kiss, came at her from another direction to settle his mouth more firmly over hers. Her soft lips clung to his and her fingers came up to grip his head, as if afraid he'd pull back if she didn't hold him in place. She tangled her tongue with his, and he groaned deep in his throat.

It could have been mere moments or hours later when he disengaged his hands from her hair and slid them slowly down her body until his fingertips brushed the high hem of her skirt. Curling his hands around the fabric, crushing it between his fingers, he tugged the stretchy material up her thighs and over her hips. Then it was bunched around her waist beneath the tail of his purloined shirt, and his fingers were snaking beneath the flimsy material of her panties. Suddenly he held a sweet, warm, volumptuously rounded cheek in each hand. He hauled her up until her legs were wrapped around his hips and that hot, damp, feminine place at the apex of her thighs was nudging his sex, cradling it as he rocked against her in a mindless fever.

Catherine moaned low in her throat and tightened her grip on Sam's hair. His mouth on hers was demanding, his tongue aggressive, and his handling of her was nearly presumptuous, as if he had some God-given right of dominion over her body. She should have hated it, but instead it excited some subterranean demon she'd never dreamed was a part of her. She felt as if every move she'd made these past few days, every word spoken, or angle played with this man, had all been leading to this one fiery moment. All sensation, she felt as if she'd been thrust into a crucible of unrelenting heat that threatened to burn her alive. His mouth, his big hands on her bare skin, his body pressing hers up against the wall, all fed the flames. His erection was pressed hard between her legs, and his hips kept moving, moving, moving, in slow, tight, smooth oscillations that accessed nerve endings she'd never known she possessed. Dark sounds, disturbing in their neediness, reverberated in her throat as she clung to him, thrusting her pelvis against his as best she could given the tight confines between his body and the wall.

Without warning, Sam ripped his mouth free. Catherine uttered a small whimper of protest and tried to bring him back, but he kissed his way across her cheek to her ear. "God," he whispered harshly. "You feel so good." He sucked her earlobe into his mouth and gripped it lightly with his teeth, his ragged pants warming her captive earlobe and sending chills down the sensitive whorls of her ear.

And all the while his hips continued to move, driving her closer and closer to the edge.

"Sam?" Catherine tightened her grip on his head and tried to turn his mouth back to hers. He obliged her with one brief, hard foray against her mouth before pulling back and determinedly kissing his way down her throat. His fingers tightening on her bottom, he raised her up slightly and his mouth nuzzled hotly along the perimeters of the white oxford cloth collar.

"Take off my shirt, Kaylee," he said hoarsely. "Ah, God, darlin', take it off. I want to . . ."

Kaylee? Catherine blinked at him in confusion. With her cognitive processes fogged by arousal, the implication was slow to sink in, and she wanted to simply let it pass. Oh, God, just this one time, and she'd never ask for anything again. She was poised on the very cusp of an orgasm, and had *no* desire to rock the boat and give it all up.

She moved against him harder, only to discover that, even with the promise of satisfaction such as she'd never known in the offing, she couldn't keep quiet. "Catherine," she whispered hoarsely. "My name is Catherine." *Say it, Sam. Please, please, just say it one time.*

For a second, he didn't respond. His mouth continued to play over her throat, his hips continued to undulate against her. Then suddenly he stilled. Lifting his head, he stared down into her face for a moment. Then his forehead hit the wall next to her with an audible thunk.

"Don't do this." His voice was as strained as hers as he ground his frontal lobe back and forth against the rough plaster of the wall. His head turned until his lips were against her ear. "Damn you, Kaylee," he said hoarsely, "don't. Can't you just allow this, at least, to be free of your lies?"

Cold reality doused all the hot sensations that thundered in her every pulse point, and it probably should have caused her to whisper thanks for her narrow escape. At the moment, however, gratitude was simply beyond her. Still stunned that she should experience such raging sensations in the first place, and fearing they were only temporarily banked, she simply rested her head against the wall and concentrated on drawing deep, calming breaths. She had to get herself together.

Sam raised his head and stared down at her. Her lips were swollen and looked bruised by the savagery of his kisses. The green of her irises was nearly swallowed by the dilation of her pupils. But her gaze, as it clashed with his, was unrepentant, and he knew damn well she wasn't about to recant her claim. He'd never met anybody so damn stubborn in his life.

It infuriated him. "I can make you want it," he said with harsh huskiness, and knew in his gut it was true. She had the look of a woman on the very edge. It wouldn't take much to push her over, and he wasn't feeling particularly charitable. "I can make you beg for it, Red, and it won't matter then *what* name I call you." Furious in an agony of frustrated arousal, he gripped her butt and moved his hips once, twice, watching with grim satisfaction as her eyes lost focus and her lids started to drift closed. Color suffused her cheeks and a faint, needy moan sounded deep in her throat. She tilted her pelvis forward.

Then she jerked it back again, and her arms dropped to her sides, her feet slid to the floor. Slowly, her lashes lifted. Eyes still dilated, still heavy-lidded and drowsy with sexual need, they nevertheless met his gaze with stubborn determination. "My name is Catherine," she said huskily. She licked her lips. "Say it." It was part command, part plea. "Please? Just call me Catherine one time, Sam. Just once, and I'll give you anything—*do* anything— you want."

Graphic visions flashed through his mind, and he was tempted . . . God, was he tempted. He could feel her nipples drilling into his chest through layers of fabric, was aware of how wet he'd gotten her, since more moisture had transferred from her panties to the fly of his jeans with each gyration of his hips. Hell, why even hesitate? All he had to do was open his mouth and say her sister's name. Just say it one time, and then he could strip her down to the skin and satisfy every single impulse he'd stifled since the moment he'd first clapped eyes on her.

It was no skin off his teeth if she wanted to play the game this way, long as he got his.

Fingers sinking more firmly into the resilient flesh of her butt, he sucked in a deep breath as he bent his head to capitulate.

Then he snarled an obscentity and stepped back. "Pull down your skirt," he commanded. Shoving his fingers through his hair, he turned away, silently cursing his outdated, inconvenient value system.

10

MADE EDGY AND uncomfortable by the vast, windswept high-desert country that stretched as far as the eye could see, Jimmy Chains stared glumly through the window of the phone booth while he waited for his call to connect. "Hey, boss, it's me," he said without enthusiasm when Hector Sanchez finally picked up the phone. "I'm here in Armpit, Wyoming, just like ya tole me."

"Arabesque," Hector corrected him.

Chains shrugged, unmindful that Sanchez had no way of seeing him through the line. "Coulda fooled me. This here's gotta be one a the butt-ugliest places I ever seen in my life. 'Cept for maybe out on the ocean, which at least is *blue*, I ain't never been in a place like this where a guy can stand in one spot and see forever." An involuntary shudder moved through him. "It's givin' me the creeps, boss, there's nuthin' here but sagebrush. I miss the neighborhood."

Sanchez ignored the complaint. "Have you made contact with Kaylee yet?"

"Huh-uh. Just been the one bus through here so

far, and she weren't on it." Catching a glimpse of his reflection in the phone booth's window, he fumbled a handkerchief out of his pocket and buffed up his chains. He felt marginally better when their reflection began to gleam. "Christ, it's dusty here," he bitched. "Seems like the wind don't never stop blowin'."

"Try to stay on track here," Hector's impatient voice commanded in his ear. "Have you checked out the territory yet, so you'll have a handle on the situation when Kaylee does arrive?"

"Yeah. There's a refrigeration shed behind the motel where I can stash the bounty hunter while I get her outta town. Once I do that, there's like a bazillion acres to choose from for stashin' her body." He frowned at his dim reflection in the glass. "You sure I gotta kill her, boss? Couldn't I just scare her? I always kinda liked—"

"I've explained this to you several times already," Hector interrupted in the cold, terse voice that meant he was losing patience, and Chains straightened up smartly. "I'll tell you again, but I want you to pay attention now, because I'm only going to say it once more. Are you listening?"

Chains nodded, his concentration focused on the need to absorb each word.

"Jimmy? Are you *listening*?"

"Yeah, boss."

Enunciating slowly and concisely, Hector said, "Kaylee knows I paid you to take care of Alice. That means we're in deep shit, Jimmy, *real* deep shit. The only thing that's gonna get us out of it is if Kaylee's not around to testify."

"Hell, she prob'ly wouldn't anyway."

"You ready to stake your freedom on that?"

Jimmy Chains took his time thinking it over. Finally he said, "Nah, I guess not," because the boss was usually right; he was a really smart guy.

"No, I didn't think so. I figured you were too intelligent for that."

Pride bloomed in Chain's heart, and he preened, but then the boss's next words completely ruined his temporary high.

"Did you exchange your silk suits for Western wear like I suggested?"

Chains looked with distaste at his plaid cotton shirt and stiff new unfaded Levi's. Shit, the shirt wasn't even properly pressed; it still had packing creases in its short sleeves. He reached up an exploratory finger to touch the only thing he liked about this get-up: the shiny silver and turquoise links that formed the band around his hard-brimmed new Stetson. "Yeah, I did," he said morosely. "I look just like a fuckin' native. Ain't seen one yet knows how to dress worth a damn."

"It's necessary, Chains. You've got to blend into the scenery."

"I s'pose." Noticing the dust that marred the toe of his alligator loafer, he picked up his foot and rubbed it clean against the calf of his other leg. He admired the newly restored shine for a moment and the subtle pattern in his silk-blend socks. His sense of fashion restored, he raised his head again.

And found himself staring straight into a pair of

soft brown eyes only inches away on the other side of the telephone booth's dusty glass.

"Holy friggin' shit!" His back hit the door of the phone booth in an involuntary attempt to put as much room as possible between himself and the creature staring in through the window.

"Chains?" Hector's voice squawked from the receiver as it bounced off the metal shelf. The phone danced and swung on the end of its silver umbilical cord. "Chains! What the hell is going on?"

"Ho!" Jimmy Chains blew out a deep breath as he slowly straightened. He reeled in the dropped receiver. "It's a horse."

He eyed the animal warily. It had skittishly jerked its brown-spotted head back at Jimmy's abrupt movement and the racket following it, but now extended its neck to thrust its face close to the glass again. "Jesus, he's a big sonofabitch." Forcing his mouth into a reasonable facsimile of a smile, he said softly, "Nice Spot. Good horse. Go home." Then he saw the reins wrapped around the post next to the booth. "Ah, man, some asshole's tied him up right next to me!"

"Will you *forget* the goddamn horse for a minute?"

"The only thing separatin' me from this sucker is a real thin piece of glass, boss—he ain't all that easy to forget." Chains dragged his gaze away from the muscular brown-and-white beast to the unending vista beyond. "Christ, not only don't they got no palm trees around here, they hardly got any kinda trees at all. It's so *brown*. And if there's a building over two stories tall in the entire fuckin' state, I'll eat my brand-new shitkicker's hat. This place is depressing."

"Well, I'll tell you what," Hector said tersely, and Chains wondered what the hell his problem was—it wasn't like the *boss* was the one stuck in this godforsaken hole. "You just do the job you're there to do," Hector commanded, "and the minute it's done we'll whip you right on home."

"Back to paradise," Chains agreed dreamily. "Where I can wear me some decent clothes again, and the only horses I have to look at are on the other side of the rails at Hialeah."

"That's right. All you have to do is take care of the Kaylee problem. Then you can catch the next flight back to the neighborhood."

Jimmy Chains smiled to himself, visualizing it. *Home.* Deep blue skies, and palm trees that were both daytime green and night black cutouts against Miami's bloodred sunsets. Neon lights and pastel buildings. Guys what knew how to dress snappy and Cuban girls with white, white teeth who strutted their stuff in bright summer dresses. The idea of getting back to the neighborhood flooded him with renewed confidence. "Piece a cake, boss," he assured Hector. "Ya might as well go on ahead and book that flight, 'cuz the job's as good as done."

Hector Sanchez carefully reseated the telephone receiver and sat back in his chair. He rubbed his aching temples. "Good as done," he muttered to himself.

The idea of Jimmy Chains on the loose with no one to guide him, and worse—God help them all—a *cocky* Jimmy Chains, sent an icy shaft of pure dread straight to his bowels. *Good as done*. The words set up a nasty, echoing clamor in his mind.

Good as done, indeed. From Jimmy's lips to God's ear.

Or they were both going to be up the proverbial creek.

For the third time in less than half an hour, Bobby thrust the gas pedal to the floor and passed yet another Rocky Mountain motorist. The single terse word he bit out succinctly expressed his opinion.

Turning away from her indifferent perusal of the scenery whipping past outside the window, Kaylee settled back in the seat of their rental car and studied him. "You know, before I took this little road trip with you," she commented mildly, "I never dreamed there were so many drivers in America named Dick."

Bobby shot her a glance before he returned his attention to the road. He was chagrined but basically unrepentant about his loss of temper, which for some reason seemed to occur with increasing frequency the longer he was in her company. "Well, dammit, baby, where do all these idiots get their licenses anyhow—Farmer Brown's School of Tractor Pulling? You don't go fifty miles an hour on an *interstate*. People get killed that way."

Kaylee quirked an eyebrow at him. "As opposed to what? Death by stroke? If you think that's somehow a better way to go than in this Farmer-Brown pileup you seem to see in your head, I'm here to tell you . . . dead is dead."

"Kaylee, honey, a guy only has to worry about having a stroke when he *doesn't* vent his frustration. What I'm doing here is minimizing the risks in order to keep myself healthy."

"Oh, please, you don't really expect me to buy that garbage, do you? Keep yourself healthy, my butt. Next you'll be flipping them all nasty one-handed gestures and telling me it's an AMA approved method of controlling your blood pressure."

He shot her a grin, and Kaylee's heart stuttered. Studying him a while through narrowed lashes, she tried to ignore the part of her that screamed, Oh, God, so handsome! Great hands! Great smile! because that only made it too damn difficult to stick to the No Sex Until We've Found Catherine rule she'd imposed on them. Now, *why* had that sounded like such a good idea again? Well, whatever the reason, she seemed to remember it had made a lot of sense at the time. And she was sticking to it, too, by God, at least as far as instigating anything herself went. She had to. To do otherwise would not only probably violate whatever her reasons had been in the first place, but make her look like a damn wishy-washy idiot to boot.

The smart thing to do, obviously, was to get *him* to break the rule. Now, that would be the perfect solution because then she could enjoy the benefits without all that nasty responsibility. And hey, how hard could it be anyhow? Guys were notorious for thinking with their dicks, and Bobby was certainly no exception. She'd developed some moves over the years guaranteed to make a grown man beg, and maybe, if she eased up on Bobby's blind side with one or two of them, he'd get so tired of the frustration, he'd throw her down on the nearest bed or other reasonably horizontal surface and do his wicked worst to her.

It made her warm just thinking about it. Bobby's wicked worst was very good indeed.

Of course, on the downside, she never had been overly fond of women who played teasing games to get their way. And Bobby did have that big ol' chivalrous streak when it came to women, so the idea of him actually reduced to using the tiniest bit of *force* to get something going between them was so unlikely as to be pretty much guaranteed out of the question.

Seduction was more Bobby's style. As long as she'd known him, she had never seen him be anything but unfailingly gentle and charming with any woman he'd ever come into contact with, and face it, that included the one or two really nasty ones he'd had to remove from the club. She had yet to see his charm slip.

Well, except with her. Swiveling to face him more fully, she wondered why that was. Gazing blindly at his handsome profile, she tried to work it out in her mind.

"*What*?" he suddenly snarled, and Kaylee gave a small start of surprise. She slapped a hand to her chest to contain her thundering heart.

"Jayzus, Bobby, you scared the shit outta me! What do you mean, what?"

"Why are you staring at me like that?"

"Was I staring? Huh, I'll be damned. I didn't realize."

He waited for several silent heartbeats and when it sunk in that she had no intention of elaborating, snapped, "Well?"

Kaylee blinked at him. "Well, what?"

"Why were you staring!"

"I told you I didn't know I was. I was just thinking about you and women."

The glance he shot her was abruptly wary. "Me and women," he repeated, careful to leave all inflection out of his voice. "Did you, uh, have any particular woman in mind?"

"No, not really. I was just thinking about how you are with all of us."

"And that is . . . ?"

Kaylee gave him a tender smile, for he clearly expected a trap. Where did he get all these suspicions? "Charming," she said gently. "Easygoing. Eventempered." Her voice trailed away as she stared at him in openmouthed amazement. "Why, Bobby LaBon, you're blushing!"

"Like hell." The color flooding his cheeks made his eyes blaze bluer than usual when he took them off the traffic to shoot her a quelling glance.

She decided, quite magnanimously if she did say so herself, to cut him some slack. "Okay, if you insist, then of course you're not." She nibbled a cuticle for a moment, then forced her hand down into her lap. "Listen, do you remember that woman you had to remove from the Tropicana last winter? The one who kept trying to join us chorus girls onstage?"

"Hell, yeah, I remember. She ripped off half of my face before I finally got her out the door."

"I always wondered why you didn't just deck her after she got in the first pop."

His head swung around, and shock, genuine and bone deep, filled his eyes as he stared at her. "She was a woman!"

"Bobby, she was drunk and vicious, and your face was infected for more than a week because of her dirty fingernails. If she'd been a man, you would've decked her in a minute."

"Well, hell, baby, what's your point? Of course I'm not gonna let a guy get away with shit like that. It's kinda fun then to mix it up a little—it gets all those aggressions worked out." He turned his attention back to the road, but spared enough time to shoot her a quick look of reproval. "But a guy sure hell doesn't go around hitting women—I don't care if they deserve it or not."

"You pointed a gun at *me*."

"But I wasn't gonna use it! That was just to get your cooperation when I still thought you were your sister."

"Speaking of which," Kaylee said with a sudden narrowing of her eyes, "I've got a bone to pick with you. Just what was all that bullshit with Catherine's—*my*—legs?"

"Huh?"

"Don't play dumb with me, Bobby. When I was trying to prove I was Cat, you gave a great big once-over to what we both know damn well you thought at the time were *her legs*. And you said *nice*." She gave the word the same deep, sexy inflection he had given it.

"What, you're jealous over a little complim—?"

"I'm not jealous over anything!"

"Uh-huh." Bobby grinned. "Well, they are nice." He glanced over at them, taking in their long, sleek length showcased by her short skirt and skyscraper heels, and his eyes went dark for a moment before he dragged his attention back to the road. "Very nice. So I just told her—*you*—the truth."

"You were flirting with her!"

"If I was flirting with anybody, baby—and I'm not admitting to a thing here—it was you."

"Yeah, nice try, Bobby, except you didn't know it was me at the time. As far as you knew I was out the door, and you sure didn't wait for the dust to settle before you started flirting with my sister."

"I wasn't flirting! I was just appreciating her— damn, *your*!—legs." He took one hand off the steering wheel and rubbed at his head. "Yours, hers, hers, yours—Christ, I'm getting a headache here. They were nice, so I said so. So, shoot me. Women like to hear these things."

Kaylee snorted. "You obviously don't know as much about the female gender as you think you do. Sure, some like to hear it. Maybe even most do. But if I really had been Cat, I would have ripped you a new one right where you stood."

"What, she doesn't like compliments?"

"She wouldn't like strangers busting into her home and then ogling her legs, that's for damn sure."

"Yeah? So what would she have done about it, you

suppose? Gotten physical with me? That makes her sound a whole lot more like you than you've led me to believe."

"Damn your black heart, even now you're dreaming about wrestling around with my sister! Well, in your dreams, Ace! She woulda ripped you to shreds with the nasty side of her tongue. Froze you into a big ole Popsicle man. Reduced you to a stammering idiot."

Bobby's eyebrows were elevated when he turned to meet her gaze. "Then I guess it's a lucky thing for me that it was you and not Catherine in that house, huh? The fire and ice twins and I got me the hot one." His brows snapped together in a sudden scowl. "Least I did before you decided to cut me off. Now all I got is a big hurkin' case of blue balls."

"Ah, poor baby. Want me to kiss 'em and make it better?"

"Yes," he growled.

The atmosphere in the car was suddenly full of the hot jitters, and they were both silent for a few moments. Then Kaylee took a deep breath, eased it out, and reached for the road map. "What was the name of that town again, where Scott said we might catch up with them?"

"Arabesque."

"I wonder if I can get a manicure there. Cat's got all my good stuff, and my nails need attention something fierce. They're a mess." She ran one down the map. When it stopped at the town under discussion, she frowned. "Why, it's nothing but a little bitty dot."

"Yeah, I guess all they really require for a lunch stop is a café."

"God, would you look at this?" she demanded, staring down at the map spread out over her lap. "There's only but one, two, three, *four* towns of any size at all in this state. I wonder what people do around here for fun."

They drove in silence for a while. Eventually, Bobby glanced over at her. "Have you given any thought to what we're going to do when we do catch up with your sister, baby?"

Kaylee looked at him blankly. "Sure. Rescue her."

"Okay. How?"

She blinked.

"It's not enough simply to find her, Kaylee. She's being escorted back to Miami by a bounty hunter, and he's sure hell not going to just hand her over to us without a fight. The guy's probably armed to the teeth."

"You've got a gun."

"Yeah, but he's probably prepared to actually use his!"

Kaylee gave her shoulders a thoughtful shimmy. "So, we'll take him by surprise."

"All right, say for the sake of argument we do that. If he gets a look at you, he might even realize he has the wrong twin." He took a hand off the steering wheel and reached over to grip her thigh just above the knee. His eyes left the road long enough to pin her in place with the intensity of his gaze. "But what makes you think the guy's gonna just give up? This is the man's livelihood we're talking about, and we can be pretty damn sure he'll come after us with everything he's got."

"Well, then, maybe we'll tie him up and get just as far away as we can before he gets himself undone. I don't know, Bobby!" she wailed in frustration. "Cat's the smart one—"

His fingers tightened on her leg. "Would you quit friggin' doing that to yourself?" he roared.

"What? Quit doing what?" She slapped at his forearm with both hands, then tried to pry his hand away. "Bobby, you're hurting me!"

"Quit implying that you're somehow stupid," he yelled. But he released his grip on her leg, bringing his hand back to clasp the steering wheel with white-knuckled fingers. He glanced away from traffic long enough to pin her in place with his fierce gaze. "Just because you didn't go to a goddamn college like your precious sister doesn't mean you're not every bit as bright as she is."

"But I'm not." He glared at her, and she reached over to touch conciliatory fingertips to his thigh. "It's the truth, Bobby. Saying so doesn't mean I think I'm dumb, because I don't. I'm not. But Catherine is the quick-witted one. She kinda had to be. Most of the time I don't even care, except maybe when I get myself in some stupid jam that I can't figure out how to get out of again without calling her first. I was always the social one. I can make friends faster than she can. Hell, I know I'm more *fun* than she is. But Cat is smarter or at least faster at thinking on her feet. It's just a fact of life, like my red hair or exceptionally pretty boobs." She watched her fingers weave abstract patterns up and down his hard-muscled thigh.

Bobby's gaze glanced off her exceptionally pretty breasts. "Maybe it's more a matter of not exercising your natural smarts."

"Huh?"

"Well, I imagine it's like any muscle—if you don't work it, it doesn't develop. You've never had to exercise your problem-solving abilities because you always had your sister there to do your thinking for you. But if we're gonna do this, baby, then we'd better put some thought into what, exactly, we plan to do when we catch up with Catherine and the bounty hunter."

"Can't we just let her know I'm nearby and ready and willing to help, and let her figure out a way to use it?"

"No. We can either give it up right here and now and save our own butts, which is what I vote for, or we can make up our minds to do it right."

Depend on her own intelligence? The very idea scared her to death. She chewed on her bottom lip, tempted to go with Bobby's vote and give up. But she took a deep breath, slowly let it out, and then said, "Okay. We do it right."

"Damn." He slapped the steering wheel. "That's what I was afraid you were gonna say."

11

〜〜〜 IT WAS BARELY eight o'clock in the morning and already it was breathlessly hot. Mirage waves had begun to shimmer above the blacktop surface of the highway Catherine and Sam trudged along.

Catherine's breakfast sat heavy in her stomach, and she cursed the whim that had driven her to put on a pair of Kaylee's spiked heels this morning. She had to quit giving into these childish impulses to spite Sam; invariably, they only rebounded on her. Tripping along trying to keep up with his long-legged stride, tugging damp, clingy Lycra away from her perspiring chest, she dreamed of loose clothing that allowed air to circulate next to her skin. Cool cotton shifts and baggy-legged shorts. Long dresses that merely skimmed her body instead of sticking to every inch of it. If she ever got back to the real world, she was going to climb into the roomiest outfit she owned and never come out again.

And why *was* she trying to keep up with him anyway? Immediately, Catherine slowed her pace. It wasn't as if it were to her benefit if they got to the bus station on time.

Sam took an additional three strides down the shoulder of the road before he realized she was no longer with him. He turned back impatiently. "What's the holdup, Red?"

"Aside from the fact that I'm hot, my feet hurt, and I'm through trotting along in your wake like a trick poodle? Not a blessed thing, McKade."

Taking a giant step back toward her, he scowled at the long, bare length of her legs. "Hey, don't blame me for your sore feet. If you'd worn your Keds instead of those dumb heels, like I suggested . . ." But that wasn't a good road to go down. It brought to mind a ruthlessly clear vision of her mincing around the motel room this morning, taking baby steps in those damn high heels and wearing his oversize white oxford cloth shirt buttoned to the throat over the little pink dress she had on now. It had entirely covered the skintight garment, which should have been a relief. Instead, it had made her look naked underneath, and between the thought of that and the memory of those smooth white legs wrapped around his waist that kept popping to mind, he'd damn near started howling.

"Suggested, my fanny, Ace—you demanded."

Okay, he admitted it—if only to himself; that had probably been a mistake. She'd immediately stuck her slender little nose in the air and plunged him into the business end of yet another one of her damn silent treatments.

And the sexy heels had remained firmly on her feet.

"Besides," she sniped, raising an arm to blot perspiration off her forehead, "if you weren't such an all-fired cheapskate, maybe we could catch an occasional ride to the bus station instead of always having to hike down the highway."

"If you didn't eat like a damn trucker, maybe I could afford to!"

She took an angry step in his direction. "Don't you *even* get started on that 'fat' business again."

"Dammit, Red!" Frustration had him taking a huge step forward, which left him looming so far over her, she had to bend back from the waist simply to see up into his face. "I never once said you were fat—not once! I said some might say you were well fed. Well trust me on this, sweetheart, you are. As the guy who's been paying for your meals, I can sure as hell testify to that." He backed off a step and watched her slowly straighten as he readjusted his grip on their bags. "Now get your butt in gear," he said through his teeth. "We've got a bus to catch." He turned and stomped off down the shoulder again.

Catherine teetered along behind him at her own snail pace.

A car roared past, kicking up dust. Coughing, Catherine stopped by the side of the road to wait for the grimy cloud to blow past, irritably waving away the grit that swirled around her head.

Sam turned and saw her standing there and uttered a phrase so foul Catherine backed up a step. He was back at her side in a few ground-eating strides, switching both bags into one hand as he walked. Without so much as a pause, he ducked, got a shoulder into her midsection, and rose to his feet with her dangling over his shoulder in a fireman's lift. Slapping a big hand to the back of her thigh to hold her in place, he turned and strode off down the highway.

"Dammit, Sam, it is *way* too hot for this." She banged a fist into the small of his back and felt sweat begin to adhere their bodies together everywhere they touched. "Put me down." Another car roared by and honked enthusiastically. Derisive hoots from what sounded like teenage male throats floated back on the heat-laden air. "Dammit, Sam, put me down! They can probably see clear up my skirt to my tonsils!"

"Like I'm supposed to believe that would bother an exhibitionist like you?"

"Sam!"

"You gonna put on your Keds like a good little girl and quit giving me grief?"

Her stomach jounced on his hard shoulder with every long-legged stride he took, and the breakfast she'd eaten a short while ago threatened to make a return appearance. His wording was enough to give her a bad case of tight teeth, but she bit back her resentment and answered, "Yes. Now put me down."

He leaned forward and eased her to her feet. Then he dropped her bag to the road and squatted in front of it. A moment later he handed her the tennis shoes. "Fork over the heels."

She passed them to him and stooped to tie her shoes. Looking up a moment later, she caught him weighing the strappy pink heels in one large hand while staring consideringly out at the shrub brush beyond the shoulder of the road. "Don't even think about it, buster," she advised. "Not unless you're prepared to part with some of your precious cash to buy me a replacement pair."

He grunted, but placed the heels in her suitcase and closed the case. Surging to his feet, he grabbed her wrist and took off down the highway. "Come on. We're not missing this bus."

Catherine was overheated and cranky by the time they reached the air-conditioned depot. She grabbed the front tail of Sam's shirt, which he wore outside his jeans to cover the gun he wore in the small of his back, and brought it up to blot the sweat rolling down her throat. He lurched in its wake, hard stomach exposed to the first rib. That brought him to within inches of her, and before he even knew what she was about, she'd plunged her hand with its fistful of shirt down the scooped neck of her stretchy pink minidress. When it emerged again, the tail of his shirt was a damp, wrinkled mess. She held it fastidiously away from her body between the tips of her thumb and index finger and dropped it like a soiled hanky. It fluttered into place against the fly of his jeans.

"I'm tired of staring out at the scenery all day long," she said sulkily. Grabbing the hem of her dress, she held it down while she discreetly wriggled in place to get everything seated properly within it. "I want something to read."

Sam looked up from a bemused contemplation of his crumpled shirttail. "I doubt they carry *Soap Opera Digest*, Red."

"Oh, very cute. Come on." She grabbed his raw-boned wrist and dragged him over to the book and magazine rack.

Sam studied the offerings and picked out a romance with the most lurid cover he'd ever seen. "Here," he said, holding it out to her. "This should be right up your alley."

Catherine flipped the book over and read the back copy. Then she turned to the teaser page inside and read that, too. "Wow. This sounds pretty good." She held it out to him. "I'll take it."

He looked at the price. "They want *seven-fifty* for a paperback?" He thrust the book back in the rack. "Pick out something else." He plucked a *True Confessions* magazine off the rack and thrust it at her. "Here. How 'bout this?"

"My God," she sighed. "You are so cheap. And your taste in reading material is really lowbrow." Ignoring the magazine he extended to her, she picked up the latest copy of *Time*. "I'll take this one." She sent him a disgusted look. "You oughta approve, McKade, since you'll get to read the thing when I'm done. Or maybe you'd prefer I pick *Playboy*."

"Hell, yeah. I can read the articles, and you can look at the pictures."

"You're so droll," she said flatly, and shrugged. "Either way, this should appease your miserly little soul, since you'll only have to fork over the cash for one magazine."

He scowled at her and grabbed the romance back off the shelf. He took it, the magazine she'd selected, their bags, and her up to the counter to pay. When the transaction was complete, he thrust the book into her hands. "Here. Shut up and read."

She blinked at him. Something in his expression gave her heart a squeeze. Had her remarks somehow hurt his feelings? But . . . no, that was a ridiculous idea; he was simply being his usual contrary self. She stole a glance at his heavy black eyebrows, drawn together over his nose, at his golden brown eyes pointedly not looking at her, and at the sullen slant of his mouth. Then she looked down at his big hand, wrapped so tightly around the rolled magazine in his fist that his knuckles stood out white against his tanned skin. *Wasn't he*?

"Thank you for the book," she heard herself say softly, and had to actually stop herself from reaching out to stroke her fingertips over that clenched fist. Damn! She'd fallen prey to a case of Stockholm Syndrome, she was sure of it. What else could explain this sudden desire to placate her captor?

Well, this wouldn't do. She looked around, determined to get herself back on track. What she needed here was a way to create a new ruckus, and more importantly, a likely prospect to help her accomplish her ultimate goal—that of throwing a crimp in Sam's precious schedule and putting a dent in his much-revered wallet.

At first the pickings looked mighty slim. Everyone

was pretty much minding their own business, and it said something about just how far she'd morally deteriorated in a few short days that that seemed like a *bad* thing. But then she spotted a young man sitting on a bench across the room, staring with dazed eyes at her breasts, and she perked up, thinking perhaps he had possibility. Testing the theory, she eased her shoulders back a bit, took a deep breath, and watched as his mouth went slack.

She sighed over the necessity of exploiting this too-lush body once again. Maybe Mama had had a point, after all. Let a woman expose too many curves all at once, and men just seemed to lose all rational thought.

And surely her willingness to capitalize on the fact was sinful.

But what could she say—a woman had to do what a woman had to do. And if some poor boob couldn't see past a pair of breasts or long legs to the intelligence that lay behind it, well . . .

She could work with that.

Sam was determined that today, come hell or high water, Red was not going to get them kicked off the bus. To that end, he kept a covert watch on her every move. For the longest time, that meant watching her read. The moment the bus left the station, she buried her nose in the book he'd bought her and didn't come up for air for a solid two hours. He had just reached the point of thinking this was possibly the best eight bucks he'd ever spent in his entire lifetime when she made her first move.

Physically he was at peak frustration level, and when she reached over and skimmed her fingers along his leg, his instinctual reaction was to get her hand off of him, pronto. It was either that or bring those long white fingers up to press over the part of him he'd really like her to touch, and that sure as hell didn't contribute to his professional image of himself. So he snatched her hand up in his and roughly returned it to her side of the armrest.

He didn't know what her game was, but he knew he'd played right into it when he saw her wince as if he'd applied far more pressure than he knew to be the case. *Aw, hell. Who's she playing to now?* He glanced around surreptitiously.

His gaze came to a dead stop at the young man across the aisle. The kid glowered back at him. Shit! Red sure knew how to pick 'em. Probably just young and dumb enough not to think twice about issuing a challenge, the boy was no doubt brimful of testosterone—primed, cocked, and ready to fire away indiscriminately and without a lot of preliminary discussion. Sam allowed his gaze to drift casually past, his mind whirling as he searched for a way to neutralize the situation before it escalated to the point where they got tossed off yet another bus.

He turned back in time to see Catherine give the young man a brave, slightly trembly smile. Wonderful. In two short moves, she'd convinced the kid she was being abused. You had to give credit where credit was due. The woman had talent.

He was careful to keep his hands to himself, despite another attempt on Red's part to provoke him.

But when she reached over a third time, he'd had time to think the problem through and covered her hand with his own, rubbing it up and down his thigh. Turning his head, he gave her a sleepy, carnal smile. Catherine's eyes narrowed and he pantomimed a kiss. He didn't dare look across the aisle, but hopefully the kid would at least be confused.

About an hour further into the ride, he saw the young man get up and head for the back of the bus. A moment later, Catherine gave him a nudge.

"Excuse me," she murmured. "I need to use the rest room."

Without a word, Sam stood up and moved into the aisle, stepping back to allow her room to get by him. He watched as she undulated down the aisle as if her hips were geared by well-oiled ball bearings. She stopped behind the young man, who was waiting his turn for the rest room, and Sam saw the kid turn in response to something she said. He took a deep breath and headed down the aisle after her.

Coming up behind her, he wrapped his arms around her waist and bent his head to kiss the side of her neck. "Hey darlin'," he said in a low voice against the warm, fragrant skin there, and snuggled her deeper into his arms. "I'm sorry I was so testy earlier." Tightening his grip around her stiffening body, he murmured, "Forgive me? Please, honey. I was frustrated, but I finally figured out that all that touchin' was just your way of letting me know the penicillin finally cured your little problem."

Catherine was looking right into the young man's face, so she could hardly fail to see the horrified comprehension written there. She felt her face flame and tried to ram her elbow into Sam's side, but he had her wrapped up too tightly to do any real damage. She skewered her nails into his warm, hairy forearm instead. "You *pig!*"

"Aw, darlin'," he rumbled into the contour of her neck, "don't be mad at me." Then he rubbed his smooth-shaven cheek up and down the side of her throat, and Catherine's stomach began to jump. "I guess I shouldn't have brought up your condition in public, but it's been so damn *long* and when it finally occurred to me what you were trying to tell me, I just got so excited . . ." His voice trailed off, and she craned her head around in time to see him give her erstwhile helper a man-to-man look. "I sure didn't mean to be insensitive, but I bet the kid here understands how I coulda been so thoughtless, don't you, son?"

"Huh?" The young man's gaze was stuck on Catherine's lush curves, but as it sank in he was being addressed, his face flushed a deep red. He jerked his gaze up to Sam's face. "Oh, uh, yeah, sure." The rest room became available just then, and he exhaled a lusty sigh of relief. "Um, 'scuse me." He escaped within, slamming the door behind him with such force it bounced open again before he caught it and carefully pulled it closed.

"Lunch stop at Arabesque, Wyoming, in forty-five minutes, folks," the bus driver announced.

Sam loosened his grip slightly. "You wanna take those claws outta me now, Red?"

"I don't think you want to be asking me what I

want right this minute, McKade." She nevertheless retracted her fingernails.

He flashed her an unholy smile as he set her loose, and, angry as she was, she was hard-pressed not to return it. She was mortified right down to the new paint job on her toenails that there was a person in this world who actually believed Catherine Mac-Pherson had had a sexually transmitted disease. Yet she couldn't help but feel a sneaking admiration for Sam's ploy—she would have used it in a nanosecond if she'd thought of it first and the situation had been reversed. There was just something about matching wits with the man that was dangerously exhilarating.

But that wouldn't do, and she arranged her features into her sternest teacher's face. "Enjoy yourself while you can, Bounty Boy," she advised coolly as she pushed past him to return to her seat. "Because I'm going to have the last laugh."

"Oh, you think so, huh?" His amusement was undisguised as he fell into step behind her.

"There's no 'think' about it, McKade, I know so." Her payoff was in knowing that when their bus ultimately reached its destination and all their skirmishes were finally at an end, her fingerprints were not going to match up with her sister's. And big, bad, bounty hunter McKade was going to have to eat crow.

Or his shorts, just as he'd promised her that first day. She shrugged. Crow, shorts—the point was, she was going to enjoy watching him choke down every single bite.

12

"I'M GOING CRAZY in here, Bobby." Kay-lee dropped the motel-room drape over the window she'd been peering out of and turned around to glare at him where he lounged on the bed watching TV. How could he be so relaxed—didn't he feel the walls closing in around them? She resented everything about him at that moment: his easy attitude, his interest in the television program, his indolent sprawl with ankles crossed, elbows spread wide, and hands cradling his head atop two stacked pillows. Pushing away from the window, she headed for the door. "I've gotta get out for a while."

That at least got his attention off *Wide World of Sports* long enough to spare her a look. "Go ahead and go out, then," he agreed easily, "if you don't mind blowing the whole element of surprise."

"I—" She opened her mouth to protest, to tell him to go to hell, to rail against the unfairness of it all, then snapped it shut without uttering another word. Flouncing over to the bed, she dropped down to sit on the edge and picked up a *Vanity Fair* magazine. She crossed her legs, jiggled her unfettered foot impatiently, and flipped through several pages of advertisements without finding a single thing to hold her interest. She tossed the magazine aside and swiveled to face him. Taking a deep breath, she eased it out and forced herself to say civilly, "I've got a bad case of cabin fever." The fact of which, after all, was hardly Bobby's fault.

He hit the remote control to kill the power on the television and rolled onto his side, propping himself up on one elbow. "I know you do, sugar, and you've been a real good sport about it, too. You just have to hang in there a little while longer. We agreed that if people saw you first, there was a real risk they might say something to Catherine in front of the bounty hunter, thinking she was you."

"I know."

"And that could wreck our only advantage—"

" 'Which is that of surprise,' " she completed in unison with him. "I know, I *know*, already!"

"Well, then?"

She growled deep in her throat in pure frustration. "I want to do this the right way, Bobby—I do. But I'm jumpin' outta my skin."

"Well, how about if I drop you off at that little beauty parlor on the edge of town—"

"Town," she scoffed. "You call this a town? It's a wide spot in the road that happens to have a café, a general store slash gas station, a tavern, and this crummy roach motel."

"Hey, don't forget the phone booth and the beauty parlor." He flashed her his patented charmer's grin, then gave her hip a friendly nudge. "C'mon, baby, it's a regular boomin' metropolis—for Wyoming."

"For Wyoming—that says it all right there. The entire state probably only has one zip code."

"Ah, but we got the town with the beauty parlor. It coulda been worse—we coulda ended up in the one with the McDonald's instead. And the minute the bus pulls in and your sister's safely in the café, you can leave this stuffy little room and head over to the Curl Up and Dye. Get your nails done. It'll be my treat—I'll even spring for the tip. Whata ya say?"

Kaylee looked down at her fingernails. "Well, they could stand some attention."

"It's a date then. I'll even walk you to Curl Up's door."

She expelled a huge sigh. "I remember back in the days when a date meant champagne and salsa dancing 'til dawn, not being walked across a dusty highway to some podunk little beauty parlor for God only knows what kind of nail job."

"Hey, they come in all shapes and sizes, baby. And we're gonna get back to the dinner and dancing kind real soon. The minute we liberate your sister."

She gave him a real smile then. "You promise?"

"That I do."

"I can hardly wait." She looked around the tiny room, with its cramped and tired furnishings, and her smile faded. "What time is it, anyway?"

"Eleven-forty-five."

"Oh, God." Her sigh of disgust was profoundly felt, a long, gusty breath dredged up from deep in her diaphragm. "That means another *loonng* fifteen minutes to get through in this crummy little hellhole before the bus is s'posta be here."

The next thing she knew, she was being tipped onto her back on the mattress, and Bobby was propped up over her, grinning that devil's grin. "I know a way to make the time pass by real quick-like," he said, and lowered his head to nuzzle at her neck.

Kaylee gave his shoulders a shove. "Quit screwing around, Bobby," she retorted testily, but the words had no sooner left her mouth when she wondered why she was allowing her bad mood to run away with her good sense. *Are you crazy, girl? Isn't this exactly what you've been angling for ever since the moment you first opened your big mouth and laid down that stupid No Touching rule?*

"Is that what you really want, Kaylee—for me to back off?" The words whispered in her ear seemed to echo her own. "Screwing around sounds just like what the doctor ordered to me, but if you say no . . ." He started to push away, but Kaylee reached up and pulled him back. He growled his approval, and said huskily, "That's my girl."

His mouth, hot and knowledgeable, moved to the angle where her jaw met the hollow beneath her ear-lobe. He'd propped himself over her with both arms, and he bent his elbows now to bring his chest down to her breasts, brushing it back and forth, back and forth, while that knowing mouth turned Kaylee's senses into a swirling, mindless cauldron. He spread his thighs around hers and lowered his hips.

"Oh, God, Bobby." Reaching down, she filled her

hands with his muscular buns and held him to her, rocking up to meet his gentle thrusts. "Oh, God, Bobby, oh . . . *shit!*"

His head jerked up. "What? *What?*" A flush colored his cheekbones as he stared down at her, and there was confusion in the eyes that burned gas-flame blue with the intensity of his arousal.

"Shh!" She sucked in her breath and held it in an attempt to hear beyond her own ragged, breathy panting. Yes, there, she heard it again. "The bus," she moaned. "That's gotta be the bus. It's here early."

With a whispered curse, Bobby rolled off of her and onto his back. He stared up at the ceiling, while Kaylee scrambled off the bed and crossed to the drawn drapes. She tweaked one aside.

"Yeah, that's what it is, all right." She was quiet for a moment, then suddenly blurted, "There she is, Bobby, there's Catherine! Wow. She looks really good. She could stand a little more makeup and add a bit of oomph to her hair, but all in all she oughta wear my clothes more often, 'cause . . ."

"For Christ's sake, Kaylee." Bobby butted her aside and looked out the window. "Where is she?"

"There, in the pink dress. Which, trust me, is a huge improvement over her usual wardrobe. Well, I don't have to tell you, you saw her picture."

"Yeah, she was a lot plainer than you, but that's hardly the main consideration here. Pink dress, pink dress . . . Whoa, daddy. Got your body, though, didn't she?"

Kaylee smacked him on the arm. "Don't even think about it, buster."

He dropped the drape and grinned over at her. "Think about what?"

"Doin' the horizontal macarena with my sister."

Humming, swiveling his hips, he executed a few gyrations, complete with complicated arm movements. Then, dodging the next smack she aimed his way, he let his arms drop to his side, discontinuing his tongue-in-cheek rendition of the dance. "Nah, I was just teasin' ya, baby. I got a feeling she's not my type at all."

"Oh, please, am I supposed to be comforted by that? It's always been my understanding that if they had a *pulse*, they were your type."

"Ah, but that was before I hooked up with you." He said it lightly, teasingly, but it scared the bejesus out of him that way down deep, on some never before accessed level, he meant exactly what he said. The truth of it made him edgy and uncomfortable, so he shoved the disturbing knowledge aside, gave her a cocky grin, and pushed his luck just a little bit. "But just out of idle curiosity, what would you do if I ever did make a pass at her?"

She looked him in the eye. "Does the name Lorena Bobbit strike a chord?"

He took a hasty step back. "It does more than strike a chord, baby, it strikes pure terror in my heart. Jesus, Kaylee, don't even joke about something like that."

The demure smile she gave him did nothing to allay the jumpiness the Bobbit name invoked, and he reached out to jiggle her elbow. "It *was* a joke, right?"

"Umm."

"Right?"

"We'd better go, Bobby. Now don't forget, this is my name sign." She demonstrated as she'd been doing for the past twenty-four hours, circling the letter K that was formed by her right hand upside down over the palm of her left hand. "Show me 'Kaylee sent me.' "

He wanted to pursue the threat to his pride and joy, but he repeated her name sign and held both open hands to the front, palms up, and brought them in toward himself.

"Good. Now show me 'meet me in the women's rest room.' "

Making the letter D with both hands, he brought his hands together from the sides, palms facing. He pointed to himself, then, with his right hand open, touched his thumb to his chin and brought the hand down to touch his thumb to his chest. He then crossed his fingers and moved it in a short arc to the right. He gave her a cocky grin. "Pretty good, huh?"

"We're as ready as we'll ever be, I guess. I just wish there was more I could do." She opened the drape a crack. "Everyone's gone inside. You set to walk me across the highway for my big date?"

They were almost to the door of the Curl Up and Dye when Bobby took her hand and said in an intense undertone, "I'm gonna do my best to free your sister for you, Kaylee." Which probably made him one crazy son of a bitch, but there it was.

She turned to face him. "I know you will, Bobby." She went up on her toes to kiss him. "Thanks. I owe you."

"Yeah? Well, listen, about that Lorena crack, then—"

"Oh, man, would you look at these nails?" she demanded. "Let's hope the Bumpkin School of Beauty can do something about them—though I suppose, considering the shape they're in, they can only be improved." She grabbed the bills he was pulling out of his wallet and opened the door to the beauty parlor. "Good luck," she said, and blew him a kiss. Then she stepped over the threshold and closed the door in Bobby's face.

"How can you eat all that heavy food in this heat?" Catherine demanded. She looked down at the salad in front of her, deliberately averting her eyes from Sam's fried chicken platter, with its attendant mashed potatoes and gravy, vegetables, and biscuits. For the first time since he'd dragged her away from her home, she hadn't ordered the most expensive item on the menu. "Are you sure that chicken's even okay? It smells kinda off."

Sam thought it smelled a little funny, too, but it tasted just fine. "It's just the heat in here," he assured her. They'd been informed upon entering the restaurant that there had been a power failure earlier. Even though everything was now up and running again, the air conditioner hadn't yet caught up with the stifling heat that had built up, and the café was still oven hot. He gave Catherine an insolent once-over, taking in her damp hairline, her shiny face, and perspiration-dewed chest, and a lopsided smile pulled at one corner of his mouth. "Why, Red, darlin', are you worried about me?"

She snorted. "Yeah, right. I don't want you puking all over me on the bus if you contract salmonella poisoning from bad chicken."

Making a face, he shoved his plate away. "There's an appetizing thought."

While he was signaling for the waitress, Catherine looked up to see a man across the room watching her. Tall and good-looking, he had hair as black as Sam's and eyes that even from here she could tell were a startling shade of blue. She sat up a little straighter. This could very well be her means of getting them tossed off the bus this afternoon.

Then she stilled in shock when he suddenly signed her sister's name sign. Kaylee? Kaylee brought him? Her gaze met his elevated eyebrows, and she gave a slight nod, her heart beginning to pound.

Pointing his index fingers in the air, he brought his hands together from the sides, palms together. Then he pointed to himself. *Meet me . . .*

A man in brand-new clothing, wearing a dude-ranch Stetson, two-hundred-dollar city shoes, and a tangle of gold jewelry walked up to the black-haired stranger just then and grabbed him by the right arm, the one he was using to sign. The two of them engaged in what appeared to be an intense conversation. A moment later, they walked out of the restaurant together.

Wait a minute! Catherine leaned forward with indignant urgency. *You can't just leave me hanging here. Where am I supposed to meet you?*

Sam looked across the table at her. "What's your

problem?" He glanced around suspiciously but saw nothing out of the ordinary. Not so much as one young man with his tongue hanging out to be seen gawking at Red's damp cleavage.

What's my problem? she thought sulkily, slumping back down in her chair. *Men. So what else is new?* But aloud she merely muttered, "Nothing." Stabbing a forkful of salad, she looked around. "Where is that waitress, anyhow? I could use a glass of iced tea."

Ah, man, Kaylee was gonna kill him. Provided Jimmy Chains didn't do the job first, that is.

"I don't want to hurt you," Chains had assured him before ushering him out the restaurant door. But Bobby had a bad feeling that Alice Mayberry had probably heard those exact same words just before she'd died.

What a fuck-up.

Man, he *knew* he should have left Kaylee to pursue this mess on her own. If he had been smart, he'd have taken himself back to Miami, where the living was easy, and found himself a new woman whose life was uncomplicated. But at least Kaylee was safely out of the way for the moment. And, dammit, he was sorry that he hadn't gotten her sister away from the bounty hunter for her. It had all been going so nice and slick until Chains showed up. Catherine had actually understood the sign language Kaylee had taught him.

Chains led him around to the back of the motel, where he let loose of his arm and took a step back.

Bobby considered going for his gun, wondering if the safety was off and if he could pull it free of his waistband without shooting his own dick off in the process. He really didn't like guns.

On the other hand, he could work around the aversion if it meant the difference between living and dying.

"I don't think this's gonna help, you chasin' after Kaylee, Bobby," Jimmy Chains said, and Bobby realized Chains didn't have a clue about Kaylee having a twin. He clearly believed Catherine *was* Kaylee. Was there an angle to be worked in that? He didn't see what it could possibly be, but for now it was all he had to go with.

"She's my woman," he said, "and she took off without so much as a by-your-leave. I can't let her just run off with another guy without at least talkin' to her about it first."

"What, you doan know? She's ain't runnin' off on you, bud—that joker's a bounty hunter."

"Get out of here!"

"No, I'm serious, man. Kaylee was arrested for grand theft auto when you were outta town—"

"Bullshit. She didn't steal no car."

"Yeah, man, she did. Then she jumped bail, and that's when the bounty hunter went after her. He's bringin' her back to stand trial."

"But why would she do that? She had to have known that I'd straighten the whole thing out the minute I got back, so why didn't she just stay put?"

"I, uh . . . dunno."

"I gotta talk to her." Bobby started to walk away.

"I can't let you do that, Bobbarino. I'm sorry."

He heard the gun cock at his back and turned back to look at it in Chains's hand. "You going to *shoot* me, Jimmy?"

"I don't want to. But if you force my hand, I'll hafta."

"Hey." He held his hands to his sides in entreaty. "Chill. I'm not forcing anything here."

"I always liked you, Bobby. Liked Kaylee, too. I don't wanna hurt anyone, 'specially not a guy just tryin' to get his girlfriend back. But the boss says . . ."

"What, Jimmy C? What does Sanchez have to say about any of this?"

"Nuthin'. Turn around."

"Hey, I don't think so. If you're going to shoot me anyhow, I'd rather you did it to my face."

"I ain't gonna shoot you, I said! Jeez!" Chains gestured with his gun. "Turn around and open that door."

Bobby looked behind him. "This door?" Until that moment, he hadn't even realized one was there.

"Yeah. Open it."

He didn't see that he had a great deal of choice. He opened it and felt a welcome blast of cold air coming from within what appeared to be a refrigeration shed. Fumbling in his waistband for his own gun, he held his breath awaiting the bullet that would end his life. Could a person actually hear the shot that killed him when it came from such close a range?

His head exploded in sudden pain, and he had just enough time to realize Chains had pistol-whipped him with the butt of his gun and not shot him after all, before the world went black.

13

CATHERINE PUSHED BACK from the table. "I need to use the ladies' room."

Hand snaking across the distance separating them, Sam pinned her wrist to the tabletop before she had a chance to rise to her feet. "You can wait for the one on the bus."

She looked down at his large hand, brown and strong-looking, holding her paler, weaker looking hand captive, then raised her gaze to meet his once again. "No, I can't. I need to use it now."

"That's tough, Red. You're just gonna have to wait."

Catherine surged to her feet, her free hand slapping down on the table as she leaned over it to stare into Sam's face. "I've had two tall glasses of iced tea and a glass of water. I have to go to the bathroom. If I do not *get* that opportunity, and I do mean soon, chances are I will piddle right where I stand." She leaned closer, until her face was centimeters from Sam's. "And if that happens, McKade, if I wet my pants in public, you can bet that this entire café will know it's because you refused to LET ME USE THE BATHROOM!"

The last several words were literally shouted in his face, and Sam was aware of heads swiveling from every corner of the diner to stare at them. He let go of her wrist. It took an effort to regroup when she had so thoroughly, efficiently, routed him, but he nonetheless thrust his hand out. "Fork over your purse."

It practically knocked him off his chair when she hurled it at his chest, but he recovered in time to watch her turn and stalk away. He could follow her progress simply by keeping an eye on the path of dropped jaws that witnessed all that furious loco-motion barely confined by a skintight pink dress.

Had Catherine still had possession of Kaylee's purse, she would have launched it across the ladies' room the moment she entered, then kicked it and kicked it and kicked it across the floor. She hardly recognized herself in this state, but *God*, he made her angry! Who the hell did he think he was, to tell her when she could or could not use the bathroom? He was lucky she hadn't stripped the skin right off his smug, arrogant face!

Catching a sudden glimpse of herself in the rest-room mirror, her furious pacing ground to an abrupt halt, and she stared at her reflection with open-mouthed wonder. One hand reached out involuntar-ily as if to touch her image, but immediately dropped to her side, spooked, when the reflection in the mir-ror duplicated the motion.

Dear God.

Her face, normally so pale, was flushed and damp. Her hair blazed atop her head where she'd pinned it up this morning, but it was listing heavily to one side, and pieces of it had slipped free, clinging in untidy tendrils to her nape, her right eyebrow, and her throat. Her body was dotted with perspiration and looked as if it might burst free of the pink dress at any moment. She looked voluptuous and wild and sexual, and she looked—ah, man, she looked . . .

Exactly like her sister. That could be Kaylee staring back at her from the mirror above the counter.

Her reason for being in the rest room in the first place suddenly became imperative and she dashed into a stall, dancing in place while she yanked up the skirt of her dress and thrust down her panties. She ripped a paper protector out of its case on the wall, slapped it on the seat and sat.

Oh God, Oh God, when had this transformation taken place? *How* had it taken place without her even noticing? When—even though she preferred the roominess of her own clothes—had she ceased to be embarrassed by Kaylee's? And how had good manners been allowed to surrender without a whimper to a competitiveness she hadn't even known was part of her nature? Everything about Sam McKade ought to be an insult to her hard-fought-for good breeding.

Instead, everything about him seemed to exhilarate her, tempt her, push her to pursue feats the likes of which she never dreamed she was capable. She longed to smack him, to get *away* from him.

To kiss him silly, yank down his pants, and climb

onto his lap. Moaning, she bent forward and rested her forehead on her bare knees.

She didn't get it. She should be appalled by all these changes that had been wrought within her in such a short span of time. Instead she liked them. Where the hell was her good sense? She banged her fist over and over against the side of her knee.

Then she sat up. *Oh, please, this is too pitiful. Can't you find a better place to have an identity crisis than sitting in a bathroom stall with your undies down around your ankles?* It was certainly getting her nowhere, and if she wasn't back out in the café soon, Sam would come banging on the door. She really didn't feel up to dealing with that at the moment.

So, big deal, she thought, trying to find a way to manage her discovery with logic. She was having a bit of fun. She'd been robbed of one vacation, so what was the harm in getting whatever pleasure she could out of the situation? And if the thought that this was loads more fun than covering Europe all alone kept sneaking into her consciousness, what, in the long run, did it actually matter? Matching wits with McKade was stimulating. And it was safe. Nobody would be hurt by it.

Standing, she straightened not only her clothing, but her spine as well. She hit the flush lever, then opened the stall door and stepped out.

Right into the muzzle of a gun that was pointed straight at her chest.

She squeaked incoherently and stumbled backwards until the man with the gun reached in the stall with his free hand and hauled her forward. Swinging her free of the cubicle's confines, he set her loose. Catherine scrambled backwards, but the counter housing the sink blocked her escape, its sharp corners cutting into her hips. She reached back to grip its edges with both hands. "What . . . ?"

It was the same man who earlier had interrupted the stranger trying to sign her—and it was a damn good thing she'd just emptied her bladder, because looking down the bore of that black gun would have resulted in a sizable puddle at her feet otherwise. "Wh . . . what do you want with me?" She spread her hands on either side of her to display her purseless condition. "I'm not carrying any money." Then a truly terrible thought occurred to her. *Oh, please, please. Let him be a robber and not a rapist.*

"Doan play stupid, Kaylee."

Her heart slammed up against her ribs. He thought she was Kaylee? This was not some random act of violence, then; it was aimed specifically at her sister. *Oh, God, Kaylee, the bounty hunter wasn't enough? You had to get me involved with a gun-toting goon, too?*

Catherine saw the amiable lack of intelligence in the man's eyes. She noted his incongruous footwear, urban-cowboy hat, and an easy thousand dollars worth of gold jewelry, and queried tentatively, "Jimmy Chains?"

"I'm sorry 'bout this, Kaylee. I don't wanna have to do it, but the boss insists you can't keep your mouth shut, and I really gotta get back to the neighborhood. All this wide-open space and good ol' boy bullshit is making me nutzoid."

She edged down the counter in the direction of the door. "I can keep my mouth shut."

"That's what I tol' him, Kaylee! But Sanchez says ya can't."

"Well, go back and tell him he was wrong."

"Are you crazy? I can't do that."

"So what's the alternative then, Chains? Are you gonna shoot me?"

"I don't wanna!" he said defensively, which scared her worse than an out-and-out threat would have, because she could see that he truly didn't want to, but that he would do so all the same.

"Aw, come on, Kaylee, doan cry." He reached out an expensively manicured fingertip to brush away the tears that sheer terror had sent spilling over. "Hey, it's not like I'm gonna do it right here or nuthin'."

How comforting. She sucked in a deep breath and clamped a lid on her emotions. Exhaling softly, she looked him squarely in the eye. "The bounty hunter is not going to just sit by and let you waltz me out the door, Chains."

"I know, but I got a plan for that. The door to the kitchen's just across the hall. I'm gonna take you out through there." He gave her a big dumb smile. "Pretty smart, huh?"

"Yes," she agreed through tight vocal cords. "Very smart." Her heart felt as though it were trying to beat its way out of her chest.

He reached out his non–gun-toting hand and gave her arm a little thump of approval. "I always liked you, Kaylee."

"I, uh, always liked you, too."

"I'm real sorry it's come down to this. But I gotta do what the boss man says. He's a really smart guy, you know."

"Well, that's certainly true. But you're smarter, Jimmy."

He beamed. "Ya think so?"

"Oh, yeah. Just ask"—oh, God, what was Kaylee's guy's name again?—"uh, Bobby! Sure, ask Bobby. I've said as much to him many a time."

He looked guilty for a minute, but before she could begin to figure out why, his expression had smoothed out. He shook his head. "Nah, that's mighty nice of you to say so, but I really ain't that smart. Hector, he's the one."

Catherine edged a little farther down the counter. "Oh, I think you seriously underestimate yourself."

"Well, I am a snappy dresser."

Catherine felt her jaw sag, which Chains must have seen, for he rushed to say, "Oh, not this sorry getup—this here's just my cowboy disguise. But— you know—ordinarily and all."

"Um, right. Right! Can't argue with that." *Said Alice down the rabbit hole.*

The door swung open just then and several women barreled through the opening, chatting noisily. Chains whipped his gun down to his side where it was hidden from view, and Catherine, taking advantage of the sudden confusion, pushed through the knot of women and out into the hall.

"Hey!" she heard one of them say edgily as they undoubtedly caught sight of Chains. "What do you think you're doing in here? Were you bothering that woman? Why, I have half a mind to call the cops!"

Catherine spared the swinging kitchen door across the hall a single tempted glance, then ran past it. It made her feel unobservant that Chains had plotted a halfway intelligent escape route when she hadn't even noticed the darn thing, but this was clearly not the time to be on her own. For once she was going to do her utmost to *stay* in Sam's company. At least he had a gun, which was more than she possessed in the way of protection. She burst out of the hall into the main body of the cafe.

Catherine skidded to a halt at the table, where McKade had been brought to his feet by her rather dramatic entrance. She grabbed him by the biceps, sheer will alone stopping her from hurling herself into the protection of his brawny arms. "McKade, my God, you're never gonna believe—"

Sam felt the muscles she clutched grow hot and rigid as he scowled down at her. He was tired of this constant lust that boiled just beneath his surface. Her meagerest touch brought it to the fore, and the renewed knowledge made him strike out blindly. "What the hell took you so long, MacPherson? It's a goddam ladies' room, so for once it can't have involved an impressionable male. Unless—no, wait, don't tell me—some guy forced his way into the ladies' room, held a gun to your head, and said, 'Show me your feathers and G-string, baby.'" He glowered down into her huge green eyes, which had gone blank with shock at his attack. He knew he should leave it alone then, but couldn't seem to stop himself from continuing, "To which, of course, you re-plied"—his voice went falsetto—" 'Why, sugar, you don't need a gun for me to take off my clothes.' "

"You son of a bitch." The story of Chains dammed up in Catherine's throat. What point was there in telling him now? McKade wasn't going to believe her; he considered her a congenital liar. Oh, and a slut, too, she mustn't forget, but first and foremost a liar. She tugged on the biceps still beneath her hands. All she wanted now was to get out of here before Jimmy Chains with his very big gun hunted her down. "Let's hit the road, McKade."

Sam stood his ground. Taking in her suddenly pale face, he felt a belated flash of remorse for his crack. Hell, who Red was, or what she did with her life, had nothing to do with him after all.

Then he shrugged the guilt aside. She'd live. The important thing, thinking back, was the realization that she'd been on the verge of telling him something before he'd jumped all over her. There had been an element both edgy and excitable in her tone. "What's going on?"

"Not a damn thing you'd be interested in. I'm ready to go back to the bus is all. Let's move."

Black eyelashes narrowed over his golden brown eyes. "What the hell are you up to now?"

"Three minutes, folks," the bus driver called.

She tugged on his arm with the one hand and smacked him on the opposite shoulder with the other. "Excuse me? *What am I up to now*? Man, you're so suspicious all the time. You gotta kick back, McKade, alleviate some of that stress. You might even want to try doing it in a manner that doesn't involve trashing me," she added with an equanimity that was pretty damn commendable, if she did say so herself. The way her heart was racing, she feared congestive failure might bring it to a screeching halt in a moment. She glanced over her shoulder, but Chains hadn't appeared yet. Turning back to Sam, she gave his arm an encouraging tug. "So, let's go then, huh? Here, give me my purse."

Sam handed it over, but it was clear he still suspected her motives. Well, the hell with him. Catherine didn't give a rip what he thought, as long as he *moved*.

He finally did, but Catherine could practically feel his chivalrous impulses kicking into gear as they passed an elderly woman at the cash register who seemed to be in some sort of distress. Catherine took a firm hold of Sam's arm and steered him around her. "Don't even think about it, bud. Not today. Somebody else is going to have to play guardian angel to the Golden Girls of Greyhound for a change."

He looked down to where she hugged his arm to the side of her breast. The heat was enough to burn a hole through his biceps. "What's with you?" He scowled at the blank innocence in the big green eyes she turned up to him. "I know you're up to something, Red—I just can't figure out what the hell it is."

Tell him! Catherine's conscience screamed. *He's got a gun, he can protect you—tell him!*

But she didn't. She was still reeling from the knowledge that she had just narrowly escaped being dragged from the restaurant to her death, and she wanted to put as much distance between herself and Jimmy Chains as possible. If she sicced Sam on the man, God alone knew what might happen.

Supposing she could get McKade to believe her in the first place, which was a mighty big if.

And even if she did somehow win his belief, what if Chains shot McKade before McKade could get a handle on the situation? Then where would she be? Right now, following this blind urge to get herself miles down the road beyond a killer's reach was extremely compelling.

Stepping outside was like walking directly into a blast furnace. She'd almost become acclimated to the stifling heat of the diner, but this was something else again. The air was viscous and hot, and it was difficult to draw enough of it into her lungs to satisfy the need for oxygen. Luckily she had released her grip on Sam's arm the moment she'd safely navigated him beyond the little old lady, for the temperature was wilting, draining, and combining another person's body heat beneath the relentless glare of the sun would have been intolerable. As it was, Catherine felt her dress adhere damply to every inch of skin as she picked her way carefully across seams of tar that had softened along the blacktop. The adrenaline of her confrontation with Chains abruptly dissipated and it took massive effort simply to cross the short expanse of parking lot.

The bus, by contrast, was wonderfully cool, and she sank down into her seat with relief. It was foolish to feel safe just because a layer of steel and tinted glass separated her from the threat of Chains, but nevertheless she experienced a sense of comfort. Which indicated to her that she needed to think. She had to pull herself together and *think*, because unless she could convince Sam she'd been threatened, she was on her own.

She stared out the window, keeping a close watch on the diner's front door. The other passengers boarded the bus and settled into their seats, the driver climbed on board, closed the front door with a pneumatic whoosh, and started up the bus. Chains did not appear.

Sam touched her arm. "What the hell are you searching for, anyway?"

Catherine snatched her arm beyond his reach, her entire body jerking away in repudiation of his touch. The strength of the bitterness that surged through her caught her by surprise. Turning to look at him as the bus finally pulled away from the café, she said incredulously, "You've made it more than evident you think I'm nothing but a lying slut. Why the hell would I bother confiding anything to you even if I had a problem?"

As far as Sam was concerned, she'd gotten in more than her fair share of licks this trip, so he refused to feel ashamed of his behavior. He gave her an insolent once-over. "Because I'm all you've got, Red."

A crack of what might have passed for laughter exploded sharply out of Catherine's throat. Her head fell back against the headrest, and she shook it slowly from side to side as she stared up at the ceiling. "Then God help us all."

*   *   *

Jimmy Chains had fled the lynch mob in the ladies' room by bulling his way past the angry skirts and escaping through the kitchen. His first inclination, when he heard the bus pull out of the lot out front, was to jump in his rental car and follow it. But Kaylee had said he was smart, and he'd noticed over the years that smart people usually stopped and thought about the stuff they did instead of just jumping right in and doing it.

So he tried that. He stopped and thought about it. And it occurred to him that sooner or later someone would probably take notice if his car was forever trailing along in the bus's wake.

But how else was he supposed to know where to hook up with Kaylee again if he couldn't follow the bus? He supposed he could always call the boss to get his opinion, but at the moment that seemed like a piss-poor idea.

He stopped and thought about it some more. Then he walked around to the front of the café and let himself in the front door.

It was quiet after the rush, and he chose to make his inquiry from one of the teenagers busing the tables. "Hey," he said, walking up to a young woman with a long brown ponytail. She unloaded the industrial-grade crockery from the table to her wheeled cart, wiped her hands on the grubby white apron tied over her jeans, and looked up at him.

"I'm, uh, not sure how I missed connecting up here with my sister like I was s'posta, but somehow I did," he improvised. "I wonder if you could tell me where the bus'll stop next."

"I'm not sure about all the stops," she replied, leaning forward to wipe down the table, "but I know dinner's at the Diamondback in Laramie."

"Thanks, kid. Appreciate it. Here." He thrust out a twenty. "Buy yourself somethin' nice."

"Wow." The teenager stared down at the bill in her hand. Then she took her eyes off her work for the first time to grin up at him. "Thanks, mister."

He felt pretty damn good. Kaylee was right; he was smart. And being an intelligent kinda guy, he decided that now might be a good time to get out of town. He'd just as soon not be around when Bobby was discovered in the refrigerator shed. He left the café and walked straight to his rental car. Having already checked out of the motel, he climbed in and started it up. Then he sat for a moment, waiting for the air conditioner to catch up with the built-up heat.

When the temperature had reached a tolerable level, he put the car in gear and cruised out of the lot. He drove with caution up the main highway to the interstate.

Then he put the pedal to the metal and pointed the hood ornament toward Laramie.

14

Before Kaylee heard the rumble of Catherine's bus starting up, she'd divided her time between keeping a watch on the café parking lot where the vehicle was parked and admiring the fine new paint job on her nails. The Curl Up and Dye might be located in Back of Beyond, USA, but its owner knew manicures. Kaylee's fingernails hadn't looked this hot in a gator's age.

It had been an unexpectedly great hour. Maydeen, owner and head cosmetologist of the C U & D, was Kaylee's kind of stylist. They'd talked fashion, they'd talked men, and Kaylee felt she'd found a regular soul sister when they discovered they even watched the same soap opera. The relationship was cemented when Maydeen emphatically agreed with her that the pregnancy-of-not-quite-twin-babies-from-two-different-fathers, which had been a featured story a couple years ago, was to this date still the main contender for the weakest plot line in history award. Upon the arrival of Maydeen's 1:45 appointment, Kaylee had moved over to the window to keep a watch for Bobby. She had nevertheless continued to hold up her share of the conversation.

Then the bus had pulled away from the parking lot down the street, heading for the interstate, and she'd gotten down to business. She'd peered through the miniblinds covering the plate-glass window and waited expectantly for her first sight of Bobby and Catherine.

And she'd waited.

And waited.

"Dammit, Bobby." She pressed her nose closer to the blinds. "This had better not be a payback for one harmless little joke."

"You say somethin', hon?" Maydeen looked up from her shampoo.

"Yeah. Damn men."

"Uh-oh. Boyfriend late picking you up?"

"Yes, dammit." Kaylee spared a glance from her vigil at the window to look back into the main body of the shop. "What do we see in them, anyway, Maydeen? It's not like we can live with the creatures . . ."

"And the law don't allow us to castrate 'em," the cosmetologist agreed, then heaved a commiserative sigh. "I hear that, girlfriend."

"Actually, I'm afraid that might be part of the problem, right there," Kaylee admitted, speaking over her shoulder but keeping her attention on the view out the window. "Just before he dropped me off, I, um, evoked the dread name of Lorena Bobbit."

"Oops. Men do seem to lose all sense of humor

when it comes to that woman, don't they? And her such an artiste with a knife and all."

But Kaylee had stopped listening. Her attention was riveted on a man walking from the back of the café to the establishment's front door. She felt her hands go cold and knew it owed nothing to the salon's air-conditioning.

She knew that walk. And she was positive those intermittent flashes, set off by the noonday sun, came from the gleam of gold.

It was Jimmy Chains.

Oh, shit. She drew back with involuntary skittishness even though he'd already disappeared into the café and couldn't possibly see her standing behind the tilted blinds inside the Curl Up and Dye. And that was supposing the man had even known to look for her there in the first place.

Shit, shit, shit, shit, *shit.* That brought up a whole new question she didn't even want to think about. *Did* he know to look for her? *Oh, Jaysus Jean, where is Bobby?*

Chains's presence in this small Wyoming town added brand-new immediacy to the question.

Chains came back out the diner's front door a short while later, and once again Kaylee jerked back in pure reflex. Shifting to keep him in view, she watched him cross the lot to the motel, where he climbed into a silver sedan. Her heart did a flip. Holy mama, had he had a room there last night, too? It was a flaming wonder they hadn't bumped into each other.

God, please let Bobby and Catherine be all right, she prayed.

Kaylee headed for the door the moment Chains drove from view. She was nearly through it before she remembered to call, "So long, Maydeen. I'm taking off now."

"Your boyfriend here, hon?" Maydeen fastened the perm rod she was rolling and straightened, one fist going to the small of her back as she stretched out her spine. "That's one guy I sure wouldn't mind getting a peek at."

Kaylee forced a casual smile. "The bum didn't show. I guess I'll meet up with him at the motel." Or so she fervently hoped. *Please, please, let him just be lying low.* "Thanks for the nail job. It's one of the best I've ever had."

The stylist patted the pocket where Kaylee's healthy tip resided. "My pleasure, hon."

Kaylee broke into an awkward trot the instant the door closed behind her back. By the time she reached the motel room, her cleavage was awash in perspiration.

"Bobby," she called softly as soon as she let herself into the dim room. "You in here? Cat?"

Neither the dingy room nor its tiny, cramped bathroom was occupied.

"Jaysus, Jaysus." She sank onto the side of the bed. Arms hugging her waist, she bent low over her knees, rocking back and forth. Where was he? Had Chains gotten hold of him? *Oh, please, let that not be the case.*

Sucking in a deep breath, she held it, blew it out,

and forced herself to sit up straight. She had to think. She had to think like Catherine would, and work this thing through.

Kaylee sent a prayer winging heavenward that Chains had not gotten his hands on Cat, either. She'd never be able to live with herself if he had.

She inhaled another breath and forcefully exhaled it. She shook out her hands. For just a second, her attention was snagged by the beauty of her manicure, but then she fisted her hands, buried them in her lap, and focused on a dreary wall across the room. Okay, now. *Think.*

There were only so many places to check in this town. So, maybe, the smart thing to do would be to start at one end and simply work her way through to the other. If—God forbid—that didn't turn up anything, she could always cross the road and do the same over there. Even if she already knew Bobby wasn't anywhere near the beauty parlor, which was the only building that side of town.

She left the room, keeping an eye on the road in case Jimmy Chains should come back as she made her cautious way along the uneven sidewalk. For the first time in her life, she cursed her fondness for tall-heeled shoes, but finally she reached the gas station/general store that defined one end of town. A bell rang over the door when she opened it, and the young man behind the counter looked up.

He had a prominent Adam's apple and it bobbed convulsively at the sight of her. "Kin I help ya?" he inquired of her breasts as she approached.

She reached across the counter and hooked a finger beneath his chin, tipping it up until he met her eyes. "Keep your eyes up here, sugar, and pay attention," she said, tapping a crimson-tipped finger on her temple parallel with her own eyes. He turned red, which ordinarily would have amused her. Right now, all she felt was an unaccustomed, testy urge to snarl that she didn't have time for this shit.

If there was one thing Kaylee knew inside out, however, it was men and their sometimes fragile egos, so instead she gave him a gentle smile and rubbed her thumb across his jaw before dropping her hand. "You look like an observant kind of guy. Have you seen a woman around here today looks just like me?"

Adam's apple working furiously up and down his throat, he shook his head. His gaze kept wanting to wander, but he brought it diligently back into line time and again. "No, ma'am. I sure woulda remembered that."

She flashed him an aren't-you-just-the-cutest-thing smile. "How 'bout a guy, about six-foot-two, black hair, and blue eyes? Seen him?"

"No, ma'am."

"Damn. Well, thanks anyway." She was almost out the door when a thought occurred to her and she turned back. The young man's gaze was glued to her ass, but it immediately bounced up to her face. She hid a rueful smile, but really, you had to adore young men. They were so trainable. "How about a man, just a little under six feet, has brown hair and wears a lot of gold chains?"

The kid's expression lighted up, clearly pleased to

be able to supply a positive answer. "Yeah, him I saw. Dresses weird. He's been in a couple times the past few days."

It really was pure dumb luck that she and Bobby hadn't run into Chains before. "Thanks, sugar," she said to the clerk. "If he comes back, do me a favor and don't tell him I was asking about him, okay?"

"Gotcha."

She took the time to flash him her hundred-dollar smile. "You're a prince."

She was off the store's lot and headed toward the tavern when she turned back and eyed the telephone booth that sat on the boundary line between the two. Chances were slim to none that someone could be on the floor of the booth, but the bottom half, door included, was made of some kind of metal, which made it impossible to know for sure from a distance that it was, indeed, empty. She walked over to it and gave the door a push.

It opened into the booth easily.

She was turning away when her eye was caught by the Dumpster behind the store. Her heart gave a huge thump, and she had to reach out a hand to brace herself against the rail that ran adjacent to the telephone booth. Then, girding her loins, she pushed upright and picked her way over to the receptacle.

Her pristine new manicure looked out of place against the battered green metal as she grasped the hinged lid and heaved upward. Holding it open as far as the reach of her arms allowed, she raised up on tiptoe and leaned forward to peer inside—only to immediately sag with relief to find it contained nothing it shouldn't. She let the lid drop with a clang.

Mopping sweat from her forehead with the back of her forearm, she patted the soft fullness over her heart with her free hand and tried to control its racing beat with a couple of slow-breathing exercises. "Jaysus, girl, you've got to get a grip here. I think your first grey hair just sprouted."

Entering the tavern's dim interior a few moments later did nothing to relieve her stress, but it was at least a break from the sun's relentless glare. She stood just inside the door and waited for her vision to adjust, ignoring the headache beginning to kick up behind her eyes. As shadows slowly separated into individual details, she looked around and took inventory.

Two men sat at the bar, a couple more talked over beers at a booth in the back, and a long, lean drink of water bent low over the pool table, solitarily running it of balls. He looked up at her without straightening, thumbing back his Stetson the better to give her an appreciative once-over. For once in her life, Kaylee felt no gratification at being the recipient of a man's admiration. Accompanied by the jukebox's soft wail of a woman who had her daddy's money and her mama's good looks, she made her way to the bar.

The bartender was a rare individual who kept his gaze strictly on her face as she asked her questions. His courtesy was appreciated, but that was about the only satisfaction she received. He hadn't seen Bobby or Catherine.

A little over an hour later, Kaylee had circled back

to the motel and was trying her very last option, the refrigeration shed behind it. She found the door locked, its knob badly bent, which seemed a pretty strong indication to her that no one, let alone Bobby, had been in there today. She rested her forehead in defeat against the door's solid panel.

She had talked to what seemed like the entire population of Arabesque, Wyoming. And the only person who remembered a man answering to Bobby's description was the cashier in the café. She recalled seeing him leave with someone who sounded suspiciously like Jimmy Chains.

She had to face it. Bobby might not have been the victim of foul play. She'd checked every place where a body could be conveniently dumped. She had seen Chains with her own two eyes as he'd driven off by himself, and she couldn't spot so much as one questionable mound of dirt that indicated a hastily dug grave. No matter which way she looked at it, she was left with only one conclusion.

Bobby was in cahoots with Jimmy Chains and had been all along. What else explained Chains's ability to track them to this town? Ordinarily, he was a guy who would have a tough time finding his ass with both hands and a flashlight.

She was unprepared for the pain of betrayal, but it seared like acid through her stomach. She'd been telling herself that Bobby was just another guy to share a couple of laughs and some dynamite sex with, but somewhere along the line he'd managed to sneak beneath her guard and become more than just a good-time lover. She thought it probably had to do with the way he'd agreed to help her find Catherine, even though Kaylee had cut off the sex he found so important and in spite of his own obvious reluctance to get involved.

And hadn't he played her like a fish, though? Acting so unwilling, which had only served to endear him to her all the more when he'd nevertheless stuck by her and done his best to help. God, he must have laughed his fool head off every time she thought he was off collecting their meals from the café and he was meeting instead with Chains to plan her downfall.

She slammed her fist against the door. "Damn you, Bobby!"

"H'lo?"

It was a husky whisper, so faintly spoken that at first she thought she'd imagined it. She gave a snort of self-derision. *You chump. You just want all these nasty suspicions to be untrue. Well, get a clue, sweetheart.*

There was a faint scratch low on the other side of the door, and another barely audible whisper of sound. "Somebod' there?"

Her head snapped up. "Bobby?" She pressed her ear to the door, her heart drumming so furiously with renewed hope that she could barely hear above its roar. "*Bobby*? You in there?"

"Yeah."

"Oh, God. Are you hurt?"

"Hmm." There was a long pause, then he mumbled, "Cold."

Kaylee rattled the knob and put all her weight behind the shoulder she rammed against the panel.

It didn't give any more than it had when she'd tried it earlier. "The door's stuck. I'll be right back; I'm gonna get help."

There was no answer, and she hesitated a moment in an agony of indecision, her ear pressed up against the panel. "Bobby? You hear me, sugar? I'm gonna go get help."

Still he didn't answer, and she was just beginning to feel the first faint pinch of panic when he finally said in a barely audible whisper, "'Kay."

She raced around to the front of the motel, barging through the office door with enough force to keep the miniblinds on the door bouncing long after she'd reached the desk.

No one manned it.

She slammed the dinger down on the little free-standing summons bell, and when that didn't get immediate results, did it again. And again.

She kept on slapping it in a cacophonous frenzy.

"What the fargin' hell is going on out here?" The owner came barreling out of the back room, swiping at a smear of spaghetti sauce near one corner of his mouth with the napkin in his right fist while he used his left to yank free another one that had been tucked bib-style into his collar. "Quit that racket." He snatched the bell out from under Kaylee's palm.

"Come quick!" she urged. "There's a man stuck in the refrigeration shed out back."

"What?" He glared at her. "No one's s'posed to be in that shed."

"He's not there because he wants to be!" She all but danced beneath the force of her impatience, willing this skinny little duffer to shake a leg. "Come on, dammit, will you *move*? We gotta get him out."

The owner was a little rooster of a man, and her tone ruffled his feathers. He drew himself up with affronted dignity. "Don't you go swearing at me, young lady. You think just because this here's a small town, we're all a bunch of rubes? Well, think again. I'm in the middle of my supper and don't have time for your city-slicker rudeness or your games." He turned back toward the doorway that separated office from living space.

Kaylee rounded the counter in three of the longest strides she'd ever taken in her life. Grabbing his shoulder, she whirled him around and grasped him by two fistfuls of shirt, hauling him forward with all her strength. In high heels she was close to six feet tall, and by the time the little proprietor had quit stumbling forward his nose was buried an inch deep in her cleavage. She fished him free, hauled him up onto his toes, and lowered her head until they were eyeball-to-eyeball.

"Listen, you little pipsqueak, this is no game. My man is stuck in your refrigerator shed. It wasn't his idea to be put in there, and if anything happens to him because you refused to haul your skinny little ass out there and check, never mind *get him out*, I'll slap you with a negligence suit so huge you won't see the light of day through the paperwork until you're in your sunset years!" She turned him loose and executed an about-face on one stiletto heel. Without so much as a backward glance, she headed for the door. "Now move your ass!"

He moved his ass.

His outrage flared anew when he saw the condition of the doorknob, which Kaylee was beginning to suspect was the handiwork of Jimmy Chains.

"Look at this," he cried. "Just look at this! Somebody's going to pay for this. Some—"

Kaylee could only assume he got a good look at the expression on her face, for he swallowed the rest of his tirade whole. "I'll have to get some tools," he muttered.

"Make it snappy." She didn't wait to watch him leave, but crowded up close to the door. "Bobby? Sugar? Can you hear me?"

There was no answer and she pounded her fist against the panel. "Bobby! Oh, Jaysus, please, please, answer me."

"C . . . cold, lady," she heard him say weakly.

"Just you hang on, sugar. We're gonna have you out in just a minute—two at the most. Then I'm gonna warm you right up." She looked around frantically. "Oh, God, where is that little pissant?" Throwing back her head, she began screaming for help at the top of her lungs.

It was no doubt the sheer volume of the racket she made that garnered such swift results. The motel owner came running with a box of tools, simultaneously, the café's kitchen staff poured out the diner's back door. A second later, a man Kaylee took to be a rancher also came running, a gnawed toothpick stuck out of one corner of his mouth.

It was he who took command of the situation, cutting through the babble of questions to ask with calm authority, "What have we got here, Irv?" The inquiry was directed at the motel owner.

"Some city boy got himself stuck in my 'frigeration unit," Irv replied sourly as he fiddled without noticeable results with the bent doorknob.

Kaylee, who recognized a doer when she saw one, turned the full force of her attention on the rancher. "Please, mister," she implored. "Get him out. He's not in there because he wants to be, and I'm scared to death he's been injured bad."

The rancher eyed the door. "I suppose I could kick it in."

Irv immediately puffed up, but Kaylee cut off what she feared would be a tirade on the sanctity of his property before it had a chance to develop. "No," she reluctantly refused. "You might end up hurting him worse. It sounds like he's on the floor right behind it."

The rancher squatted down and pawed through the toolbox. When he'd selected whatever it was he'd been looking for, he rose to his feet and stepped forward. "Move aside, Irv," he directed.

Irv did, and the rancher took his place. Several moments later he had the door open as far as it could go before Bobby's inert body blocked its path.

Kaylee eased inside. "Bobby?"

He lay facedown on the floor, and a moan of distress escaped Kaylee's lips when she saw the swollen goose egg on the back of his head. At its center was a deep gash that was black around the edges with crusted blood.

"Jaysus." She dropped to her knees by his side.

His bare arm was cold to the touch when she reached for it. "Bobby?"

"How you doin' in there, miss?" The meager shaft of light that came through the doorway was temporarily eclipsed by the rancher's sturdy body as he squeezed through the opening. "He all right?"

"No. His skin is freezing, and he's not answering, and . . ." She ran out of breath and couldn't seem to drag enough of it into her lungs. Panting, she felt hysteria threatening to seize control. She reached a hand out to the rancher. "Please," she implored him helplessly between wheezy breaths. "Please."

"Okay. It's all right." He stuck his head outside the door. "Somebody get me a paper bag." Swiveling back, his leather-tough hand closed around hers and he helped her to her feet. "Step outside, miss. Let me bring him out so we can see what we're dealing with."

He laid Bobby down on the hot concrete a moment later, using his own pristine handkerchief to shield the head wound from contact with the gritty ground. Kaylee squatted at his side, dying to lend her assistance. Unfortunately, she was about as helpful as the man stretched out at her feet as she wheezed and struggled for air, and when a line cook ran up waving a brown paper lunch sack, the rancher snatched it from his hand, shook it open, and handed it to her.

"Hold that over your mouth and nose and breathe into it, miss. You're okay. You're just hyperventilating."

Kaylee did as directed and watched over the top of the bag as he thumbed back Bobby's eyelids one at a time, checking for pupil reaction to the strong afternoon light. He then pressed two fingers to the artery beneath Bobby's jaw and sat back on his heels, looking over at her.

"I'd say he's got himself a case of hypothermia that's been aggravated by blood loss from the blow to his head. Got a concussion, too."

Kaylee lowered the sack. "Is there a doctor or clinic nearby?"

"By Wyoming standards. Let's get him loaded up in your car and I'll draw you a map."

"Thank you." She reached across Bobby to touch the rancher's hand. "You've been so great."

Bobby's eyes opened then and he looked around until his unsteady gaze slid past Kaylee's face, then backtracked to lock on it. His mouth crooked up in a shadow of his old charmer's grin, and it rocked her right down to the ground. Immediately on the heels of that emotion came a punch of guilt delivered by the remembrance of what she had believed of him.

"Oh, God, Bobby, I'm sorry," she whispered. "I'm so sorry for what I thought." She picked up his limp right hand in both of hers and brought it up to cover in kisses. She then cradled it reverently between her breasts.

"Hey. No prob'lm," he slurred. He blinked at her several times, his gaze sliding in and out of focus. Finally, he seemed to get a bead on a point in her face that he could focus on. He stared up at her, mouth loosely smiling, brows drawn together in puzzlement. "Do I . . ."

His voice trailed off but then he seemed to gather his strength to repeat, "Do I . . ."

Once again his voice trailed into silence, and without relinquishing the grip that held his hand buried to the wrist between her breasts, Kaylee leaned over him. She gazed lovingly into his blue eyes. "Do you what, sugar?"

He blinked up at her. "Do I know you?"

15

꩜꩜⌒ THE BUS PULLED off the interstate onto a scenic overlook. It had left the Great Divide Basin behind and was starting the climb into more mountainous terrain.

"Fifteen minutes, folks," the driver announced over the loudspeaker. "Take advantage of it to stretch your legs and enjoy the view."

Catherine was wary and on guard as she climbed off the bus. She kept glancing around, expecting to see Jimmy Chains pop up at any moment, brandishing his gun. Sam had a firm grip on her arm, and for once she welcomed his complete lack of trust. She didn't even care that he had been such an ass back at the restaurant. All she wanted was to stick close to him, and did so even when he relaxed his hold and eventually dropped his hand from her arm altogether.

With each uneventful moment that passed, however, her edgy nerves eased. The overlook was little more than two lanes that took a half loop off the interstate. One was designated as a parking lane and the only other vehicle parked in it aside from their bus was a minivan currently disgorging a family of five. The overlook area to the right contained a sanican and a small enclosed hut to the side of the parking lane—a waiting room for passengers catching the bus, and their reason for stopping.

It was still hot at this elevation, but a cooling breeze flirted intermittently with the idea of offering relief. Overall, it was quiet, and peaceful, and, lulled from her constant vigilance, Catherine wandered from Sam's side, drifting with the milling crowd toward the overlook.

For several minutes she admired the view of the mountain range to the south, but eventually she began to feel hemmed in by the press of bodies and edged away. She strolled back toward the bus, taking her time and enjoying the freedom of being on her own, even if only for a moment.

The car came at her out of nowhere. One minute she was alone in the lane as she headed for the bus, and in the next a sedan had appeared off the freeway. Moving much too fast, it roared straight at her.

She froze in middle of the road, watching as a ton of steel bore down on her. Then a hand, age-spotted and crisscrossed with soft, ropy veins, reached out and gripped her wrist, hauling her out of harm's way. The car blew past without stopping, missing her by a hairbreadth.

She stood, breasts heaving as she struggled for breath, gazing blindly after the disappearing car. Then she turned to stare down into the face of a small-boned, white-haired old lady who was a good five inches shorter than she and so slender that it looked as if a stiff breeze might blow her away.

"Damn teenagers." Her rescuer released Catherine's wrist and flapped a hand to disperse the swirl of grit that had been kicked up in the wake of the car's high speed pass. "Oughtta have their licenses yanked for a stunt like that."

"My God, thank you," Catherine said fervently as she finally gathered her wits about her. "You saved my life." The woman's words sank in then. "It was a teenager? You saw the driver?" She hadn't caught so much as a glimpse, herself.

"Not really, but who else drives like a bat out of hell like that?"

Sam came tearing up, skidding to a halt in front of Catherine. He grabbed her by both shoulders. "Are you all right? Jesus, I just turned my head for one minute, and when I turned back a car was screaming down the road and someone said it only missed you by an inch." She dived into his arms and he clamped them closed around her, holding her close. His stomach gave a nasty lurch.

"Damn teenagers," reiterated the little old lady pithily.

Sam looked at her over the top of Catherine's head. "Did you get their license number by any chance?"

"Nope. Happened too fast."

"She saved my life, Sam," Catherine muttered into his chest. "If it wasn't for her, I'd be splattered all over the road."

"You have my thanks, ma'am."

"Hell." The woman shrugged. "Anybody would've done the same."

"Maybe, but not just anybody did." Sam looked her over. That air of fragility was clearly deceptive, and he grinned down at her. "You must be stronger than you look. Red's a whole lot of woman for a little thing like you to be yanking out of the path of speeding cars."

She cocked an arm, causing a surprisingly sturdy bicep to leap to life. "Life of ranching, fifty years of cross-country skiing, and three days a week at World Gym since we sold the spread."

"For every one of which I give a heartfelt thanks." Catherine twisted out of the comfort of Sam's embrace and turned to her rescuer. She reached out to grasp the woman's hands. "Thank you so much. I can never repay you."

"No payment needed, dearie. I'm glad I was there to help."

"Time to board, folks," the bus driver called.

Catherine thought about her near miss as the bus continued on its journey. In all likelihood her rescuer was correct to assume the driver was a teenager, someone young and inexperienced enough to panic at discovering he'd nearly hit another person.

But Catherine didn't like coincidences. And two brushes with death in a little over an hour struck her as very coincidental indeed.

She had given it great deal of thought before this rest stop, and she'd come to the conclusion that the man who'd signed to her in the café today had to be Bobby LaBon. He fit Kaylee's description, at any rate. Question was: was it true he'd been sent by her erstwhile two-timing twin, or was he part and parcel of the hit squad with Jimmy Chains?

The latter idea wouldn't quite jell. She couldn't discount having seen the two men together, but a conspiracy theory would surely fly a little better had the Bobby-person actually finished arranging a place for them to meet, for she'd have done her utmost to be there.

So, if Bobby wasn't with Chains then, and Kaylee really had sent him, did that mean her sister had also been nearby? Had she come to rescue her?

Catherine told herself it was self-defeating to get her hopes up. The sister she knew and loved had never exactly knocked herself out to get other people out of trouble.

But a tiny kernel of hope nevertheless warmed her.

She couldn't seem to stick with any single emotion for long, however. An entire barrage of them kept bouncing back and forth, with first one attempting to attract her attention, then another. The most persistent was guilt.

Catherine knew she had a responsibility to inform Sam of Chains's attack. Like a puppy with a knotted rag, she'd been worrying the knowledge since they'd left Arabesque, and the incident with the car only served to reinforce it. She could gnaw on it and nose it around and search futilely for a loose end that would somehow magically unravel an alternate option, but the bottom line was clearly defined. She *had* no other choice—not when a similar attack could come from out of the blue, in any place, at any time.

And perhaps already had.

She dreaded the thought of getting into it with Sam, though. His lapse back into aloof silence said louder than words that his show of concern at the overlook had not been for her, so much as a desire to keep his investment intact. And he was so obstinately, determinedly *blind* in his view of her that she knew getting him to believe her would be an uphill battle.

Nevertheless—she heaved a long-suffering sigh—there was no time like the present. She supposed.

Sam felt it when Catherine turned toward him. She'd been squirming around in her seat since they'd got back on the bus, and all that motion was making him queasy. Without opening his eyes, he reached out and clamped his nearest hand over her thigh to hold her still. "Will you quit that?"

"What?" she demanded acerbically. "Breathing?"

"Works for me." It was a knee-jerk response, but he didn't want to spar with her. He just wanted her to quit wriggling. Cold sweat broke out on his forehead, pooled clammily on his chest and in his armpits, and a fresh wave of nausea rolled up his throat before mercifully receding. "Quit rockin' around, dammit."

"I have something I have to tell you." She plucked at his fingers where they gripped her bare thigh, and Sam removed his hand. For once the feel of her skin beneath his didn't even register. She gave him an impatient nudge of the elbow, and he had to suck in a deep breath to combat another wave of sickness.

"McKade, will you pay attention?" she demanded. "I said I've got something to say."

"And I'm sure every word that drips from your lips will be a pearl beyond price," he agreed through his teeth. "But do you mind? Save it." He was beginning to have a bad, bad feeling that eating that chicken at lunch had not been his greatest move of the day.

"Trust me, I would like nothing better," she snapped. "However, as time is of the essence . . ."

"I said save it!" He opened his eyes and everything seemed too bright, the colors too garish. When the hell had Red's dress taken on that sickening Pepto-Bismol hue? Swallowing hard, he glared at her. "I'm not in the mood, got it?"

She acquiesced to the snarled warning with a full complement of her usual good grace. "Well, too damn bad, Bubba, because I'm not in the mood to be murdered in my sister's stead!"

He narrowed his eyes at her. "What the hell are you yammering about now?"

"Jimmy Chains, the guy I told you about who killed that woman in Miami—which, you might recall, caused Kaylee to skip bail and brought *us* together—was in Arabesque today."

"Oh, for chrissake." Like he really needed this shit on top of the way he was feeling. "And you expect me to just take your word for it, I suppose. Now that we're a hundred miles down the road with no way for me to check out your story for myself. Next you'll be telling me that was him in the car that nearly ran you down."

"I've been wondering about that myself."

He glared at her in disgust. "Man, you really do

take me for one stupid son of a bitch, don't you?"

"Oh, I've never said you were stupid."

All right, he'd left himself wide-open for that one. Mopping cold sweat from his brow, he inquired sarcastically, "And just where did this Jimmy Chimp—"

"Chains! Jimmy Chains."

"—Chains guy magically show himself? In Arabesque." Sam had to swallow hard against an encroaching wave of nausea, and it fueled his anger. He was in no mood for her games. "What was he doing, lounging at a nearby table while we ate?"

"No, he—"

"*You're* the only one who saw him, I imagine."

"As a matter of fact, an entire group of—"

"And just supposing for a moment that I might be so gullible as to actually buy your bullshit story," he interrupted once again, unwilling to subject himself to the tangle of fact and fiction he knew she'd weave with her glib tongue if he gave her half a chance, "what is it again that makes you think he wants to kill you? Aren't we getting just a tad melodramatic?"

She jerked rigidly upright with one enraged motion, and he nearly lost his lunch right then and there.

"I don't know," she said furiously, "are we? I don't find it particularly melodramatic to believe I might get killed when someone shoves a gun in my face. But then, that's me. Perhaps for a big-time, fearless *bounty boy* like yourself, it's merely your average, everyday occurrence."

Some still-functioning, logical corner of his mind

tried to tell him there were tidbits of information in this conversation that were important, and he should be focusing his fast-dwindling resources on them. His pure gut reaction, however, got tangled in the contempt she invested in the words "bounty boy." Hell, she might just as well have been saying *baby molester*.

He thrust his face aggressively near hers, ignoring the renewed wash of sweat the movement caused him. "You think I *enjoy* being a bail enforcer?" he snarled. "You think I like spending my every waking hour in the company of thieves and lowlives?"

"I think you revel in it. And my sister is not a lowlife! Neither is she a thief."

Cautiously, he pulled back far enough to make the insolent once-over he subjected her to that much more effective. "No, your sister sounds like a regular productive, law-abiding citizen. You on the other hand . . ."

"Oh! You are such a prick!" Catherine gave his shoulder an indignant shove. The fact that it merely rocked him in his seat increased her frustration and fury. "Well, just suppose for one moment that I buy into your self-deluding fantasy that I'm Kaylee MacPherson. What the hell gives you the right to sneer at what *she* does for a liv . . ."

She found herself talking to thin air. With a choked oath, he'd abruptly rolled from his seat and hot-footed it down the aisle to the back of the bus.

Catherine's mouth went slack and she slid over into his seat on the aisle, craning around its high back to see what on earth he was doing. As she watched he practically ripped the rest room's door from its hinges before disappearing into its depths, and with a huff of exasperation she faced forward again.

Well, for crying out loud. If that wasn't just typical of him to be so rude. No "excuse me" for this guy. He had to use the facilities so he just hopped up and used it. It wouldn't have killed him to have said something, but then that was probably the idea. She had been making a valid point and rather than admit she could be right, he'd taken a hike. She moved back into her own seat with a flounce and picked up her book.

It was a highly entertaining one, so she barely glanced up when a man made his way down the aisle from the front of the bus sometime later. The conversation his approach elicited, on the other hand, caught her attention.

"If you're headed for the bathroom," she heard someone behind her say, "you might as well save yourself the trip. There's a guy been in it for nearly half an hour."

"Someone's going to have to talk to the driver," another voice chimed in. "From what I hear, it's fast approaching critical stage for a couple of the ladies back there."

Catherine glanced at the unoccupied seat next to her and saw with a start that Sam had never returned. Reluctantly setting aside her novel, she moved over into his seat to peek once again around its back. The first thing she saw was the line that had formed outside the only rest room.

Sam was not one of the people standing in it.

She didn't stop to question her sudden concern for his welfare; she simply acted upon it. She was out of her seat and down the aisle in an instant.

"Please," she queried of the first person she came upon in the line. "What's going on?"

"Some guy's in there pukin' his guts out," a young man replied, and Catherine realized it was the same kid whose help she'd hoped to recruit this morning before Sam had blown her plan out of the water.

Begging pardon over and over again, she worked her way to the front of the line and tapped on the rest room door. "Sam? Are you in there?"

"Go away, Red." An instant of dead silence followed those unencouraging words, and then the unmistakable sound of violent retching came through the door.

"Oh, Sam," she whispered. She turned to the people in line. "It must have been the chicken he ate at lunch. I thought it didn't smell quite right."

They were sympathetic but had problems of their own, the most imperative of which involved a dire need for the rest room themselves.

She turned back to the door. "Sam? A whole line of people are out here waiting to get in."

He surfaced from his misery long enough to utter a truly offensive suggestion as to what said people could do.

"He doesn't mean that," she assured those near enough to hear, but she could see that with a few words Sam had completely destroyed the sympathy factor, and those waiting were rapidly losing pa-

tience. A few people farther down the line looked in
the mood for an outright riot. "Perhaps I'd better talk
to the driver."

Twenty minutes later the bus had parked in front
of a run-down motor court in a small Wyoming
town, and the driver was at the back of the bus,
pounding on the door. "Sir! Please open up. I have
to insist you free up the rest room. It's the only one
we've got, and your occupation of it has generated
quite a need out here."

Sam lifted his head away from the door where it
had been resting. "I can do that," he agreed weakly.
"But then I'm gonna be vomiting all over your nice
clean bus."

"We got you an accommodation for the night, sir.
Your wife collected your bags and she's in the room
now, waiting for you."

His wife? Sam rose shakily to his feet and rinsed
out his mouth with water from the tiny sink. What
in hell was this idiot talking about?

Then it hit him and Sam swore. The deluded fool
must be referring to Red.

He pulled the door open and staggered out.
"Where is she?" Stupid question. Probably six miles
down the road by now.

"Right inside the room, sir. Here"—a beefy arm
reached out to guide him—"Let me give you a
hand."

"My wife . . ."

"Is just fine. She must not have eaten whatever
you did. She's a fine, accommodating woman, sir.
You're a lucky man. Why, a lotta women would have

made a fuss about being put off the bus, particularly at a place like this. Watch your step here, sir. But your wife said for me not to worry about it, that she'd make do just fine."

Sam would have curled his lip if he'd had the strength. He just bet she had—right before she'd boogied off down the road.

"The cost," he mumbled, but in truth at the moment he didn't really give a shit. The nausea that had temporarily abated was beginning once again to make its presence felt.

"Greyhound will take care of it, sir. Don't you worry. Here, step up. And another. And here we are."

"Bathroom," Sam mumbled. "Quick."

"Through here, Sam."

His head jerked up at the sound of Red's voice. Those big green eyes of hers were soft with concern, but he didn't fool himself into believing it was actually for him. It was an act for the driver's benefit. Of course she wasn't going to split with an audience around to see; he should have known that. She'd wait for the bus to leave.

Nausea slammed into him hard, and he stumbled for the bathroom.

Catherine thanked the bus driver and closed the door behind him. It was stifling in the tiny unit, the antique cooler in the window more proficient at producing noise than cooling the air. She could barely hear over its racket as the bus started up and pulled away. Mopping an arm across her forehead, she rummaged through her suitcase until she found shorts and an abbreviated top. She quickly changed, then went to render what assistance to Sam she could.

She found him sitting on the floor with his back to the door, long legs crooked around the toilet and arms crossed over the rim of its bowl. He was the picture of exhaustion as he rested his forehead against his forearms.

His big body swallowed up most of the available space in the tiny room, but she managed to squeeze inside. Looking down at his shirt, which was transparent across his back where he'd sweated through the material, she reached for a thin washcloth with one hand and turned on the faucet with the other. She soaked the cloth with cold water, wrung it out, and formed a compress.

"Here," she said, kneeling behind him to press it against the back of his neck. "This'll make you feel better." Reaching around, she fumbled to undo the buttons on his shirt.

He reared up with a jerk, which in the confined space pressed his back hard against her stomach. "What the hell are you doing here?" he demanded with unfeigned surprise. "I thought sure you'd be miles down the road by now."

Catherine realized with an unpleasant start that it hadn't even occurred to her to take off and leave him to his own weakened devices. Disgust for her own sentimentality and such unmerited concern for a man who'd done his utmost to make her life miserable made her voice acerbic as she lifted the compress off his neck, rewet it, and applied it to his forehead. "The day is young, McKade."

His head sagged back against the bolstering fullness of her breasts. "I s'pose it is at that."

She had just peeled him out of his soaked shirt when the next wave of sickness hit him. For the next hour and a half she watched the muscles in his bare back heave violently beneath his skin as he bent over the bowl. One bout followed hard on the heels of the one before, with very little respite in between, and she could practically see him turning himself inside out until ultimately there was nothing left in his stomach to bring up. The last paroxysm finally faded and he slumped back against her. She wiped him down once again with the cool rag.

"We should probably get you to a hospital."

"No." His head rolled side to side in denial. "Can't afford a hospital."

"Can you afford to *die*?"

A faint smile tipped up one corner of his mouth. "Not gonna die." He tilted his head back, pressing it deeper into her cushioning breasts as he sliced a gaze up at her. 'Sides, I would've thought that'd make your day."

"Oh, yeah," she agreed sarcastically. "The idea of explaining your moldering corpse to the authorities gives me a real thrill." She started to give him a shake, but his distressed moan and immediate loss of the little color he'd managed to retain caused her to drop her hands guiltily to her sides. "This is no time to be cheap, Sam."

"Gotta be," he mumbled. " 'Sa only way I'll ever get that lodge for Gary."

Catherine's eyebrows furrowed in her brow. "What lodge? And who the heck's Gary?"

16

He settled in against her. "Friend. Gary 'n me were MPs together."

Catherine's eyebrows shot up. "MPs? As in military police? As in the U.S. Army?"

"Yeah."

"Sam McKade, you had a real job, and you gave it up to be a *bounty hunter*?"

"Had to." His upper body slumped heavily against hers as he relinquished the last of his strength. "Gary took a bullet meant for me. Left him paraplegic. Someone had to take care of—" He broke off with a curse as a new bout of nausea sent him sitting forward to lean over the toilet bowl again, racked by convulsions that culminated in nothing.

Catherine looked at the butt of his gun sticking out of his waistband and the bulge of wallet in his back pocket. She liberated both and he was so preoccupied with his own misery he failed to even notice. Setting them aside, she rose up to freshen the washcloth with cool water. A few moments later he once again slumped back against her as if she were his own private easy chair.

She patted the cool compress against his forehead, his throat, his shoulders. "So why was the bullet that injured your friend meant for you? Did you piss somebody off?" She could easily visualize that.

"No, I was the ranking noncom in command. Shoulda had control of the situation."

She waited, but he didn't elaborate. "That's it? You should have had control of a situation but you didn't; therefore, the bullet that paralyzed your buddy ought to have hit you instead?"

"Yeah."

"You didn't make anybody mad, which caused them to shoot your friend by mistake when they were actually aiming for you?"

"Jesus, Red." His tone was invested with a wealth of disgust. "No."

"But it's nevertheless your fault he was injured."

"Yes!"

Feeling his agitation, she wet the cloth again and stroked it soothingly over his shoulders and along his wide collarbones. "I don't get it. Maybe if you explained what happened."

"See, this tanked up Spec-4 ran the base gates—"

"Wait a minute, wait a minute," she interrupted. "What's a Spec-4?"

"Specialist, fourth class. The guy's rank, Red: more than a private, less than a sergeant."

"And by tanked up I assume you mean—"

"Knee-walking drunk. Plus, we found out later he'd been freebasing. But all we knew at the time was that he'd run the gates and the marines on guard duty had called for the MPs—that was me 'n' Gary.

We tracked the soldier down to the parade grounds where he'd left his Jeep. The guy was staggering all over the green, yelling and occasionally shooting off a pistol he had no business having."

Sam closed his eyes, visualizing it as if it were yesterday. The humid night, the full moon that wheeled in and out of banked clouds. The erratically parked Jeep, with its engine still running, its lights left on, and the driver's door hanging open. The silence when the cicadas stopped singing in the face of human disturbance. "I talked to him, trying to calm him down. At the same time we instigated a flanking maneuver." His head rode the wave of the sharply inhaled breath that lifted Red's breasts, and he could practically *feel* the question before it ever formed. A slight smile pulling at one corner of his mouth, he provided the answer without making her ask. "That's where one party—me—moves to one side, holding the quarry's attention, while his partner moves to the other. It makes for a smaller, or at least divided, target for the quarry to take aim at and gives the MPs more options for disarming him."

"So, was Gary somehow forced to follow this flanking maneuver against his better judgment?"

"No, it's standard operating procedure. And generally very effective."

"Only this time . . ."

"Only this time I fucked up," he said flatly. "I lost the Spec-4's attention. He'd been swinging back and forth trying to cover both of us at once, but mostly it was on me where it belonged, and I thought I was making inroads at calming him. I almost had him talked into giving up his weapon. But then I did something, said something, wrong, because he suddenly went apeshit and started howling and firing off rounds. I hit the ground and came up firing." His breathing grew labored beneath the weight of his failure. "Took him down, too, only it was too damn late. He'd already gotten Gary."

There was a moment of silence, then Catherine asked, "So, why was it your fault?"

"Because I was the master sergeant, dammit!"

She felt his turmoil in his tensed muscles everywhere they touched. "And Gary was . . . ?"

"Staff sergeant."

"Not as lofty a rank, I take it."

"It was my responsibility to secure the situation, and I lost control of it. As a result, a man who was not only under my command, but my best friend, lost the use of his legs."

Catherine thought she was beginning to understand. "And Gary blamed you?"

His laughter was short, sharp, and unhappy. A deep desire to offer comfort, to wrap him in her arms and rock him like a baby, caught Catherine by surprise.

"For maybe six, eight months, Gary was mad at the world. He blamed the Spec-4, the marines who didn't stop him at the gate, the U.S. Army in general. Hell, he blamed *God*. For some dumb reason, though, he never did blame me." And he sounded as if the lack tortured him.

"Maybe that's because he accepted it for what it was: a tragic accident."

"No. It's because he's a better friend than I deserve." It was stated flatly, in a tone proclaiming that the conversation was at an end.

Then he shifted. "I think maybe the puking's finally stopped." He was weak as a kitten and felt chilled to the bone—which, considering the trapped heat in here, indicated to him he was dehydrated. He nonetheless struggled out of his warm resting spot against Red's body. It felt dangerously comfortable, and that wouldn't do. "And this floor is sure as hell no place to be sittin' around. Let's get out of here." He struggled to his feet.

Wondering where the lodge came into the story, Catherine absentmindedly picked up his wallet and gun and followed him into the unit's main room. He was fiddling with something from his duffel bag when she walked up to him, but it wasn't until he turned that she realized it was his handcuffs.

"I'm sorry, Red," he said, reaching for her. "But I'm too weak to be chasing you down. I gotta do this."

"*No!*" Betrayal was a knife in her heart and without thought she slammed her hands against his chest, shoving with all her might. He went down like a felled tree onto the bed behind him.

She shook as she stared at him sprawled out on the mattress. "You lousy Judas pig! I stayed and took *care* of you, and now you want to lock me up like a dog on a chain?" She hadn't cried once since he'd dragged her from her home, but now tears rose in her eyes, and furiously she dashed them away. She would not let him see her reduced to this, damned if she would.

Sam struggled up on one elbow, feeling shaky and frail. Rubbing at his chest where she'd struck him, he stared up at her flushed cheeks and furious green eyes, made huge by unshed tears. Jesus, what had she hit him with, a hammer? Then he saw what was in her hand and he went very still. "Put down the gun, Red."

"What?"

"Put. Down. The gun."

She looked down at the weapon in her hands as if she'd never seen it before, very nearly bobbling it as shock robbed strength from her fingers. Oh, God, she'd forgotten she even held it. She'd had his comfort in mind when she'd taken it out of his waistband, nothing else.

In the face of his betrayal, however, she took a deep breath and rearranged the weapon in her hand until she had a proper hold on it. It was heavier than it looked and swayed in a wobbly figure eight as she raised it up to point at him. She brought around her other hand to lend assistance and saw that it clutched his wallet. Shaking, she tucked that into her cleavage and used the freed hand to support the weight of the gun.

"You stay right where you are, McKade." Edging over, she grabbed her suitcase off the bed. Then she scuttled back. His golden brown eyes watched her steadily, and even though his face was pasty and he made no overt move, she didn't trust him not to rise up off of the mattress and forcefully detain her.

"You should have left the cuffs out of it," she said shakily. "We would have been okay if you'd just left the cuffs out of it." She backed up to where she'd deposited her purse and stooped, keeping her eyes and the wobbling gun on him while she felt around with one hand until her fingers brushed the strap. She snagged it, swinging it up into place over her shoulder. Fishing Sam's wallet from her scooped neckline, she dropped it in the bag, picked up her suitcase again, and backed toward the door.

"I'm going to be more humane than you and leave you free. In case you get sick again." Opening the door, she backed through it, then hesitated a moment, staring at him. His face was leached of color but his eyes burned at her, and his naked chest, arms, and shoulders radiated a power she wouldn't underestimate. "I'm sorry about your friend," she whispered. "I really don't think it was your fault."

Then, stuffing the gun in her purse, she fled into the burning sunlight.

"Son of a bitch!" If frustration equaled volume, it would have been roared like a lion. Instead the words emerged from Sam's throat as barely more than a croak.

He struggled to sit up, but by the time he made it to the side of the bed, he had to acknowledge to himself that his strength had been severely undermined. Chasing after her was out of the question, at least for the moment.

He swore a blue streak.

Then he forced himself to his feet. It wasn't out of

the question, dammit, and he'd better get his butt in gear or she'd be long gone.

His chance for the lodge had just sashayed out the door, and it didn't do a thing for his sense of self to know the regret uppermost in his mind was that now he'd never get the chance to use even one of the condoms he'd been collecting from rest-room dispensers for the past couple of days. He was a real deep guy, a true professional.

Shivering, he collected a clean shirt from the duffel bag and shrugged it on. Then he sat down on the side of the bed to gather his strength. He knew he should be forcing fluids—he'd stopped sweating some time ago, and it was the dehydration more than anything that made him wobbly as a newborn colt. But when he ran water at the bathroom sink for a drink a few moments later, its slight mineral smell caused his stomach to flip-flop rebelliously, and he set the glass down untasted. He shuffled off in search of his toothbrush and toothpaste, brushed his teeth, and then tried again.

He gagged.

The hell with it. Just get going. Automatically, he reached for the small of his back to check the placement of his gun. And swore when he recalled where he'd seen it last: weaving unsteadily in Red's hands. Damn. He could sure use a smoke right about now.

A humorless laugh escaped him. You had to give credit where credit was due, she sure as hell was some piece of work. She'd kept his attention so firmly trained on her the past few days that this was the first time in quite a while he'd even given a thought to cigarettes. Give the little lady a cigar.

But, hell, man, that was nothin'. Deflecting a craving for nicotine was chump change compared to the way she'd gotten him to spill his guts about Gary and then blithely tripped on out the door, trailing streamers of my entrails behind her.

Remembrance of the look in her eyes when she'd seen the handcuffs rose up to haunt him; it had been anything but blithe. Furiously, he shook it off. Big deal. He already knew what a dandy little actress she was.

Her last words to him, however, were not so easily dismissed.

It had flat-out knocked the pins out from under him when she'd told him Gary's condition was not his fault before boogalooing out the door and down the highway. Sam propped himself against the wall to catch his breath for a minute.

Why would she go and say something like that? She'd had the upper hand at the moment, her shaky handle on that gun notwithstanding, so it wasn't as if it had gained her a damn thing. Why, then, had she said it?

Man, he didn't get her, didn't get her at all. But come hell or high water, he was getting that goddam lodge for Gary, and for that he needed her. Therefore he would get up off his butt and go fetch her back.

In a minute. Just as soon as he regained a bit of his strength.

Jimmy Chains slumped on his tailbone on the seat of the rental car, absentmindedly rolling a toothpick from one side of his mouth to the other as he watched passengers climb off the bus. He waited for Kaylee to put in an appearance. It was time to wrap things up and get back to the neighborhood.

Then, sitting up with a jerk, he spit the toothpick on the floor. The last passenger must have gotten off the vehicle, because the driver was closing the doors. *What the fuck is this?*

Climbing out of the car, he slammed the door and stomped across the lot to intercept the driver, who was headed for the diner. "Hey," Chains said. "I was s'posta meet my sister here—she said she'd be on your bus. Redhead, good-looking, killer body—ya seen her?"

"Huh?" Blinking, the driver gaped at the man who'd appeared out of nowhere, then collected himself with a shake. "Oh, the redhead. Yeah, her husband got food poisoning. I had to let them off at a motel." He started to walk away.

The bounty hunter was sick? Chains mentally rubbed his hands together. This was good; it would make his job that much easier. "Wait a minute!" He took a couple huge strides to catch up with the driver. "What motel? Where?"

"I'm sorry, sir, I'm not allowed to give out that information."

"She's my fuckin' sister!"

The driver stiffened, shooting him a look of distaste. "So you say," he said stiffly, and studied Chains as if searching for the resemblance. Insincerely, he reiterated, "I'm sorry. Those are the rules."

Chains considered kicking the information out of

the little turd, but it was way too public, and the boss had said to keep a low profile. Son of a friggin' bitch, though, now what was he supposed to do?

Well, a man had to eat, so he supposed he might as well catch a bite as long as he was here. Something would probably come to him while he was refueling the ol' engine. He was a smart man, after all.

Kaylee said so.

Nothing shook loose while he tucked into chicken fried steak and a baked potato. He racked his brain until his head hurt but came up blank while putting away a slice of apple pie and a cup of coffee.

It was while the waitress was refilling his coffee cup that he overheard the conversation at the next table.

He'd taken only the vaguest of notice of the teenage girl who had stopped by the tiny table next to him. It was occupied by a boy maybe two or three years older than her, and the sweet young thing clearly had an urge to catch the kid's attention. Chains could give a shit about young love, but his ears perked up when she began to speak.

"Hey," she said shyly. "What was the deal with that man and woman who were put off the bus? I'm Belinda." She gave the boy a slight smile and shrugged. "I figured you'd, like, probably know, 'cause I saw you talking to her earlier."

"I'm Joel." The kid, too, shrugged. "I didn't really know 'em or anything, but I know the dude was pukin' his guts out in the can and no one else could get in to use it. So they put them up for the night in that motel."

Chains leaned back in his chair, startling the teenagers with his sudden appearance in their conversation. "What was the name of the place they was dropped?" he demanded. "That was my sister, and I was s'posta meet her here."

The kid looked annoyed to have his budding flirtation interrupted, but he answered readily enough. "Don't know, man. I had to use the can so bad I wasn't paying much attention."

"I didn't see either," the girl contributed. "It was about a two-hour ride from here, though,"

"Nah, more like an hour and forty-five minutes," the kid disagreed.

She turned to him, clearly willing to defer to his greater knowledge. "You think?"

"Yeah, an hour forty-five. Definitely."

Well, all right. Chains shoved to his feet, dropping tip money on the table. "Thanks, kid," he said. He reached for the bill that lay facedown on the young man's table. "Here, let me get that for you."

"Hey thanks, dude." The young man grinned up at the girl. "Want some dessert? My treat, now that I've got a couple of extra bucks."

Chains picked up a new toothpick at the counter as the cashier totaled the two tabs. He stuck it in the corner of his mouth and grinned as he made his way across the parking lot to his car. Kaylee was right.

He was one smart guy.

How stupid can one woman be? Catherine stormed back up the shoulder of the highway, a brown grocery sack clutched fiercely to her stomach. She didn't believe this; she just plain didn't believe she was going back to that motel room.

Voluntarily putting herself back in Sam McKade's double-crossing clutches.

She could have made a clean getaway. She'd talked to the owner of the local garage, and he had a car he was willing to rent her. She had Sam's money to pay for it and could have been long gone, back to her safe and orderly life. That's what a smart woman would have done. Just jumped in that car and headed for home.

But she hadn't been able to forget Sam's awful coloring or the dry, parched look of his mouth. She was ten kinds of fool for worrying about the man, and had told herself exactly that several times. But had that smartened her up or directed her attention back to her own problems, where it rightfully belonged? Hell no.

That spelled "sucker" in her book, no two ways about it.

The niggling truth was, Sam McKade held a fascination for her that she couldn't seem to dispel. So here she was, with a bag full of clanking bottles of Gatorade and a box of saltine crackers, going back to play Nurse Nancy to a man who'd probably have her handcuffed to the nearest piece of furniture before she could say, 'How ya feeling?'

What a dolt.

She found him sitting on the floor, sound asleep, slumped against a wall. Setting down the bag, she squatted next to him and reached out a hand to gently shake his shoulder. "Come on, Sam," she murmured. "Come on, sugar, this is not the best place to recuperate. Let's get you on the bed."

"Mmph." He opened his eyes and rubbed a hand over his sandpaper jaw. He tried to lick some moisture into his lips, but his tongue was as arid as the rest of his mouth. Red assisted him to his feet, and his efforts to help were clumsy and largely ineffectual. He tumbled weakly onto the mattress, where he lay blinking up at her. "Hey. Dreamed you took off."

"Did you?" She pulled off his shoes and socks and then left him. He heard her go into the bathroom, but she came right back out and there was a rustle of paper, the clink of glass kissing glass. A few minutes later she was back, sitting down next to him and sliding an arm beneath his shoulders to raise him and brace him. "Here. Drink this."

Liquid slid cold and refreshing down his throat and Sam gulped it down greedily until she pulled the glass away.

"Easy," she murmured. "You don't want it to come right back up again." She brought the glass back to his lips and forced him to consume it in unsatisfyingly small increments until the cup was empty.

"Good." He looked up at her. "More."

It took three more glasses, which she only let him have a niggardly sip at a time, before his thirst was slaked. Finally, he slumped back onto the pillow. The last thing he heard was her voice murmuring something about crackers.

Then he fell headfirst into a bottomless black pit.

Catherine watched over him, not sure if she should

call in a doctor or not. The point was most likely moot, since she doubted one could be found out here in the middle of nowhere. But that didn't stop her from worrying.

Sam awoke every hour or so with a raging thirst and she poured more Gatorade down him, after which, like a man stepping off the side of the world into deep space, he'd once again immediately be swallowed up by a deep, consuming sleep. Awake one moment and comatose the next—it wasn't normal. And when he was awake he complained of being cold, which in this heat *really* wasn't normal. Gradually, however, his color improved and the worst of the dryness left his lips. His skin remained dry, however, and he kept shivering, so she wrapped him up in blankets. She was limp with relief when, around nine o'clock, he broke into a light sweat and awoke long enough to swear fretfully at the coverings piled on top of him, tossing them onto the floor. She coaxed him to eat a few crackers, and when he dropped off to sleep this time it seemed to be at a more natural level of unconsciousness.

Sitting on the bed next to him, Catherine allowed her head to thump back against the wall. For the first time in hours, she felt he was going to be okay.

She should get going.

The idea of gathering up her purse and suitcase and figuring out a plan of action, however, was just too much effort. And the honest-to-God truth was, she really didn't want to. Somehow, her safe and secure life in Seattle just didn't have the same allure it had a few short days ago. Try as she might, she could no longer hear it calling her.

Besides she was sure to awaken before Sam in the morning, so she might as well get some rest, see how she felt in the light of day, and deal with it then.

"Oh, God." Catherine's voice was faint and laced with an undercurrent of hysteria. She thumped her head against the wall once, twice, three times. She was in big, big trouble if she was reduced to the Scarlett O'Hara defense. *Fiddle-dee-dee, Rhett, I'll think about that tomorrow.*

Damn. She was an independent woman. She didn't need any outdated, antebellum, Southern belle justifications and rationalizations. She made well-thought-out decisions and acted upon them. She . . .

Oh, the hell with it. She slid down on the mattress next to Sam. She was too damn tired for this—she really would think about it tomorrow.

In less than a minute she was sleeping like the dead.

17

IF JIMMY CHAINS could have gotten his hands on that punk kid who'd told him Kaylee was in a motel somewhere an hour and forty-five minutes west of Laramie, he'd have busted him in half, broken both arms, and kicked his fuckin' teeth down his throat. He'd canvassed one nowhere little burg after another without success, and in the process he came to appreciate the aggravation that must have set off his own father's temper all those years ago. Maybe the old man'd had a point after all. Maybe fists were the only thing a smart-ass teenage boy understood.

The kid had played him for a fool and he hated it when people took him for stupid. Few men ever did so twice, at least to his face, because he always responded promptly—with his fists, his feet, with a broken bottle, knife, or gun. He'd never liked hurting women, but he'd agreed to kill Alice Mayberry when Sanchez shopped the idea, and never in this man's lifetime would he'd a done it just for the money, either.

The bitch had called him big, dumb, and ugly one time too many. So how smart did that make her?

Kaylee, now, she was a different story. He sure didn't like the thought of having to hurt her, even knowing it was necessary. Maybe she hadn't talked to him all that often back at the club, but she'd always had a friendly smile, a wisecrack, or a 'How-ya-doin'?' for him when they did cross paths. She'd never made him feel slow or dim like some'a the other girls did.

And today she'd told him he was smart. Nobody had ever said that to him before.

It was true, though, he wasn't the dumbshit everyone seemed to think he was. Nobody as stupid as some folks made him out to be could dress this sharp, for one thing. And when he'd needed to take a piss and had pulled off at that scenic overlook, spotting Kaylee right smack dab in the middle of the road in front of him like the goddamn answer to all his prayers, hadn't he jumped on the gas?

Would'a got her, too, if not for the old bat. Who would'a thought someone so little and creaky-looking could move so fast?

Chains shook himself as he pulled into the lot of yet another run-down motel just as the skies opened up and it began to pour. Point was, he'd thought fast, the way smart people did, and he'd taken advantage of the situation, doing what needed to be done.

Hell, a *dumb* guy wouldn't a thought to eat at the restaurant where the bus stopped for dinner in the first place, and so would'a missed overhearing the conversation about the woman he was looking for. He opened the car door and dashed through the rain toward the darkened motel office.

His face heated up and his fists clenched. Okay, it probably wasn't such a hot idea to think about the conversation in the restaurant right now. He tried the office door and then pounded on it when he found it locked. Thinking about it just got him all bent out of shape all over again. It was nearly two o'clock in the morning, and he still hadn't found the motel that was supposed to be a mere hour and forty-fucking-five minutes from his starting point. He'd like to get his hands on that punk asshole. And to think he'd picked up the little turd's dinner tab, too.

He was just getting ready to put his fist through the door's window and help himself to the guest register when a light went on in the back room. A man shuffled out, squinting against the glare of the light he switched on as he came to the door.

A bell rang over it when he pulled it open. "Nasty night," he greeted Chains. Yawning, he shuffled back to the desk. "You want a single?"

"No, man. I want information."

The man's head came up warily.

Chains was tired and fed up and wanted to go home where there were palm trees instead of this bullshit shoot-out-at-the-OK-Corral scenery. Seemed to him this was a situation private enough that he could beat whatever information he needed out of the guy, without pissing off the boss. His willingness to do violence must have shown, for the man opened the register without a word and set it on the counter, turning it for Chains to read.

Neither Kaylee's name nor the bounty hunter's was in there, but he was smarter than to expect it would be. "Redhead with show-stopper tits, tall guy with black hair," he snapped. "Ya seen 'em?"

"No, sir."

Chains leaned over the counter. "You wouldn't lie to me, now would ya?"

"No, sir." The man swallowed hard, but met his eyes without flinching.

Chains swore. Then he blew out a weary breath. "The hell with it. I'm beat. Give me that single."

He'd catch a few hours' sleep and find her in the morning.

Sam awoke to an empty room. He jerked up in bed, the sheet spilling down around his lap. Where had Red gone? She'd come back last night, unless he'd dreamed it. But where was she now?

Then, over the patter of rain on the roof, past the roar of blood in his ears, he heard a muted noise and sagged back against the lumpy pillow. She hadn't left; she was in the bathroom. He could hear only the faintest of sounds—sort of a muffled chink, chink, chink—but it definitely came from inside the unit, and unless they'd gotten mice in here overnight, it had to be her.

His bladder made its needs known, which he took as a good sign since it meant last night's dehydration was a thing of the past. But although he tossed aside the covers, he only moved as far as the side of the bed. He sat there, feet planted wide apart on the thin carpet, hesitant to get up and go into the bathroom.

He had the makings of a huge problem on his

hands. He was beginning to wonder if he'd snatched the wrong twin.

Rubbing the flat of his hand over his jaw, the rasp of his heavy morning beard barely registered over the hard thump of his heart, the sudden clamoring of his emotions. Jesus, what a piss-awful thought. But it was one he had to consider. There were . . . inconsistencies about her that he'd been ignoring.

She had a vocabulary on her that wouldn't quit, for one thing. What was it she'd said the other day, that she had planned to tell people he was transporting her across state lines for salacious purposes? What kind of showgirl said salacious purposes, for chrissake?

Not to mention she was smarter than his original impression had led him to expect. Loads smarter. Hell, she thought faster on her feet than he did and turned the smallest opportunity to her own advantage.

He also hadn't failed to notice that, except for that one time, she ignored nine-tenths of the makeup in her bag. Or that she was friendly to women and children while ignoring every guy who tripped over his own two feet trying to get next to her—unless it was to enlist his help in getting away from *him*.

And . . . she'd come back last night.

That was the real kicker, the one he couldn't quite get around. When she'd left, he'd sure been in no condition to hunt her down. She could have been a state away in any direction, which would have given her a decent head start. He might have found her again, but maybe not. And even if he had, odds were it would have been too late or would have run him through too much money to do him any good. So, why hadn't she just kept going?

Could it be that she didn't have a thing to lose because she was exactly who she'd insisted she was all along, and a simple fingerprinting at the end of the road would prove it?

Oh, shit, McKade. The very idea made him sick, and it wasn't simply the money he'd have to kiss good-bye or the knowledge that he'd once again let down Gary.

It was remembering every word he'd spoken, every action he'd taken. All of which had been made under the assumption he was dealing with a dim-bulb showgirl. A *lying* dim-bulb showgirl. And a car thief.

Not a respectable teacher of the deaf.

He surged up off the bed. Okay, if he'd been wrong about her, he'd apologize. Would an apology be enough, though? *Doubtful, buddy boy, extremely doubtful.* Well, he'd return her to her home. He'd . . .

The sight that greeted him when he pushed open the not-quite-latched bathroom door stopped every thought in his head.

She was standing with her back to the door, one foot up on the toilet seat, leaning over to carefully stroke a razor up her lathered leg from ankle to knee. She twisted slightly to swish the razor clean in the sink, tapped it against the sink's edge with a chink, chink, chink that knocked the excess water from it, and then turned back to apply the razor to a fresh patch of lather. She was wearing his shirt again, but its tail rode up each time she leaned forward to ply the razor, exposing and then concealing a portion of the panties beneath.

Panties that consisted, from what he could see, of a single, satiny thong that rode the division of her round, firm cheeks. They were lipstick red. Fitting, that.

For they matched the little pursed lips of her tattoo.

The tattoo that wordlessly invited all comers to kiss her lucious butt.

The tattoo of a chorus girl, not a teacher.

Relief he didn't care to examine too closely raced through his veins. Jesus, what an idiot. Okay, sure, maybe he'd made an assumption or two that was on the clichéd side . . . like showgirl equals dumb. But he hadn't entirely lost either his mind or his touch. He nearly laughed out loud. Then he got a closer look at the razor in her hand, and the crazy surge of relief segued into irritation.

"Hey," he groused, shoving the door more fully open, "that's mine."

She jumped, letting out a shriek. "Holy Mary, mother of God!" A hand slapped to her heart, she dragged in several gulps of air, then twisted her head around to glare at him. "Are you trying to give me a heart attack? Get out of here!" Reaching a hand back to yank the shirttail firmly over her bottom, she turned her attention back to finishing up her leg, muttering under her breath about inconsiderate men who sneaked around like cats in an aviary.

"Gimme that." He reached for the razor in her

hand, but she twisted away, blocking him with an upraised elbow. Her razor hand didn't miss a stroke up a virgin patch of lather. He watched the endless swath of smooth leg that appeared in its wake while flecked white lather built up on the blade. "Dammit, Red, that was my last one, and now it's gonna be useless."

Catherine spared him a glance over her shoulder. "Feeling much better this morning, I see. You're right back to your usual charming self." She swished, rinsed, and tapped. Applying the razor once again to her skin, she blocked another attempt to grab it away from her. "Will you stop that! You're gonna make me nick myself."

"Shit." He straightened up and stared at her. "It's ruined. I might as well shave with the top of an old tin can now." He raked his hair off his forehead and scowled at her. "A rusty tin can. One that's been opened by a knife."

"Oh, poor baby. I can't remember the last time I heard such a pitiful, sad story."

He stormed out of the cramped little room but a second later was back. A smooth white object with coils at one end was thrust into Catherine's line of vision. "Here," he growled. "Use your own damn razor."

She shouldered it away, twisting around to reach the last remaining stripe of lather on the back of her leg. "That's an Epilady, McKade."

"Yeah? So?"

"So it doesn't whisk the little hairs off nice and neat like your mother's electric razor; it rips them out by the roots. You use it. I'm not into that kind of pain."

"Then why'd you pack the damn thing?"

She whirled around, mouth opening to hurl a few well-chosen words in his face, but he waved a big, imperious hand at her.

"Never mind, I don't even want to get into that." He twisted his head to peer at the long underside of her calf. "You about finished there? I can't just stand around here holding it all day long, Red; I gotta use the can."

"My God." She gave him an incredulous look. "I don't *believe* you."

"What's not to believe? If ya gotta go, ya gotta go."

She made a sound like steam escaping. "Fine." Tossing the washcloth she'd used to wipe away the last of the lather into the sink, she shoved past him. "It's all yours, you ingrate."

She was into the main room before his voice stopped her. "Red."

"What?" She didn't turn around. Damn him, she should have just left while she'd had the opportunity.

"Thanks. For last night." His voice was low, rough, and reached out to wrap itself around her. "I don't pretend to know why you came back, but I *am* grateful. I feel fine this morning, and I know I owe it to you." Then he pushed the door between them closed.

Damn. Catherine stared blindly at the rain rolling down the window through a part in the curtain. He was making her crazy. He was so arrogant. Infuriating. Too damn stubborn to see past his own blind preconceptions.

Exciting.

Ah, face it. She had pretty much made her decision this morning anyway, so why keep pretending otherwise? She was sticking around to see where this strange trip led.

For years she'd believed she wanted to live a *Leave It to Beaver* kind of life. Something that was normal and safe. But maybe she was a lot more like Kaylee than she'd ever imagined. And maybe that wasn't such a terrible thing.

She was beginning to realize just how consistently she'd repressed and denied integral parts of her personality over the years. Cutting loose wasn't necessarily the road to ruin. And acknowledging her sexuality didn't automatically have to equate with irresponsibility. Clearly there were parts of Kaylee that were parts of her, too. Parts she'd secretly envied. Perhaps it was what she *did* with those parts that really counted.

She sorted through her suitcase slowly, thinking about it. By the time Sam emerged from the bathroom, she'd figured out at least one aspect.

"I was right," he grumbled as he walked out. "You destroyed that blade. Women's legs and men's faces were never meant to share the same razor." Scowling at her offending limbs, he touched a long finger to a miniscule dab of toilet paper that was stuck by a dot of blood to his jaw and then indicated the others that decorated his face. "Look at this! I'll probably be scarred for life."

"Aw, you poor, poor thing." Her heart began to pound, but she didn't hesitate; she crossed the room to stand right in front of him. Mere inches was all that separated their bodies.

Looking up to find him regarding her with a challenging wariness, she almost chickened out. If this bombed, she was going to feel like the worst kind of idiot. But she had to give it a try.

Eyes on the slight wound beneath his sullen lower lip that was her ultimate goal, she reached out to grip his shoulders, raising up onto her toes. "Here." Hearing the lowered sultry timbre of her voice, she dabbed a nervous tongue at her lower lip. If he but knew it, for the first time, she truly sounded like Kaylee.

"Let Mama kiss it all better."

18

SAM WENT VERY still as Catherine pressed soft, pursed lips first to the tissue-patched spot he'd pointed out to her, then to another one on his opposite cheek. Finally she kissed the one just south of his lower lip.

Was she toying with him? He could feel her heat, smell her scent, and his mouth hardened determinedly. Fine, then, two could work that angle. He liked contests. "You wanna play games?" He snaked an arm around her waist, yanking her flush against his torso. His free hand speared into her hair to hold her head still. "Play this." He slammed his mouth down on hers.

Like fire to gunpowder, emotions exploded between them with instant combustion. Differences of opinion, individual worries, thoughts of one-upmanship went up in flames. A deep, hungry sound rumbled in Sam's throat, and he widened his mouth over hers, seeking her flavors with the tip of his tongue. His fingers dug into her scalp, his arm tightened around her waist, and he leaned into her as the kiss climbed out of control, bending her farther and farther backwards, until all that prevented her from falling onto the floor was his grip at head and waist.

Catherine wrapped her arms around his neck and hung on, but the strain shot arrows of discomfort through the fog of her arousal. She ripped her mouth free. "My back," she panted. "Sam, I don't think it was intended to bend in this direction."

"What?" A veil of sexual arousal hazed his golden eyes and only gradually did cognitive reasoning pierce it. Black lashes blinking lazily, he gazed down at her contorted posture. "Oh. Damn."

His tongue slicked over his full lower lip. Then he straightened, easing her upright. Without a word, he dropped his arms but reached out long fingers to manacle her wrist and pull her over to the bed. There he set her free, but his head immediately lowered once again, and touching her with nothing more than his mouth, he kissed her softly. Then, with a husky growl, he kissed her more firmly.

It was rapidly sliding into something hot and out of control, their bodies plastered in each other's arms again when, moaning softly, Catherine reached for his T-shirt at the small of his back. She pulled it free of his waistband, worked it up his torso, and, feeling his arms raise, pulled it off over his head. That broke the kiss, and she stood blinking, staring with aroused befuddlement at the fan of black hair on his muscular chest while his fingers rapidly worked the buttons on the oxford cloth shirt she wore.

His knuckles brushed her skin as he worked his way down the placket, but despite the stimulus, without his mouth on hers she began to regain the tiniest degree of sensibility. Then he bent his knees and applied his mouth to her throat. His lips were hot and skilled, and her eyes slid shut as she plunged back into the tempest. Anchoring herself by hooking her fingers through the belt loops of his jeans, she hung on. A moment later her shirt lapels were spread apart, the material pushed from her shoulders to hang from her elbows, and Sam's mouth ceased its debauchery on her throat as he raised his head.

All motion came to an abrupt halt. Even sound seemed to cease, as Sam's breath caught raggedly in his throat. Confused, Catherine slowly raised her eyes. Why had he stopped? Had she put him off by standing here like a dolt, letting him do all the work?

It had nothing to do with her lack of expertise, she realized the moment she looked at him. His golden brown eyes were all over her, and their hot intensity as they stared at her breasts, her waist, her hips, caused a blush to heat up her chest and climb toward her face. Her arms dropped to her side, causing the shirt to drift to the floor.

Sam felt as if he'd been kicked by a horse. His hand rubbed at the spot over his heart as he stared at her, unable to tear his eyes away. "God," he said through tight vocal cords. "You are so . . ." He cleared his throat and tried again. "I have never seen anything so . . . Christ, so incredibly . . ."

"Sinful?" Catherine supplied drily when he seemed at a loss for words. "You can go ahead and say it, you know. It's no more than what Mama always called it."

Sam snorted. "Oh, yeah, Mom's the person to judge a daughter's figure, all right." He reached out a reverent finger to the tip of one pert beige nipple. It beaded up tight beneath his touch, distending nearly half an inch while the aureole around it twisted and shrank until it all but disappeared. He shivered and stroked both hands down her sides to encircle her waist. His fingertips nearly touched. His gaze lowered to the deep indentation of her navel, the full, sweet swell of her hips, and lower still to the scrap of red satin that was all she was left wearing above those long firm thighs. "If you ask me, darlin', a body like this is more of a religious experience. I know that I could spend days on my knees in front of it." Then his eyes took a leisurely tour back up to her face. The color warming her chest stopped him cold, and he jerked his gaze up to her face. "Are you blushing?"

The incredulousness in his tone made her deny it. "Who, me? Of course not."

He pressed a brown finger to her chest, staring at the white spot that stood out for a moment in the surrounding field of hot color when he lifted it. "The hell you're not. You're blushing." His tone wasn't exactly accusing. But it was close.

"Don't be ridiculous." Her chin angled up at him. "Women like me display our naked bodies for dozens of lovers. We wear G-strings and feathers and strut our stuff in front of hundreds of men. *Thousands*. We don't blush."

It was no more than a confirmation of everything

he'd ever thought. Why, then, did he suddenly find her statement doubtful?

You really want to think about that right now, Boscoe?

With a soft curse, he jerked her into his arms, then hissed through his teeth at the feel of her breasts flattening against his diaphragm. Gripping a slippery fistful of hair, he pulled her head back. "Shut up," he muttered. "Just shut up, Red, and kiss me."

Her green eyes flashed defiance but her mouth raised to his in instant compliance. It was soft and sweet, and he made love to it with his tongue, sliding in and out in an increasingly compulsive motion. Within moments her arms were clinging to his neck and one long leg had raised to hook around his hip as she did her best to climb his body.

Sam growled deep in his throat and tipped them onto the lumpy mattress. He rolled on top of her, spreading her legs to make a place for himself between them. He wedged his erection hard up against her cleft.

Sensation rocketed through Catherine, and she mewled into his ravaging mouth. An instant later she was left panting as he ripped his lips away and moved down her body. She tipped her pelvis up, but his sex had been replaced by hard stomach muscle and the satisfaction level was simply not the same. "Oh, please," she pleaded, widening her thighs and rubbing herself against him. "Please, Sam."

"What do you want, darlin'?" He stroked his cheek against the side of her breast, watching her. "This?" Opening his mouth, he took a gentle bite out of the fullness. Then he released it and moved an inch inward and a little to the south to open his lips over fresh territory. "This?" Sinking his mouth into her pale, pale flesh with its faint tracery of blue veins, he drew a section hard against his teeth.

Her nipple distended, blindly seeking similar treatment. Sam's mouth went slack. "God," he whispered hoarsely. He went after it like a zealot after an unclaimed soul. He wrapped his lips around the proffered morsel and sucked, while his long brown fingers caught and plucked at its unattended mate.

His name left her throat in a long, attenuated moan. She pushed her mound restlessly against his stomach. "Oh, please. Oh, please."

He growled and opened his lips wide around her nipple, and Catherine watched helplessly as he extended his tongue to lap as far down the full curve as he could reach without losing his place at its beaded peak. His big, dark-skinned hand stroked and molded the other globe.

Since the day she'd developed, her breasts had been a source of embarrassment to her. But this morning, for perhaps the first time in her life, she liked them, was proud of them. Seeing him pay homage to the generous curves as if he wanted to consume them gave her an incredible rush of power.

She'd never realized what an aphrodisiac that could be.

His fingers released her and he gauged her expression closely as he insinuated his hand between their bodies and slid it, palm flat, down her diaphragm, her stomach, lower. He stopped with the heel of his hand resting feather-light against her pubic bone as he probed her navel with the tip of his forefinger. Then he slowly rotated his hand, and his fingers slid beneath red satin onto her downy mound.

It rose eagerly to his touch, and his middle finger divided slick feminine folds with unerring accuracy, zeroing in like a heat-seeking missile on the slippery pearl of her clitoris. Feathering it with his fingertip, he simultaneously clamped his lips around her nipple, sucking it firmly into his mouth.

With a soft shriek, Catherine arched up off the bed. For a moment, only the back of her head and the heels of her feet anchored her to solid ground.

Sensations throbbed and roared, clamoring for completion. Never in her life had she experienced feelings like this. The few times her sexuality had threatened to run away with her in the past, she had firmly clamped a lid on it. But the passion that whipped through her blood now had absolutely no intention of being denied, and whimpering, she fisted her hands in his black hair to hold him to the breast she thrust upward. Hips involuntarily instigating their own bump and grind, she spread her thighs to experience more of the magic of his fingers. "Oh, please, Sam. Please. I want you." His touch slipped and slid between her legs and she chanted mindlessly. "Want you, want you, want you."

Releasing her breast with an audible pop, Sam pushed up onto his knees between her legs. He slid his hand from her panties and stared down at her. Her eyes were dark with arousal, her nipple wet and ruddy from his mouth. "God, you're sweet," he muttered, and reached out impatient hands to peel the scrap of satin from her hips. Gaze drawn to the triangle of downy curls gracing her mound, he stilled. Oh, sweet Jesus. She was a redhead all right.

All over.

He touched the bright curls with reverent fingertips. "Where?" he demanded hoarsely, stroking his thumb along her cleft. "Where do you want me, Red?" He lightly circled her opening, pressing without penetrating. "Here?"

"Sam?" She moved convulsively against his hand.

He caught her chin in his free hand and tilted it until she looked at him. His thumb continued to torment her. "Tell me where you want me."

"Inside me?" She licked her lips. "Please, Sam, I want to feel you inside of me."

He ripped at the fastenings on his jeans, then shoved to his feet on the bed to stand between her sprawled thighs as he shucked out of his pants and shorts. He saw her eyes zero in on the erection that sprang out proud and eager above her. Watched as her big eyes rounded and the little yearning movements of her hips stilled. Saw her swallow hard.

His brows pulled together. He was hardly a stallion, just a guy with an average, run-of-the-mill-sized cock. One he could drive nails with at the moment, maybe, but nothing she need regard as if it would rip her asunder. It must be the angle.

That didn't compute, though. Even if he appeared hung like a horse from her viewpoint, why would that give her pause? Well hung was generally the experienced woman's preference. Unless . . .

No. He rolled his shoulders uneasily at the thought that cropped up in his brain, made even more uneasy at the emotion it prompted. Hastily he dropped to his knees between her thighs. No second thoughts.

Second, third, and fourth thoughts assailed Catherine as she watched Sam reach for protection and roll it down, down, *down* the length of his penis. She didn't know if the thing was truly as massive and capable of doing damage as it appeared to be, or if it had simply been so long since she'd seen one of those bad boys that she'd lost all sense of perspective.

She almost laughed. Yeah, right. Like she'd ever seen all that many in the first place—never mind actually inspected one this closely.

Nerves were definitely gaining the upper hand and she was on the verge of calling the whole thing off when he fell forward over her. He caught himself on his palms and propped himself up on stiff arms. She found herself staring up into his golden brown eyes, mesmerized by the intensity that burned in their depths.

"We sorta lost momentum," he murmured huskily, and bent his elbows, lowering his chest to brush back and forth across her breasts. Black hair brushed her jaw as his mouth attached itself to the side of her throat with soft suction.

Catherine's nipples, newly softened, sprang to full, erect attention, and sensations she'd thought killed deader than a doornail by her nerves roared like an out-of-control freight train back to life. She arched her back, flattening the aching globes of her breasts against his chest.

Sam's head reared up at the contact and she saw his mouth pull back from his teeth. His eyes stared blindly at the wall as he moved against her like a huge domesticated cat, rubbing himself up and down, side to side, shoulders and arms flexing with his efforts. Then his sex bumped hers, and he inhaled sharply through his teeth. His chin lowered, and slits of gold gleamed at her demandingly through narrowed black lashes. His hips pressed forward.

"Let me in."

She'd have been helpless to resist even if she'd wanted to. Pulling her knees back, she opened herself up to him.

It made her as vulnerable as a woman could be, but he pushed into her slowly, with care. Blood-rich tissues, swollen and sensitized, parted to accommodate him, then immediately closed around every inch of the thickness that invaded her. He pulled back slightly, dragging against the hugging sheath, then thrust a little deeper. A whimper of need shuddered in her throat, and she hooked her ankles behind his thighs. Her hands gripped his buttocks and gave a shy, encouraging little yank.

"Oh, yes." Sam pulled his hips back and then slammed them forward, seating himself fully inside her. He held himself still, fighting for breath. Looking down into her face, he saw a strand of bright hair that had flopped across one eye, and he brushed it away. "God. You. Are. So. *Tight.*" It was like being squeezed into a hot, wet, velvet glove one size too small. Rocking his hips with shallow, subtle strokes, he watched the parade of emotions that crossed her face. The desire for more. The helpless wonder. She licked her lips and clung to him and returned his gaze with dazed eyes.

He thrust into her harder, deeper, and her nails sank into his butt. Sucking in a sharp breath, he slammed into her, snaked his arms around her, and rolled them over.

She sprawled across his chest and a grin crooked his mouth at the wide eyes that stared down at him, and the startled look that flashed across her face. "If ever there was a woman built to be on top, it's you." He adjusted her legs on either side of his hips, appreciating their sleekness beneath his own rough-skinned hands. Then, gripping her taut thighs, he thrust up into her. "Ride me."

He watched heat spread across her cheeks at his command, but she pushed herself up until she was sitting astride him, raised her hips experimentally, then slid back down his rigid sex. She repeated the motion. A look of startled pleasure scudded across her eyes. Rising and falling upon the erection wedged firmly up inside her, she raised languorous arms over her head, folded them, elbows high, and rested a cheek against one bicep. Her eyes slid closed.

And she smiled, licking her lips.

Sam's penis jerked. "Oh, man, I think I've created a monster." His hands reached for her breasts, and his hips came up off the bed. She slapped down on him in perfect rythmn. He plucked at her nipples, gritting his teeth against the need to drive like a pile driver run amok to his own completion. "You really like it up there, don'tcha?"

"Sam?" Her head fell back and she rose up his length a little faster, thrust down a little harder. Reaching behind her, she braced her hands on his legs. "Oh, God, *Sam*? I'm going to . . . uh! Oh, God, I want to . . ."

"Come," he growled, and delved a thumb into the wet tangle of curls above where they were joined. Locating her magic button, he pressed and felt an unholy grin split his face when her low moan spiraled several octaves higher. "That's it, darlin', let it go. I want to hear you. I want to see ya come for me."

His gaze was firmly on her face when all that screaming, throbbing sensation inside her suddenly coalesced, grew hotter, then hotter yet, and then blew sky-high like the grande finale at a Pyrotechnics of America convention. Jerking convulsively as wave after wave of ecstasy hit her, she threw back her head and groaned at the top of her voice.

Hearing her, seeing her, *feeling* her clamp down around him again and again with each contraction, Sam lost it. He started to slip his thumb free of its creamy nest, but Catherine grabbed his wrist to hold it in place and started contracting crazily around him all over again.

His breath left his lungs in an explosive, "Hah!" and he grabbed for her bottom with his free hand and gripped it while his hips shot up off the mattress. He slammed into her once, twice, three times, then impaled her with one final thrust that lifted her high, and staring up at her flushed cheeks, slumberous green eyes, and tumbled red hair, came in scalding pulsations. His hips jerked as he came and came with bone-rattling satisfaction, and despite the teeth he kept gritted against it, a name rumbled in his chest, surged up his throat, and roared its way past his unlocked teeth.

"Catherine!"

He collapsed back onto the mattress, wrapping his arms around her and holding her tightly when she slumped down atop him. Rubbing his chin against the top of her head, he stared up at the ceiling.

Uneasiness warred with a simpleminded sort of happiness and gradually won out. As much as he longed to tell himself differently, he knew who he had in his arms. Knew it beyond a doubt this time.

The chorus-girl tattoo might have stacked up against all the other reasons he'd already trotted out for reality not fitting her appearance. But it tumbled into dust against her blushes, tight, untried body, and undisguised expressions of wonder. She was Catherine MacPherson. Respectable teacher of the deaf.

He might not know how she'd ended up with the same kiss-my-ass tattoo as her twin sister. But he knew this: he'd really fucked up this time, and he didn't mean the position he'd assumed while violatiing that sweet, sweet body.

He'd gone and snatched the wrong friggin' sister.

19

FROM A PRONE position on the bed, Bobby watched Kaylee prowl the room. When the silence grew so oppressive he couldn't stand it any longer, he demanded plaintively, "Aren't you ever gonna talk to me again?"

She gave him a scathing look and he repeated for what felt like the sixth or seventh time, "Baby, I'm *sorry* I didn't know who you were, okay? But it's not like it lasted all that long, and ya gotta cut me some slack, here. I didn't plan to lose my memory, and I sure as hell didn't get my head bashed in just to ruin your day."

She continued to ignore him, striding from the window where she stopped only long enough to drum her fingers against the sill and pout out at the rainy morning, to the table and two chairs in the corner, to the bathroom, and back again. Bobby watched, feeling his tension mount. His head throbbed savagely, he felt embarrassingly feeble all over, and still he desired her a little bit more with every long-legged stride she took. Worse, he wanted her approval, and that had the effect of making him downright irritable.

The neediness of his feelings aside, he knew damn good and well that the odds were great he wasn't going to get her approval anytime soon. All that unexpressed ire, which practically stood her red hair on end, made that evident.

The fact that she wouldn't accept his apology, however, really began to grate on his nerves. "Dammit, Kaylee," he burst out after watching her complete yet another circuit. "I had a concussion! Hell, I probably still *have* a concussion. And it wasn't only you I forgot."

At least he got her attention. Eyes flashing, mouth sulky, Kaylee whirled to face him. "You don't," she snapped.

He blinked at her in befuddlement. "I don't what?"

"Still have a concussion."

"Yeah?" Belligerence rose at her unequivocal tone. "And how the hell would you know? My head's still pounding somethin' miserable."

"Remember that doctor at the clinic? He told me what to look for, and your symptoms went away about midnight."

He barely remembered the doctor or the clinic. He recalled coming to, colder than death except where his back touched a patch of hot concrete and where his forearm was burrowed to the wrist between the most luscious set of tits he'd ever seen in his life. He remembered his hand, emerging from said tits, being clutched by a gorgeous redhead who'd hung over him in concern.

And he sure as hell recalled the way she'd dropped it like a disease-infested sack of garbage when he'd asked if he knew her.

The drive through the countryside to the clinic remained a blur, though, as did the examination that followed. He thought there'd been another drive after that, but the details were gone. He did know the redhead had woken him up periodically, and that it was late when she'd finally left him to sleep in peace.

He'd awakened this morning to find most of his memory restored and himself in Kaylee's arms. But when he'd given her a sleepy smile and greeted her with his lazy, familiar, "Hey, baby," she'd flown off the bed like a scalded cat. And she'd been silently, solidly furious ever since. When *he'd* been the one to have his head caved in for reasons he couldn't even fully recall.

Go figure.

"Here." Her scarlet-tipped fingers were suddenly thrust beneath his nose. "Take these."

He put a hand out in automatic response and had three aspirin dropped into his palm.

"I'll get you a glass of water," she said coolly, and turned and left the room.

Kaylee let the water run, and with her hands braced on the countertop, stared blindly at her reflection in the mirror while she fought to get herself under control. Bobby was right. She had to cut him some slack.

But, Jaysus, it was a hard, hard thing to do when

her emotions kept running amok the way they'd been doing for the past twenty-plus hours.

Never in her life had she been petrified like that for someone else. She'd been frightened for herself plenty of times and scared of situations in general, but she'd never experienced the gut-wrenching terror that came of fearing for another person's safety.

Yesterday, Bobby had regained consciousness just about the time it had begun to dawn on her that her feelings for him were serious. The last thing she'd been in any frame of mind to discover was that, while for the first time in her life she was quite likely in love, he didn't even know who the hell she was.

She'd gotten him to a clinic, and that had been a nightmare all its own. It had taken the doctor and nurse what seemed like forever before they'd stablized his body temperature and felt it was safe to release him, and then it had been with a list of instructions as long as her arm. She'd never dealt with that sort of responsibility for herself, let alone somebody else.

She'd been terrified to the bone all night long, certain she would screw up somehow and do something to send him spinning down into an irreversible coma. Then, when he'd awakened this morning as if nothing out of the ordinary had gone before, fear had transformed into anger.

She felt like she was coming unglued.

Much as she'd adore to stay pissed at him, however, the fault truly couldn't be laid at Bobby's door. The back of his head still sported a nasty bump, for God's sake, whose dimension had only shrunk somewhat during the night. Damn. She supposed she really had no choice but to get over it.

But she didn't have to like it.

She filled a glass with water and turned off the faucet. Carrying it back to the room, she sat down on the side of the bed and handed it to him. "Just how much do you remember about yesterday?"

Bobby's eyebrows furrowed. "I knew who you were as soon as I woke up this morning. But as far as the rest of it goes, I get bits and pieces and flashes of stuff, and it's like seeing them through a piece of cheesecloth."

"Can you lay out for me what you do remember?"

He concentrated. "Okay. I remember going into the café to make arrangements to meet with your sis . . ." Stricken blue eyes flashed up to meet her gaze. "Ah, shit, baby, your sister. I can't believe I forgot all about her. I let her get taken away, didn't I?" He abruptly shoved himself up on an elbow and Kaylee watched as the color drained right out of his face. "Chains! I was signing the stuff you taught me to Catherine when Chains showed up." He swore roundly and rubbed at his head. "That son of a bitch. He's the one who hit me. He didn't get her, too, did he?"

Kaylee hugged herself. "I don't know. I didn't hear any fuss over a missing woman while I was looking for you in Arabesque, but as far as anything that's happened since then . . ." She shrugged helplessly. Then she added with studied casualness, "I guess he probably thought she was me, huh?" She wanted desperately to hear otherwise.

Her wish was not fulfilled. "Yeah." Events were starting to unfold more clearly in Bobby's mind obviously. "He had no reason to believe otherwise. And, baby, he's here under orders from Sanchez."

Kaylee moaned at the mess she'd made of everything. But when Bobby tried to sit up, she pressed her hands against his chest to stay him. "Where do you think you're going?"

"To get your sister back for you."

"Oh, for crying out loud, don't be an ass!" *Oh, good, Kaylee, attack the ego. That's bound to make him receptive to good sense.* "That is, that's just real sweet of you and all, but you're in no condition—" *No, no, no, no, NO! What is it with you, girl? You knew how to handle men better when you were twelve.* "Uh, what I mean to say is, the doctor said you have to stay quiet for a couple of days. He said it was absolutely—what was that word he used?—oh yeah, *imperative.*"

Bobby rolled out from under her hands toward the other side of the bed. "Screw imperative," he suggested. "And screw the doctor, too."

Kaylee had had a truly awful night. Temper igniting, she knocked him flat on his back, and it was a measure of how much had been taken out of him that she could so easily do so. "Screw them? *Screw* them?" Climbing on top of him, she straddled his stomach to glare down into his face. "Does that apply to me, too?" Slapping her hands down on his shoulders, she leaned her weight against them to keep him pinned in place. "Do you have any idea how *scared* I was, Bobby? It must have been a hundred flippin' degrees in that car, but you were wrapped to the teeth in a blanket, *freezing* to death! The doctor said we'd be much better off in a city that was 150 miles away in case you needed emergency medical treatment, so I bundled you back in the car and drove like some demented stock-car racer to this cow-town Gotham City. But he'd also said not to let you sleep for more than a half hour at a time, so I had to keep stopping to wake you up and check your pupil reactions, and every damn time you smiled that stupid, charming smile of yours and asked me who I was. Oh, and yes, you let me know how very much you admired my t . . . tits."

Her hands gripped his shoulders and gave them what would have been a fierce shake had he not been so firmly anchored to the bed by her weight. She looked him dead in his handsome blue eyes.

"Well, let me clue you in on something, bud—I've had it up to my eyeballs, and I'm not taking any more shit off of you. I don't have the first idea how to take care of *myself*, but somehow I managed to take care of you anyway, and I'll be *damned* if I'll let you run around acting out some comic-book macho fantasy and undoing all my hard work. As long as I have breath in my body, that ain't gonna happen, so you can just live with it, buster—and your male ego be d . . . damned!"

She didn't realize she was crying until he reached up and brushed the tears from her cheeks with his fingertips. Then he gave her inner elbows a poke to make her arms bend and pulled her down on top of him, wrapping her up in his brawny embrace. "Shh," he crooned, tucking her head into the crook of his neck and anchoring it there with his chin in her hair. She flung her arms around his neck, and he stroked her everywhere his hands could reach. "Shh, shh, shh, now. It's okay, baby. You did real good, and I'll do whatever you say."

"I was so scared, Bobby."

"I know, baby, I know." He tipped his chin down. "But you handled it. You did what had to be done. Just like your sister would've."

She tilted her head back to look up at him. "I've screwed up so bad. I've gotta find Cat and get her out of this mess."

"You called Scott yet?"

"No. *No*! I forgot about him." She struggled free of his arms. "I'll do that right now."

She hung up the phone fifteen minutes later. "They were put off another bus, but this time Scott doesn't think it was because of anything Cat did. There's a note in the Greyhound computer to pay their motel bill and not only to reissue their tickets but have the next bus through make a special stop to pick them up. It's due in Laramie at five tonight." She started tossing her few items of apparel not already packed into her suitcase.

Bobby struggled up on an elbow. "What are you doing?"

"I'm going to meet the bus."

"And you need your suitcase for that?" He didn't like the uneasy sensation that crawled in the pit of his stomach.

Kaylee stopped what she was doing and looked at him. "If I can't get her away from the bounty hunter any other way, I'll have to turn myself over to him."

"No!"

"What else can I do, Bobby? Let Catherine get killed in my place?"

"Yes! No. I don't know. But we'll think of something."

"Unless we do in the next couple of hours, this is the way it's gotta be. I have to leave in time to drive back to Laramie."

"Where the hell are we now?"

"Cheyenne."

He scrubbed his hands over his face. Lowering them, he looked at her. "There's got to be another way, baby."

"I'm certainly open to suggestions. My mind's a blank. The only clear thought I have is that I'm really and truly going to have to do this, and it scares me to death." She rammed her fingers through her hair and blew out her breath. Meeting his eyes, she tried to explain. "All my life I let Cat take care of business. I just accepted it as my due, as if that were the natural order of things. Well, last night I got a taste of what it must have felt like for her, and I had hours and hours to think about how young she was to be accountable for so much. No kid should ever have that kind of responsibility, but none of us—not me, not my dad or my mom—thought twice before unloading all our messes on her to clean up."

Struggling to an upright position, Bobby moved to sit on the side of the bed. "I wish my damn head would quit pounding," he muttered. "I can't think straight." Dropping the hands that rubbed at his temples, he looked over at her. "I had sorta thought maybe you and me would go to Vegas and start over. There's all kinds of opportunities there for people like us. Lots of shows and revues for someone with your talent, and hell, I bet I could even work my way up to pit boss in some big casino."

Kaylee stared at him in agony. She'd always thought of him as a good-time sort of guy, but here he was offering her so much more than she'd ever expected from him. She wanted badly to grab it with both hands.

And yet . . .

"I can't let Catherine get hurt in my place, Bobby. I've walked the line between right and wrong more times than I care to think about, but that's one thing I don't think I could ever live with."

Bobby didn't know Catherine, so if it came down to choosing who had to take a fall, he quite frankly would rather it was her than Kaylee. He argued until he was hoarse, but nothing he said changed Kaylee's mind, and he was forced to sit by and watch her trip out the door in her four-inch heels several hours later. His last sight before the door closed was of the swivel of her well-rounded, spandex-clad hips, the sun blazing in her hair, and her suitcase bouncing off the doorjamb to knock against her shapely calf. She gave it an impatient tug, and the door clicked closed.

He sagged back on the bed, cursing. He didn't like this urge to do something stupidly noble, but it kept popping into his head. He had an awful feeling that he'd act on the damn thing, too, if he felt the least bit stronger. Because, even less did he like the sick churning he got in his gut wondering when he'd see her again.

As it turned out, it was sooner than he thought.

Kaylee burst back through the door at six-forty that evening. She dumped her suitcase at the door and tossed her purse on the bed.

Bobby felt a grin split his face as he surged up off the bed. "You're back!" He reached for her, hauling her into his arms. "Damn, it's good to see you." He couldn't seem to keep his hands off her. "You know that No-Sex-Until-We-Get-Catherine-Back rule? Well, baby, the minute I get the rest of my strength back, it's toast."

It belatedly occurred to him that she wasn't waxing as enthusiastic as he, and he tilted his chin down to peer into her face. "What happened?" He stiffened. "Oh, shit, not Chains?"

"No. At least I hope not." Kaylee snuggled into his embrace. "She wasn't there, Bobby. The bus came, but Cat and the bounty hunter weren't on it."

"Why do I get the feeling this doesn't mean we can head for Vegas now?"

"The driver said he stopped to pick them up like he was instructed, but he left when no one was waiting at the café where he was told he'd find them."

"And?"

Leaning back in his arms, she raised her gaze to search his face. "And I'm worried, Bobby. Where the hell can she be?"

20

It HAD NOT been Sam's intention to fall asleep again, but that was what he'd done. And so had Catherine, he discovered when he awakened to find it well after two o'clock in the afternoon. They were tumbled together in the middle of the mattress like a couple of puppies sleeping off an energetic tussle, and he slowly disengaged himself from her long legs and soft arms. Sitting up, he scrubbed his hands over his face. Then he lowered them to his thighs, where they gradually curled into fists as he stared down at her.

God, he was such a prince. Forget the lodge; he'd be lucky if she didn't hit him with a mess of legal charges. No sense prettying it up; he'd kidnapped her. Hell, kidnapped her, dragged her around like a piece of ratty luggage, and insulted her time after time.

After time.

Shit.

Flipping a section of the spread over the most distracting of the curves sprawled across the mattress, he got up. A hollow feeling gnawed deep in his gut,

273

and there was no way of knowing if its source was the fact that every bit of sustenance he'd put in his body in the last twenty-four hours had been spewed back out again, or the royal mess he'd made of everything—but he suspected the latter.

Well, it was a done deal; there was no use standing around whining about it. He'd better throw his clothes on and go pick up some food to bring back to the room. Catherine was bound to be hungry when she woke up, even if he doubted he'd ever be able to swallow again past the heavy mass sitting so squarely in the middle of his chest.

Catherine awoke to an empty room.

Chilled, she grabbed for a corner of the spread that spilled to her lap when she sat up, and absentmindedly wrapped it around her. "Sam?" There was no answer, but she wasn't worried. Wherever he'd gone, he'd be back, and this time he hadn't left her handcuffed to the bed frame to wait out his arrival. Life was good. She looked out through the crack in the drapery, saw the rain had been reduced to a drizzle, and, stretching beneath her covering, smiled.

She felt great.

He'd called her Catherine. They hadn't talked after they'd made love—she'd been too limp with amazement to put her feelings into words, and Sam had simply held her quietly and stroked wherever his hands would reach until both of them had drifted off to sleep. But everything was going to be okay now.

He knew once and for all who she was.

She hadn't expected the knowledge to make him

wary as a mongrel expecting a kick, but she saw the
minute he came through the door that it had.

He stopped just inside and shook his head like a
wet dog. The rainwater beading his dark hair flew
in all directions, and one big hand paused in the act
of scraping it back as his gaze alighted on her. His
eyes were cautious behind their screen of black
lashes. "Hey," he said, his other hand tightening on
the aromatic bags that dangled from it. He thrust the
bags forward. "I, uh, got you some food."

"Thanks." She crossed the room, decently covered
once again by his oversize shirt and Kaylee's red
panties. "I'm starved." She took the packages from
him and set them down on the little table in the corner, ripping them open. "What've you got here? Not
chicken, I bet."

"Catherine."

The seriousness of his voice brought her head up.
To her amazement, color was creeping up his brown
throat and onto the smooth skin of his jaw.

"I, uh, guess I owe you a big apology." He cleared
his throat. "A huge one. You tried to tell me who
you were from the very beginning, and I wouldn't
listen."

Ah, vindication. It was sweet. She observed the
flush that colored his cheeks, listened to him stumble
for words, and gave herself a big old mental hug.
Swallowing back her grin, however, she rounded her
eyes at him in a look of faux reproach. After all, she'd
earned a little fun at his expense. "You owe me a
whole lot more than an apology, McKade."

Those solemn green eyes hit Sam hard, and he

missed seeing the amusement that lurked beneath the surface. "Yeah. I know." His palms itched to reach for her, and he rubbed them against the seams of his jeans before stuffing them into his front pockets. Hunching his shoulders, he swallowed hard. Against all odds, he'd somehow hoped he wouldn't have to do this. "I'll, uh, start making arrangements to send you home right away."

Catherine choked on the piece of bread she'd just bitten off. Swallowing it barely chewed, she dropped the baguette onto the table. She'd been about to remind him of a certain offer to eat his shorts, but his announcement knocked the words right out of her. If her expression was anywhere near as stupefied as she felt as she stared at him, it must be some sight to behold. "Excuse me?"

"I said I'll . . ."

Indignation roared through her veins. "My God. I don't *believe* you, Sam!"

"Listen, I know it's little enough reparation—"

"You consider that reparation? What kind of man are you? If you believe I'm Catherine and not Kaylee, then you must know I've also been telling you the truth about Jimmy Chains. The man's trying to kill me, but you're going to cut me *loose* to deal with the problem on my own? Well, sure, why not," she decided with a bitter twist of her lips. "It's not like anyone else has ever believed I could use a hand dealing with life's little messes."

Poleaxed, Sam stared at her. Amidst the revelation that she wasn't Kaylee, everything except the thought of how badly he'd handled everything had been knocked clean out of his mind.

He took a step toward her, then stopped. "I forgot. Christ," he said, shaking his head in self-derision, "I've taken you from your home, humiliated you, called you a liar at every turn, seduced you—"

"I rather liked that part," she said sulkily.

He was so immersed in his own misery that her interruption failed to penetrate. "Then when I discover your bond's not going to get me Gary's lodge after all, I offer to leave you alone to deal with the danger I've created. You must think I'm such an asshole." She opened her mouth, but with a harsh laugh he held up a forestalling hand. "No, don't tell me— you've always considered me an asshole."

Catherine's good humor was restored. He didn't need her to revile him; he was doing such an excellent job of it all on his own. The man certainly took his responsibilities very seriously. She wondered if he'd offer to buy her a lodge, too. "Actually, I was going to say you didn't create the danger. That was strictly a by-product of Kaylee's being in the wrong place at the wrong time."

His mouth twisted. "That's very generous of you."

"Yeah, that's me, all right, generous to a fault. Sam, tell me something." She waited until his eyes focused on hers. "You say you forgot about Chains. Did you remember him before you made the offer to return me home?"

"No, but . . ."

"Then, for God's sake get over yourself. You take on way too much; not everything in this world is your responsibility. Come on." She began setting out the food "Let's eat."

His expression was priceless. Obviously confused, his automatic response to the emotion was irritation. His big hands stuffed in his pockets, he regarded her with a sullen mouth and wary eyes. He nevertheless stepped forward when she jerked her chin peremptorily at the food she'd set out.

A short while later, she finished blotting her lips and set down her paper napkin. "So, what do we do now?"

She watched Sam swallow the bite he'd just taken. His eyes were still cautious as he looked at her across the small table, but he wiped his mouth with the puny paper napkin clutched in his fist and demanded with his usual arrogance, "Tell me everything you know about Chains."

She did so and sat back to await his response.

"We definitely have to stick together." Sam pretended to himself that didn't give him a huge rush of satisfaction. "I guess the big question is, where do we go next?" He studied her through narrowed lashes. "Do you want me to take you home?"

"No." The decisiveness with which she shook her head sent several strands of red hair wrapping around her pale throat. He watched as she hooked them with her fingers and tucked her hair behind her ears. "I get the impression Chains doesn't have a clue about me," she said, "and frankly, I'd just as soon keep it like that. No way do I want to lead him straight to my door. Besides." Her green eyes were level as they locked on his. "I've been dragged into this now. You're not getting rid of me until I see how it finally ends up. I've earned the right."

Hey, that worked for him. Planting his feet, he gripped the seat of his chair, and by raising his butt and swiveling, thumped it down a few feet closer to Catherine's. He wanted to reach out and touch the smoothness of her thigh just below his shirttail, but clenched his fingers around the seat instead. "Fine. As long as you understand I'm the one in charge here." He'd probably forfeited everything else in this debacle, but he'd be damned if he'd forfeit control. He was responsible for this situation; he'd damn well see it handled right from here on out.

"Why, certainly, Sam," she replied, and the very mildness of her tone had him narrowing his eyes in suspicion. "I wouldn't have it any other way."

He should have known it was too good to be true. Hell, he *had* known, but fool that he was, he'd allowed himself to be sucked in anyway.

"Dammit, Catherine, I'm telling you we can't afford this," he said twenty minutes later. He nevertheless found himself striding alongside her toward the town garage, shoulders hunched against the drizzle.

"We can't afford to do otherwise," she argued. "Chains is looking for us on the bus. Renting a car will be cheaper in the long run than running into him." She turned those big green eyes on him. "Trust me. Have I been wrong so far?"

"Damn. The guilt card." He rolled his shoulders. Then, as graciously as he could manage, conceded,

"Ah, what the hell—I suppose you're right. Gary's lodge is history anyway."

"And look on the bright side, Sam. Greyhound's picking up the tab for last night's lodging, and you can most likely cash in the remainder of our tickets. That should help defray the cost." She shot him a glance from under her lashes. "It's too bad we don't have camping supplies. You could cut way down on the expense of lodging, then."

He studied her guileless expression. "You really get a kick out of making me feel cheap, don't you? I'm not, you know. I simply had a budget and a deadline, and I did my best to stick to both in order to attain my goal."

That tugged Catherine's heartstrings. His goal was shot, and he had accepted the knowledge matter-of-factly. Not once had he moaned about it the way she would have been tempted to do.

She also knew he wouldn't appreciate her appreciation. He was firmly entrenched in his professional mode, his manner remote. She said breezily, "Well, that's good to hear. Then you won't mind buying me some clothes of my own, will you?"

She wasn't sure she appreciated the way his eyes lit up. "Something really loose?" he demanded. "Like that blouse the little guy spilled grape juice on the first day?"

"Yes."

"Well, all right! But don't go crazy on me now. I don't have a huge budget."

"Oh, sugar, don't I know it. There must be a Kmart somewhere in this state."

* * *

They found a discount store in Laramie, which was as far as the garage owner was willing to let them take his car. Leaving it with a national car rental agency that had a reciprocal agreement with the man, they rented a slightly roomier vehicle to accommodate two sets of long legs and made the stop to buy Catherine her new clothes. Then they headed out on a secondary highway for the Colorado state line.

An hour and a half later Catherine rested her elbow on the open window ledge, breathed in the aromatic Colorado mountain winds that blew through her tied-back hair, and felt at peace with the world.

A large part of her euphoria stemmed from once again wearing clothes that didn't cling to every atom of her body. She looked down at her pleated khaki walking shorts, with their roomy cuffs that ended a little below mid-thigh, and the loose, matching T-shirt. The top wasn't as boxy as most of the items in her wardrobe at home, but then again she didn't feel as self conscious about her body as she had a week ago.

Life was sweet.

"You goddamn stupid idiot."

Catherine tore her gaze from the spectacular scenery out her side window and glanced at Sam in surprise. His black eyebrows were gathered over the thrust of his nose and his attention kept jumping between the road that wound up the side of the mountain and the rearview mirror. Glad to know he wasn't referring to her, she twisted in her seat to see what had caught his regard.

A large silver car was roaring up on their tail. Even as she watched, the distance between the two vehicles narrowed.

"Stupid son of a bitch," Sam snarled. He spared her a quick glance. "You buckled? Good." His eyes back on the road, he let up slightly on the gas. "Idiot's bound to try to pass us, and there's bugger-all room right here."

The words were barely out of his mouth when their car was rammed from behind. Catherine screamed, but it emerged as no more than a squeak through paralyzed vocal cords. Sam swore and tightened his grip on the wheel, correcting the swerve the car made toward the dirt shoulder and the rail-free drop-off beyond that.

Once again the car behind them came screaming up and rammed their back bumper. Metal screamed against metal, and the tires on Catherine's side of the car spewed up a storm of dust and grit as they skidded off the highway onto the shoulder.

"My God, is he drunk? Why is he doing this?" Her demand was breathless, and once again she twisted in her seat to try to see into the other car.

It roared out from behind them and accelerated into the oncoming lane, pulling abreast.

"Oh my God, oh my God," she whispered. "It's *him*, Sam, it's Jimmy Chains. How did he find us?" She watched the other car pull even with their car and saw Chains raise his arm straight up from his side. "Sam, look out! He's got a gun!"

Taking advantage of Sam's divided attention as he tried to both drive and hunch down to provide a smaller target, Chains wrenched his steering wheel toward their car. His heavier vehicle slammed them broadside, shoving them onto the shoulder.

Sam fought to keep the car from getting too close to the brink. Dust boiled up from beneath the spinning tires and he had the front wheels under control when Chains dropped back and rammed their back fender. It spun the still-canted rear end toward the verge. One minute there was hard-packed dirt beneath their back wheels, and the next the tires were spinning in space. For an instant, the car hung suspended over the mountainside. Then, with an attenuated creak, gravity exerted its pull and the front tires lifted off the ground. A second later the hood was pointing skyward.

"Ohmygod, ohmygod," Catherine repeated mindlessly as they began sliding backwards. She reached for the dashboard, digging her fingers in and pressing her full weight hard against it, as if by exerting enough pressure she could prevent the car from flipping over backwards and turning end for end in their headlong rush down the mountainside. Sam was hunched as far over the steering wheel as his seat belt would allow.

The car slid and bumped with lightning speed and horrendous noise down the almost-vertical slope. The front wheels left the ground several times, but somehow the vehicle avoided flipping over. Catherine's stomach, however, felt as if it were turning cartwheels.

As the slope became less vertical, brush and slender branches tore at the painted metal and whipped in and out of Catherine's open window. Stones bounced with loud, metallic clangs off the car's underside, and green blurs flashed past the windshield.

Suddenly the car slammed into a boulder with a rending screech, and whipped around as if upon an axis. It teetered just long enough for them to get a clear view of the massive evergreen that sat dead in the middle of their path down the hill, and then slid free. As they hurtled down the steep slope, Catherine said a silent prayer that her death would be a quick and painless one. With the impact of a freight train meeting a brick wall, they hit the tree head-on.

Two airbags exploded out of the dashboard and mashed them back in their seats.

A breath of incredulous laughter exploded out of Catherine's throat. "Oh my God," she panted. "Oh, my God, do you believe this? Are you okay? Sam, we're alive!" She reached out to touch his strong hand, resting on the seat between them and panted, "I completely forgot the car came equipped with these. Oh, God, Sam, we're alive." She raised her trembling hand to his jaw. "*Alive.*"

His eyes were all over her, assessing her condition. Then his black brows met over his nose and he sniffed. And sniffed again. "Do you smell gas?" Suddenly he began to swear and tore open his seat belt. "Shit! That rock must have torn a hole in the gas tank." He turned his fierce regard on her. "Unbuckle your seat belt, Red." When she simply regarded him blankly for a second, he snarled, "*Move.* We've gotta get the hell out of here."

She moved, and once free of the restraints, reached

for the door handle. His voice stopped her.

"No," he said. "Go out the window. There's bugger-all way of knowing what kind of damage was done to the doors, and one spark could blow us sky-high."

She stared at him as she battled her way free of the airbag and pushed back evergreen branches to clear a space for herself in the window opening. "A spark from what?"

"Metal striking metal, darlin'. Just takes one and boom! We're barbecue."

"My God." Catherine paused to stare at him. "You're just full of cheery tidings, aren't you? How do you know these things anyway?"

Sam's teeth flashed with feral whiteness in his tanned face. "Hey, we're alive, sweet cheeks—it doesn't get much cheerier than that. And I don't know how I know. It's a guy thing, I guess."

She cocked a skeptical eyebrow. "Absorb it through your penis, do you?"

"Big guy's been known to do some of my best thinking," Sam agreed, and gave her leg an appreciative pat as she eased up onto the window ledge. What the big guy was thinking right this moment, however, he acknowledged as he watched her pull herself out, was hardly appropriate to the circumstances.

The thing was, he'd been so busy beating himself up this morning for all the ways he'd screwed up that he'd lost sight of the fact that Catherine was nobody's pushover. Somehow he'd gotten it into his head that along with everything else, he'd taken unfair advantage of her inexperience. But if Red hadn't wanted to make love with him, she sure as hell wouldn't have.

Damn. He fought a dippy smile . . . and lost.

"Hand me my purse." Her face appeared at the window. "What are you grinning at? I thought you were worried about becoming the featured item at the barbecue."

"Gasoline doesn't just spontaneously combust." He passed her handbag through the window. "Stand back." Reaching up, he grasped a heavy overhead branch and hauled himself through in her wake. "We should be fine as long as we don't create any sparks."

He ducked beneath the branches and went around to the back of the car to inspect the trunk. Given the abuse it had taken, it looked surprisingly unscathed and should be safe enough to open to retrieve their bags. He inserted the key.

That's when the shooting began.

"Son of a bitch!" Abandoning the trunk, he grabbed Catherine's wrist and dragged her behind the tree, using it as a shield between them and the shooter. "Run!"

"Is that Chains?" She dragged against his hold as she kept glancing over her shoulder, trying to see how close the danger was. "Is he coming?"

"No, I think he's still up top." He gave her an impatient yank. "Come on, Red, move it. Trust me when I say it's in our best interests to put a lot of distance between us and the car."

"But he's too far away for a hand gun to have an effective range, isn't he?"

"Yeah . . . unless he hits a rock up the hill and sets off one of those sparks I was talking about. The tank left a trail of gasoline all the way down to the tree, so we could be that barbecue yet." He spared a glance over his shoulder as he dragged her deeper into the woods. "You willing to risk that?"

Catherine passed him in a burst of speed. "Huh-uh, no sir. I am not."

21

"Do you have the vaguest idea where we are?" Dusk was setting in, and Catherine was nervous as a cat. Her legs sported scratches from ankle to thigh, and both they and her arms were covered in bites. Slapping at yet another mosquito trying to liberate her of more of her blood, she followed closely behind Sam, just narrowly avoiding tramping on his heels. "You ever do any camping as a kid?" she demanded. "I've never been camping in my life." She tilted her head back to look up through the towering evergreens, anxious to see a slice of the sky. "We're lost, aren't we? This is way too much great outdoors for my taste."

Sam stopped and turned, catching her by the shoulders to steady her when she bounced off his chest. Stepping back a pace, he held her at arm's length and studied her expression. "We'll stop and make camp for the night," he said decisively.

"Oh, good idea." She looked around and saw that they were in a tiny clearing. "How does one do that, exactly? Set up a tent, I suppose, except we don't have one. Should we forage for berries? But what if they're poisonous?" She wished she'd shut up. The more she chattered, the more she scared herself. But this vast wilderness was very much outside her range of experience.

Sam stroked a big hand down her hair. "We're not lost, Red. We have to spend the night here, but we'll reach a town tomorrow. Collect some firewood. I'll forage for the berries."

She desperately didn't want to let him out of her sight, but she bit down hard on the inside of her cheek to prevent all the disgraceful pleas she felt clogging her throat. She was a self-reliant woman, dammit, always had been. She took care of people— she certainly didn't need anyone to take care of her. Watching until he disappeared into the trees, she took several deep breaths to stem her panic. God. She was practically hyperventilating. This was too pathetic.

But she had a very bad feeling that all this rampant nature was simply teeming with many-legged creatures ready and willing to crawl across her exposed skin.

She wandered the perimeters of the clearing, gingerly picking up fallen branches and inspecting them for wildlife before carrying them back to a growing stockpile in the center of the glade.

When the gunshot abruptly sounded in the not-too-far distance, she nearly wet her pants. Hand clamped over her thundering heart, she slid into the shadows of an evergreen, where she hovered anxiously until she heard Sam's voice.

"Catherine? Don't be nervous, darlin', that was

only me catching our dinner. I'll be there as soon as I dress it out."

Dress it out? She shook her head. She didn't even want to know.

An hour later, however, she was feeling more relaxed. Sam kept a small fire burning in the circle of stones he'd collected, and the rabbit he turned on its makeshift spit sent up a heavenly aroma. After repeated assurances that they would reach civilization in the morning, her current worry was of the eight-legged variety.

Darting a nervous look into the darkness over her shoulder, she scooted closer to Sam. "You think there's a lot of spiders in these woods?"

He kept his attention on the rabbit. "We're in Colorado, Red. They don't have spiders here. Kind of like Hawaii and its lack of snakes."

She sagged against him in relief.

Until she thought about it.

"You are so full of it, McKade." Giving his knee a smack, she straightened away from him. "I'm arachnophobic, not stupid."

He turned his head, golden eyes gleaming in the firelight as they met hers. "I don't know how to break this to you, honey, but being arachnophobic is kind of stupid."

"Oh please! And I suppose you're not afraid of anything, logical or illogical."

"Hell no." His fist thumped the center of his chest. "Me big strong man."

She made a rude noise and cast another nervous glance into the darkness.

Sam grinned and slung an arm around her, pulling her close again. He found himself charmed by her vulnerability, as it wasn't a side of her he'd seen often. And damned if it didn't generate the craziest surge of protectiveness.

"You don't believe that, huh? Well, believe this." He snugged her up under his arm and tilted his head back to look up at the stars hanging low in the sky. Then he pulled his gaze away to look into her face. "You're not going to find many spiders at this elevation. And if we do happen to stumble across one, I'll get rid of it before it can come anywhere near you."

"But what if it sneaks up on me from behind? From the dark?"

"Catherine, spiders are more afraid of you than you are of them."

She gave him a look, the one only women seemed to be really good at, and he backpedaled. "Okay, let's compromise and say they're nearly as afraid of you as you are of them. Bottom line here is, they're basically shy creatures. They don't pounce on people out of the dark. They practice avoidance."

She emitted another sound of disbelief, but he felt her relax. "Hungry?" he asked. "I think this rabbit's about done."

They ate it with their fingers and drank creek water from a beer can he'd found lying on the forest floor. "People can sure be slobs, but in this case it came in handy," he said when Catherine asked him about it. "I scrubbed it up as best I could, and it's been lying around long enough that I doubt any germs survived."

With a full stomach and Sam's lean bulk warming her right side, Catherine began to feel not quite so desperately out of her element. She couldn't shake the feeling a spider was going to crawl up her unprotected back at any moment, however, and kept shooting nervous glances over her shoulders.

Sam suddenly reached out to grasp her wrist. "You're not going to relax as long as your back's exposed, are you?" he demanded. "Well, c'mere, then." He pulled her around to sit between his legs. Settling her with her back against his chest, he wrapped his arms around her waist. "So, what grade do you teach, anyway?"

For the first time since he'd dragged her away from the familiarity of the car, she relaxed completely. Warmed by his body heat, she snuggled a little deeper into his loose embrace and stared into the fire. Never could she recall anyone taking pains to make her feel safe this way, especially over something as inconsequential as a phobia. There was something very . . . nice . . . about it. Comforting. "Seventh and eighth," she replied.

"God, pubescent teenagers? No wonder I couldn't get anything past you. What subject?"

"Language arts, primarily."

She dug at an itchy welt on her calf while she answered further questions about her work. A while later, they fell silent. As she stared drowsily into the fire, it occurred to her that their entire conversation had been about her. She tilted her head back into his shoulder to catch a glimpse of his profile. "Can I ask you something?"

"Sure."

"Why is it so important to you to buy your friend a lodge?"

He stiffened for a moment, but then she felt his muscles loosen as he shifted on the ground behind her. His warm hands rearranged her infinitesimally to fit the new configuration, and he rested his chin on top of her head. "Gary and I always talked about buying one when we retired from the service," he said in a noncommittal tone of voice. "It just happens that a lodge on the market now is the same one we used to go to on furloughs."

"Which makes it pretty special, I imagine." Her brows furrowed. "So why don't you ever refer to it as *your* lodge?"

"What? Sure I do."

"No. You don't." She could tell by the way his arms tightened around her that she'd hit a nerve, but felt compelled to persist all the same. There was something to this—she knew there was. "You always call it Gary's lodge, as if it has nothing to do with you at all."

All of Sam's desires, which for the past three years had been kept neatly buried, welled up inside him. There were things that, given different circumstances, he would have liked to do with his life. And the fact that she'd somehow tapped into what he'd managed to keep hidden even from himself infuriated him. His arms dropped away from her.

"Isn't it amazing," he said sardonically, reaching

for a stick to feed into the fire, "how you can fuck a woman once and she thinks she knows every last detail about you?"

The words reverberated in his head the instant they left his mouth, and he was appalled. He may have been brought up poor, but his mother had raised him to treat women with respect. He felt Catherine's immediate withdrawal and tightened his thighs on either side of her hips, wrapping his arms around her once again to hold her in place.

"I'm sorry," he said hoarsely. "That was uncalled for—I don't know what came over me."

"No, you're perfectly correct," she replied with cool civility. "You don't owe me any explanations. We're barely more than strangers, after all."

"Bullshit." His arms drew her tighter against him. "The last thing we are is strangers. You . . . hit a nerve, is all, and I wanted to hit back."

"Because?" Her voice was cool, disinterested.

"Because you're right." He exhaled sharply and looked past her averted profile into the heart of the fire. "Gary and I always talked about buying a fishing lodge, but it was just a dream—you know? Something that seemed way off in the future."

"And now here it is, huh?"

"Yeah." His chest moved against her back. "Something like that."

She looked up at the stars. "So, what would you rather be doing?"

"Nothing." He shrugged again. "What I'm doing is fine."

"Dammit." She twisted around to glare up at him.

"Tell me to mind my own business, if you don't want to talk about it. But don't tell me 'nothing' and then turn around and use it as an excuse to say something offensive because you're an unhappy camper. Now, what would you rather to be doing?"

"None of your damn business."

"Fine." She faced forward again and sat stiffly between his legs.

"I'd like to be a cop, okay?" Sam swore and freed a hand to rake back his hair. "I really liked being an MP. I liked the structure and the order." His stomach twisted up in knots at the thought of never again realizing that level of satisfaction, but he took a deep breath, expelled it, and sat a bit straighter. "But you don't always get what you want. That's life."

Her voice was gentle, full of warm interest again, when she asked, "What will you do now?"

"Hell, who knows? See if I can scare up a bounty that's worth running down before the option on the lodge runs out, I guess. I know what I *don't* look forward to."

She tilted her head back to look at him. "What's that?"

"Having to break it to Gary from the next phone we find that I loused this up."

They awoke at dawn, chilled, stiff, and, on Catherine's part, at least, out of sorts. Disengaging herself from Sam's arms, she rose to her feet and dusted herself off as best she could. She missed her toothbrush and tormented herself for a moment or two with the thought of hot water and clean clothes. A long shower and a new toothbrush would be her reward when they reached civilization again, which, oh, please, God, would be *soon*.

She did her utmost to fight the call of nature, intimidated at the idea of entering those woods by herself. Eventually, however, the need grew too imperative to ignore. With a long-suffering sigh, she slipped into the trees.

Sam watched as she disappeared. He, too, felt out of sorts.

What the hell was he doing?

Somehow his relationship with Catherine had veered so far from what was acceptable, it was nothing short of ridiculous, and it was past time to get the damn thing back on track. He'd known her for—what?—all of six days? Hell, he knew without a shadow of a doubt that the minute he got the Jimmy Chains/Hector Sanchez situation straightened out, he wouldn't see her for dust. She'd return to her life and her cozy little house and her upscale job, and that would be that. He'd never see those big green eyes again.

So, this was it, time to quit screwing around. No more sexual advances, and definitely no more spilling his guts to the woman. From now on, he was the ultimate professional. Kicking dirt on the few embers that remained in the fire pit, he ignored the leaden feeling in his gut. It might pinch a bit, but it was the right decision and he knew it.

It was a resolution that was blown clean out of his mind when Catherine's bloodcurdling scream ripped through the forest.

*   *   *

He entered the woods in a running crouch, his gun extended in one hand and braced by the other, sweeping the woods to cover as much territory as possible until he could find the danger. Catherine stood shivering, her arms wrapped around herself and one foot stacked on top of the other, but he saw no sign of Jimmy Chains. Eyes scanning the surrounding trees, he worked his way over to her. "Are you okay? Where is he?"

"There," she said in a wavery voice, and pointed at the ground. "Right there."

Puzzled, both his gaze and the barrel of his pistol followed her trembling finger. There was nothing to be seen.

Except a spider.

It took a full minute for the significance of that to sink in. Then his gun hand dropped to his side. "Oh, for God's sake . . . *that's* why you were screaming the woods down?" Granted it was a decent-sized wolf spider but . . . "Christ Almighty, Catherine, I thought Chains had gotten his hands on you."

The finger she pointed at the insect trembled. "Shoot it!"

"It's a spider, doll. You don't go around shootin' spiders."

She gave him a look of pure incredulous indignation. "You shot a helpless bunny!"

"For Chrissake, Red, that was different. That was dinner."

"*Shoot it!*"

"Look," he said reasonably, "the thing's sitting

right on top of a rock. Bullet hits rock, it ricochets. Then we could all be in a world of hurt."

"Oh, God, it's got such fat, hairy legs." She raised huge eyes to his. "*Please*, Sam."

Sam stomped the spider into paste.

She dived into his arms and he hooked an arm around her neck, pressing her cheek against his chest. She clutched his waist, trying her damnedest to meld her trembling body to his. He stared off into the woods over her head.

Christ Almighty. How the hell was he supposed to have a prayer of remaining professional when she persisted in doing stuff like this?

He peeled her off his chest and held her away at arm's length to study her.

The trek through the woods and a night spent in the open was a minor inconvenience to him. The experience had been far less kind to her. She was scratched and bug-bitten, her skin was even paler than usual, and half her hair was tumbled out of the bun that listed to the right of her crown.

He roughly finger-combed her hair away from her left eye. "You okay now?"

She took a deep breath and blew it out. Then her elegant little chin firmed up, her shoulders squared, and she nodded curtly. She stepped back from him, beyond the reach of his grooming fingers.

His hand dropped to his side. She had guts, he'd give her that. "Good," he said gruffly. "Let's break camp, then, and move out."

Catherine trudged along in Sam's wake for what felt like days. Periodically, she'd glance up from her careful scrutiny of the ground to glare at his back. The way he strode along, arms swinging, shoulders easy, *whistling* for God's sake, they could have been strolling an upscale mall instead of picking their way through a vast forest in the middle of nowhere. It was highly irritating. Why didn't it produce obstacles to trip *him* up the way it kept doing to her? And he couldn't whistle for beans, either.

She was so busy watching where she put her feet, one in front of the other, that she failed to realize when he stopped. She walked into him with enough force to flatten her breasts against his back.

Steadying herself, she peered around him, amazed to find them right back where they had started, at their crumpled rental car with its hood ornament of an evergreen tree. She shot Sam a dubious glance.

"Is this wise?"

Sam went to the trunk and opened it. "I don't know about wise, but its probably the safest place for us right now. The fumes have had time to dissipate."

"But what about Chains?"

He tossed her Kaylee's suitcase and slammed the trunk. Pulling a map out of his duffel bag, he shook it open and spread it across the trunk, anchoring it with one big hand.

"Look," he said, pulling her forward for a clearer view. "Close as I can figure, this is where he drove us off the road. I considered walking this way"—his long finger traced a route that bisected the highway farther along—"but the more I thought about it, the more I realized that's where he'd expect us to come out." He turned his head, and his voice growled directly in her ear when he said, "So, grab the stuff you can't live without and leave the rest in the car. We're going out here."

She looked up the steep, steep slope they had somehow managed to careen down alive. *"Here?"*

"Here. And when I say pack light, Red"—his golden brown eyes pinned her in place—"I mean it. Take only what's absolutely necessary. You're going to want your hands free, and there's no way in hell I'm carrying out any pink high heels."

Kaylee's wallet went into Catharine's back pocket. She selected clean underwear, a hairbrush, toothbrush and toothpaste, deodorant, and a bottle of moisturizing lotion. Then, sighing, she pulled a clean outfit out of the bag. Looked like she'd be back to wearing Kaylee's clothes again. She dumped her selections in the discount-store bag and handed it to Sam.

Pawing through it, he handed her back the bottle of moisturizer. "I said only what was absolutely necessary."

"That is necessary. It contains sunscreen." She displayed her scratched arms for his consideration. "Just because you have hide like a rhinoceros doesn't mean I won't fry to a crisp. I'm fair-skinned, Mc-Kade; I burn easily."

For just one moment his gaze was all over her, taking in every inch of exposed skin. Then he grunted and tossed the moisturizer in the plastic bag and added a few items of his own. He tied it to his belt. "Here," he said, digging through his duffel bag one last time. He handed her a squashed candy bar. "Breakfast."

"Oh, God, chocolate! Who said you don't know how to treat a girl right." She ripped it open and took a hungry bite. The bar was more than half consumed before it dawned on her that he wasn't eating as well. She lowered her hand. "What about you?"

"I'm fine."

She'd seen the amounts of food he could consume. With a final look of longing, she extended the remainder of the bar to him. "Here. Kill it off."

The glance he shot her was impatient. "I'm fine, I said."

"Take it, Sam." She thrust it out at him. "I don't deal well with guilt."

That was something he could identify with and he took it, wolfing it down as he watched her clean melted chocolate from her fingertips with delicate, catlike laps of her tongue. He cleared his throat. "Thanks."

"Don't mention it." She gave a comic groan. "Please."

He grinned at her. "You're a good sport, Red. You ready to move out?"

"Ready as I'll ever be, I guess."

It was an arduous climb but not truly difficult until they neared the top. Panting, Catherine pulled herself over another hillock by a grabbing a fistful of brush. She wiped stinging sweat from her eyes with the back of her hand, then stared in dismay at the steep cliff that towered above her as Sam pulled himself up to join her. "Oh, God, look at that. It's impossible."

"No it's not. You're doing great. And there are a lot more hand- and footholds than it appears at first glance." He took her shoulders in his big hands and turned her slightly to the left. "Look, over here. Reach up and grab that rock. Good. Now, put your foot right there."

He guided her hand by hand, foot by foot up the cliff. After several yards, the slope tilted inward, much to Catherine's heartfelt relief. The new angle made it feel a little less as if she were hanging out over a sheer drop.

Then, suddenly, she was at the top. Hooking her elbows over the verge, she found a last foothold and thrust herself up and over, rolling to lie on her back on firm ground. A moment later, Sam joined her. Staring up at the sky, she laughed breathlessly, then turned her head to look at him. "We made it." She laughed louder. "Dear God, we made it!" She rolled over on top of him and kissed him soundly.

His hand wound in her hair as he kissed her back. Then they pulled apart, sat up, and grinned at each other. He pushed to his feet, extending a hand to help her up.

They were brushing themselves off when footsteps sounded behind them. Smiles fading, they slowly turned.

"Welcome back," Jimmy Chains said. The gun in his hand pointed steadily at Catherine. "Sure took your own sweet time about it."

22

CONTRARY TO SAM'S expectations, it had never occurred to Chains to check a map to see where the highway connected up again in case Sam and Catherine decided to hike out in another direction. After watching them scramble to safety at the bottom of the ravine yesterday, he had briefly considered climbing down to complete the job. But one look at the rugged terrain and another at the fine finish on his loafers had discouraged that idea.

So he'd waited. It had been boring, and his clothes were badly crumpled, which annoyed the hell out of him, but all things considered, he was pretty pleased with both himself and the situation.

Damn. All these years and he'd never realized it, but he had the makings of a goddamn genius.

He wagged the gun at Catherine. "Come over here."

Catherine didn't think so. She thought she'd just huddle here at Sam's side, behind the comfortingly wide protection of his shoulder. But then she remembered what he had said—was that only the night before last?—about the technique employed by the military police. She sighed in resignation.

"Flanking maneuver," she said sotto voce as she left Sam's side and thus divided the target they presented.

"Red, get your butt back here!" Sam made a grab for her, but she sidestepped his reach, and Chains's gun swung away from her to cover him.

Well, hell. That wasn't what she'd intended. Sam was the one with the weapon, and in order to give him an opportunity to use it, she needed to keep Jimmy Chains's attention firmly on her.

"You hear how he talks to me, Jimmy?" she demanded petulantly. The morning sun glittered off the hit man's tangle of gold jewelry and picked out the gleam of his pristinely polished shoes, and Catherine slapped unproductively at the dirt on her own clothing as she widened the gap between herself and Sam. "And would you *look* at this? I'm filthy. Not that it was much to begin with, but at least it was clean. It'll never be the same now."

Jimmy Chains turned his head to inspect her. His gun, however, remained pointed at Sam. "Doesn't look like a big loss to me, Kaylee. Where'd you get it, Kmart?"

"Exactly. Can you imagine? But Junior G-man here doesn't like chorus-girl clothing, and he tossed out all my cool stuff. He thinks I'm a bimbo."

"There's no 'think' about it, Sister," Sam growled. "You are a bimbo if you think this little ploy's gonna get you anywhere."

She pointed an accusing finger at him as she edged farther away. "You drag me through the woods and

make me sleep in the dirt, and *I'm* the dumb, unciv-
ilized one? There are *spiders* out there, Chains. Big,
black, hairy ones." She didn't need to fake a shudder.
"I *hate* all this nature. My idea of roughing it is leaving the salt off the tequila glasses. I want to go home,
where people know how to act. *He* certainly doesn't
have a clue." She shot Sam a dirty look and took the
step that would force Chains to choose which person
he wanted to cover.

Jimmy Chains finally turned to face her fully, and
his gun sagged at his side. "Man, Kaylee," he said
plaintively. "You sure make it hard to do what a
guy's s'posta do."

She saw Sam's hand go to the back of his waistband. Simultaneously, she heard car tires crunch to
a stop on the gravel of the shoulder behind him. The
vehicle was partially hidden from sight by the curve
of the road and a low sweep of evergreen branches.
She stepped into the road to see who had stopped,
and nearly sang a hosanna when she saw the swirling lights atop a Highway Patrol car. "The police,"
she murmured reverently.

Then she turned an incredulous grin on Sam . . .
and noticed Jimmy Chains had disappeared. Whirling around, she heard a car roar off down the highway behind her. "Hey," she protested indignantly,
but Sam was at her side practically before the objec-
tion left her mouth, reaching out a strong hand to
grip her wrist with punishing force. Her gaze shot
up to his and she saw murder in his golden brown
eyes.

Directed at her, for God's sake.

"Keep your mouth shut and let me handle this," he said under his breath.

"But he's getting away!"

"So, what was I supposed to do to stop him, Red, pull my gun? I was in full view of the Smokey while Chains was out of sight—that's a good way to get myself shot. We'll tell the cop about him, but if Chains has half a brain, he's already found himself a little side road somewhere to pull off and wait for the heat to die down. Now, would you, for once in your life, leave it to me?"

A patrolman stepped out of his cruiser. "You folks need help?"

"Yes," Sam agreed at the same time Catherine said with fervent sincerity, "Officer, are we glad to see you!"

Sam squeezed her wrist. "We got run off the road yesterday—"

"By a *maniac*. We're lucky to be alive." Catherine wrenched her arm out of Sam's hold before he could inflict further damage on her bruised flesh. She didn't know what his problem was, but he wasn't taking it out on her—she'd sustained enough abuse for one week. "Tell him about Chains taking off just now."

"Dammit, I'm trying, if you'd let me get a word in edgewise."

The highway patrolman's eyes weren't visible behind the reflective lenses of his sunglasses, but there was no mistaking the sudden alertness of his posture. "Someone ran you off the road? Deliberately?"

"Yes, sir, and he was still waiting for us here when

we climbed out today. He just took off a minute ago when he saw you arrive."

"Wait a minute, he ran you off the road yesterday and then hung around waiting or you to climb out? Why? Where?"

"The why is a little complicated. But it was over here." Sam led the way down the highway to the spot where they'd left the road.

Catherine broke out in a sweat seeing the evidence of their hurtling journey down the mountainside. There were skid marks on the asphalt, the verge was chewed up, and all down the cliff and hillside scarred rock, flattened brush, and broken saplings gave mute testimony of the path the vehicle had taken. The back end of the car, foreshortened from this distance, was visible beneath drooping evergreen limbs.

The patrolman whistled. "You're right, you are lucky to be alive. I think you'd better explain."

Sam did so concisely without going into a great deal of detail. The officer wrote everything down and checked Sam's ID and gun permit. He was clearly unhappy. "You at least get the license plate from his car?"

"No, it happened too fast," Sam said. "It was a newer model silver Chrysler, but I was too busy trying to keep us on the road to read its plate." He reached out for Catherine's hand and pulled her to stand in front of him. Pushing a tumbling strand of hair away from her eye, he inquired gently, "How about you, Catherine? You get the number?"

He might look solicitous to the highway patrolman, but Catherine could see the fury deep in his eyes. She didn't understand it, and for the moment didn't try. She simply answered and reanswered numerous questions.

"Listen," Sam finally said. "It's been a rough twenty-four hours. Ms. MacPherson's beat. Do you think you could take us to a hotel? I'd like to get her settled before I start all the arrangements with the insurance and car rental and towing companies. I'll be happy to answer any further questions you have in the car."

In little under an hour, the cruiser pulled into Fort Collins. "Pick your poison," the patrolman said as he drove past several motels, indicating accommodations whose prices ran the gamut from low end to top dollar.

"That one," Catherine said, pointing to the nicest place she saw, and the patrolman pulled into its lot. When Sam's hand closed warningly on her thigh, she murmured for his ears alone, "This one's on Kaylee. It's the least she owes us, and frankly, McKade, I'm tired of staying in dumps."

His grip relaxed.

The highway patrolman stopped Sam a moment later as he started to climb out of the cruiser in Catherine's wake. "If you'll just read over this report and sign it, sir, we can start the search for Mr. Slovak."

"I'll get us the room," Catherine offered. She thanked the patrolman for his help and walked into the office.

Sam was still talking to the officer when she'd completed the transaction, so she gave him a key and made her way to the room. Letting herself in, she tossed Kaylee's wallet on the bed and stripped, dropping her clothes to the floor in a careless trail from bed to bathroom. She turned on the shower, stepped into the tub, and with a sigh of pleasure, stood under the pounding, steaming spray.

She'd just finished rinsing the shampoo from her hair when the shower curtain was yanked back with a clatter of rings. She whipped around, hands and arms slapping with automatic protectiveness over exposed feminine body parts. Sam stood on the other side of the tub, the plastic curtain bunched in one big fist, a black scowl pulling his eyebrows together.

"What the *hell* were you trying to do out there with Chains?" he snarled. "Get yourself killed?"

He'd managed to keep it all bottled up while they dealt with the cop, and now he wanted nothing so much as to reach across the tub, grab her by her slippery white shoulders, and shake her until her pearly little teeth rattled. "Christ Almighty," he roared. "You 'bout gave me a friggin' heart attack! Or was that your plan? Maybe you weren't trying to kill yourself at all, maybe you were trying to kill me." His fingers on the curtain were so tense the knuckles stood white beneath his skin. "Dammit, Red! I had visions of you in matching wheelchairs alongside Gary. And I'm telling ya, I don't think I can bear up under that burden one more time."

She quit shielding her breasts and reached out a hand. He felt the soft slide of her fingers along his jaw. "We're really going to have to talk about your overweening sense of responsibility one of these days," she murmured.

Then she launched herself at him, and he found himself in a sudden stranglehold of damp arms and dripping hair, with 130 pounds of lush, wet redhead plastered to his front. "God," she whispered, her breath hot in his ear. "I thought we were dead for sure when Chains showed up."

"So you thought you'd just offer yourself up as a sacrifice?"

"No, my thinking was more along the lines of dividing the target, the way you told me." Her hand tangled in his hair, pulling his head back, and her mouth blindly sought his. "I don't want to talk about this now. Kiss me, Sam."

He'd promised himself no more sex, that from now on he was going to act professional.

It was a pledge he broke without a qualm.

His mouth moved the fraction of an inch necessary to make contact with hers, and he groaned at the softness of her lips, at the hot, sweet flavors his tongue collected when those lips parted.

His hands were grappling for purchase on her slippery back, seeking to pull her closer, when she laughed against his marauding mouth and pushed away.

She slicked a tongue over her bottom lip. "You have on way too many clothes, McKade," she said, reaching for the button on his waistband. He yanked his shirt over his head while she wrestled with his fly. Toeing off shoes, shedding underwear, seconds later he stood naked before her. She gave his arm an urgent tug, and he stepped up into the tub, jerking the curtain closed behind them. Water poured over his head, slicked down his back.

"Turn around," she whispered. "I'll wash your back."

Cleanliness wasn't exactly his top priority, but he turned away obediently and braced his hands against the enclosure wall. Head hanging, he struggled to catch his breath as sudsy hands slipped and slid over his shoulders, his back, his buttocks. Busy, soapy fingers slithered between his cheeks, touched his testicles, and he widened his stance.

Then Catherine's lush breasts flattened against his back, her mound and her thighs nestled spoon-fashion into his backside, and her slender hands slid around his waist. His stomach muscles jumped beneath the froth of lather she worked up on their surface, and he rose up on the balls of his feet, willing those industrious hands to go a little lower, please, ah, God, just . . . a . . . little . . . lower.

Then they did, and his breath exploded from his lungs. He pushed into her touch and looked down to see himself emerge dark and angry-looking against the white lather of soapsuds and long, pale fingers. He contracted his hips and disappeared into her fisted hands. Then he thrust forward again. "Oh, God, Red," he muttered. "I want in you."

He spun them both around and Catherine found herself with her back to the enclosure wall and Sam in a half squat between her legs. His big hands swallowed up her breasts. They massaged, and pressed, and pulled, then shifted until her nipples popped through spread fingers. His fingers closed, and the massaging, the pressing, the pulling began again. Little mewling sounds crawled up her throat.

His mouth kissed, licked, sucked its way down her stomach, her waist. His tongue probed her navel, then he kissed her abdomen. A moment later he was crouched between her feet, looking up at her, his eyes glints of gold between narrowed black lashes. "Spread your legs for me, Catherine."

Flushing, she did as he commanded, and then bit her knuckles to muffle her cry as his mouth moved up to kiss her there, too, his agile tongue lapping apart sensitive folds of flesh.

"Sam, ohSam, ohSam, ohSam," she repeated over and over, and her hands tangled in his dark hair, attempting to pull him away one moment and then holding him fiercely in place the next, before he raised his head again and sat back on his heels. Licking his lips, he stared up at her with burning eyes. Then, surging to his feet, he grasped her hips, lifted her against the wall, and buried himself in her in one smooth, controlled motion.

"Ah, Jesus, Catherine," he growled in her ear. "You feel so damn good."

She wrapped her arms around his neck but didn't quite know what to do with her legs. The position raised her onto her toes and she tentatively hooked one leg over his hip, bracing the sole of her foot against his calf. That felt a bit more secure but still awkward.

"Both of 'em, darlin'." He grasped her bottom and hiked her up. She gasped to feel her feet leave the ground. Clutching at his neck, she instinctively raised both legs to grip his hips as well, then whimpered at the fullness inside that stretched her to capacity.

"Yes. Like that," he approved, and started to move. "Just like that."

Hot water hit her underarm and the side of her breast; it drummed against her waist, trickled over her outer thigh and cantilevered knee. Sam's hands gripped her bottom, his chest hair rasped her nipples, and the emphatic thrust and retreat of his iron-hard sex abraded oversensitized nerves deep inside. She was immediately ready to explode but longed to make it last. Panting, tightening her grip until she feared she'd strangle him, she tried to pull herself to a plane where the feelings weren't so intense in order to hold back.

Sam wasn't having it. "Oh, no you don't," he muttered hoarsely. He bent his knees for better leverage and surged into her, reaching for the heart of her with every thrust. He felt the rhythm lift and drop the full globes of the breasts pressed hard against his chest, felt the clamp of smooth arms around his neck and firm thighs around his hips. Lowering his head, he laved her ear with his tongue and encouraged her to come with dark, whispered urgings.

Savage satisfaction burst deep in his gut when her head thunked back against the wall and his name emerged from her throat in a low wail. He watched a flush spread over her pale cheeks, her eyes darken and lose focus, and felt a sense of power that owed nothing to his size or strength. Then the tight, hot sheath clasping him, milking him, sent him over the edge in her wake. Gritting out her name between clenched teeth, he thrust deep, a guttural groan wrenched from him with each scalding pulsation he jetted into her.

He sank to sit cross-legged on the floor of the tub, with Catherine draped astride his lap, her long legs loosely crossed behind his back. Her arms flopped over his back, her chin rested in the angle where his neck met his shoulder. He accepted her full weight, running a gentle finger up and down the bumps in her spine as she sagged limply in his arms.

"Wow," she whispered several minutes later, without bothering to raise her head. She felt as if someone had removed her entire skeletal structure. Enervated to the point of inertia, her limbs were heavy, her muscles lax, only the persistent after-twinges in the nerve-rich passage that still encased him showing signs of life. Lazily, she tightened interior muscles to prolong the feeling.

And felt him pulse once inside her.

"Oh." She repeated the exercise and felt him do the same. What had been half-hard was suddenly three-quarters hard.

And gaining strength.

"Sam?" she whispered.

In reply he pressed his thighs toward the tub floor, the movement sliding her down his phallus, burying him deep. Relaxing his knees made his thighs raise off the floor and lifted her up a few inches.

Her twinges became a full-fledged throb. "Oh my God. Sam?"

With lazy precision he butterflied his splayed thighs up and down. "Reach behind you and turn off the water, Red."

When she found the strength to comply, he bent his head to nuzzle the breast the action thrust forward. "We may be here a while," he said roughly. "I wouldn't want you to drown."

23

BOBBY HAD JUST maneuvered himself into a little slice of heaven when the phone rang. He had Kaylee with her skirt rucked up around her waist, facedown on the bed, where he was busy complying with the invitation extended by the pursed lips of her little red tattoo.

He raised his head at the unexpected interruption. "I don't suppose you're gonna let me ignore that."

She was tempted. Lord was she tempted! His mouth, fitted so precisely to the lips on her rear, was soft, hot, and it had been sooo looonnng.

However . . .

She rocked up onto her hands and knees and reached forward to grab the receiver off the phone on the nightstand. "Hello," she said just as Bobby's mouth resumed its activity. But this time, his fingers joined in the game just a few inches to the southeast, and she had to bite back a moan.

"Kaylee, it's Scott," said the caller. "Your sister just used your Visa to charge a room at the Mountain Crest Inn in Fort Collins, Colorado."

She reached back to grasp Bobby's wrist and halt

his marauding fingers. "Was she alone?"

"I don't know, but it was her who signed for it, not the bounty hunter. And if prices are anything to go by, the place is a lot nicer than the usual dives he's been checking her into."

"Oh, my God, Scott, thank you." She reseated the receiver and flipped over. "He found her." She grinned at the hot-eyed male crouched at the foot of the bed. "Bobby! He found her! And it's possible she's alone."

She started to scoot off the bed, but he grabbed her ankle and yanked her flat. He swarmed up the mattress to loom over her, his warm hand stroking down her stomach.

"Not so fast, baby. That's real good news, but another ten minutes isn't going to make or break the schedule." His fingers slid back to their warm nest between her legs.

"Come on, Bobby, this is serious." She dislodged his hand and rolled away.

"Damn!" He flopped onto his back. "I'm starting to seriously dislike your sister."

Kaylee's hands stilled. She set down the top she had picked up to fold and turned to look at him. Frustration rolled off him in waves as he glowered back at her. "Ah, don't be like that. Please. None of this is Catherine's fault."

He looked less than convinced, and it struck her that she was harboring some serious frustrations of her own. Which left her, oh goody gumdrops, with another adult-type decision to make. This being responsible was stressful stuff. How did Cat deal with it on a daily basis?

But back to the decision. Well, let's see. She could snap Bobby's head off for failing to fall in with her plans with better grace . . . or she could take care of the source of the problem for both of them.

She felt a slow smile tug up the corner of her mouth. Big contest.

"You know what? You're right." She laughed and dived back onto the bed, rolling to lie on top of him. "I mean, what can I say, big fella—when you're right, you're right." She wriggled around, nestling her breasts on his chest, and grinned down at him. "Ten minutes one way or the other's not gonna make or break the schedule."

Sam's fingers had been drumming out a nervous rhythm against the tabletop ever since he'd sat down in one of the easy chairs, tucked the phone receiver between his ear and shoulder, and punched out his Florida number. Breaking off mid-drum, he brought his little finger up, wiggled it in his free ear and withdrew it, inspecting its perfectly clean tip. Clearly he'd heard exactly what he thought he'd heard. Nevertheless, he said in disbelief, "You started what?"

"Computer classes, man," Gary's voice replied down the line. "I told you a couple a weeks ago I'd signed up for 'em. Damn, you gotta pay more attention when I'm talkin' to ya."

"Computers," he repeated blankly. His fingers slowly resumed their rhythm against the laminated surface of the tabletop. What was this? Gary had always scorned any job that would keep him indoors.

"Yeah, who'd a thunk it, huh? Turns out I have a real aptitude for the suckers. And it's a great way to meet chicks, Sam—more than half the class is sweet young things. There's this especially fine little blonde, sits next to me—the girl's really strugglin' to comprehend this stuff. I've helped her out a couple of times, and now she thinks I'm smarter 'n Alex Trebek." Gary's raspy laugh scratched its way down the line. "We're going out Friday night. So, hey, how about you? Still got the showgirl chained to your bed?"

Sam's fingers once again stilled. Shit. This was the part he'd been dreading. He levered himself upright and stretched the phone cord over to the window. "Uh, about her, Gare. There's sorta good news and bad news. The good news—for me, anyhow—is that she's pretty much in my bed voluntarily now."

"No shit? Way to go, Sambo."

"Yeah, but, uh, the bad news is, turns out she's not the showgirl after all. She's her twin sister."

There was dead silence for a moment. Then Gary said in a strangled voice, "You grabbed the wrong sister?"

"Yeah."

"Dudley Do-Right McKade *grabbed the wrong sister?*"

Jaw clenched, blind to the view on the other side of the glass, Sam braced his forearm against the window frame. His fist rose up, then thumped down, once, twice, three times.

Gary's laughter rolled down the line. "Oh, God,"

he gasped. "That's beautiful. So, if this one doesn't strut her stuff in minimum clothing for a living, what does she do?"

"Teaches the deaf," he mumbled.

"Say what? Ya gotta speak up, Sam, I didn't quite catch that."

"She teaches the deaf!"

Gary laughed himself sick.

"I'm glad you're so amused," Sam interrupted. "Because this means I'm gonna get bugger-all as bounty for her. And that means that unless I can find something else pretty damn pronto, the lodge is history."

The laughter stopped. "Ah, shit, man, have you been worryin' about that?" Before Sam could even begin to formulate a reply, Gary blew out a breath. " 'Course you have. Sam, listen to me," he said in a suddenly serious voice. "That's probably just as well."

"Dammit, Gare, you don't have to spare my feelings. I know I really screwed this up."

"Fuck your feelings, man. How the hell am I supposed to meet women in the wilds of North Carolina? Fishing lodges are usually chock-full of men—how many times did we ever go to that place when there were any chicks? Once, right? And the girl could cut bait, no doubt about it, but she chewed Red Man, Sam."

"You loved it there."

"Sure I did; it was a great place to get away . . . when I was meeting women on base or in town. But it's not the place for me now. Screw the lodge, man. Go join a police force somewhere."

Sam was still standing in the same place, in shock, brooding over the conversation, when Catherine let herself into the room fifteen minutes later. She smiled at him and wafted two fragrant bags in his direction.

"Barbecued beef sandwiches," she said. "Nice and sloppy." Noticing the phone still in his hands, she quirked an eyebrow. "You get hold of your friend?"

"Yeah."

She observed the sullen slant of his mouth, the moody eyes, both of which were a far cry from the lazy satisfaction of the man she'd left just a short while ago, and paused in laying out the food. "Uh-oh. He was furious, huh?"

"No, ma'am." Sam came over to the small table. Picking up a sandwich, he peeled back a corner of the wrapper and tore off a huge bite. Jaws working furiously, he chewed, and then swallowed audibly. He impaled her with furious golden eyes. "He says it's just as well the financing's going to fall through on the lodge, because it's not what he really wants anyhow."

She lowered her own sandwich and swallowed the much daintier bite she had taken. "But . . . that's good, isn't it?"

He looked at her as if she'd said something unutterably stupid. "It's bullshit, is what it is."

" 'Scuse me?"

"I said it's bullshit. I'm supposed to believe he doesn't want the place after all, because he can't meet women at a fishing lodge?"

That arrested her attention. "Oh! Can he still . . . ?" She made a vague movement with one hand, glancing instinctively at Sam's crotch, then hastily away, embarrassed to be so curious about someone else's sex life.

"Hell, yes he can still"—his explicit hand gesture mocked the genteel movement hers had made. "The man lives for pussy; he always has." He noticed the slight wash of color that rose in her cheeks and felt a flash of shame for his crudeness. "Sorry," he muttered. Still, the basic premise was true, and he thrust his chin out at her. "But it's a fact, dammit. It's the one thing that hasn't changed since the day we met. He's a hound for women and he's pursuing 'em as diligently as ever."

"So . . . I don't get it. What makes it so difficult to believe then that he might want to stay in a place where they're more readily available?"

"Come on, Red, *computers*?" He ripped off another bite of sandwich and chewed furiously.

Her eyebrows furrowed. "You've lost me."

"He says he's discovered a fuckin' aptitude for computers!"

"And this is bad, because . . . ?"

"Because he lived for the challenge of police work every bit as much as I did. And he always said he'd rather be dead than work at an indoor job!"

"For crying out loud, Sam!" She stared at him, incredulous that a guy so savvy could be so obtuse. "The man's life is not what it used to be, and it never will be again. But, bless his heart, he's getting on with it all the same. He's still chasing women—

which has to take guts from a wheelchair—and he's actively pursuing something to replace what he used to do. What part of that, exactly, don't you understand?"

"The part where he told me to screw the lodge and go join a police force somewhere!" He threw the remains of the sandwich into the sack. "Don't you get it, Red? He's doing this for me."

"Uh-huh. Well, let's just agree for a moment with that interpretation. You're going to—what?—throw his generosity back in his face? Save him in spite of himself?" She set down her own sandwich. "My God, there's nothing wrong with your ego, is there?"

"I don't know what you're talkin' about."

Because she could see that he honestly didn't, she tried to rein in her rising impatience. "You assume way too much responsibility for other people's problems," she gently pointed out—only to be immediately interrupted.

"This isn't about 'other people,' " he said impatiently. "This is about Gary. Whose life I messed up."

"Arrrgh!" She clutched fistfuls of her hair and tugged until her eyelids stretched. She glared up at him. "Dammit, Sam, you are the most stubborn pain in the ass I have ever met!"

He looked thoroughly insulted. "Because I don't shirk my responsibilities?"

"Who asked you to shoulder the damn things in the first place? Gary? I doubt that." She poked his hard chest with an irate finger. "He's a fully adult male. Who the hell are you to decide he's not competent to know what he wants?"

"I never did that," Sam roared. He took a large step forward, pushing his face close to hers, as if he could intimidate her by sheer size and proximity into taking back the accusation.

She pushed right back, angling to get her nose up under his. "In a pig's eye—that's *exactly* what you're doing. You're always so damn ready to take on everybody's problems. Well, maybe you should trust and respect your friends' abilities. Maybe we'd like to be accountable for our own actions. Did that ever occur to you? Huh? Did it, huh?"

He grabbed the finger jabbing him in the sternum and stared baffled into her furious green eyes. "Whataya mean, we? When did I ever step on your precious accountability?"

"Good God, Sam! What was it you said this morning—that you didn't think you could bear up under the burden if Chains shot me?"

"Well, shit, I couldn't."

She made a sound like steam escaping a teakettle at full boil. "When did *my* actions become your burden to bear? It was *my* decision to instigate the flanking maneuver. You have no control over what I do, Samuel McKade."

"I *told* you about the damn flanking maneuver. And I've been dragging you around the countryside for days—you wouldn't even be here for Chains to hurt if I hadn't snatched you from your house."

"My sister ditched me, knowing damn well you'd mistake me for her. So why isn't it *her* fault? Or no, wait, let's take this back even further. My mother gave birth to me. Since I'm not responsible for my own actions, I guess everything that's happened to me since the day I was born must be *her* fault."

"Christ, I'm getting a headache." He was also fully aroused, he realized. She might be totally infuriating, but he couldn't deny she was one exciting woman. He quit massaging his forehead and slid the flat of his hands down her warm, round ass, sinking his fingers in to pull her near. Leaning back from the waist, he looked down into her flushed face and then lower still. She was wearing her sister's revealing clothing again, and he presented her with his most reasonable expression as he rotated his pelvis lightly against her. "Life's too short, Red. What say you and me quit sweatin' the small stuff and . . ."

"I don't believe you!" She was a sudden flurry of elbows, knees, and shoving hands, and the next thing he knew, he was standing outside the motel room, staring at a closed and locked door.

"Red?" He thumped it with his fist. "Catherine! Let me in." Silence greeted his command, and he hit the panel harder. "Open the damn door, I said."

An anatomically impossible suggestion was the only reply he received, and, swearing, he shoved away from the door. Clearly there was no talking to her while she was in such an unreasonable mood.

He found a coffee shop downstairs and sat down to brood over the illogical emotionalism of women. Damn—why couldn't they be more like men? Analytical, rational. But, no. To hear them tell it, a guy would think taking his responsibilities seriously was a bad thing.

"Damn, son, you gotta pay more attention when I'm talkin' to ya."

He rolled his shoulders uneasily and nodded a curt thanks to the waitress who stopped by the table to top off his cup.

He paid attention.

Didn't he?

Hell, yeah. Just because he didn't want to see his friend's entire life messed up, merely so *he* could shrug off what he knew was his duty to run off and join the police force, didn't mean he wasn't paying attention. That was like saying he should stand by and watch a train wreck, when he could prevent the damn thing by kicking the debris that would derail it off the tracks. *Seeing* the frigging debris *was* paying attention.

Maybe you should trust and respect your friends' abilities. Maybe we'd like to be accountable for our own actions.

Sam's fist slammed down on the tabletop. Silverware clattered and several people swung around to see what the commotion was. A flush climbed his throat. Hunching his shoulders, he stared down into the impenetrable black surface of the coffee in his cup.

Damn her. Why couldn't she leave it alone? He was just trying to do what was right here. He was striving to pay off a debt that could never be repaid. He was . . .

Shit. He was an arrogant ass. Dudley Do-Right McKade, who thought his opinion was the only one that mattered, riding to the rescue once again.

Even if nobody needed or wanted to be saved.

Ah, man, what a joke. *You're not in the army now, boy. You're no longer the senior ranking noncom whose motto is The Buck Stops Here. Get used to it.*

Oh, God, and had he really tried to run an end play around Red's arguments with the suggestion of sex?

He was a dead man.

He sat and stewed about it over another cup of coffee, trying to find a way out of the hole he'd dug himself.

Flowers. Maybe if he got her some nice flowers, she'd let him back in the room some time today. All women liked posies, didn't they? Maybe he should call Gary back—his friend had always been lots better with women than he was.

He asked at the desk, but there wasn't a florist shop anywhere nearby. Big surprise—that would have been too simple. Well, that was that, then. Even though the chance of Chains putting in an appearance now was slim to none, only an idiot would waltz off and leave a threatened woman unprotected. He'd just have to go back to the room empty-handed.

Then the girl at the desk told him about a supermarket down the street that sold fresh-cut flowers. He could be there and back in five minutes, she said.

He almost leaned over the desk and kissed her on the spot. You just had to appreciate someone who'd quite possibly just saved your sorry butt.

Catherine heard the knock on the door and scowled. She'd seen Sam's key sitting on the tabletop after she'd thrown him out—did she really want to let him in?

No, she did not; she was still angry. On the other hand, what choice did she have? They were in this thing together, and besides, she could hardly drive how *stupid* he was being through his thick head if she made him stand out in the hallway all afternoon. With a long-suffering sigh, she yanked open the door.

And jumped in surprise to see her twin standing on the other side.

"Surprise," Kaylee said in her trademark throaty voice.

"Déjà vu," Catherine retorted blankly. Looking beyond her sister to the tall, black-haired man behind her, she added, "Except you weren't here the last time we did this. The much revered Bobby LaBon, I presume."

Kaylee tripped across the threshold and threw herself into her sister's arms, and Catherine hugged her back convulsively, suffused with a fierce joy that Kaylee had come after her.

"I'm sorry, Cat," Kaylee murmured in her ear as she gripped her fervently to her lush breast. "I'm so sorry I threw you into the middle of this."

"Yes, about that," Catherine said in sudden fury, pushing back to stare into her twin's face. "Do you know that Jimmy Chains Whatshisname has been trying his utmost to *kill* me? Look at me!" She spread her arms so her sister could take a look at the scratches and bites that marred her skin.

"I know, you look great!"

"*Great*? I rode a car down a cliff, I got dragged through the woods where I had to spend the night, I had a close encounter with a *spider*, and you say I look great? Look at me, Kaylee! I'm a mess!"

"Oh, my God, a spider? Ah, Catherine, I'm sorry."

"And well you should be—it scared the bejesus outta me. If Sam—"

"But those little bitty scratches hardly even show, and Sis, you look so *good* wearing some decent clothing for a change. Speaking of which, where's my suitcase? The weather these past few days has been hell on my complexion, and you've got all my good cosmetics."

"How do I break this to you, Kaylee? Your precious cosmetics are in the trunk of the car Jimmy Chains forced over the cliff."

She watched her sister pale as the reality of Catherine's situation apparently sank in for the first time. Bobby, who had been observing the byplay between them like a spectator at a tennis match, grasped Kaylee above the elbow and steered her away from the door, which he closed behind them.

"She gets a little sidetracked sometimes," he told Catherine. "But she's been bustin' her hump trying to get to you."

"He drove you off a cliff?" Kaylee wailed. "What else?"

"Pointed a gun at me a couple of times. Tried to run me down." She shoved a hand through her hair. "At least I think that was him. Look, come in out of the hallway," she invited. "We can talk. I'm really glad to see you, Kaylee. It means a lot that you came after me."

She led the way into the motel room. Bobby flopped down into a chair, but Kaylee remained standing, staring at Catherine in distress.

Her first words, however, were ones of admiration. "The way you slowed down the bounty hunter was nothing short of genius, Cat. I didn't know you had it in you to break so many rules."

"Guess I'm more like you than either of us ever would have thought, huh?"

Kaylee grinned. "Guess you are. And you're never gonna believe this, but I've actually got some of your less than exciting characteristics myself. So, how did you ever get away from him?"

"Get away from whom?"

"The bounty hunter, of course." Kaylee looked at her in sudden horror. "Oh, my God, Cat. You did shake him, didn't you? Please. Tell me he's not still here."

Sam should have figured five minutes was an optimistic time frame. It was closer to twenty by the time he stepped off the elevator and made his way to their room, a bunch of tulips clutched in one hand. He knocked on the door and wasn't surprised when Catherine failed to answer it.

He had a feeling she was going to make him work to regain her approval.

Well, he'd never get anywhere standing out here in the hall. He used the key the desk girl had supplied when he'd confessed he'd locked himself out, and opened the door. "Red?" he called softly. "I come bearing peace offerings, darlin'."

He walked down the short hallway. The drapes were open over the large window dead ahead, and he found himself looking almost directly into the sun. Raising the cellophane-wrapped tulips to shade his eyes, he squinted against the glare.

He was all the way into the motel room before he saw the dark-haired man seated in one of the easy chairs. And standing next to Catherine, he saw as his eyes adjusted, was her double.

Red's twin held a gun in her hand. She had about as much expertise as her sister in the handling of firearms, but it was nevertheless pointed determinedly, if less than steadily, right at his chest.

24

⌒⌒⌒ CATHERINE HAD DROPPED her bombshell only moments before, and its sheer unexpectedness had caught Kaylee flat-footed. With no time to recover from the shock, she'd snatched Bobby's gun out of her purse when she'd heard Sam's voice, ignoring both Bobby's and Cat's protests. Then, before she could even say "boo," the bounty hunter was suddenly in the room as well. He was big and dark and terrifying, despite the incongruous bunch of flowers in his huge fist and the soft tone of voice for her sister.

Though her heart was trying its utmost to pound its way out of her chest, he didn't seem particularly fazed. "Kaylee MacPherson, I take it," he drawled. He slowly lowered the flowers shading his whiskey brown eyes, which narrowed behind their screen of black lashes. "Put the gun down before somebody gets hurt," he commanded curtly. Ignoring her entirely, as if her compliance was to be taken for granted, he turned to Catherine and extended the cellophane-wrapped tulips. "Here," he growled. "These are for you. I'm sorry about earlier—I guess maybe I was a jerk."

Catherine reached out to accept the offering thrust at her, and clutched the damp bundle to her chest. Her nervous gaze remained glued to the wobbling gun. "Kaylee, please," she implored.

Kaylee wasn't accustomed to having a man totally disregard her. "Listen up, bud," she said to Sam's profile. "We aren't looking for any trouble. We're just going to collect Cat and then we're outta here. There's no need for anybody to get hurt."

Sam turned his head to look at her. "Get a new plan, lady. You're not taking her anywhere."

The blazing determination in his eyes sent Kaylee stumbling a hasty step backward. Then she caught herself and drew erect, thrusting out both chin and chest. "Listen, mister, *I've* got the gun here. You're not the one calling the shots."

The next thing she knew, she was staring down the barrel of *his* gun. Jayzus Jean, where had that come from? She hadn't even seen him draw the thing. "*Bobby*." To her eternal humiliation, her voice squeaked several octaves higher than normal, cracking on the first syllable.

Bobby came half out of the chair, but Sam's quiet command to sit down and the unwavering hand pointing the gun at Kaylee caused him to sink back onto the cushions.

"Sam!" Catherine wailed in protest, but he ignored her, too.

He looked at Kaylee, wondering how he'd ever

confused Catherine for her. They looked alike, yes. But once you knew the individuals, the differences were more striking than the similarities. "Bend down nice and slow and put the gun on the floor," he instructed her. She didn't respond quickly enough to suit him, and he snapped, "Do it!"

She did it.

"Now, push it over here with your foot."

Sulkily she kicked it across the carpet.

He picked it up and tucked it, along with his own, in the waistband of his jeans at the small of his back. Then he straightened and grinned with impartial cheer at the three people in front of him. "Well, now, this sure is an interesting situation, isn't it?"

"More interesting than you might'a thought," came a new voice from the doorway, and Sam, uttering a vicious, low-voiced obscenity, slowly turned.

Jimmy Chains walked down the short hallway. He raised a hand to shield his eyes as he stepped into the main body of the room, but at the same moment Sam realized the man's vision was impaired, Chains swung his gun around to cover him.

"Don't even think about it," he barked. "In fact, I'd think twice, if I were you, about taking a really deep breath. Even half-blind you make a big enough target to hit, and frankly, asshole, you're beginning to seriously hack me off."

"Don't want that," Sam muttered, but Chains wasn't listening. He was staring beyond him, his mouth agape.

"Twins?" he croaked. "Y'all are friggin' twins?"

"Well, I'm not sure that's the adjective I'd use,"

Catherine began, only to have Kaylee clamp a hand around her forearm and squeeze warningly.

Chains wasn't even listening. "Which one of y'all's Kaylee?" he demanded.

The sisters exchanged glances. Then, in unison, they turned back to Chains and said, "Me."

"Catherine," Sam snapped, at the same time that Bobby muttered, "Ah, shit."

Chains turned to the men. "So, who's who, then?"

Both men gave him a flat stare, and he snapped, "I'll fuckin' shoot 'em both."

"No you won't," Bobby disagreed. "Kaylee's sister's got nothing to do with this—she just got caught up in the mess. The Jimmy Chains I know could never gun down an innocent woman in cold blood."

"Yeah, well, maybe you don't know me as well as you think you do." But Chains didn't pursue it. He waved the gun at the men. "Get up, Bobby. And you, asshole, turn around." He made a circling gesture with his gun. "Assume the position, both of you."

Sam and Bobby placed their hands flat against the nearest wall and spread their feet, standing still while Chains patted them down for weapons. He removed the two guns from Sam's waistband. "Got me a righteous little arsenal," he murmured happily as he tucked them into his own waistband and stepped back. He pulled a length of rope from his pocket.

"You're gonna have to lend me a hand here, girls." He handed the rope to Catherine. "You two," he said to the men. "Lie back-to-back on the bed, hands behind you. Tie their wrists," he instructed her. "Shit, what do we use for their ankles? If I'd knowed there was gonna be two, I'd'a brought more rope." He looked around the room and crossed to the open drapes. Using his pocketknife, he cut the draw cords and thrust them at Kaylee. "Here. Tie their feet."

Several minutes later the men were neatly trussed, and Chains stood at the side of the bed to observe them with satisfaction. Hah! If all the assholes who'd ever called him stupid could only see him now.

Grinning, he stepped back. "Ladies." He gestured expansively, indicating the twins should precede him down the hallway. "After you." He laughed out loud as he closed the motel-room door behind them.

He wasn't nearly so pleased an hour later. Damn. He couldn't just keep driving around with two really built redheads in the car. They were way too conspicuous, and for all he knew the cops could be hot on his tail. He needed to get off the road and come up with a plan.

Twins. Man oh man, who the hell woulda thought it? And what the fuck was he supposed to do with the one wasn't Kaylee? He'd barely resigned himself to doing what had to be done to *her*, and it sure wasn't something he looked forward to. After all the frustration of chasing her around the country, it didn't seem quite as impossible as it had when he'd set out from Miami, but he didn't fool himself into thinking that it was gonna be easy, either.

He sure as hell didn't want to have to do the other one, too. So where did that leave him? And how did he figure out just who was who?

He pulled into the parking lot of a nice chain motel. If they had to be holed up for a while, it wasn't going to be in some fleabag, backwoods motor court. Parking close to the office, he turned to face his prisoners. "I'm gonna check us in. You two sit tight." He pinned them in place with a fierce stare. "I mean it. If I have to come chasing y'all down, I'll just friggin' shoot ya both and call it good. I'm tired of these nowhere burgs in goddamn Pioneerland. I wanna go back to civilization, and I ain't gonna be held up no longer than I gotta be." He climbed out of the car and slammed the door.

The sisters immediately turned to each other. "Are you all right?" they demanded simultaneously and then Kaylee added, "Jayzus, Cat, I'm sorry. This is such a mess."

"So, what do we do to make it better? I've got Sam's handcuffs. I took them when Chains was fooling around with the drapery cords." Catherine hooked a finger into her cleavage and pulled them out a fraction of an inch to show her sister, then tucked them back in. "I don't have the key, so if they get into his hands we're sunk. If we get a chance to use them first, though . . ."

"I slipped Bobby my nail scissors," Kaylee said. "It might take 'em a while to hack through those cords, but they'll be after us soon."

"How will they find us, though?"

Kaylee told her about their computer genius.

"Well, that's all fine and dandy," Catherine agreed. "But it'll only be effective if Chains uses a credit card to pay for the room. He'd have to be a total idiot . . ." She saw her sister's raised eyebrow and felt a slow smile crook up one corner of her mouth. "Okay. It's beyond dumb to think he can leave all the witnesses he's leaving and still get away with this, so I guess using a credit card is not outside the realm of possibility. He really isn't very bright, is he?"

"He's dumb as a post, but don't *ever* suggest that to his face." Kaylee reached over and gripped Catherine's thigh as if to underscore the importance of her warning. "I really don't think he's naturally mean, but I've seen him stomp bruisers the size of pickup trucks into paste for making fun of his stupidity."

"Then it's just as well that I told him he was smarter than Sanchez. And he said he'd always liked you, Kaylee. Maybe we can use that to our advantage."

"That and the fact he thinks civilization ends at the Florida border. There's gotta be something we can do with that."

They fell silent when they saw Chains come out of the office. He climbed into the car a moment later and drove them around to a unit at the back of the motel. "Everybody out," he commanded tersely.

They were barely inside the room when he grinned at them, clearly pleased with himself. "Hey, I just figured out how to tell y'all apart," he said. "Drop your pants."

"Excuse me?" Catherine demanded icily.

"Drop your drawers, girly-girl. Kaylee's got a tattoo on her butt."

"We *both* have a tattoo on our butt."

"Yeah, right," he scoffed. "Drop 'em."

She rolled her eyes but complied, easing her shorts down one cheek. More than that was unnecessary, since all Kaylee's panties had thong backs. Looking over her shoulder, she watched Chains' eyes light up.

"Hot damn! I knew it!"

"Uh, Jimmy?" Kaylee said. While he'd been busy looking at Catherine, she'd bared her own butt. He left off congratulating himself long enough to glance over at her.

"Shit!"

"We're twins, Jimmy," Catherine said gently while she and Kaylee straightened their clothing.

"I *know* you're twins," he snarled. "But why the hell wouldja wanna get the same friggin' tattoo?"

She shrugged. "It was a teenage rebellion against our mama."

He swore again and jammed his fingers through his hair. "I was hopin' to avoid this, but I guess I gotta call the boss."

"Ooh, Jimmy." Kaylee shook her head at him. "I don't think that's a good idea at all."

"Why the hell not?"

"Because it's really not in your own best interests. Hector arranged this whole thing so that you'd take the fall if things went wrong."

"Hector wouldn't do that—he's my friend."

"Or so he'd love you to believe." She reached out to give his arm a compassionate little pat. "But Hector's only friend is Hector."

"Things are kind of falling apart here, Chains," Catherine contributed in a sympathetic voice and he swung around to stare at her. She stepped a little farther away from Kaylee. "Are you prepared to kill both of us?"

"If I have to."

"Here, in this room? The desk clerk saw your face. Won't he connect you?"

"Uh . . ."

"And what about Bobby and Sam?" Kaylee queried, and Chains swung back. "They're witnesses now, too. You can't kill everybody. And you know what Hector will say? He'll claim to know nothing about it. He'll leave you twisting in the wind when all you did was try your very best to help him out. Worse, he's going to say something mean about your intelligence."

"The hell he will! You're full of shit and I'm gonna prove it right now!" He stepped away from both of them and picked up the telephone. Glaring from one to the other, he punched out the number of the Tropicana Club.

"Dammit, LaBon, would you take a little care? That's the tenth time you've jabbed me."

"Hey, I'm sorry, but these aren't the most ideal circumstances, ya know? I'm doin' the best I can."

"Well, try to do it without letting any more of my blood, huh?"

"Believe it or not, McKade, that's my goal. You keep bleeding all over the place, and I'm not gonna be able to keep a grip on these stupid little scissors."

Sam snorted. That hadn't exactly been his primary concern.

He and Bobby had set to work on their bindings as soon as the door closed behind Chains and the twins. The cords around their ankles had been fairly simple. They'd managed to keep a good deal of space between their feet when Kaylee tied them up; she was lousy with knots; and Chains hadn't checked her work. The bindings on their wrists were a different story. Catherine had left them as much slack as she'd dared, but it wasn't enough to work their hands free. So, they'd maneuvered themselves to an upright position and now sat back-to-back on the bed, while Bobby blindly and clumsily manipulated the manicure scissors between them, snipping away at the cords that bound their wrists.

Sam strained with impatience. It was all he could do to sit still and keep his mouth shut, when what he really wanted was to bellow his rage and assign blame. Nevertheless, when the implement slipped and once again stabbed into the underside of his wrist, he gritted his teeth and kept his complaint to himself.

"There!"

The exclamation was unnecessary, as Sam felt the thin ropes loosen, then sag over their wrists. Awkwardly, they fought their way free and then leaned against each other for an instant, as they painfully straightened their stiff shoulder joints to rotate their arms back to a more natural position.

Finally free, Sam found himself strangely paralyzed. He looked down at his nicked wrists. "Will he kill them?" he demanded rawly.

"Not if they're careful, I don't think."

"Great." A hoarse bark of laughter escaped his throat. "Catherine's never careful."

Bobby craned his neck around. "According to Kaylee she is. And smart, too."

"Yeah. She's damn smart."

"So's Kaylee, but Jimmy Chains isn't. They'll be okay." Bobby straightened his back away from the support of Sam's. "I'm going to call Scott." He climbed off the bed and turned to look down at him. "You'd better clean those cuts. By the time you're finished, I'll be done with the phone and you can call the cops."

Sam felt a fierce compulsion to be the one to rescue Catherine, but pushed it down as he climbed to his feet. To reject the help of either Bobby or the police would be irresponsible.

And while he was beginning to understand that at times his need to be fully accountable and play by the book was a bit obsessive, today it was crucial. This was no time to start running around half-cocked like some steroid-fed hotdogger.

Besides, it wasn't his sense of responsibility that Red had questioned—it was taking on the entire burden of responsibility when things went wrong. But nothing would go wrong this time.

It couldn't.

Jesus, God, please, don't let it.

For he had this sick, tangled feeling deep in his gut that told him if anything happened to Catherine, he would never recover.

* * *

As Chains punched out numbers on the phone, Catherine caught Kaylee's eyes. Using sign language, she quickly explained the basics of Sam's flanking maneuver and mapped out a possible use for it.

Kaylee's right hand, palm up and fingers bent, moved up and over to touch her fingertips to her left palm. *Again.*

Catherine repeated the plan.

"Why the hell are you flapping your hands around?" Chains suddenly demanded, looking up from the phone.

"Sorry, I'm nervous," she retorted, and shook them out before bringing one up to rub the back of her neck. "It calms me." She watched Kaylee take advantage of having his diverted attention to sign back that she understood. But then she added a variation.

Catherine mouthed No! but then forced the contours of her mouth into a sickly smile when Chains frowned at her.

"Well, knock it off, 'cuz it *annoys* me. Hi, Hector?" Jimmy dismissed the women as his attention was drawn back to the phone. "It's me, Chains."

"I trust you're calling to report satisfactory results on the Kaylee situation," came the cool reply.

"Well, about that, boss"—he cleared his throat—"I've got a slight problem."

There was an instant of silence. "What problem?" Hector demanded coldly.

"Did you know she's got a twin?"

"What!"

"A twin. And she's here."

"So, what's the problem," Hector snapped. "Take care of both of them."

Jimmy Chains straightened away from the wall he'd been leaning against. "I can't just kill some innocent woman," he protested. "Besides, there's the matter of LaBon and the bounty hunter. They know I got the girls, boss. If I start killing everyone involved, there's gonna be bodies stacked up like cordwood. It's gettin' kinda complicated."

"Listen, you fucking idiot, I sent you there to—"

"What did you call me?" Chains interrupted, a mist of red rage starting to rise behind his eyes.

"A fucking idiot," Hector yelled. "I gave you an assignment Simple Simon could've handled, and what'd you do? You turned it into a goddamn circus! Well, listen to me good, Chains, because I'm not taking the heat on this—"

Chains slammed down the receiver and stood, chest heaving and eyes blindly staring, trying to suck air into his lungs.

"I'm sorry, Jimmy," Kaylee said softly, and his eyes slowly focused to find her watching him with what he took to be pity. "He's going to leave you holding the bag, isn't he?"

He took a step forward. In the same motion, he drew his gun and pointed it at straight at her heart. "Not if I take care of the situation the way I'm s'posta."

"That will certainly work well for Sanchez," Catherine said, and he swung around to aim the gun at her. "Inevitably you'll be connected to one of the bodies, and he'll simply claim you went off on a rampage."

"Shaking his head in sorrow that any employee of his could do such a dreadful deed," Kaylee added. When he swung back to cover her, it seemed she was farther to his right than she'd been a moment ago.

"I'll fuckin' bring him down with me!"

"Who's gonna believe you, Jimmy, if it's only your word against his? He's a respected businessman in the community, and you're just a bouncer. I'm the only one who could back up your story, but then I'll be dead, won't I?" She took a step closer to him. "And you know what the worst part is? They're gonna stick you in a prison right here in Palookaville, and you'll never see Miami again."

Chains blanched.

"You could turn state's evidence, though," Catherine said, and, gun sagging at his side, he whipped around to see that she'd somehow drifted all the way behind him. "If you turned yourself in, you could cut a deal in exchange for your testimony."

"Even if you had to do time, it would be in *Florida*, Jimmy," Kaylee said, and he turned around yet again. She was standing directly in front of him. "You're an intelligent guy. Think about it. I bet they'd reduce the sentence down to practically nothing if you cooperated."

"Ya think?"

"Oh, yeah, I do. And why should Hector get off scot-free while you do the time?"

"Yeah," Chains agreed belligerently. "That don't seem fair."

"It's not." She extended her hand. "Can I have the gun, Chains?"

He stiffened up. "Hell, no."

"I'm sorry to hear that, because I was really hoping for a little dignity here. But I guess we're reduced to the Three Stooges routine."

He felt a corner of his mouth kick up. He'd always loved the Three Stooges. "What the hell you talkin' about, girl?"

"This."

And thrusting his gun hand wide of his body, she gave him a hard shove. Simultaneously, Catherine kicked his feet out from under him. He went over like a toppled tree, the gun spinning across the room when his hand cracked against a chair leg on his way down.

Roaring with rage, he started to roll up onto one hip so he could grab the spare gun in the small of his back. A high-heeled shoe clamped down on his crotch, the leather sole pressed firmly to his dick, the spike grazing his scrotum with unmistakable threat.

He froze, staring up a long white leg, past thrusting breasts, to Kaylee's face peering solemnly back at him. He barely breathed, knowing the least amount of weight could drive that spike deep.

Turning him into a permanent soprano in an instant.

25

"PLEASE," KAYLEE SAID gently. "Don't move. I truly don't wanna hurt you, Jimmy. But I will, if you push it."

With exaggerated, nonthreatening slowness, he spread his hands to either side of his head. "I ain't movin'. See here? I'm just lyin' here nice an' quiet."

Catherine squatted by his side and slid her hand beneath his back to relieve him of his weapons. Setting them aside, she scowled up at her sister. "Dammit, Kaylee, you weren't supposed to keep diverting his attention away from me like that. He could have shot you!"

"Fish out the handcuffs, so we can tie him up, Sis, and grab a rope for his ankles. I *told* you there would be a slight variation on your big plan. This was my mess, so why should you be the one put in danger? Jayzus Jean, Cat, you've been whining forever about—"

"I do not whine!"

"—me taking responsibility for my actions. Well, I took responsibility, but now that doesn't suit you either. Make up your damn mind."

Catherine snapped a cuff on one of Chains's wrists and eased it down by his side. She tapped his shoulder. "Put your other hand behind you and roll over a bit so I can fasten them together." Then she looked up at her sister. "You're right, you're right; I'm sorry. I'm beginning to sound just like Sam, and that's not what I want." She smiled. "You did really well, Kaylee. I'm proud as punch of you."

"That's more like it."

Sliding her fingers gingerly into Chains's front pocket, she extracted his knife. Then she looked at the three-inch-heeled shoe that rendered him very, very docile and grinned up at her sister. "Now there's a piece of anatomy you just gotta love, huh, Kaylee? It's simply one of those delicious little ironies that makes life so very rewarding, don't you think?"

"What the hell are you babbling about, little ironies?"

She gave her sister's threatening foot a gentle pat. "Why, sugar, how man's greatest asset can turn into his biggest liability in the blink of an eye, of course."

Kaylee grinned down at her. "Oh. Yeah. That delicious little irony. That is a peach, isn't it?"

Catherine cut the drapery cords and firmly bound Chains's feet. Kaylee slowly withdrew her spiked heel and watched as he took his first truly deep breath. "How y'doin', Jimmy—you want to sit up or anything?"

"Nah. I'll just stay right here, if it's all the same to you."

"Sure enough. You know, we weren't just jerkin'

your chain earlier. You really should try to cut yourself some kind of deal in return for testifying against Hector. Don't let him get away with treating you like a fool, because you're a whole lot smarter than he gives you credit for."

"Yeah, I'll think on that."

"I called the police," Catherine said softly from over by the bed. "And I'm going to try the room at the Inn." She hung up a moment later and joined her sister. "There's no answer, so I talked to the front desk. They'll notify security and send someone up." Leading Kaylee away, she said in a low voice, "You do know, don't you, that you're going to have to turn yourself in now, as well?"

Kaylee blew out a breath, and, gripping the hem of her spandex skirt, gave a thoughtful little full-body undulation to distribute the material evenly over the lush landscape of her curves. "Yeah. I know. I guess I'll let your bounty hunter take me back." She cocked her head and observed her sister with speculative eyes. "Speaking of which, Sis . . ."

"I bet we can get those auto-theft charges dropped," Catherine said.

"Oh, I'm counting on it. What *you* shouldn't count on is changing the subject. What's the story between you and Tall, Dark, and Dangerous?"

Catherine looked left, right, and sideways. Finally, she met her sister's eyes. "Oh, God, Kaylee, I think I'm in love. No." She shook her head impatiently. "There's no think about it; I know I am, and isn't that *crazy*? It's only been—what?—five or six days? I've lost all track of time. At first, when he snatched me from home, I just wanted to make him pay for turning my nice, orderly world upside down. Then I tried to hinder his progress in any way I could, to make it cost him in both time and money. But, God, he's so damn sexy, and he's sweet to little old ladies, and can be depended on *way* beyond good sense to be accountable for his actions—"

"Which would make him your soul mate for sure."

"And now I want to have his *babies*, and I don't have a clue how he feels about me or what he wants out of this relationship. What if it's merely to screw my brains out until we hit Miami?"

"Is he any good at that?"

Catherine's eyes glazed. "Oh, God, yeah."

"And from the looks of him when he looks at you, I'd say you are, too. Which I gotta tell ya, Sis—even if you are my twin—kinda surprises me." Her shoulders hitched in a little shrug. "Still, that's good news. Guys are a lot like kitchen floors—lay 'em right the first time and you can walk all over them for years." She gave her sister a grin and a companionable bump of her hip. "Trust me, Cat, you've got nothing to worry about. This one's in the bag."

Catherine's bark of laughter was tinged with hysteria. "I think you've got that backwards. I mean, I never knew it could *be* like that."

"That may be, but you obviously haven't let it turn you into one of those idiot women who immediately give up their own identity to become some guy's doormat. The man was bringing you flowers and telling you he was a jerk, for God's sake. This is a very good sign."

Catherine waved her words aside. "Oh, that's just because we had a fight over his ridiculous compulsion to shoulder the blame every time something goes wrong. Well," she admitted, "that and the way he thought he could use sex to make me drop the subject when I called him on it. Not exactly romantic."

"Honey-chile, flowers are always romantic. Besides, you didn't see the look in his eyes when I told him Bobby and I were there to take you away. I did, and it scared the shit outta me."

"About Bobby." Catherine latched on to the excuse to divert the subject. "For a guy you never bother to talk to, he certainly seems to know you inside and out."

Kaylee came as close to looking diffident as she ever got. "Actually, we've been doing quite a bit of talking this week. He thinks we should move to Vegas together." If her shrug was intended to convey indifference, her eyes told an entirely different story. "'Course, that might prove a tad difficult if I get my butt tossed in jail."

"I meant it when I said we'd get that sorted out, Kaylee. And I'm happy that your relationship with him is working out. He seems to care about you a great deal."

The police arrived a few moments later, and the twins were caught up in a whirlwind of activity as their statements were taken and Chains was led to a far corner of the room, where he was kept under close guard. It was into the midst of this that Sam and Bobby burst onto the scene.

Sam searched through what appeared to be a huge crowd of people until he zeroed in on Catherine. With Bobby hot on his heels, he plunged into the room, making a beeline straight for her. Grabbing her by the upper arms, he hauled her onto her toes and held her at arm's length while he surveyed her from head to foot, searching for injuries. He wanted to yank her into his arms and wrap her in a full-body hug the way Bobby was doing to Kaylee, but he felt constrained not only by his sense of responsibility for putting her in this predicament in the first place, but by the roomful of observant strangers. "You okay?"

It didn't escape his notice that she didn't launch herself into his arms, either. She merely stared back at him with unfathomable green eyes and nodded.

"So, what happened? LaBon and I have been worried." He glanced over at Bobby and Kaylee, who unlike him seemed not at all averse to putting on a public display. Just when he thought he was going to have to search out a damn fire hose, however, they pulled apart and joined him and Red. He thrust his fingers through his hair and gave Catherine a helpless stare. "How the hell'd you get away?"

She and Kaylee took turns explaining, tripping over each other's words.

She was so bright and inventive, and his last legitimate reason for keeping her at his side was fast slipping away. "Has anyone called in the feds?" he asked, and when Cat and Kaylee informed him they didn't think so, he reluctantly turned away to seek out the man in charge.

Within an hour, the FBI had arrived and everyone's statements had either been taken or gone over once again. Matters were finally sorted out to all of the various agencies' satisfaction, and Chains was led away after assurances he would be extradited to Miami. Gradually, the room cleared of law-enforcement officers.

Sam rejoined Bobby and the twins. Stopping in front of Kaylee, he said, "I have to take you back to Florida." That was bound to make him real popular with Red.

"Yeah, I know," Kaylee agreed.

He glanced at Catherine, but she was looking at him as if expecting him to say something germane. His gut in an uproar and his mind sluggish and dull, germane was simply beyond him. "I'll, uh, just make some reservations on the first flight I can find back to Miami, then."

"Make one for me, too," Catherine said quietly. She reached out to grip her sister's hand, giving him a look he couldn't even begin to decipher.

"And one for me," Bobby agreed.

Feeling hunted and in the wrong and not quite sure why, he snapped, "You're paying for your own, LaBon."

"Whatever." Bobby shrugged it aside as a minor detail and turned to Kaylee. "I'll turn myself in the minute we get there, baby," he promised her urgently. "You aren't going to pay for my screwup a minute longer."

She flung herself in his arms. "Oh, God, Bobby, what a mess. I love you, you know."

"I love you, too, baby."

Her laugh was short on humor. "Fat lot of good it does either of us."

"Speak for yourself, baby. It does me a lot of good."

"Yeah, but Bobby, I sure liked the idea of Vegas. Instead," she said glumly, "one of us is going to rot in jail."

"Nah." He gave her a squeeze. "That's not gonna happen." Leaning back, he rubbed his hands up and down her hips and flashed her his charmer's grin. "Trust me, baby. We'll see Vegas yet. I'm going to work it all out."

Bully for you, Sam thought sourly as he tried to catch Catherine's eye, only to be summarily ignored. The criminal's gonna get it all worked out.

The good guys's gonna get bugger all.

"Hector Sanchez?"

Hector gave the man in the cheap suit an impatient look, but broke off giving instructions to his bartender to attend to him. Seeing there was not one but two suit-and-tie-clad men awaiting his attention gave his nerves a twinge, but he said coolly, "I'm Sanchez. How can I help you gentlemen?"

"You're under arrest for soliciting the murder of Alice Mayberry. You have the right to remain silent—"

"That fuckin' Chains," Hector snarled under his breath. Starting to sweat, he looked at his bartender, who gaped at him as one of the cops pulled Hector's arms behind his back and cuffed him while the other droned the Miranda warning. "Call my lawyer," he instructed as he was led away. "His number's in my Rolodex on the desk. You hear me, Rex?" he snapped as the man continued to stare in openmouthed shock at the scene that was unfolding. "Call my friggin' lawyer."

"You're an idiot, Sam, you know that?"

Sam glared down at Gary, then executed a precise about-face on his heel and strode away.

Gary wheeled along in his wake. "So, you gonna just let her go back to Seattle without a fight? You even bothered to declare yourself, man, or state your damn intentions?"

Sam swung around to face him, belligerence written in every clenched muscle. "Maybe my intentions were just to get me a red-hot piece of ass and then get the hell outta Dodge."

"Yeah, right. That's why you've been prowling around here for the past day and a half, snappin' and snarlin' and generally making it worth a guy's life just to try to get near you."

"So get the fuck away then, why don't you," Sam roared. He jammed his fingers through his hair and stared down at Gary with an abject misery he desperately tried to pretend he wasn't feeling. "Jesus, Gare, a cop I know downtown tells me LaBon sweet-talked the woman whose car he stole clean out of pressing charges. Don't that just beat all? He's gonna skate without a single repercussion."

"What the hell's that got to do with your teacher?"

"Don'tcha see? Her sister's life is gonna be all settled. I doubt Red'll stick around long after that."

"Chrissake, man, why should she? Have you even bothered to try to *talk* to the woman?"

"Yes, dammit, I have! I went over there this afternoon to do exactly that, even though the facts pretty much speak for themselves—"

"And how d'you figure that?"

"Hell, you haven't seen her seeking me out, have you? She's probably ten kinds of relieved to see the last of me, but I went to talk to her anyhow, because I admit I have a history of making some assumptions that are all wrong."

The sound that emanated from Gary's throat was one of heartfelt agreement, but he resisted adding his two cents' worth. They'd been over what he wanted out of his life, as well as his refusal to take Sam's bounty money, too many times already. "And . . . ?"

"And nothing, Gare. She wasn't home. So I put the return ticket I bought her in Kaylee's mailbox."

"I hope you took particular care wording the note so she knows you don't really want her to use the damn thing."

"Huh?"

"Ah, Christ, Sam, tell me you didn't just leave her the ticket. You left a message to go with it, right?"

Sam stared down at him in frustration. "What the hell am I supposed to say in a note?"

"Shit." Gary reared back on his wheels and spun the chair around. Wheeling furiously across the floor in the opposite direction from his friend, he snarled over his shoulder, "Like I said before, Sam. Sometimes you can be a total fuckin' idiot."

26

〰〰 "YOU ASK ME," Kaylee said as she and Catherine approached her salmon-colored stucco apartment house, "the man's a total freakin' idiot. And it surprises me, frankly, because he strikes me as someone who goes after what he wants, and I know damn well he's hot to own you."

"Oh, there's pleasant imagery," Catherine said.

"Well excuse the hell outta me, but I saw the guy's eyes and trust me, he definitely had ownership on his mind." Kaylee let them into the miniscule lobby and then unlocked her mailbox. Scooping out the contents, she stuffed everything into her purse. She turned to her sister. "You sure you won't change your mind and come out celebrating with us?"

"Positive."

"It'd do you good."

"No, you guys go ahead. You and Bobby could use some time alone, and I'm really not in the mood to party anyway."

"Okay, then." Kaylee opened her apartment door and preceded Catherine into the living room. "Just let me find that spare key. I don't know why I didn't think to do this earlier."

"Probably because we've been together practically every waking minute." Catherine was anxious for her sister to leave, in desperate need of a little privacy. "Listen, if you can't find it, it really doesn't matter," she said. "Where am I going to go?"

"You never know—ah, here it is." Kaylee tossed it into a dish atop the end table. "It'll be there if you need it. Well, I guess we'll see you later then, huh?"

"Yeah, have fun." Go, go, *go*. "Don't *worry* about me, Kaylee," she urged as her sister hesitated at the door. She pasted on a smile. "I'll be fine, honest. Go have a wonderful time—you've earned it. I'm really proud of you, you know. You did all the right things for all the right reasons."

Kaylee smoothed the stretchy Lycra fabric that hugged her hips. She met her twin's eyes. "I'm kinda proud of me, too. I've learned a helluva lot in the last week, not the least of which is that I'm not as dumb as I always thought I was. Well!" She fluffed up her bouffant hairdo and thrust out her breasts. "Let's not get all sickeningly mushy here or the next thing you know, my mascara's gonna be all over the place and I'll look like a damn raccoon. I'm outta here." She turned to the door but then turned back, reaching into her voluminous bag. "Oh, here. Separate out the mail for me, wouldja?" She handed it over, wiggled her flame-manicured fingertips at her sister in a jaunty wave, and tripped on out the door.

Catherine's smile disappeared. Tossing the mail onto the end table next to the key, she flopped down on the couch, leaned her head back, and stared up at the ceiling, expelling all the air from her lungs in one harsh, unhappy exhalation.

God, she'd forgotten how miserably humid Florida got in the summertime. The nearly palpable air was hot and heavy, and it made her feel downright ill.

A bitter laugh escaped her as she raised her arm, using the back of her wrist to blot beading sweat from her forehead and cheeks. Yeah, right. Like the weather was what ailed her.

What the hell had happened here? Kaylee wasn't the only one who'd expected Sam's intentions to run deeper than a temporary shack-up. Yet it seemed that one minute they'd been making love in the shower, and in the next, events had taken off like a runaway freight train. By the time matters were under control again, he'd reverted into the one-track-minded, sullen-mouthed man she'd first encountered a week ago. How could she have so misjudged the situation?

And how on earth was it possible for her life to have gotten so thoroughly scrambled in such a brief span of time?

She wanted to go home. To the comforting familiarity of her own house, where she'd be free to lick her wounds in private. To a wardrobe that didn't thrust every blessed inch of her body into prominence, and a life that was safe and carefully planned out.

Okay, maybe it sounded just the tiniest bit . . . boring. But things were bound to seem different once she got back to her real life.

Blotting her face with the crook of her elbow, she went to the thermostat and punched up the air. Then she returned to the couch and reached for Kaylee's mail. She'd sort it as requested, then search out the phone book and call a few airlines to see about flights.

She had flipped through a phone bill, a credit-card offer, and a postcard from New Hampshire wishing Kaylee was there, before her hands stopped at the airline folder with her name printed on the front. Going very still, she simply sat for a moment, staring at it. Then she flipped it open and extracted a one-way ticket to Seattle. It was scheduled to leave Miami the day after tomorrow.

It was a no-brainer to figure out who'd left it for her, and she was suddenly engulfed in fury. Pure, mindless, white-hot fury.

She had no idea how she reached Sam's apartment. She didn't remember calling a taxi, and she couldn't recall the ride from Kaylee's. One minute she'd been sitting on her sister's couch staring with mind-screaming rage at the ticket in her hand . . . and the next she was pounding on a screen door, her breath coming too quickly as her free hand curved over her eyes to block out the sun, straining to see down a darkened hallway.

She gave the panel a furious kick when her summons was not immediately answered. "Open the damn door, you lousy coward!"

*   *   *

Gary propelled his chair out of the kitchen and into the hallway. The relentless clamor at the front door was starting to scrape on his nerves. "I'm coming, I'm coming already," he snapped. "Hold your damn horses."

Wheeling up to the door, he leaned forward to slap the screen's handle, unlatching the door and bumping it open an inch. It was immediately grabbed from the other side and yanked wide, and the sight before him made his jaw go slack.

"Ho-ly sh . . ." Swallowing the imprecation, he stared with undiluted admiration at the redhead on his doorstep. Sam was right, she had real white skin. He hadn't bothered to mention, however, that she was tall and built to stop a strong man's heart. Color high, her hair blazing under the harsh afternoon sun, she glared down at him with eyes turned a brilliant green by temper.

"No wonder he's been draggin' around here like a 'gator with a bad tooth," he murmured. Rolling back from the doorway, he waved her in. "I take it y'got the ticket."

"Where is he?" Blotting her brow with the back of her forearm, Catherine looked around as if expecting Sam to materialize out of the woodwork. She strode over to the nearest open door and yanked it open, calling out his name imperiously.

Gary rolled along in her wake. "He's not here, miss. He ran down to the store to get a pack of smokes. You want a beer?"

For the first time she looked at him as if she actually saw him. Her eyebrows gathered over her nose. "Sam doesn't smoke."

"Yeah, actually he does, or did, anyhow—up until a couple weeks ago. He's been kickin' the habit, but then about fifteen minutes ago he decided why bother."

"Yes, he apparently thinks 'why bother' about a lot of things," Catherine agreed bitterly.

"Now, I can't say I agree with you there." Before he could formulate a defense to save his friend's butt, however, he heard the screen door creak open and then bump closed again. Ah, hell, too bad—he could have used a little time to get the redhead cooled down. He spun his chair around to intercept his buddy, but it was too late. Sam appeared in the doorway, eyes moody, an unlit cigarette drooping from the corner of his mouth. "You got company," was the best Gary could do to warn him.

Sam had already spotted Catherine, and he stopped dead, his heart beginning to surge heavily against his rib cage, every sense suddenly, painfully alive. God, it felt like months since he'd seen her last, instead of just two days ago. But she was here.

That was the good news.

The bad news was, she was clearly furious. Damn, he should have listened to Gary—he could see that now. He sent his friend a quick glance to see if he had any bright ideas to bail him out of the mess he'd made. Apparently not; Gary was wheeling himself out of the room.

Straightening, he watched warily as Red stalked across the room toward him. Okay, so it was a mistake not to have left a message with the plane ticket. But she was here now and he could fix it. "Now, Catherine," he began in a placating tone.

She slapped the offending ticket against his chest and thrust that imperious school-marm nose up at him. The cigarette he'd forgotten poked against the belligerent angle of her chin and she batted it out of her way with her free hand. Cheeks flushed and eyes flashing green fire between narrowed lashes, she glared up at him, and against all reason, he felt better than he had in the past forty-eight hours.

"You wanna know what you can do with this, McKade?" She demanded, grinding the ticket into his pectorals.

"Burn it?"

"Oh, you can set it on fire, for sure. And while it's in full flame, why don't you just shove it where the sun don't—"

Fingers sliding into her hair to clasp her head in both hands, he stamped his mouth over hers, cutting off the rest of her suggestion. Her eyes flared wide and she grabbed his wrists, pulling on them, but he held fast and took advantage of the fact that her mouth was open mid-rant. It was enough to slide his tongue in, and . . . *there*, yes, right there. God, she tasted so good. He wasn't letting her go this time without a fight.

He kissed her until the rigidity left her spine and she slumped against his chest. Kissed her until her eyes slid closed and her mouth went soft and hot in response. Then he backed her against the nearest vertical surface and kissed her some more.

Eventually he pulled his mouth free and kissed her cheekbone, her cheek, her chin, her throat. "I'm sorry," he said, and his voice felt rusty as old pipe. He cleared his throat but still sounded hoarse when he said, "God, Red, I'm sorry—I screwed up. It's just that I felt so responsible for getting you into that mess and I was scared—no, Christ, I was terrified— that Chains would hurt you. And it would have been all my fault."

She slugged him in the chest. "We've *had* this conversation. You aren't responsible for the world!"

He wrapped his fist around hers. "Yeah, I know that . . . here." He brought her entrapped hand up and tapped it against his temple. Then he brought it down and unfurled her fingers, pressing them to his chest. "But here, I'm still working it out, ya know? I get tunnel vision sometimes and forget to look at the big picture. Then just when I think I've learned all these important new lessons, they get all scrambled up, and I revert to my old ways." He tucked her against his chest and ground his chin against the top of her head.

She fiddled with his faded T-shirt where it tucked into his waistband. "You weren't just sulking because you didn't get to do all the rescuing?"

"No!"

"I know how you like to be in charge of every last detail."

"I was proud of you. Hell"—the noise from his throat was half snort, half laugh—"I was even proud of your sister. Y'all not only got the best of a man who had three guns; you talked him into turning state's evidence while you were at it."

"You didn't act proud," she disagreed. "You acted as if I didn't exist. Bobby was kissing and carrying on with Kaylee and what'd you do? Gave me a quick once-over and then set me aside so you could go play cops. I wish you'd just join the darn force for real."

"Hey," he said, stung, "you didn't exactly throw yourself into my arms, either."

"Yes, well, that was because . . ." She bit off whatever she'd intended to say, and he felt a sudden tension in her posture. He leaned back to peer into her face.

"It was because what?"

"Nothing, never mind. You know what?" She thrust her chin up at him. "Maybe your reasons are just so much baloney. Maybe the truth is, you had my sister and your stupid bounty and didn't need me anymore. You sure as hell dumped me fast enough."

Even though part of him recognized it as a diversionary tactic, it nevertheless worked. Brilliantly. "Bullshit!" he roared, letting her go. "You *know* that's bullshit! Maybe I'm not good at spilling my guts in front of a crowd like your sister's precious Bobby, but I was going to talk to you on the plane. Then our seating assignment got all screwed up and I didn't get a chance, and I guess I, uh . . . lost my nerve, okay? Chickened out. I blamed me for the whole lousy situation and figured you did, too, and I backed away from putting my feelings on the line."

Catherine stared up into his golden brown eyes,

watched as he plowed his big hand through his hair in frustration. She took a deep, calming breath. Then, easing it out, she summoned all her nerve.

Instead of demanding to know exactly what those feelings were, she took the biggest risk of her life and gave him hers instead. "I love you, Sam."

"What?" He went very still, his hand arrested mid-sweep in his dark hair, elbow pointed to the ceiling.

"I love you. That's why I didn't throw myself in your arms back at the motel room. I'd just sorta admitted to *myself* how I felt, and then suddenly you were there—but you were all businesslike and aloof, and I didn't think you'd want to hear it."

Slowly, his arm lowered. "Oh, yeah—I'd want to hear it. I'd definitely want to hear it." He swallowed, and his Adam's apple slid up and down the length of his throat. "I kept telling myself it's not possible to fall in love in a week. But I want to rush you in front of a preacher, change the laws to outlaw divorce, and bind you to me with as many legal ties as I can find or invent. Jesus, Red, I've been so miserable. I thought you were gonna leave and go back to your life and forget all about me, and it paralyzed me. You could have anyone you want—what the hell would you want with me?" He bent his knees to bring his face to her level. With gentle fingertips he slid her hair behind her shoulders, then ran his hands lightly up and down the bare length of her arms. "But I love you, Red. God, I love you so much." He picked up her hand and gave her a crooked grin. "So whataya say: you wanna get married?"

"Well, I don't know." She looked up at him through a screen of lashes. "I just learned you're a smoker. I *really* don't like smoking." He could have a three-pack-a-day habit and she'd still jump at the chance to make him hers, but she didn't have to tell him so. "I could have anyone I want, remember," she murmured modestly. "You told me so."

A corner of his mouth kicked up and he eased his pelvis against hers, giving her a subtle rub while his hands continued their feather-light seduction up and down her arms. "Who says I'm a smoker? That's a damn lie. I've reformed."

"I saw the evidence myself. You came in here with a cigarette sticking out of your mouth." She gave a delicate shudder. "Disgusting habit."

"Didn't see it lit, didja?"

"Well . . . no."

"There you go, then. You and me, we're gettin' married. There's no good reason not to."

She tilted her nose in the air. "Maybe I'm not ready for that kind of commitment."

"Don't make me get tough, Red."

She pursed her lips and blew out a little *pfft* of disdain.

"Okay, don't say I didn't warn you." Sam narrowed his eyes at her. "I know where the really big spiders live. And I can find one—just . . . like . . . that." He snapped his fingers in her face.

She blinked. "You'd use my deepest fear against me to get your own way?"

Giving her an insolent grin, he ran his tongue

along the edges of his upper teeth and wagged his black brows at her.

"My God. That's reprehensible. You are such a low-down, despicable *snake*." Leaning back, her face was a study in mock horror as she stared up at him. Then a slow, wicked smile began to unfurl across her lips.

"I really *like* that in a man."

Epilogue

"WHOA NELLIE, I thought I was gonna have a heart attack trying to make it here on time." Kaylee arrived breathless at the church dressing room. "Our plane was late, and then the baggage got held up. Did we hold up the show?"

"No, there's still time to dress." Catherine gave her sister a hug. "It's good to see you."

"I know. I wish we were gonna have more time to visit, but it's been a crazy week. I'll tell you about it when we get a minute."

"Let me introduce you to my bridesmaids." Catherine did so, then stood back, awaiting the expected reaction.

Kaylee didn't disappoint her. "Dammit, Cat!" Her hands fisted on her shapely hips as she glared at the pale green gowns worn by Catherine's two other attendants. "When you said 'trust me to pick out the perfect matron of honor's dress,' I took the big gulp and let you ... even though all my instincts screamed I was makin' a big mistake." The bridesmaids, stifling smiles, murmured excuses and drifted out of the room, and Kaylee turned back to her sister.

369

"I should have known your wedding would be pitifully anemic."

"I prefer to call it elegant," Catherine replied calmly, and gave her twin a wry smile. "Although I do admit it must seem sorta tame compared to the Hunka-Hunka-Burning-Love Chapel. And of course our officiant is just a regular old minister, not the snazzy Elvis impersonator you had."

Kaylee grinned, her eyes dreamy with reminiscence. "Wasn't that just the greatest?"

"Umm," Catherine replied noncommittally. Then she returned her sister's grin. "Anyhow, Kaylee, you oughtta have a little faith in me. You think I don't know your taste by now?"

"Not if those simpy dresses that just walked out the door are anything to go by." Kaylee reconsidered as she eyed her sister's wedding gown. "Although I gotta admit, *you* look really fine. Your dress could be the teeniest bit tighter and it could stand more beads, for sure, to add a little flash. But all in all, Caty-girl, you did all right. It shows you off."

"I know. Isn't it great?" Catherine stopped to admire herself in the full-length mirror. Complementing her hourglass figure, the gown was form-fitting without being skintight, a long, slim tube of creamy white. It was cut low between her breasts for a strapless appearance beneath the beaded illusion that stretched from her shoulders to her waist, where it nipped in before skimming the flare of her hips and draping softly to the floor.

She felt beautiful in it.

She met Kaylee's gaze in the mirror and cocked an

eyebrow. "Okay, so you ready for yours? Close your eyes."

"That ugly, huh?" But Kaylee obediently did as she was told.

Catherine unzipped the garment bag hanging from a hook on the door and removed her sister's dress. Holding it up against herself, she said, "You can look now."

Kaylee's eyes opened. "Oh!" Her breath caught in her throat. "Oh, my God. OHMYGOD!" She started ripping her street clothes off, dropping them where she stood. "It's beautiful. Sis, it's so beautiful!"

"Didn't I say you could trust me?" She carefully lifted the emerald green gown away and extended it to her twin. "I told the seamstress to think Jessica Rabbit, but she hasn't been in the country long and didn't get it. So I just had her add a lot of extra beads. And I told her to fit it to me 'til I couldn't sit down."

"Perfect," Kaylee breathed.

"Yeah." She grinned as she watched her twin hug the gown to her breasts. "I thought you'd like it. Put it on. It's almost time to rock 'n' roll, and I want to see how you look."

Down at the altar several minutes later, Sam hooked a finger under his bow tie and tugged. "Christ," he said. "Isn't this shindig ever gonna get on the road?"

The minister had led him and the groomsmen out a minute ago, then just left them there to sweat it out in front of a sea of strangers.

Gary looked up at him. "Getting a little jittery, son?"

"Big-time."

Bobby, who was still adjusting his cummerbund, said out of the side of his mouth, "Breathe deep. You'll be okay once you see her."

"Man, from the looks of things," Gary observed, looking out over the church, "I'd say you spent a pretty penny on this affair."

"Yeah, I guess it's just as well you refused to take any of the bounty money. I had no idea you could finance a small country for the same amount of money you put into a wedding and reception. If I'd known, I might've stripped Jimmy Chains of his jewelry before we turned him over to the feds."

"Speaking of which, he 'n' Sanchez have been all over the news back home lately," Gary said. "Y'all gettin' the coverage up here?"

"Nah. Seattle could care what's happening in Miami." Sam tugged at his tie again and kept his gaze glued to the door at the end of the aisle.

"Kaylee's not gonna have to testify after all," Bobby contributed. "We've been talking to the DA all week and just found out for sure yesterday. Sanchez's attorney accepted a plea bargain. It's a huge load off, I gotta tell ya."

The organ started up, but the door remained closed. Sam's gut churned.

"They gave him twenty to twenty-five years," Gary said. "Chains made a better deal. He got like fifteen to twenty."

The doors opened, and Sam quit attending to the conversation. His gaze went past the two bridesmaids in pale green, past Kaylee in flamboyant emerald, straight to Catherine. Her upswept hair blazed beneath the subdued overhead lighting, and she was a vision in white, pale and serene. Catching her eye, he watched as she broke into a radiant smile.

It took his breath away, and his nervousness disappeared, replaced by a fierce pride. She was smart, she was beautiful, and she was his.

"Oh, darlin'," he murmured under the swell of organ music, feeling a smile tickle the corners of his lips. "Come to Papa."

The reception was in full swing when Gary wheeled up to the groom. "How 'bout a dance with the bride?" he demanded. Sam had been a mite possessive of Catherine since the moment she'd walked down the aisle, and even now made a growling noise of dissent. "Ain't askin' to kiss her, Sambo, just want one dance."

Catherine laughed, gave Sam's cheek a pat, and hiked up her skirt to climb on Gary's lap. Giving his friend a maniacal grin, he tilted the chair back on its wheels and spun them around, then wheeled hell-for-leather to the edge of the dance floor. Once there, he slowly cruised its perimeter.

"I've never seen Sam so happy," he said. He looked up at Catherine's radiant face, and she gave him such a sweet, satisfied smile that he laughed. "You look pretty damn happy yourself."

"I am," she agreed. "And I'm happy to make him happy. But it's not only because of me, Gary. It's going to the Academy, too." Much to her satisfaction,

Sam had applied to the Police Academy right after following her out to Seattle.

"Yeah, that was one decision that was long overdue. I'm glad he finally saw the light."

Catherine touched his forearm, which bunched and flexed muscularly beneath her fingertips as he propelled them in slow, lazy loops. "He misses you, y'know."

"Get him a dog. He just needs something to take care of." Gary gave her a rakish grin. "Or better yet, make him a kid." He watched her carefully as he said, "On the other hand, it's nice out here. I just might have to move once I finish up school. There's Sam and you. And there's Microsoft. I sure wouldn't mind workin' there."

Catherine hooked her arm around his neck and smiled. "We'd really like that."

"Give me back my wife, Proscelli."

They both looked up at Sam with identical smiles on their faces, and Gary tipped an imaginary hat. "Your smallest wish is her command."

"I live for that day." Sam assisted Catherine off of Gary's lap, then quirked an eyebrow at his friend. "There's a good-lookin' woman over by the buffet. If you hurry, you might be in time to hit on her." He watched Gary spin the chair around and wheel off. "With luck, she'll keep you too busy to hit on my wife," he added under his breath.

Red slipped her arm around his waist and hugged him to her. "You aren't going to be one of those dreary jealous husbands, are you?"

He pulled her into his arms and swayed in place

to the beat of the music. "Maybe just today. And during the honeymoon. Then I'll settle down."

"Good. Because I love you and only you, you know."

He looked down into her bright eyes and brought a hand up to gently trace his fingers over the flushed curve of her cheek. "I do know. And I'm crazy in love with you, Red. So, I'll tell you what." He saluted Kaylee and Bobby as they danced past, then turned his attention back to his bride. "After the honeymoon, men can look all they want. 'Course, if any of them tries to touch you"—he ran possessive hands down the sweet curve of her butt and wiggled his hips, sucking in a breath when she followed his movement perfectly—"Honey, I just may have to get ugly."